Drink to the success of

A TASTE FOR IT

BY

MONICA McINERNEY

A FRESH NEW TASTE IN FICTION!

Win a case of mouth-watering Clare Valley wine kindly donated from Mangans Keencost Cash 'n Carrys, who stock the widest range of quality wines from the Clare Valley in South Australia

TO WIN ANSWER THE FOLLOWING QUESTION

Q. Is Shiraz red or white wine?

A. _____

ANSWERS ON A POSTCARD CLEARLY MARKED
A Taste For It competition to:
Poolbeg Press, 123 Baldoyle Industrial Estate,
Baldoyle, Dublin 13.

Closing date for all entries 26th January 2001, the prize will be drawn on 1st February 2001. The judges decision is final.

MANGANS KEENCOST CASH 'N CARRYS: Castlebar, Ennis, Galway, Letterkenny, Sligo, Tipperary and Tullamore.

A TASTE FOR IT

MONICA McINERNEY

POOLBEG

Published 2000
by Poolbeg Press Ltd
123 Baldoyle Industrial Estate
Dublin 13, Ireland
E-mail: poolbeg@poolbeg.com
www.poolbeg.com

© Monica McInerney 2000

Copyright for typesetting, layout, design
© Poolbeg Press Ltd

The moral right of the author has been asserted.

1 3 5 7 9 10 8 6 4 2

A catalogue record for this book is available from the British Library.

1 84223 043 3 (Irl.) £6.99

Cover design by Slatter-Anderson
Typeset by Patricia Hope
Printed in the UK by Omnia Books, Glasgow

Author Biography

Monica McInerney was born in the Clare Valley of South Australia. She has lived in Australia, Ireland and England and worked in book publishing, public relations, arts marketing, children's television and Irish music pubs.

She currently lives in South Australia with her husband. *A Taste For It* is her first novel.

Acknowledgements

Thanks to Mary and Steve and all the McInerneys, Nancy and Joe and the Drislanes, the Dolan family, Anita Ruane, Kate Strachan and Stephen McInerney of Inchiquin Wines, Maeve O'Meara, Marea Fox, Jane Melross, Karen O'Connor, Bart Meldau, Kristin Gill, Felicity O'Connor, Janet Grecian, Christopher Pearce, Michael French and Annie Kaczmarski.

Thanks to everyone at Poolbeg in Ireland and Penguin in Australia.

Thanks to my friend and agent Eveleen Coyle in Dublin.

And special thanks to two people: my sister Maura McInerney, for not only letting me borrow her name but also for her eagle eye and constant encouragement, and my husband John for everything.

For my Dad

Chapter One

Maura picked up her wineglass and spoke in a low, sexy voice. "I'm rich and full-bodied and you'll savour my taste for a long, long time."

"It's a wine label not *Playboy* magazine," her brother Nick said under his breath, not looking up from his writing-pad.

Maura took another sip of red wine and tried again. "What about 'fruitier than Carmen Miranda's hat and a lot easier to carry'?"

Nick didn't even smile. "Maura, you're not taking this seriously, are you?" He ripped out another page of scribbled notes from his writing-pad and threw it onto the growing pile on the floor.

She *had* been taking the label-writing seriously. For the first four days anyway. But they were now into day five of the process and she was rapidly running out of adjectives.

They went through this several times a year, when

the various blends Nick made in their small winery were ready for bottling. Nick was usually very easy-going, but he fell into a high anxiety state when it came to his labels. He was convinced the perfect combination of words hinting at full flavours and bursting taste sensations produced extra sales.

Maura softened as she looked at her brother's worried expression. "Nick, your wine is so good, it doesn't matter what's written on the label. Let's just tell it like it is. 'Here's a fantastic Shiraz. It was made in South Australia. We hope you enjoy it.'"

"No, far too straightforward. This is the wine industry, remember?" He looked up at her with a glimmer of a grin. "Besides, I want it to be extravagant. There are three years of my life in those bottles."

There was silence again as they both bent back over their notes. Maura surreptitiously checked her watch. She had half an hour before she had to start preparing for today's lunch crowd. She picked up her glass again, letting the morning sunlight stream through the deep red wine.

"What about 'ruby rich in flavour, colour and appeal, a gem among Clare Valley reds'?"

"Now, that's more like it." Nick actually smiled, scribbling down her suggestion.

The sudden peal of the telephone made them both jump.

Maura got to it first. "Lorikeet Hill Winery Café, good morning." Her voice warmed. "Joel, hello! How are

2

you?" Nick looked up as Maura walked out into the garden with the portable phone. That would be the last he'd see of her for a while, if her usual conversations with Joel were any guide. Maura and Joel had become friends when she had lived in Sydney, where Joel worked as a freelance food writer. He moved from office to office, usually finding time to ring Maura for a good long catch-up at some editor's expense.

Nick was surprised when she came back into the reception area less than five minutes later, a mischievous smile on her face.

"I've got some news," she said.

That was no shock. Joel was the gossip king of the food world. Nick waited.

"The Diner, the *OzTaste* magazine food critic, is coming here today."

"What! *The Diner!* How on earth does Joel know that?"

Maura sat down. "He was calling from the *OzTaste* office. He just happened to see a confidential list of the critic's restaurant visits this month. And he just happened to read it closely and notice we're the lucky one for today. Apparently The Diner's travelling around the country with his wife reviewing regional restaurants."

Nick looked worried. "That's really bad news, isn't it? Isn't he the one who closed down Gemma's restaurant?"

Maura nodded. Several years previously her friend Gemma had opened a small bistro in Sydney. All had gone well until The Diner had visited and written a vicious – and factually incorrect – review. Overnight it had destroyed her trade. Gemma had demanded an apology from the editor, and had received a well-hidden two-line retraction in the next issue. But the damage had been done. The customers had stayed away in droves.

"Did Joel have any good news?" Nick asked.

Maura smiled broadly. "Today's review will never be published. *OzTaste* magazine is closing down. Joel's heard the publisher's been taken over by some international magazine group and there's going to be a big change in direction. But it's still hush-hush and The Diner wouldn't have heard the news yet."

"So he'll soon be out of a job?"

"Just like Gemma was when he closed her restaurant."

They were silent for a moment.

"If this is going to be his last free meal, we really should make sure it's one to remember, shouldn't we?" Maura said thoughtfully.

"Make sure he never forgets us, do you mean?"

"Pull out all the stops," she grinned.

* * *

As her kitchen and waiting staff began to arrive, Maura took great pleasure in explaining the situation, promising a fifty-dollar bonus for the most inventive revenge tactics.

Her head waiter Rob was especially taken with the idea. "He's an arrogant pig, apparently," he said with feeling. "He made a waitress friend of mine in Melbourne cry once, he was so rude to her. Leave him to me."

In the kitchen, Maura cast an eye over the list of

dishes her other customers would be choosing from: a warm garlic, herb and mushroom salad, made with herbs from the Lorikeet Hill garden; a Thai-style beef salad with mint, coriander and peanuts; grilled lamb cutlets with potato and parsnip mash; tangy yoghurt chicken with roasted capsicum and garlic; and a zesty fruit sorbet served with poached nectarines. The dessert was one of her favourites, and was always a hit with the customers. Ironically, she had adapted it from a recipe she had found in an old issue of *OzTaste*.

Thinking of the magazine, she suddenly recalled an article The Diner had written a year or so back, in which he'd included a list of his dining-out pet hates. She and Gemma had laughed about it, wondering how the editor had kept the list to one page. With an idea hatching, she hunted for the issue in the box of magazines she kept as reference.

There it was. Maura frowned as she read his article again. It was people like him who gave food writing a bad name, she thought, as she skimmed through the pompous introduction to his article.

Australian food has certainly come on somewhat in recent years, but far too many times I have had the misfortune of being served food better suited to seventies dinner parties or countrywomen's association annual dinners, invariably delivered by drop-outs from a second-rate catering college.

Maura quickly scanned his list of six pet hates. Perfect. She'd be able to manage them all easily. She'd get her waiter Rob to explain to the critic that they were trialling a new style of dining. They'd serve him a number of small dishes, in a Lorikeet Hill version of the famous Spanish tapas style. It would work a treat.

By 1.30 pm the café was about three-quarters full of a mixture of local people and visitors from Adelaide, up for a day of fine Clare Valley food and wine. Out in the reception area, Maura smiled goodbye as a couple left, carrying half a dozen of the newly released Lorikeet Hill Cabernet Sauvignon.

Maura mused for a moment, wondering where that wine would be when it was opened. She loved the whole winemaking process. Lorikeet Hill was right in the middle of the vineyards of the Clare Valley, one of the most beautiful parts of South Australia, and she saw the vines through all the seasons, from the bare branches of winter, to the sudden blast of light green in the spring. She liked to imagine the whole process as a fast-forward film – the grapes flourishing, swelling from tiny seeds to plump ovals on the vines, the early morning sight of groups of grape-pickers, moving down the long, long rows, like flocks of birds eating all the fruit . . .

The noise of a car engine outside caught her attention. Looking out from the reception window she watched a car with interstate number plates manoeuvre into the small carpark. This had to be him.

She watched as the passengers took great pains to engage the car alarm and carefully lock the doors. Just as well, Maura thought. The possums around here were notorious car thieves.

She caught a glimpse as a couple made their way up the tree-lined path. A tall, dark-haired man, with an equally tall, very slender young woman beside him. Her hair was styled in a stark, angular bob and she was wearing a close-fitting bright-pink dress. As for the King of Critics – he was hardly the stooped, overweight, gout-ridden elderly gentleman they'd been expecting, Maura thought in surprise. He didn't even look forty. Thirty-five maybe. At least six foot tall, she judged, watching as he ducked under the garden arch. Dark, maybe even black hair. And from this distance his physique looked more like that of an athlete on his day off than a man who ate for a living.

Moments later the doorbell jangled as the couple walked in. Maura nearly laughed aloud – the man was carrying a copy of *OzTaste's* guide to regional restaurants. Well, that was subtle. She'd heard of some critics who insisted on anonymity. This one was obviously the opposite, dropping hints so he'd get the best treatment.

She took a moment to look at him closely, taking advantage as their eyesight adjusted to the dim, cool light of the reception area. She nearly wolf-whistled. He was gorgeous.

Beautifully dressed in a white linen shirt and close-fitting dark jeans. Tanned, lean features, yet his face looked lived-in, not male-model smooth. He and his wife looked like they had just stepped off the set of an expensive aftershave commercial.

It wasn't fair, she thought, suddenly feeling a rush of

dislike for him. Not only did he make his living wreaking havoc on poor restaurateurs like Gemma, but by the looks of things he lived a glamorous, charmed life as well. Maura thought cheerfully of the imminent closure of *OzTaste*. A taste of his own medicine at last.

Still, Maura decided on one last check before it was all systems go with what they had dubbed 'Gemma's Revenge'. Heaven knows she didn't want a poor innocent couple from Adelaide to go through this particular experience. Joel had been unable to give her a detailed description of The Diner but had alerted her to his distinctive voice. "He grew up in New York," Joel had hurriedly explained on the phone that morning, "and he's still got traces of an American accent, even after years here in Sydney. I've heard him being interviewed on the radio. But I'm sure he'll stand out – by all accounts he's not the easiest of customers."

He was right. These two stood out like sore thumbs.

She decided on two quick tests – if she managed to hear his American accent and find out they'd driven from Sydney, then it was full steam ahead.

"Good afternoon," she said brightly. "Welcome to Lorikeet Hill – can I help you?"

The stylish woman answered in a drawling voice. "Yes, we'd like some lunch – I sure hope we're not too late."

"Oh, there's no such thing as time in the country," Maura answered lightly. "Have you driven a long way?"

The man answered, in a deep, almost musical voice.

"We've come from Sydney, but we've broken the trip over a few days." Maura strained to catch his accent, but he'd spoken too low to be sure. But they'd come from Sydney . . .

"Sydney?" Maura repeated, almost shouting. "How lovely! Well, you're both very welcome to the Clare Valley and Lorikeet Hill. Your table will be ready in just a moment. But could I just ask you both, if I may be so bold, are those American accents I hear?"

"Yes, I'm from New York," the woman replied, in a bored tone of voice.

"And you, sir?" Maura pressed.

"I lived there for a number of years," he answered, looking a little puzzled at the sudden interest in accents.

"Ah, America, land of the free – and you've just driven down from Sydney, well, that's terrific!" Maura felt her voice get slightly high-pitched. "Just one moment please and I'll have someone escort you to your table."

'Have someone escort you to your table?' What had come over her? She'd never said that in all her years in restaurants. She walked quickly back into the kitchen, where her staff waited.

Maura gave a big wink. "Thank you, Rob – if you could please show our most honoured guests to their table."

"My pleasure, Miss Carmody," Rob said with a wide smile.

The staff peered around the kitchen door to watch.

The sleek woman was checking her reflection in the glass-framed photographs by the door, while the critic was reading the food and wine reviews pinned to a noticeboard on the wall.

Rob coughed politely, and as they turned around, greeted them with a shocking grimace, far removed from his usual sweet smile. Maura watched as the couple tried not to react. "Bon jour, madam and mizure, pliz follow me to ze table we 'ave chosen for you," Rob said, adopting an appalling stage-French accent.

Rob was a born actor, Maura thought. He chattered away as he led the couple through the entire café, weaving in and out of every table in the dining-room, before returning to the first table they had passed on their tour. "Sit 'ere, pliz. I 'ope you enjoy ze special taste sensations we 'ave pre-pared for you today. Zee wine waitress, she will be wiz you shortly." With a flamboyant bow, he placed their napkins on their knees and flounced off.

Pet hate one – fussy, fake French waiters – done, Maura thought to herself. She came out to the reception desk again and eavesdropped as the couple settled into their seats.

"What on earth's going on here? This isn't a French restaurant, is it?" she heard the woman hiss.

"It's supposed to be modern Australian," the man replied, checking the *OzTaste* guide. "But didn't that waiter say something about the Spanish tapas style?"

"Well, by the look of these decorations it's more like

a fake Irish pub," the woman sniffed. "We'll have tin whistles playing jigs and reels next."

"Thanks for the idea," Maura whispered to herself. Fake Irish, indeed. The white walls of the café were decorated with the originals of a series of beautiful paintings Fran, Nick's wife, had done for their wine labels. Depicting musicians and Irish scenes, the paintings reflected the Irish heritage of the Clare Valley.

Maura moved over to the compact disc player and lowered the volume on the classical CD playing. "The lady in pink over there has just told me she's Irish and very homesick and I just want to play her some music to cheer her up," she explained to one of the larger groups.

The customers nodded and smiled – *Riverdance* had done wonders for the popularity of Irish music and they had all been lulled by the fine Lorikeet Hill food and wine.

Maura found a CD called *Tin Whistle Favourites for All the Family* that Nick had given to her as a joke the year before. The shrill sound of the whistle began to fill the café, concentrated on the table in the corner. How unfortunate that Mr and Mrs Critic have been seated there, Maura thought, as she moved the volume control higher and higher.

The other guests tapped their toes as the squawking increased. The guests of honour moved angrily in their seats, trying to get a staff member's attention and shouting over the music to make themselves heard.

Turning down the music to a dull squeal, Maura

mentally reviewed the hit-list again. Pet hate two, loud background music. Two down, four to go, she thought with pleasure. With a wink, she sent her star wine waiter Annie into the fray.

For someone who had just graduated top of the class from a wine appreciation course, Annie did a terrific job of pretending to be completely ignorant about all the wine. She deliberately misheard every question either of the two asked her. She spoke about Riesling as though it was made from Shiraz grapes. And to top it off she made sure she was clearly visible as she filled their glasses from a cheap cask of mass-produced wine Rob had rushed out and bought that morning.

"Number three done with perfection, Annie," Maura whispered. Now, time for the food.

Rob delivered their first course with great pomp and ceremony – two huge platters of deep-fried canned asparagus spears coated in breadcrumbs. The dish would have looked perfectly at home on the cover of a seventies cookbook. The can of polyunsaturated oil she had used certainly delivered the critic's pet hate number four too – several times over.

Back in the kitchen, Maura put the finishing touches to their next course – chicken à la paprika. But Maura felt her hand accidentally slip as she was adding more of the spice. Now it was more paprika à la chicken. And a bit of fresh chilli always went a very long way, she thought, adding three teaspoons of freshly cut red chilli, seeds and all. Number five – tick, she thought gleefully.

Having removed the untouched asparagus Rob delivered the chicken dish to their table with great pizzazz, placing the plates in front of them with dramatic flourishes, *voilà's*, hoopla's and every other vaguely French-sounding word he could remember. Maura and the kitchen staff waited as the couple took their first mouthful.

The spluttering began in seconds. She heard their coughing from inside the kitchen, and peeped through the glass doors leading into the dining-room in time to see the woman grasp the napkin to her mouth and make a dash for the bathroom.

Maura took the chance to beard the lion in his den. The critic seemed to be suffering a silent coughing attack, his eyes streaming, his voice hoarse as he tried to say something.

"Oh, I am sorry," Maura said in a saccharine-sweet voice, as she walked over to his table. "Was that a little too spicy for your delicate palate? How awful! And I understand your sixth pet hate is having to ask for water in restaurants. Here, let me save you the trouble."

She actually hadn't planned her final action. But a memory-flash of the trouble he had caused Gemma suddenly made her see red.

Almost in slow motion, she picked up the large vase of flowers standing on the cupboard beside her, took out the flowers and poured the cold liquid slowly over his head.

"It comes with Gemma Taylor's compliments," she added for good measure, deciding it was time to come clean.

The only sound he made was a deep gasp, but that was enough to attract the attention of the other customers. They began to whisper and giggle at the sight of the man dripping water, with Maura standing beside him, vase in hand.

She had to admire his coolness, but really, with a back full of water she could hardly expect anything else. He gave her a long slow look.

Maura had intended to give him a passionate lecture on the importance of getting his facts right and the severe effects his reviews could have. But a shriek from his companion as she flounced back to their table stole the moment. She took a breath as though she was about to begin shouting when the man laid a hand on her arm.

"Thank you, Carla, but I don't think there's anything you can add to this very strange situation. Are you ready to leave?" The man rose from his seat, giving his head a slight shake, which only spread the water further. "I had hoped after the asparagus and paprika that this meal couldn't possibly get any worse, but now I wouldn't like to bet on it."

"Well, we're certainly not paying for that garbage!" the young woman almost spat at Maura. "This is the most appalling restaurant I have ever been in." She strode to the door. "You should be reported!" she shouted over her shoulder as they made a noisy exit.

Rob and Annie hurried out of the kitchen, congratulating each other.

"Gemma would have loved it," Nick said, still laughing. "Revenge accomplished. We should have hired a video camera."

Maura smiled with them, but didn't feel as elated as she had hoped. There was something in the man's gaze which had unsettled her. She mentally shook herself. It was just the surprise of him being attractive, when you were expecting an overweight old boor, she told herself. You've been out in the sticks too long – you're not used to handsome, sophisticated men.

As she heard the front door open again, Maura went out to greet the new arrivals. She tried to ignore the sight of Rob giving a reprise of his French waiter's act, with his fifty-dollar bonus clenched between his teeth. The kitchen assistants were in hysterics.

The newcomers, an elderly couple, looked over in a puzzled manner at the noise.

"You all seem very happy today," the man said in a slightly drawn-out, disapproving voice.

"Oh, I think it's the country air," Maura explained as she led them to the newly reset table. "Now, can I show you the menu?"

Chapter Two

"So I could show the slides first, and then do my talk. Or maybe start with the talk and the wine-tasting, then follow that with the slides. Or – "

"Talking to yourself again, Morey?"

"Just for a change," Maura answered with a grin. She turned around as her sister-in-law Fran came into the room, carrying a large cardboard box overflowing with sketches and designs. Fran was a talented illustrator, and had designed a bestselling series of children's books as well as all of Lorikeet Hill's wine labels.

"Fran!" Maura leapt from her chair and took the box from her. "You're not supposed to lift anything, let alone heavy boxes like that. You know what the doctor said."

"You're as bad as your brother," Fran grinned, as she slowly eased her heavily pregnant body down into the one comfortable armchair in Maura's tiny spare room, which doubled as a guest-room and office. "If you'd both had your way, I would have been lying in bed for the past eight months, propped up on feather pillows and sipping on little cups of tea. And I'd have gone slowly mad with boredom."

"He's just worried about you, and I am too. I'm sorry if it feels like we're bossing you around or at you all the time to take it easy. It's just . . . well, you know why," Maura tailed off, not wanting to mention the two miscarriages Fran had suffered in the past few years. Busying herself, she tried to find room on her cramped desk for the box. In the process she nearly knocked over the huge bunch of flowers that had arrived as a thank-you from Gemma the day after the critic's lunch, nearly a week ago now.

Fran looked affectionately at her sister-in-law. "Really, stop worrying. I'm nearly there now, just a month to go. Don't worry about me, or you'll spoil your trip."

"I will worry about you, until I get that call in the middle of the night telling me I'm an auntie at last," Maura smiled back. "You have got all the phone numbers in Ireland, haven't you? The one in the Dublin hotel, and Bernadette's car-phone and her number in County Clare?"

"Presumably they haven't changed since you gave them to us last week? And the week before that?" Fran teased.

Maura gave an embarrassed smile. "Sorry . . . honestly, I'm carrying on as if I'm going to the moon rather than Ireland for a month. Of course you'll be okay, and of course Nick will remember to ring me when the baby is born and of course Gemma will cope perfectly well in the kitchen here."

Fran copied Maura's singsong voice. "And of course you will manage to make all the winesellers in Ireland fall head over hills in love with Lorikeet Hill wine, and we can all retire rich and happy in twelve months from now. That's what happens after these export trips, isn't it?"

"I wish," Maura smiled. "I've just had another e-mail from Rita Deegan, the lady in Dublin organising the whole trip. She's added another two bottle-shops to my itinerary."

"So how many is that all up? You must be into double figures by now." Fran stretched out her legs as she spoke and began moving her feet in slow circles, eyes closed in pleasure.

Maura scrolled down her computer screen, trying to find the final itinerary that had arrived during the night via e-mail from Rita.

"Let me see. I arrive on a Sunday, there's a cocktail party that night, a wine-tasting in Dublin the next day, then I'm off to the West of Ireland with Bernadette for the assault on the bottle-shops," Maura counted under her breath. "Eleven bottle-shop visits – or off-licences as I have to learn to call them – and four talks and wine-tastings, half with slides, half without. Then, thank God, I can stop pretending I know anything about making wine, and move on to three weeks of cooking at

Bernadette's very swanky house in the glorious Irish countryside."

Maura spun around in her chair with her last words, finishing with a wide grin in Fran's direction.

"You're not still nervous about talking about the wine side of Lorikeet Hill, are you?" Fran asked, looking over and knowing Maura well enough to guess the anxiety behind the high spirits.

Maura suddenly looked serious. "No, not any more, though I was terrified at first. But I knew there was no way Nick would leave you so close to your due date. I'll be fine. And Nick has coached me so hard I'm dreaming about winemaking in my sleep."

"You'll be great," Fran said encouragingly. "The two of you have worked so closely together these past few years, I bet you'll find out you know heaps more than you realise."

A knock on the front door stopped their conversation. "Oh God, it's that reporter," Maura whispered, looking at her watch.

"What reporter?" Fran whispered back.

"From one of the local papers. They're doing a story on me, about the Irish trip. Photo and all."

"Good luck to him with that," Fran smiled wryly to herself, as Maura moved down the narrow hall toward the front door.

"Good morning," Maura said brightly as she opened the door to welcome a smartly dressed young man. "I'm Maura Carmody, you must be the new reporter." Hired

19

straight from a crèche by the looks of things, she thought.

"Hello, Maura, yes, Gary Lewis is my name." He suddenly leaned forward and grasped her hand in a firm shake that nearly pulled her off her feet.

She smiled a welcome, quickly rescuing her hand. "Let's go on up to the winery and café – are you happy to walk or would you rather drive?"

She saw him look nervously out through the vineyards and long dry grass that surrounded her cottage and guessed what he was thinking. "There are only a few snakes and I'll go first and beat them off," she added kindly.

She obviously convinced him, and they set off along the well-trodden path that linked Maura's old stone cottage with the Lorikeet Hill Winery Café.

"Have you been up here before?" Maura asked as they walked along, both kept busy swatting the flies away from their faces.

Gary was stepping very gingerly, keeping close to Maura and practically treading on her heels. "No, but I've heard lots about it. I only arrived in the Clare Valley from Melbourne last week, but I'm hoping to work my way around all the wineries and restaurants."

"That'll keep you busy for a few months," Maura wasn't surprised to hear he was a city boy. "Would you like to sit outside and we can talk?"

The young man followed Maura as she led the way onto the front verandah. An enormous walnut tree in the centre of the garden shaded them, sending dappled-green light onto the grass and the front of the building. As they sat down at one of the tables, a pair of bright green and red birds darted swiftly along the edge of the verandah, making Gary jump.

He really was terrified of the wildlife, Maura thought. "They're lorikeets – the inspiration for our business name," she said. "They're a sort of parrot – this garden and the hill behind us have been home to a family of them for years. Beautiful, aren't they?"

Gary nodded politely, but she noticed he was sitting very stiffly, as if expecting them to swoop down and peck out one of his eyes. He coughed nervously as he withdrew his notebook from a bag he was carrying.

"Perhaps you could give me a bit of background on Lorikeet Hill, before we talk about the trip to Ireland?" he asked, his pen poised.

Settling onto the wooden bench opposite him, Maura briefly explained that Nick had set up his winery just outside their home-town nearly five years before, after serving his apprenticeship at other wineries in South Australia.

"I joined him about three years ago. I'd been working as a chef in Sydney, came home for a holiday and Nick convinced me to go into business with him and open the café here as well."

And that's as much background as you're going to get, young fellow, Maura said to herself. The newspaper's readers weren't going to get all the juicy details of her break-up with her boyfriend Richard, the real reason she'd come running home from Sydney. There'd already been enough gossip in the town when she first arrived back. She didn't want to set it alight again.

Gary was scribbling down her every word. "And are you older or younger than Nick?"

"Nick's thirty-two and I'm four years younger."

"And can I just double-check the spelling of your first name – it's quite unusual isn't it?" he asked.

Not for the first time, Maura slowly spelt out her name. "It's an Irish version of Mary," she explained.

"Oh, were your parents Irish?" Gary asked.

For a fleeting moment, Maura debated whether to give him the complete story of her parentage, but decided against it. "Oh, there's Irish blood in the family tree, for sure," she answered vaguely. "But one in five Australians can say that."

"And is that why Lorikeet Hill was chosen to be part of this Irish trade trip?"

Maura shook her head. "Just coincidence really. But I think it helped that we had links with County Clare already – do you know about those?" she asked.

Gary nodded. His editor had filled him in that morning on the twinning arrangement between Clare and the County of the same name in Ireland.

Maura explained that a group of Australian wine exporters had teamed with an Irish wine society to promote sales of Australian wine in Ireland.

"Lorikeet Hill was chosen to represent the Clare

Valley, and there'll be other winemakers from the other wine areas around Australia. We're all touring different parts of Ireland, leaving no stone unturned and no bottle unopened." She grinned.

"And you're doing some cooking in Ireland as well, is that right?" he asked.

"That's right. After the wine trip I'll be guest chef at Cloneely Lodge in County Clare." She explained that in the early preparations for the trip she had learned that the wine society member she would be travelling with also owned a well-known residential cooking school and country house restaurant, south of Ennis, the main town in County Clare.

"Her name's Bernadette Carmody – and no, no relative," she added quickly. "Just a common surname, I guess. We talked a lot while we were working out the itinerary for the wine trip, and realised it was a great opportunity to promote Australian food as well as wine. I'll be teaching Bernadette's students during the week, and then cooking in the restaurant for real-life diners each weekend."

Gary closed his notebook. "That all sounds great. It'll really help put the Clare Valley on the map, won't it?" he said earnestly. Maura smiled at him. She suspected he was parroting his editor's words but he was right. It was a brilliant opportunity to promote the Clare Valley and Lorikeet Hill and get great experience herself. She didn't mention her other personal reason for wanting to visit Ireland, and County Clare in particular. That idea was still tucked firmly away at the back of her mind.

"Now, I need to take your photo for the article as well, if that's okay?" Gary asked.

Maura nodded, inwardly groaning. She hated having her photo taken and hated even more seeing the results. Nick had inadvertently made her even more self-conscious, after seeing her in a recent set of photos. "You're actually very good-looking in a kind of gypsy way," he'd said, "but you always do look weird in photos."

"Thanks very much, Nick," she had said crossly.

"No, really, you do look better in real life. You need to have a still sort of face to look good in photos – you're too lively-looking."

"And my hair is too messy and my eyes too green as well?"

Nick had taken her question seriously. "Well, I wouldn't say messy exactly," he'd said, inspecting her almost waist-length dark-red curly hair. "More unruly. And there's not much you can do about your eye colour – unless you want to try those coloured contact lenses?"

But the main problem was that she seemed to have a reflex reaction to the sound of the camera shutter. Every time it clicked, she shut her eyes, unless she really concentrated. It meant that photos of her either featured her with eyes tightly shut, or wide open and staring glassily. Only occasionally did a half-decent one make it through.

Gary had now switched from cub reporter to high fashion photographer and was wandering around the café trying to find the ideal backdrop.

"What about in front of the photos in the reception?" he asked. "They looked interesting."

"Sure," Maura said, leading him to the wall in the reception area that was covered in all sizes and styles of framed photographs.

She briefly took him through each one. They had been taken over the past four years and showed the transformation of the ramshackle old house to the ivy-covered winery and café it was today.

"Is that you?" Gary remarked, pointing to one of Maura standing next to Nick in front of the verandah. "Had you been sick? You look terrible."

Wait till your photos come out, she thought, quite taken aback at his comment. She looked at the photo in question. It had been taken just after she arrived back from Sydney. The last stressful months with Richard had certainly taken their toll on her. She did look terrible. But at least her eyes were open. She waved his comment away, though. "No, just too long living in Sydney, breathing in all that smog, you know the story, the stress of the rat-race."

"And is that your mother?" he asked, pointing to another photo of Nick and Maura standing with their arms around a small, fair-haired woman. Maura nodded. "You don't really look like your brother or mother, do you?" he asked. "Does she work here too?"

Where exactly had he studied? Maura asked herself. The Melbourne School of Insolence?

"No, we don't look alike," she answered in a steady voice. "That's because I was adopted. And no, my mother Terri doesn't work here. She passed away nearly six years ago. And her husband left us more than twenty-five years ago, in case you were going to ask about that."

He had the grace to look a little embarrassed. "Oh, sorry."

Maura softened at the sight of his unease. "You weren't to know. Terri had cancer. By the time we found out, it was too late to do anything."

By his sudden silence Maura guessed that Gary was too uncomfortable to ask any more questions. Blinking away the ripple of grief the memory of Terri's death always gave her, Maura turned back to him and changed the subject.

"Now, what about this photo of yours? I've got nearly a full house in for lunch today, so I'd better get a move on."

Gary lined up his camera and moved Maura to the left and the right until he seemed happy with the background.

Click. Her eyes shut tight. Great, she thought. One more to add to the collection.

Chapter Three

Sitting at her desk, the phone tucked under her chin, Maura looked up and smiled at Gemma as she refilled her champagne glass. "I won't be long," she mouthed.

"That all sounds fantastic," she continued her conversation with Bernadette in County Clare, who had just outlined the last of the arrangements for the cooking school. "I honestly didn't think there'd be such a response, especially for three sets of classes."

"Oh, it's my flowery descriptions in the brochure, pet – wait until you try to live up to them – *Flavours of the outback, a melting pot of the best of Asian and European ingredients cooked with Australian pizzazz* . . . and that's just the introduction. And the dinner bookings are coming along well, too. It's just a shame you can't import some of that good weather with you as well, so we could have the whole authentic Australian experience."

Maura looked out of her open office window. It had been a beautiful February day with bright blue skies and now, at almost seven pm, the air was still warm. She could see Nick, Fran and Gemma out in the garden, preparing for her farewell dinner tonight.

Gemma had arrived the night before, having taken a month's break from the corporate catering business she had set up to serve the head offices of Sydney. Maura smiled as she saw her, dressed in faded blue jeans and a light t-shirt, laughing and talking with Nick and Fran as they stood around the ground-level old stone barbeque. She described the scene to Bernadette.

"A barbeque, you lucky things. We can hardly walk outside, let alone eat. The weather has been monstrous," Bernadette groaned. "There were rumours there could be at least a glimpse of blue sky during your visit, but I've just heard the forecast and we've a few wild days of storms ahead of us. Hopefully, you'll miss the worst of it while you're flying."

"The weather's the last thing on my mind," Maura said. "I've been too busy trying to track down huge quantities of bush-pepper and wattle seed and sundried bush tomatoes. Why worry about a little thing like the weather!" She looked down at her watch. "Bernadette, you'd better go, this will cost you a fortune!" Their final phone call was supposed to have been a five-minute checklist, but had stretched out for nearly thirty minutes as invariably happened when she and Bernadette got on the phone to one another. There always seemed to be more to talk about than just food or wine.

As Gemma came up to the window and waved the wine bottle in her direction, Maura hurriedly said her goodbyes. She hung up, still smiling. Here she was in Clare, South Australia, on a Friday evening and she'd be in Dublin in time for a drink with Bernadette on Sunday night. After months of planning, the trip suddenly seemed very real.

She joined the others in the garden, enjoying the smell of the charcoal from the barbeque. Gemma had insisted on taking charge of Maura's farewell dinner, as well as looking after the kitchen for the lunch crowd that day.

"I'm not going to have you around for a month, so I may as well get used to it. You go off and finish your packing, or file your nails or whatever it is you high-flying businesswomen do at times like this," she had teased. Maura had taken her up on the offer. Gemma had been to Lorikeet Hill several times before and managed with ease in the kitchen, as Maura had known she would. They had trained together, worked together and knew each other's methods very well.

Gemma also knew how to cook a great barbeque. She had prepared her own speciality, Scotch fillet thickly coated with her home-made thick pesto-style crust, a delicious mix of fresh basil, pine nuts, parmesan cheese, farm butter, garlic and olive oil. The meat was cooking over the embers, the pesto topping crisping nicely. The tree-trunk beside the barbeque served conveniently as a table and held foil-covered baked potatoes and a huge bowl of salad greens, sun-dried tomatoes, olives, herbs and feta cheese, all produced in the Clare Valley.

Nick gently eased out the cork from a bottle of Lorikeet Hill's premium wine, a rich, full-bodied Shiraz, and with great ceremony presented each of them with a glass. It was their most expensive wine, made in only a small quantity each year from a very small vineyard of Shiraz grapes that adjoined the Lorikeet Hill property.

Taking a sip, Maura looked around her with pleasure. This was her favourite part of the day, when the sun was almost set, the vines bathed in a warm glow. It had been a long hot summer and it looked like it would go on for some weeks yet. After a very dry season, with near-drought conditions, the grapevines were the only spot of green on the countryside, standing out against the dry, brown paddocks.

Gemma interrupted her day dreaming. "Right, you three, dinner is served. And my talents tonight do not extend to waitressing, so you'd better come help yourselves."

They filled up their plates, Nick solicitously taking care of Fran. Maura was pleased to see her looking so well and relaxed.

She caught Maura's eye and lifted her glass in a toast. "I promised myself one glass of wine this pregnancy and it's in your honour. Here's to a wonderful trip," she said, smiling.

Nick and Gemma echoed the toast, and then settled

themselves down on an old garden bench to enjoy the meal.

"So, are you and Bernadette all organised, Morey?" Gemma asked, as she passed around the salad bowl.

"As much as we'll ever be," Maura replied with a grin. "It sounds like Bernadette's got all the cooking side of things sorted out. And she's raring to go on the wine side too. She said she's had her car especially polished, so we look the part arriving at all the bottle-shops and public talks."

"You're a very generous brother, Nick," Gemma looked over at Nick with a cheeky expression. "Passing up a chance like this to spread your knowledge around the world."

"I'm sure Maura will manage to uphold the tradition and the glory of the Carmody name," Nick said mock-seriously. "Of course, she's blatantly ignored all my suggestions for her talk presentations. Really, these young upstarts, you give them a whiff of power and they run off with it."

Fran picked up the tale. "It really is a shame. We had pictured Maura arriving into each talk, the strains of 'Waltzing Matilda' echoing around her . . ."

"From a cleverly concealed speaker in her hat . . ." Nick interrupted.

"Modelled from papier mâché into the shape of a kangaroo," Fran added.

"Then she would show a compilation videotape of highlights from *Neighbours*, *Home and Away* and the

Foster's beer commercials to really grab everyone's attention," Nick continued.

"Give everyone a free bottle of Lorikeet Hill Riesling, and a stubby holder . . ."

"Then ride out on the back of a specially imported merino sheep," Nick added, waving his arm with a flourish.

Gemma shook her head from side to side, laughing at them. "And she didn't take you up on your suggestions? Heavens, I can't imagine why."

"See what I've been up against, Gem?" Maura joined in. "Where is their sense of occasion, sense of purpose? I am going to Ireland as a cultural representative of Australia. This isn't a wine trip, this is a diplomatic mission."

"And maybe even more than that," Nick added, with a challenging look at Maura. "A family reunion perhaps . . .?"

She quickly looked over at him, and shook her head. She didn't want to talk about that tonight, even though both Fran and Gemma knew all the details of her adoption. She covered the moment by standing up quickly and opening another bottle of wine, against her own better judgment, but with full support from Gemma.

Nick tried to bring the subject up again later in the evening, as she walked him and Fran to their car. "I'm not pressuring you, Morey. I guess I just want to make sure you won't turn down the opportunity if it comes up. And you'll be so close . . ."

"And so busy selling your wine. Please, Nick, leave it for tonight. Maybe we'll talk about it on the trip to the airport tomorrow."

But maybe we won't, she thought, giving him a hug to soften her words. Right now that whole question was just too hard to think about.

Maura waved as their car drove down the dirt road heading further into the surrounding hills. Nick and Fran's old stone house was about ten minutes' drive away, high on a hill with beautiful views of the valley around them. As she walked back down the driveway towards Gemma and the barbeque, she watched as their car lights dipped and shone, before finally disappearing.

Gemma had busied herself adding some logs to the barbeque coals to get the flames going again. It was warm enough to sit outside without a fire, but the flames added to the atmosphere, their colours flickering and reflecting off the white walls of Maura's cottage.

She looked up as Maura pulled her chair closer to the fire. "How did you go with selling your travel story, by the way? I meant to ask you last night."

Maura brightened. "Oh, it was a brainwave of yours, thanks very much. They agreed – they'd like a four-thousand-word article, with photographs if I take any that are good enough."

Gemma had suggested Maura contact one of Australia's bestselling travel and lifestyle magazines and offer to write an article about her Irish trip. To her pleasure, the features editor had readily agreed.

"That's good," Gemma nodded, opening another bottle of red wine, despite Maura's raised eyebrows. Gemma gave her an innocent look. "How can you expect to go overseas and sell the pleasures of Clare Valley wine if you haven't got up-to-the-minute experience?"

"You are a bad influence," Maura said severely, as she held out her glass to be refilled.

"That article will be great coverage for you," Gemma said sagely. She was a canny operator herself, having achieved lots of publicity for her restaurant in Sydney, before the critic's review had turned it all upside-down.

"If it means even a dozen extra customers and wine buyers, I'll be happy," Maura said.

Gemma picked up the worried tone in Maura's voice. "Are things bad?" she asked in surprise. "The bookings register looks great – you've got a full house for most of the next month. And Nick said the wine sales are on the up too."

"It's going okay, we're covering our costs, but we're at the stage where we really need to do some serious rebuilding. Nick's just about run out of room in the winery. And the kitchen's serviceable, but the stove's not going to last that much longer." She sipped her wine. "That's why this trip is such a bonus, the export sales could be just the boost we need. Nick doesn't talk about it much, but I know he's a bit worried, especially with the baby about to arrive."

"Well, it will be a success, won't it?" Gemma said in a determined voice.

"It sure will be," Maura answered. They clinked their glasses to mark the moment.

They were both silent in their thoughts for a few minutes, looking into the flames of the campfire. When Gemma spoke, her voice was soft in the darkness.

"I've heard some news about Richard, if you're interested?" she said.

Maura looked up, expecting to feel the usual rush of hurt at the mention of her ex-boyfriend's name. "Do you know, I hardly ever think about him any more," she said in surprise.

"Well, hallelujah for that! It's a shame you couldn't have got all memory of that ratbag surgically removed from your brain."

Maura laughed. "Gemma, you're terrible."

"No I'm not, I can remember the state he left you in. That's why it's so good to see you like this again, believing in yourself."

Gemma had been with Maura through the thick and thin of her relationship with Richard. They actually owed their own friendship to him – they had first met when they began work as apprentices in Richard's first restaurant in Sydney. He had already been making a name for himself then, five years ago, as much for his arrogant behaviour as his innovative approach to cooking.

He and Gemma hadn't hit it off though, and she had left after a month. Maura had been in his thrall by that stage, and their professional relationship had developed into a personal one. She'd even moved in with him.

Looking back, she saw pitfall after pitfall, but at the time it had all seemed exciting. The long hours they worked ensured it wasn't a normal relationship anyway, and their busy working lives had helped paper over the cracks for the first year or so.

But a combination of her finding her own feet and his increasing notoriety had caused the cracks to widen. At home they'd argued more than they'd talked, with Richard choosing to spend any free hours sitting in front of the television.

"I used to get so wild with him," Gemma said now. "The way he used to talk to you, and talk to all his people if it came to that."

Maura remembered one night in particular. The tension between them at home had spread into the restaurant kitchen. He had started to find fault with her and tell her off in front of the other staff in the kitchen. "Stop talking to me like that," she had shouted at him. "You make me look stupid in front of everyone else."

She could still remember the look he had given her. "I don't make you look stupid. You and your cooking make you look stupid."

The final straw had come the night she had returned from a week's holiday in Clare. She had always known that the easy charm and boyish looks that had attracted her also attracted other women. What she hadn't known was that Richard had been reciprocating their affection. Unpacking in their bathroom, she had found a bottle of perfume that didn't belong to her.

She had confronted him but he had just laughed it away and gone back to watching his television programme. When she had persisted in seeking an explanation, the mood had suddenly turned ugly.

"Oh for God's sake, Maura, you're turning into a fishwife before my eyes," he had taunted her. "Get used to it, it's not my fault I get bored with you."

She had gasped at that. "So you admit it – you've been sleeping with someone else, here in our bed?"

"Actually, it's my bed, if I remember rightly," he had answered, hardly looking up from the television. "Remember, you moved in with me? Your country-bumpkin side is showing through, Morey," he'd mocked her with her pet name. "You're in the big city now – you don't have to be so straight."

"I'm not being straight, I'm being honest. I would never do this to you." Her mind was a-tumble. She couldn't believe he was sitting there so calmly while admitting he'd been unfaithful to her. She had suddenly realised it mustn't have been the first time.

He was still talking. "Ah, but you don't get the opportunity like I do, do you? How can you say for sure you wouldn't do it, especially if it was handed to you on a platter? Pardon the pun." She heard rather than saw his smirk.

The fight had escalated into a full-scale shouting match. With tears streaming from her eyes, she had hurriedly repacked the suitcases she had only minutes previously emptied, and dragged them toward the door.

Richard's parting words had echoed in her mind for a long time after the door had slammed between them:

"You'll regret this, you're useless without me, Maura, don't you know that? You haven't got any talent, you've always ridden on my coat-tails."

She had felt chilled to her heart, knowing in that moment it was over. She had driven in a daze to Gemma's house.

Her friend had taken one look at her face and pulled her indoors into a hug. "It's about time you left him," she had said firmly. "I'm not even going to attempt to be kind. God only knows how it lasted this long."

Gemma had soothed her, shielded her from Richard's abusive phone calls, even given her work in her own small bistro. Then The Diner's *OzTaste* review had had a devastating effect on their trade.

Overnight the numbers had fallen and within a fortnight Maura had given Gemma her notice. She knew her friend was struggling financially and she also knew it was last on, first off. And she had also had a sinking feeling that Richard had somehow arranged the *OzTaste* review.

Gemma snapped her fingers in front of Maura's face, bringing her back to the present with a start.

"Sorry, I was miles away," Maura said, looking over at Gemma. "It's weird, when I think about that time it's like remembering someone else's life, like I was my own silly little sister then, or something." She tried to laugh.

"I'd still like to give him a taste of his own medicine," Gemma said. "But it looks like everything's not wine and roses for him in London after all."

Maura's interest was pricked, despite herself. "What's happened? Last I heard he was the toast of the town. There was a whole segment on him on one of the radio food shows about six months ago."

"When he was at Dray's?" Gemma named one of the hippest London restaurants.

Maura nodded. The radio segment had featured the current vogue for Australian chefs in London and highlighted Richard's rapid career rise as a prime example.

"Well, it seem Mister Hillman got a little too big for his boots and a little too fond of the marinating wine, and he and Dray's have parted company."

"Really?" Maura said, surprised. "They sacked him?"

"Officially, no, and he apparently got work at another of the owner's restaurants very quickly, but the word from my friend over there – and this is all hush-hush – is that he's just too erratic, especially when the drink is involved. And maybe not just the drink."

Maura wasn't surprised to hear it. Richard had been very fond of a drink when they had been together, and she'd seen a different side of his personality the times he had overindulged. It hadn't been a nice sight. "So is he about to come slinking home, with his tail between his legs?"

"I'll let you know," Gemma said. "Then you can sharpen your best knife, meet him at the airport and cut that tail right off."

"Gemma!"

"No, really, it would be the perfect situation. You can cause a stir in Ireland just as he falls from grace, and then you can slip over to London and take his position. And I can stay here in country bliss and keep little old Lorikeet Hill bubbling along. Perfect." Gemma took a determined sip of wine.

Maura laughed. "You've got it all sorted out then? I'm not sure I can imagine you permanently in the country, a flash Sydney girl like you."

Gemma went solemn. "No, actually I mean it, and this isn't just the wine talking. I'm getting a bit sick of Sydney. The business is doing well but, each time I come here, I just feel so much better and much more relaxed."

"Well, if I get snapped up by Terence Conran while I'm away," Maura said, naming the famous London restaurateur, "I hereby bequeath my tiny four-ring stove and all my cracked plates to you, my friend."

Their glasses clinked again.

Chapter Four

Maura opened her eyes as the captain announced that her flight from Heathrow would shortly be arriving in Dublin. After a long and uncomfortable flight from Adelaide to London, and the flurry at Heathrow as she ran to make her connecting flight, she had fallen asleep almost as soon as she found her seat on the Aer Lingus flight to Dublin.

Nick and Fran had seen her off at Adelaide airport, still laughing at her pale face. They had been decidedly unsympathetic when they had collected a quietly hungover Maura from her cottage early Saturday morning, in plenty of time for the two-hour drive south to the airport.

Gemma had surfaced just at the last minute, coming out in her pyjamas to give Maura a big farewell. Maura had laughed to see her. "I can't believe I'm trusting this reprobate in my kitchen, I must be mad," she had said, shaking her head.

The excitement had banished her slight headache by the time they reached the airport.

"Just think," Fran said, as they hugged each other goodbye, her pregnant stomach making it quite a feat. "Next time you're here there'll be three of us to meet you."

Smiling at the memory, Maura looked out of the window as the plane began the descent into Dublin Airport.

So this is Ireland, she thought. She cast her mind back to her conversations with Nick, his urging of her to use her time here to continue her search . . .

She half-expected her heart to begin beating stronger, or her skin to goosebump, or some familiar spirit to call through the ages to her. But all she felt for the moment was excitement about seeing another country and the trade trip starting at last. A sudden gap in the clouds beneath the plane allowed a glimpse of bright-green landscape. The travel books were right, she admitted. It was a different shade of green, like nothing she'd ever seen in Australia.

She leant back against the seat, shutting her eyes again. She wouldn't have a lot of time to get over any jet-lag. The cocktail party tonight was the start of the busy schedule. She was looking forward to that, not only because she'd be meeting Bernadette, but it seemed like such a celebratory way to start the trip.

She had been through a lengthy immigration process at Heathrow Airport in London. But there didn't seem to be any security check at Dublin Airport, just a broad smile from a man behind a desk, waving her through. Her baggage was among the first off the plane, so with a trolley loaded high, she moved out into the airport.

Dozens of expectant faces looked up as she came through the door then fell in disappointment when they realised she wasn't their visitor. Rita Deegan from the Wine Society had assured her in her final e-mail that she would be collected at the airport and taken to her hotel, so she dutifully found her way to the Meeting Point in the terminal.

Twenty minutes passed and she was the only person left standing under the Meeting Point sign. She began to worry slightly that the plans had gone awry. Not that she minded too much – she had changed some traveller's cheques at Heathrow and had an adequate supply of Irish punts. She was perfectly able to hire a taxi and she could see that there were plenty outside.

She had decided to wait for just five more minutes when she heard footsteps running across the lobby and turned in time to see a young man running up to her, red-faced and with a worried expression.

"Oh God, I'm sorry – are you Maura Carmody here from Australia?"

Maura nodded.

"I'm so sorry, I've kept you waiting, haven't I?" the young man apologised again. "And there's you probably exhausted after the long trip and dying for a long bath and a cup of tea or maybe a drink – this is hardly any welcome to Ireland at all, my name is Aidan by the way, you're very welcome to Dublin, Miss Carmody. *Céad Míle Fáilte,* that's Irish for a hundred thousand welcomes, and they're better late than never!" His words poured out in a tumble, punctuated by a wide grin and a proffered hand.

Maura grinned back, warming straight away to his accent and enthusiasm. "Thanks for the welcome, Aidan, it's very nice to be here. And please call me Maura, not Miss Carmody."

"You'll feel right at home here with a name like that," Aidan spoke in a rush. "You look quite Irish too," he added. "You must have some Irish blood in you."

"Me and a few million other Australians," Maura said with a laugh. She almost ran to keep up with him. Coming out of the airport she gasped as the chill February air hit her. She pulled her coat in tight around her body. Aidan kept walking as fast as he spoke, reaching a car parked illegally just outside the main doors of the airport building.

After settling Maura and her luggage into the car, Aidan kept up a torrent of chatter as they drove out onto the road heading into Dublin. Maura tried to take in the scenery around her. It was certainly greener than South Australia, and the road signs were in English and Irish, but she was amazed and slightly disappointed that her first proper view of Ireland didn't immediately match up to her expectations.

Though I was hardly going to see rows of thatched cottages and dancing maidens on the main highway, was I? she scolded her own imagination. Enya videos had a lot to answer for. She pulled her attention back to Aidan as he explained that his family had been wine merchants in Dublin for years, and still ran a wine store not far from where she would be staying in Dublin.

"I'm actually studying for a marketing degree at UCD – that's University College Dublin," he added kindly, "but I'm working part-time for the Wine Society this year and finding out how the export markets work. You Australians seem to be leading the pack here in Ireland, it's brilliant isn't it?"

Maura nodded, smiling at his enthusiasm. She was really looking forward to seeing bottles of Lorikeet Hill wine on sale in the shops here. Some of the other winemakers on this trade trip had been exporting for years, and would be blasé about their Irish sales, but she was thrilled at the prospect.

She'd promised Nick she'd take a whole roll of photos of his wine at the different outlets around the country. He'd protested that it wasn't worth the film, that a bottle of wine looked like a bottle of wine whether it was in Australia or Ireland or on Mars, but she knew that secretly he'd love to see it.

Aidan was still chattering away. "Now are you exhausted after that long flight – what is it, forty hours or something, unbelievable, bring on time-travel I reckon – or will I take you for a quick spin through the city or perhaps you'd like to go straight to the hotel? There's a cocktail party on tonight to welcome you and all the other winemakers but luckily it's in the hotel where you're staying so there won't be any bother finding your way there. And it's not until seven so you've about five hours to yourself if you want to have a look around. Anyway, I'll leave it up to yourself." He took a breath and grinned at her engagingly.

She blinked, trying to remember what his question had been. "Maybe I should go straight to the hotel?" she said.

"No problem," Aidan smiled across.

They were soon driving right into the middle of Dublin city, with Aidan keeping up a relentless stream of tourist-guiding anecdotes and pointing out landmarks at a rapid pace. Maura let most of it wash over her. She planned to explore the city as much as she could herself, on foot, with a guidebook to hand, the best way to see a new place. For the moment she was struck by the age of the buildings, by the crowds, even on a Sunday, and by the misty winter light that seemed to give everything a softer edge.

"That park there's called St Stephen's Green," Aidan said as they drove beside a big park enclosed in an ornate iron fence. "It was a gift to the people of Dublin from the Guinness family. Your hotel is just up here, the Shelbourne, one of the grandest hotels in Dublin, only the best for our Aussie guests."

As Aidan deftly pulled the car into a tight spot right in front of the hotel, Maura certainly felt very grand as two uniformed men came onto the pavement, one to take her luggage, the other to open the car door. She stepped through the ornate revolving door into a very plush foyer and immediately felt as though she had stepped back in time.

Waitresses smartly dressed in black and white uniforms were bustling around a room to her right, in which small groups of well-groomed people were sipping tea and talking in low voices, all the while keeping a close eye on every new arrival.

Maura followed Aidan and the porter to the reception desk where she gave her name to the smiling woman behind the desk.

"Ah, Miss Carmody, part of the Australian winemakers group – you're very welcome to Dublin. We're very fond of Australian wine here in this hotel!" As she was handed her room key, Maura suddenly felt a wave of tiredness sweep over her. What she badly wanted was a shower and a change of clothes.

Aidan noticed her sudden weariness and with a warm handshake headed off, promising to see her at the party that night.

Her room was lovely, cosy and old-fashioned, and the bed looked very inviting. But she had read all the travel tips and knew the best thing to do was stay awake as long as possible until as close to the local bedtime as she could manage. She decided to shower and change, and go for a walk around the centre of Dublin to get her bearings.

The rush of water felt lovely as she washed the grime from the flight out of her long hair. She shook out the formal dress she had bought especially for tonight's function and was pleased to see the creases fall easily from the rich red fabric. She didn't bother to unpack everything, but hurriedly pulled on a pair of her favourite jeans and a close-fitting floral shirt. Too impatient to wait for her hair to dry completely, or to use her hairdryer, she wound it up into a loose bun on her head, allowing a few tendrils to escape around her face. She'd pay for it tonight, she knew – her hair sprung into an absolute riot of curls if she didn't dry it properly.

Revived again, she picked up her long coat and set off down the stairs, passing several elegant women heading into a beauty salon. The foyer was full of little groups of people chatting or waiting for friends and she peeped into a tiny curved bar. She flashed a smile at the smartly dressed porter who once again gallantly held the door open for her.

She stepped from the relative quiet of the hotel into a cacophony of traffic sounds. Cars, vans, buses, taxis and cyclists were speeding past. Maura joined the flow of pedestrians and quickly found herself at the top of Grafton Street, which seemed to be the main shopping area. It was teeming with people.

She had been expecting the Irish accents but couldn't believe all the other accents and languages she was hearing. It was like the United Nations on parade.

She let the flow of people guide her route, avoiding the temptation of actually going into any of the shops, but making mental notes of inviting-looking jeweller's and bookshops.

Standing by a tall sculpture depicting Molly Malone and her cart at the bottom of Grafton Street, Maura stopped to catch her breath and check her guidebook. She had a list a mile long of places she wanted to see, and souvenirs she'd been asked to bring back. Waterford crystal for Fran. Irish poetry for Gemma. And Irish knitwear for herself.

Enjoying a cup of coffee and a break for her exhausted feet at a sidewalk café she looked at her watch and realised she'd been walking around for almost two hours. If she didn't hurry she'd be late for the function. As she stood up to make her way back to the Shelbourne Hotel, a wave of tiredness came over her again.

She was looking forward to the party, knowing she'd get a second burst of energy once she'd showered and changed again. She'd met some of the other winemakers before at other industry functions in Australia. Some were terrific and down-to-earth, some not so down-to-earth. There was an old joke that had more than a ring of truth in it, she'd always thought. 'What's the difference between God and a winemaker? God doesn't think he's a winemaker.'

Most of all she was looking forward to meeting Bernadette and setting off on their trip. Bernadette had assured her that their week driving around to the wine merchants in the west of Ireland wouldn't be too strenuous – " One part hard work to five parts fun, my girl, that's the secret of a good business trip."

And then the three weeks in Bernadette's beautiful old country house would begin. It would be her first experience of teaching at a cooking school, and she was looking forward to it, especially knowing she'd have Bernadette's back-up. She was particularly looking forward to the weekend restaurant nights. The ideas for menus of Irish produce cooked with Australian innovation had been crowding her head for weeks. She'd had to stop her exploring several times that afternoon to jot down an idea or two in the little notebook she always carried with her. Some of Lorikeet Hill's most popular dishes had come to her suddenly like that. She and Bernadette could use the time spent in the car driving around in their first week to fine-tune the menu even further.

***

Maura pulled on the red dress. It was much closer-fitting than most of her clothes, but the deep rich colour and the soft fabric had made it impossible to resist. It was an off-the-shoulder design and showed plenty of her pale skin, and she dressed it up with a shimmering wrap in a richer shade of the same colour.

She was certainly paying for her earlier impatience with her hair-drying – the curls were out of control.

There wasn't time to sort them out, she decided, quickly winding them back into a loose bun. She applied a dusting of powder to her face and a bold-coloured lipstick, finished with a quick spray of perfume, and decided she was ready.

The invitation in her welcome folder from the Wine Society included directions to the function room, just a floor down from her bedroom. As she came into the corridor she was pleased to see Aidan just ahead of her. He gave her an admiring look, and a low wolf-whistle. "You'll be the belle of the ball, Maura, well, the peach of the party at least."

He brought her into the party which was already in full swing. In seconds she had been introduced to the trip organiser, Rita Deegan from the Wine Society, before she was swept up into a flurry of quick conversations.

Aidan introduced her to the other winemakers in the delegation. The couple from one of the Tamar Valley wineries in Tasmania had also arrived just that day, on a later flight, and they swapped stories with Maura on their jet-lag. Maura spoke briefly with the Victorian and Western Australian winemakers, who she knew slightly from the bi-annual Wine Expo in Melbourne. The final members of the party she recognised immediately – William and Sylvie Rogers of The Glen winery in New South Wales were well known in wine circles, their reputation far preceding their formidable presence.

Aidan introduced Maura to Sylvie. "Lorikeet Hill?"

Sylvie repeated, as thought it was a particularly unpleasant disease. "Oh, that's right, the little boutique winery in South Australia, now I remember it. You serve snacks or something too, don't you?" she asked condescendingly.

Maura was about to explain it was actually more like a restaurant when Sylvie gave a sudden unpleasant smile. "Now I remember where I know your face from. You were Richard Hillman's little protégé, weren't you, until he upped and left you for London? I hear he's doing wonderfully." She gave a faintly victorious smile. "And there you are in the country – isn't it funny how these things turn out?"

Maura's eyes widened at the rudeness of her remark, though she wasn't surprised to learn Sylvie knew of Richard – a society vulture like her would be sure to keep up with that sort of gossip. Richard had been one of the more high-profile young wonder-chefs and their relationship and break-up had been a five-minute wonder in some of Sydney's gossip columns.

She was about to answer back when Sylvie deliberately turned away – looking for more influential conversations, her movement seemed to suggest.

Aidan gave a low whistle. "Phew! And there I was thinking all you Australians would be laid-back," he whispered.

Maura grinned, slightly shaken by the encounter. "Not when it comes to a share of the wine market. And Sylvie's determined to get more than her share, I'd say."

As they watched, Sylvie grasped her husband William's wrist and marched imperiously up to the head of the Wine Society and interrupted his conversation.

"The poor man doesn't stand a chance with Mistress Battleaxe in full flight," Tony, the Victorian winemaker, whispered beside her. Maura smiled back. It was common knowledge that Sylvie was the powerhouse in the relationship, bossing William to within an inch of his life.

"You know, the rumour is she doesn't even let him make the wine any more? Apparently she brings in outside winemakers who are better than him, and pays them for their silence," Tony whispered.

Maura's eyes widened.

Brenda, the wife of the Western Australian delegate, joined in their hushed conversation. "That wouldn't surprise me. I've heard of her bribing bottle-shops for constant display space for The Glen ranges, can you believe it?"

Tony was about to elaborate when a tap of a pen against a wineglass called the room to order.

With Sylvie still standing uncomfortably close to him, the head of the Irish Wine Society made a charming welcome speech, followed by another speech from the head of the Australian delegation.

Maura took the opportunity to glance around the room to see if Bernadette had arrived yet. There didn't seem to be any sign of her, or anyone that resembled the out-of-focus photograph she had sent Maura in

Australia. "I know it's blurry," Bernadette had written on the back. "It's the vaseline on the lens – the only way I can get a flattering photo of myself!"

Maura touched Aidan on the arm as he rushed past her on the way to the bar as the speeches ended. "You haven't seen Bernadette Carmody here by any chance? I was expecting her to be here by now."

Aidan's hand flew to his mouth. "Oh God, I knew there was something I meant to tell you this afternoon. It slipped my mind when I was so late and thinking I'd probably have missed you and you'd have already caught a taxi into town wondering what on earth had happened to Irish hospitality."

Maura stepped in quickly. "What did you mean to tell me?"

"The roof of Bernadette's cooking school at Cloneely Lodge collapsed in the storms we had the day before yesterday. You were already on your flight by the time it happened or we would have rung and told you in Australia. They were the most ferocious storms, the weatherman was saying he thought we'd lose every tree in the west of Ireland."

"Is Bernadette all right?" Maura asked urgently, trying to halt his weather report.

"She's fine, she wasn't home at the time, but the awful thing was she twisted her ankle the next day when she was looking over the damage. But she's absolutely grand, she just can't walk on it for the next week or so, doctor's orders. But she'll be fine and don't worry about a thing, your cooking programme together will still be going ahead."

Maura was having trouble keeping up. "Bernadette's been hurt, her house has fallen down, but we're still going ahead with it?" she asked in amazement.

Aidan gave a merry laugh and looked at her as if she was a bit simple. "Oh, of course we're going ahead with it – just not in Bernadette's house. Her place will be crawling with builders for the next month, there wouldn't be room for you all. No, you and Bernadette are moving to Ardmahon House, just across the valley. Rita sorted it all out. Apparently Ardmahon House is *gorgeous*," he drew out the word, "just been completely renovated, ten ensuite bedrooms, big kitchen, the height of luxury – it's perfect. And we're really lucky, it got through the storm untouched. Apparently the howling of the wind was so bad you could scarcely hear yourself think."

Following Aidan's train of thought was like unravelling a kitten's ball of wool. She was relieved to hear Bernadette was unhurt and vowed to ring her as soon as she got back to her room. Then another thought suddenly occurred to her. She managed to interrupt Aidan, who was in full weather-forecaster mode by now. "But what about the wine trip around the West of Ireland?"

He stopped waving his arms around. "Oh, Rita sorted that out too. The owner of Ardmahon House is a new member of the Wine Society and has volunteered to take over that part of your trip as well," he beamed at her.

As Aidan paused to draw breath, Maura tried to get a word in to find out exactly what had happened, but he rushed on.

"Now, now, not another word, trust me, it's all sorted out, the owner is coming along tonight to meet you. You'll travel around together the first week on the wine tour as you would have done with Bernadette and then we'll get you and Bernadette and your students and your restaurant guests all set up in the substitute house, happy as larks." Aidan smiled encouragingly.

At that moment Rita from the Wine Society came up and caught Aidan's last words.

"Yes, it was such a shame about Bernadette, Maura, she was so looking forward to driving you around. But you'll still get to do your wine trip and then you'll meet up with Bernadette, one week later than scheduled. Actually, I think your new guide has just arrived – hold on a moment and I'll introduce you."

Maura stood dazed, trying to take it all in. The whole anticipation of the trip had been heightened knowing that she had already made a friend in Bernadette. Now she would be starting from scratch with a completely different person.

She crossed her fingers surreptitiously, hoping her new guide would be as nice as Bernadette had promised to be.

Behind her she heard Rita say brightly, "Dominic

Hanrahan, I'd like to introduce you to your travelling companion for the next seven days."

Maura turned around with a big smile, which froze as she looked up. The last time she had seen that face she had just emptied a vase of cold water over it.

Chapter Five

Rita blithely continued her introduction, unaware that the colour had suddenly drained from Maura's face.

"Thank you, Rita, but we've already met, haven't we, Miss Carmody?" Dominic Hanrahan said smoothly.

Maura couldn't stop the look of horror she knew was in her eyes. What on earth was the *OzTaste* critic doing in Dublin?

Rita seemed oblivious to the tension. "Oh, of course, you've just got back from Australia too, haven't you, Dominic?" she said with a smile. "Did you manage to get to Maura's winery café? I understand it's really memorable."

"Oh, it is indeed," Dominic answered, flashing Maura a look.

Rita continued enthusiastically. "Dominic has just completely renovated a beautiful big house in County Clare, Maura, only a few miles from Bernadette's. We were so happy he was able to step in at the last moment after poor Bernadette's mishap with her roof. We've had a great response from the food and wine writers – there are even one or two coming over from the British newspapers, I believe. You Australians are really causing a stir."

"And severe heartburn," Dominic murmured so only Maura could hear.

"I'm looking forward to meeting the British critics," Maura looked directly at Rita. "I understand they have great integrity and know their subject, unlike some other critics I've met."

Rita gave a nervous laugh, picking up on the tension but not sure why it was there. "Oh, surely you haven't had bad reviews, Maura. I've only heard great things about the food and wine at Lorikeet Hill," she said hurriedly.

"Not personally, no," Maura said, smiling at her, before turning toward the man beside her and letting the smile slip. "But as I'm sure Mr Hanrahan knows, the restaurant and wine world is a small one and everyone knows everyone else's business."

Dominic was about to speak when they heard a drawling voice behind them. Maura recognised the accent straight away – it was the critic's glamorous wife. "Introduce me to the wonder-child of Australian wine and food, darling. I've been dying to meet her," the woman breathed, as she slipped her arm around Dominic's waist.

Dominic nodded at Maura. "Maura Carmody, may I

introduce Carla Thomas. I don't think you were formally introduced before."

Carla looked at Maura. *"You!"* Carla's shriek made heads turn. She gave a nasty laugh. "What a joke! Yours was the worst meal I've ever had in my life."

Maura's hackles rose. I guess it would stand out, she thought. The woman looked like she'd only had about six meals in her life.

Carla pointedly ignored her. "Oh, Dominic, you can't have her cooking in Ardmahon House. It will ruin your reputation. I've only just finished telling Janice all about our shocking experience at her restaurant in South Australia. Wait until she hears about this – it'll make a great piece in her newspaper column tomorrow!"

"Oh, we can't leave our visitor in the lurch, Carla," Dominic replied calmly. "And I'm very interested to see if there is any substance to all this hype and pretension about Australian food and wine."

A mixture of jet-lag, nerves and shock suddenly hardened into a flash of hot temper. Maura found herself reacting sharply to his sarcasm.

"You're a fine one to talk about hype and pretension, Mr Hanrahan. Presumably that is your real name, or perhaps you have another alias to hide behind here in Ireland?"

Rita stepped in again nervously, completely bewildered by the strange turn in the conversation.

"Well, isn't this a great party and I'm sure you'll have plenty of time on your car journeys to argue this out," she said hastily, smiling at them in a faintly desperate way. "And believe me, Mr Hanrahan, we really are so grateful to you for stepping in at the last moment. You really have got us out of a tight spot."

Maura realised her flash of temper must have seemed very ungracious to Rita. She turned to explain the situation and say that it would be impossible for her to work with Dominic Hanrahan, but, before she could, Rita drew Carla away to a group nearby. To Maura's dismay, she watched as Carla struck up a conversation with Sylvie Rogers. She heard Carla whisper something, and then both of them turned and looked over at Maura.

With a deep breath Maura turned back to Dominic Hanrahan. A part of her brain registered again just how striking he was, but she pushed the thought aside. With difficulty, she kept her voice steady. "I'm sorry, Mr Hanrahan, but this really is an impossible situation. I would find it very difficult to travel with you or work in your house. If I'd had any idea you were connected with this trip, I would have thought twice about even being part of it."

"I agree that it might seem like an impossible situation for you, Miss Carmody," he said. She realised he was mocking her formality. "But I think the Wine Society would be very surprised at your lack of professionalism if you were to back out of the trip now."

Her lack of professionalism? That was rich, coming from him. Maura decided attack was the best form of defence.

"But it's your fault that it's come to this. It was your review in *OzTaste* that nearly sent Gemma Taylor bankrupt and started this whole situation."

"Ah, yes," he said smoothly. "Who is the mysterious Gemma? I remember you chanting her name like some spell as you tipped the water over my head, but beyond that the details are a little sketchy."

Maura gave a surprised laugh. "Don't tell me you've forgotten that review. Of course you know who Gemma is."

"I'm sorry, but I don't. And while I've eaten in many restaurants I've never actually written a review of one."

"Oh, please," she almost snapped, impatient now at his stubbornness. "The next thing you'll be saying you're not connected with *OzTaste* at all!"

There was a slight pause, then he answered. "I am connected with *OzTaste* but I'm not the food critic."

"Oh, I see," she said sarcastically. "You own the magazine, of course, how silly of me."

"Well, yes, I do now, as a matter of fact."

Maura felt a strange sensation like a slow electric shock run down her spine. She suddenly had the most horrible feeling that he was telling the truth.

There was silence for a moment as they looked at each other.

Maura spoke first. "You're not the food critic from *OzTaste*, are you?" she asked in a very quiet voice, her eyes wide with alarm.

"No, I'm not," he repeated. "I'm Dominic Hanrahan.

And, in fact, from next month there won't be a magazine called *OzTaste*. We decided to close it when we realised it's been dragging the rest of the company down for years."

"So why were you in the Clare Valley?" she whispered in an even smaller voice.

"It's called tourism. Apparently you usually welcome visitors."

Maura's hands came up until they were nearly covering her face. She suddenly spoke in a rush. "I was told the critic from *OzTaste* was coming to Lorikeet Hill and that the review would never be published because the magazine house was being taken over. You and your wife fitted the bill, you'd come from Sydney, you had American accents . . ."

"Wrong on three counts, Miss Carmody. I wasn't the critic, I'm Irish, not American, and Carla isn't my wife. Though you're right on one point, we had travelled down from Sydney." The smooth exterior suddenly dropped and his voice was quite sharp. "Who told you about the takeover? That was inside knowledge until a week ago."

"My friend Joel rang . . . he's a freelance food writer in Sydney." Even as she spoke Maura wished the ground would open up and a huge tunnel would transport her through the earth back to Australia.

She had probably just blown Joel's chance of getting any work with the company run by this man. Even more probably, she had blown her own chance of making a success of this trip.

Maura took a deep breath, about to attempt an

apology. As she opened her mouth to speak, Carla sidled back up beside them. "Still wasting your time here, Dom?" she drawled. "Surely you've explained to this Australian woman that the trip is off?"

Dominic looked down at Maura, before turning his attention slowly back to the American girl. "Oh, not at all, Carla, the trip most definitely is on. I'm sure Maura is more than keen to prove that she knows something about wine and that she really can cook."

Maura's intention to apologise evaporated in an instant. Her eyes narrowed. She had had enough of this sort of arrogance with Richard and she'd be damned if the trip she and Bernadette had slaved over would go to pieces because of this man.

She glared up at him, oblivious to the flush in her cheeks and the amused look he was giving her. Switching her gaze, she gave his companion her full attention. "Oh yes, Carla, it most definitely is on. In fact, I can't wait to get started."

Carla picked up the unspoken challenge between Maura and Dominic and patently didn't like what she saw. Without warning she jerked her hand so that the glass of white wine in her hand shot forward and spilt onto Maura's dress.

Maura gasped in surprise.

"Oh, I'm so sorry, how clumsy of me," Carla said triumphantly. "It must be contagious. You're lucky there wasn't a vase of water close by. You'll just have to go back to your room and change now, won't you?"

With that, Carla took Dominic's arm in a firm grip and marched him away. Seconds later, Aidan came up beside Maura and immediately misunderstood the situation.

"Oh, did you spill your drink, you poor thing, you must be dying of the jet-lag. Here, let me get you a cloth to wipe it down. Luckily it doesn't show too much on your dress."

"Yes, luckily," Maura said, suddenly almost too weary to stand up. What on earth had she done to deserve all this? she thought. Wasn't this supposed to be a straightforward business trip?

As Aidan and Rita fussed around her, Maura looked around the room, unable to stop herself from seeking Dominic out. She was disconcerted to find his eyes meeting hers, until Carla stepped between them, breaking the contact.

Overwhelmed by the whole situation, Maura explained to Aidan and Rita that she was going to call it a day.

Rita was very sympathetic. "Absolutely, you poor thing, you probably don't know if you're coming or going. Hold on just a moment and I'll just check that Mr Hanrahan knows when to collect you. I'll be back in a moment."

"Rita is looking for me, is she?" The sound of Dominic's voice right behind her made Maura jump. She cursed her reaction. The last thing she wanted was for him to realise how much he unsettled her.

He didn't seem to notice. "I saw from across the

room that you were leaving. We need to confirm the arrangements for our trip together."

She noticed an amused glint in his eye and tried to ignore it.

He continued. "Our first appointment is in Sligo at lunchtime. I'll collect you from the foyer here at nine o'clock on Tuesday morning, if that suits you?" He gave her a sudden sympathetic smile, as if he had realised how unsettled she was by the changed plans.

Maura gave a tired nod, suddenly too weary to argue any more. In a daze she let Rita lead her to the door and escort her to her room. She wanted to ring Bernadette to check that she was okay and call Nick to fill him in on everything, but the sight of her turned-down bed proved too inviting. She simply pulled off the damp red dress and fell straight into a twelve-hour sleep.

Chapter Six

When she woke up it was nearly noon. She stretched luxuriously, glad of the long sleep. She felt refreshed and optimistic and ready to face the new situation. She would simply explain to Dominic how sorry she was for his treatment at Lorikeet Hill and try to make light of the case of mistaken identity. Hopefully that would dispel the strange tension between them. She would even apologise to Carla – if she had to.

Her good intentions were flung out of the window just minutes after she picked up the newspaper that was delivered with her room-service brunch.

Carla's gossip columnist friend had written a spiteful piece about Carla and Dominic's experience at Lorikeet Hill, without any explanation about the case of mistaken identity. She had made Maura sound like a cross between a madwoman and a drop-out from a high-school home economics class. God only knew how, but she had even managed to dig up details about

Maura and Richard's restaurant in Sydney, adding that Richard was now living in London and enjoying great success there.

Maura couldn't imagine how she had known about Richard. Then she remembered Carla talking to Sylvie. The old witch must have filled her in on the whole story.

As Maura read the article again, her heart sank further. The columnist hinted that Maura's growing reputation in Australian food circles owed much more to Richard's influence than any talent she had herself. There was even a quote attributed to Dominic, saying that he was always willing to give people a second chance. How dare he be so patronising! As if she would make a habit of serving that sort of food or emptying cold water over complete strangers!

Maura resisted the temptation to crawl under her bed and not come out until the four weeks were over. This make-or-break trip for Lorikeet Hill was certainly off to a flying start. *Céad Míle Fáilte*, Aidan had said to her yesterday. A hundred thousand welcomes. A hundred thousand nightmares more like it.

She felt like howling in frustration. It had taken nearly three years at Lorikeet Hill to rebuild her confidence and to believe in her own abilities. The growing success of the Lorikeet Hill Café was proof that she really did have what it takes. She had hoped this trip would finally banish Richard's ghost for good and help her make her own name. And now this.

If she were back home in the Clare Valley, she'd be sitting at her desk writing out her menus, or out in the sunshine digging in her herb garden. Instead here she was, stuck in Dublin on the trip from hell. In one remark she had ruined Joel's career chances. Poor Bernadette was injured and her house a wreck. Even the weather was reflecting the change in her fortunes. Yesterday's dry skies had faded away with the night and she could see a constant fall of rain from her window.

"Brilliant, keep raining," she said aloud. "Bring on the torrents." With luck, Dublin would have its worst rain in centuries. All the wine merchants would be flooded. Every bottle of Lorikeet Hill wine they had in stock would float away and the Wine Society would have no choice but to call the whole trip off. She closed her eyes and wished fervently.

Her heart leapt as the phone rang. She thought her prayers had been answered as she heard a female Irish voice, thinking it was Rita.

Then a familiar cheeky laugh made her realise with pleasure who her caller was.

"Bernadette!" Maura exclaimed. "How are you? How is your poor foot and your poor roof?"

In seconds, Maura was curled up again on her comfortable bed, hearing the whole story of the sudden storm. Bernadette assured her the damage to both foot and roof had looked worse than it actually was.

"They'll both just take a month or so to mend, and

then I'll be right as rain again. Now, tell me, have you met my proxy driver? Don't you think he's absolutely gorgeous?"

Maura smiled into the phone. "Well, they're not quite the adjectives I would have chosen." In minutes she had related the whole story, buoyed by the sound of gales of laughter from Bernadette.

"Oh, you poor thing, you must have nearly died," Bernadette said. "Don't worry about anything, especially that old gossip column. People fight for a mention in it and it doesn't matter if it's bad or if it's good, as long as you're in it. People will remember your name, not what was written about you."

"It's all right for you," Maura said with feeling. "You're not going to be stuck in a car with a sworn enemy for a week. Who is this Dominic Hanrahan anyway?"

"To be honest, I only met him myself late last year. The story is he headed off to America when he was just a young fellow. He became a big shot in newspaper and magazine publishing or something, apparently. He suddenly arrived back in the country about six months ago, with Carla in tow."

"Ah yes, the lovely, Carla, straight out of Charm School."

Bernadette laughed. "Oh, you're wicked. Yes, she's a moody young one, isn't she? She always looks as though she'd rather be somewhere else."

"What are the two of them doing in Ireland?" Maura asked.

"I'm not really sure. Dominic doesn't give much away. He said he wanted Carla to spend some time here. The local gossip is he's got some plans to set up the Clare mansion as a country retreat. It's been renovated until it's practically unrecognizable – new kitchen, ensuite bedrooms, the whole kit and caboodle. That's why we're so lucky he was able to step in when my house fell down like a pack of cards."

"I can't quite see Carla stuck in the middle of the country."

Bernadette laughed again. "No, she doesn't strike me as the rural type, either. Perhaps she plans to fill up the country retreat with famous pop stars and soccer players. Listen, enough about them, you just enjoy yourself as best you can with the wine trip. I'll be up and mobile in no time and we'll still cook up a storm together next week."

Maura hung up, feeling much more cheerful. There was no point thinking the trip was in ruins – she'd simply have to make the best of it. Besides, she couldn't let Nick and Fran down just because she was feeling a bit embarrassed and cross.

She showered and dressed quickly and tied her hair back into a loose plait. Picking up her bag and coat, she headed downstairs. She had a couple of hours to herself before the early evening wine-tasting. Time to get her bearings again, she thought.

Maura walked toward Grafton Street, planning to make a start on her souvenir-shopping and try and take in some of Dublin's tourist attractions. Then she'd have a coffee in Bewley's in Grafton Street. At the party last night Rita had assured her it was an essential experience for any visitor to Dublin.

But first she would have a look in Aidan's family's wine shop just a few streets away from the Shelbourne Hotel. She wanted to get a sense of which Australian wines were known in Ireland before she gave her first talk.

Finding the shop easily, she gazed in at the window display. She was so intent on looking at the Australian selection that she didn't notice a young man sidling up beside her. It happened in an instant – he grabbed at the strap of her bag and tugged fiercely, nearly pulling her off her feet.

Maura cried out in shock, spinning around in fright. She stared straight into her assailant's eyes, as he swore at her and wrenched at the leather handle again. They had a vicious tug of war until Maura felt a sudden rush of fury.

She let out a full-blooded scream – *"No!"* – and kicked sharply at his ankle. To her surprise he let go of the handle and tore off down the street.

Her shout attracted the attention of the man behind the counter of the wine store. He ran out just in time to see the attacker dart down a side street.

Maura leaned against the window in shock, rubbing her wrist. The fierce tugging had left a nasty welt on her skin.

"Are you okay? You were very brave – did he get anything?" The shop assistant looked at her with concern.

"I'm fine, no, I wasn't and no, he didn't," Maura reassured the man, still rubbing at her wrist.

Then her helper noticed she was trembling. "Ah now, Miss, come and sit down in here and let me give you a drink. You're a visitor, right? That's an awful way to be greeted to Ireland. But at least you're seeing the real thing. Some people spend thousands looking for a glimpse of the real Dublin and you had it come right up and say hello to you."

Maura managed a smile as he guided her into the wine store and fussed around her.

"Is that an Australian or a New Zealand accent I detected? You're here on holiday, are you?" he asked, as he fetched a glass and poured her a generous measure of fine brandy.

Maura explained why she was in Ireland and had been outside the shop in the first place.

"Ah, you're not! I'm going to hear someone give a talk about Australian wine this afternoon – I'll show you the invitation."

The young man reached behind the counter and retrieved an elegantly written card on which her name and two of her fellow Australian winemakers' names were written.

'That's me," she said, pointing to her name.

"Maura Carmody," the man read aloud. "Well, aren't I the lucky one, getting a personal audience! Well, hold on a minute now, Miss Carmody, and I'll get myself a chair and you can get started. It'll save me the bother of going all the way down to Temple Bar."

His relentless good humour and waterfall of chatter were soon helping her recover from the shock of the attempted mugging. He introduced himself as Cormac Sheehan, the manager of Aidan's family's shop.

"I know Aidan very well. Aidan's studying marketing, so of course he would do his best to get you to come and have a look at the shop. Here, let me show you around," he said with an expansive wave, as if the shop was ten times bigger than the small area it actually covered.

They fell into an easy conversation about the Irish wine market. Maura was very impressed with his knowledge of wines 'from the New World' as he put it.

Cormac explained that the French hold on the quality wine market had been gradually decreasing for over a decade in the UK and Ireland.

"It's gas how quickly Australian wine has taken off here in the last while – it used to be so exotic to drink Jacob's Creek but sure now there are whole sections of Australian wine in the off-licences and supermarkets. And Croatian wine and Argentinian wine and Chilean wine, Jaysus, there'll be Hawaiian wine yet."

She laughed aloud, holding the glass of brandy between her hands. "What's behind the sudden interest, do you think? Surely the attraction of Guinness isn't wearing off?"

"Hell will freeze over before that happens," Cormac laughed. "I suppose as people travel more, they get more adventurous in their tastes, in wine and food. And since Ireland's joined the EU and that Celtic Tiger has started running around, there's more money around. People want to try different things. And there's such a connection between Ireland and Australia, we're almost duty bound to try some of your beautiful wine."

Maura checked her watch and realised how much time had passed. Cormac looked around – the last customer had left and they were alone in the shop.

"Look, I'm due to close in twenty minutes anyway – an early finish won't hurt anyone. I can walk you down to Temple Bar. Let me show you a little bit of Dublin in return for that sneak preview of this afternoon's talk."

Chapter Seven

Maura stood outside the shop, sheltering from the fine mist of rain, while Cormac locked up. With a gentle hand on her back, he guided her down the street in the direction of Trinity College.

"So apart from getting mugged, what have you been doing since you arrived and what have the Wine Society got planned for you?" he asked. "I hope they're looking after you well, or I'll have something to say to Aidan."

She briefly explained that she'd had a few surprises since she arrived. She didn't mention the incident in South Australia but told Cormac about Bernadette's misfortune and how she'd be travelling with a completely new person.

"That's a shame, for you and Bernadette. I've known her for a few years, she's a great woman," he said, before stopping briefly and pointing out the Mansion House, the Lord Mayor of Dublin's residence. She was about to ask a few questions when Cormac changed the subject back to her trip.

"What's your new guide's name? I know a lot of the members of the Wine Society," Cormac asked. At the mention of Dominic Hanrahan's name he stopped dead in his tracks, to the annoyance of other pedestrians on the crowded footpath.

"Is something wrong? Do you know him?" Maura asked, puzzled at his reaction.

"Only by reputation, I've never actually met him. You know he's just come back from New York with some glamorous American woman?"

Maura nodded. "Yes, I've met the glamorous American woman too," she said wryly.

As Cormac set off down the road again, she had to almost skip to keep within earshot. He continued his story. "You've met Carla? A good friend of mine worked in Carla's father's company in New York. That's how Dominic first made his money – the old man heard about some street magazine Dominic had started and bought it off him. There were quite a few stories in the business pages here when it happened about three years ago. Anyway, my friend says Carla was a bit of a tearaway – you know, the usual story, only child, filthy rich, spoilt rotten."

Surprise, surprise, Maura thought.

"Apparently the old man thought Dominic was the bee's knees and tried to matchmake him and Carla."

Maura struggled again to keep up with Cormac as

they turned left and walked right into a group of people streaming from a tour bus into a large shop devoted to woollen goods and Irish crafts. Maura looked longingly over her shoulder at the beautiful glasswear in the window, but it seemed Cormac had no intention of slowing down just yet.

He turned to make sure she was keeping up with him and the story. "Her mother died when she was a kid and then the old man died last year. The gossip in the company is that the old man appointed Dominic as her informal guardian. Apparently if Dominic keeps an eye on her until she turns twenty-five he's set to inherit something like a million dollars. Even more if her marries her."

It was Maura's turn to stop walking. "What?"

Cormac arched one eyebrow. "Well, that's apparently why she is rarely out of his sight. Wouldn't you keep her close by, if you had that much money riding on it?"

"I thought they were lovers."

"Oh, apparently they are. At least, that's what the word is."

Maura was shocked. How could Dominic be so mercenary? Imagine wheedling your way into an old man's affections, seducing the daughter, just for money! It was like something out of the Dark Ages.

For a moment she almost felt sorry for Carla. Maura wondered if she knew about the deal. She gave Cormac a grateful look. "Thanks for filling me in. Forewarned is forearmed, as they say." They had reached the end of

Grafton Street and Maura could see the statue of Molly Malone across the busy street. She was on the point of asking Cormac about it when another thought struck her.

"If Dominic is that mercenary, why would he have stepped in so quickly when Bernadette's roof fell in? Surely that's a generous gesture?" she asked.

"On the surface, yes, but I bet there's more to it. I've heard he's just done hundreds of thousands of pounds worth of renovations on his house," Cormac answered.

Maura nodded. Bernadette had said the same thing.

"Well, there's talk he's planning on opening one of those luxurious country house retreats for rich Americans to come and wind down in. It's the ideal set-up for a trial run. The hard work's already been done by the Wine Society. He gets to show his luxurious new country house to all the rich young things doing your cooking course and the food writers who would otherwise have been writing about Bernadette's house. And he gets a reputation as a good guy for getting the Society out of a fix. He can't lose. And there are a few rumours floating around that someone has plans to set up a classy food and wine magazine here in Ireland. If that someone just happens to be Dominic then this could be a handy research trip for him as well."

For reasons she couldn't quite understand, Maura felt quite disappointed. She had wanted to accept Bernadette's opinion on Dominic's generosity. But from what Cormac was saying it was complete skullduggery.

Cormac looked closely at her. "Ah, I'm sorry, I've depressed you, haven't I? I'm very sorry. Really, none of it affects you – you can still talk about your wine and cook to your heart's content, regardless of who you're travelling with or what house you're in. And you'll get to see lots of our lovely countryside. And sure, maybe I'll even make the odd trip over to Clare to take you out for a bit of craic in the local pub. The pubs in the West of Ireland are the best in the world."

Maura decided that, no, she wasn't depressed, it was definitely disappointment. But why on earth would she feel disappointed by Dominic's behaviour?

Cormac was determined to buoy her up again and was practically skipping around her.

"Now, what tourist spots have you already seen, or what do I still have to show off?"

He was aghast to hear that she was leaving Dublin in the morning and hadn't had time to do any serious sightseeing. He looked at his watch. "You don't have to be at the wine-tasting for at least forty minutes. Hang on tight – I'm about to give you the fastest-ever tour of Dublin."

With that he took her by the hand and pulled her quickly across the road, expertly dodging the traffic which seemed to be coming from three different directions.

"Welcome to Cormac's Concise Tour of Dublin," he said, pulling her to a stop just outside the gates of Trinity College. "Over there, the old Irish Parliament building, now the head office for the Bank of Ireland. In front of us a statue depicting the Children of Lir. Behind us, statues of Thomas Moore and Oliver Goldsmith."

Maura spun around, trying to keep up. "And who are they all?"

"I can't tell you everything, madam, this is the Concise Tour. If you want the details you'll have to take Cormac's Longwinded Tour. Now, hurry along, we've plenty more to see."

Laughing aloud, Maura struggled to keep up with him as they ran through a little stone archway into the massive cobblestoned courtyard of Trinity College. She stopped to look around.

"Yes, yes, very old, very historic, very cobbled," Cormac said, rushing her along. "Over four hundred years old. Famous old scholars include Samuel Beckett, Oscar Wilde, Bram Stoker, even our last President – Mary Robinson. Your ten seconds here are up, this way, madam."

He took her by the hand and led her toward a nearby building and up a flight of stairs.

He gestured expansively around him. "This is the famous Long Room. And if you ask me why it's called that, I'll leave you here and now to the fate of the muggers."

Maura gazed around. The Long Room was at least 200 feet long, lined on both sides at the height of both walls with the largest collection of books she had ever seen. The high windows let in a muted, mote-filled light, which added even more to the atmosphere.

"Two hundred thousand books, apparently," Cormac whispered beside her. "I could never see the appeal of it myself. A library's a library, if you ask me. Come on, we've more to see."

She followed him down through the Long Room, tiptoeing without realising it. Cormac had bought two tickets for the next attraction before she even realised where they were.

"The Book of Kells?" she whispered.

"The Book of Kells!" he whispered back, laughing at her excitement.

She had planned to visit this famous Dublin attraction anyway, before the mugger had upset her plans. Fortunately for Cormac's schedule, there was only a very small queue into the display room. As they shuffled along, Cormac read aloud the highlights from the brochure in a comic, deadpan voice.

"A Latin text of the Four Gospels. Dating from about AD800. Named after a small town in County Meath."

"You sound more like a Dalek than a tourist guide," Maura whispered at him. As they reached the top of the queue, Maura leaned over the glass case and gazed in at the intricately illuminated pages. Behind her Cormac was humming and tapping his toes impatiently. "It was done by monks," he whispered to Maura again, but loudly enough for others in the room to hear. Several people looked up, thinking he was a guide. Catching their eye, he spoke louder. "Well, no TV, no cinema, what else did they have to do in their spare time?"

Maura gave him a mock glare. This was hardly a cultural tour of the city but she was enjoying herself hugely. She'd just have to come back again and do it all properly another time.

The rest of the tour went by in a blur, as she tried to keep up with his whistle-stop pace. They virtually ran out of Trinity College, down into Westmoreland Street, across the Liffey, into O'Connell Street, and past the General Post Office – "The headquarters for the 1916 Easter Uprising," Cormac called over his shoulder, not stopping to explain any further.

Cormac took a sudden turn left into Henry Street. "This is where the statue of Molly Malone really should be," Cormac said as they rushed past small groups of women selling everything from fruit and vegetables to jewellery, out of prams. "She'd have never gone anywhere near Grafton Street and the posh end of town."

Cormac hustled her down two more streets and across the Liffey again over the iron railings of the Ha'penny Bridge. They went through an archway into a mass of cobbled streets and colourful buildings. It was teeming with people, spilling in and out of bars, restaurants and shops.

"Welcome to Temple Bar!" Cormac said, as proudly as if he had built it himself. "It was completely run-down until about ten years ago, now it's the hottest spot in town. And here is our final destination, one of our main wine-selling rivals – but all's fair when you're promoting Australian wine."

They stepped into an old warehouse building which had been converted into a very stylish wine bar and cellar.

Maura recognised Rita, Aidan and some of the other faces from the previous night's reception. Fortunately there didn't seem to be any sign of Dominic Hanrahan and the lovely Carla or Sylvie and William Rogers. She assumed they'd be attending a similar function at another wine bar in the city. The Society seemed determined to ensure they all covered as much ground and met as many people as possible.

Rita greeted them warmly, expressing surprise to see them arrive together, until Cormac explained Maura's unfortunate brush with a mugger outside his shop.

Rita was immediately sympathetic. "Oh, Maura, what an awful thing to happen on your first day here, and you still jet-lagged and all. Do you feel like your head has caught up with your body yet? Are you up to all this?"

"Just about," Maura grinned back. "And I'm fine, honestly. I just got a bit of a shock. I'm raring to go now." She looked around the wine bar with interest.

"It looks well, doesn't it?" Rita said with a wide smile, pointing at the huge display of Australian wine in the centre of the store. "We've asked all the wine stores involved in the Australian promotion to put up a display and send us photos. There's an incentive, which may explain their enthusiasm – the winner gets a trip for two to Australia."

"And because of Aidan's connections, I'm ineligible to enter," Cormac said in mock disappointment. "And I had such great ideas – a scale-model Ayers Rock, a wire coathanger for the Sydney Harbour Bridge – it would have been spectacular."

Rita groaned, as Maura looked at the display in front of her with pleasure. The Temple Bar wine merchants had gone to a great deal of trouble. They had recreated a bush setting with an elaborate display of exotic-looking foliage, creating an effect like a huge, artistic bouquet of wildflowers. They had also hung prints of Aboriginal and other Australian art on the walls of the shop, with bottles of Australian wine placed beside each one. She was delighted to see that Lorikeet Hill wines were in the middle of the display.

Rita had also hung a huge banner over the door, inviting people to a free tasting of Australian wine that afternoon.

A commotion at the door made them all turn around. A bunch of young men already the worse for drink and wearing what looked like underpants on their heads were trying to get in. The security man at the door asked them politely to go away, to which they responded with a few rowdy choruses of 'Tie Me Kangaroo Down, Sport'.

Rita rolled her eyes. "Stag parties from England," she explained. "Dublin's very trendy at the moment – this is the price you pay."

The wine-tasting went very smoothly and Maura

was pleased to see quite a lot of sales of Lorikeet Hill wine. Her formal presentations didn't begin until the next day and she enjoyed the opportunity to chat casually to the group of local restaurateurs and wine writers. She answered their questions with an ease that surprised her, explaining Nick's winemaking methods and the differences between Clare Valley wine and the other regions in Australia.

She really did feel like an ambassador, she realised, hearing herself paint a particularly poetic picture of the scenery around their winery. She hadn't appreciated herself how beautiful it was until she saw it through other people's eyes. All the yellow paddocks, blue skies and green vineyards did sound nice. Especially the thought of blue skies, she realised, looking through the window. The drizzle was back again.

After the wine-tasting, Maura was happy to be swept along with Rita, Cormac and the others to a nearby Italian restaurant for dinner. Cormac made sure she was seated between him and a friend of his who had also been invited to the wine-tasting. "Bridget's a researcher at a local Dublin radio station," Cormac explained as he introduced them. "And the source of the best gossip in this whole town."

Bridget was very curious about her opinion of Irish food and Maura admitted she hadn't really had the opportunity to try much yet, apart from breakfast in the hotel and a sticky bun at Bewley's.

It was a bit like being a doctor at a party and hearing

about people's symptoms, she thought. When she went out to dinner, people always expected her to be overly critical of the food or especially watchful of every aspect of the restaurant's service. In fact she was the opposite. She always enjoyed going out for the company and the meal and believed a successful restaurant was one where you weren't really aware of how much trouble had gone into the whole presentation.

The sound of a car alarm outside the restaurant brought the conversation around to the growing crime rate in Dublin. Cormac entertained the group with a highly exaggerated tale of Maura beating off her would-be mugger. She laughed as he made it sound as though she had suddenly metamorphosed into Wonder Woman and zapped the mugger with a radar gun.

Bridget was particularly interested in Maura's experience. "Unfortunately yours isn't a rare story at the moment," she said, suddenly serious. "There's been quite an increase lately. It's certainly no worse than any other major city but I think many tourists come to Dublin fresh from watching *Ryan's Daughter* and forget that you have to take the same safety precautions here as anywhere else."

Maura smiled, thinking back to her own expectations.

"Is there a big problem with crime where you live in Australia?" Cormac asked.

"Not where my house is, right in the middle of a vineyard. There's more danger of a cow wandering in than a burglar. But it was a real problem when I was working in a restaurant in Sydney."

Maura explained that the restaurant she and Richard had run had been in the inner city, in an area notorious for petty crime. Muggings and pick-pocketing had grown to such a level that they had decided to attach a little printed card to each bill, reminding people to be careful of their bags when they left the restaurant.

"People coming out of restaurants are easy pickings for muggers," Maura explained to Bridget. "They're usually relaxed after a good meal and a few drinks, their guards are down, and they've usually just put their wallets or purses at the tops of their bags or pockets."

"Didn't it scare people off coming to your restaurant?" Bridget asked.

"Not at all, it was the opposite if anything. People saw we were being realistic and that we had their safety at heart."

Bridget was very interested. She mentioned that her radio programme was running a series that week on the rise of petty crime in Dublin, particularly among tourists.

"Would you be interested in doing a quick interview? You'll get the opportunity to talk about Lorikeet Hill and your cooking school and restaurant nights too," she added persuasively.

Cormac was enthusiastic. "That'd be great, you can set the record straight about your first meeting with Dominic Hanrahan too and get your own back on that gossip columnist."

Bridget roared laughing at the story when Maura

recounted it. "That'd be great, our presenter will enjoy that story."

Rita was delighted for the interview to go ahead and for the Wine Society trip to get publicity. Bridget arranged to ring her in her hotel room early in the morning, before bidding her a warm farewell.

As Maura walked through lively Temple Bar on their way back to the Shelbourne, she could feel Cormac's arm occasionally brushing her back protectively. They walked past the wine shop where the tasting had been held that afternoon and she caught a glimpse of Lorikeet Hill wine in the window display. Her heart lifted. This trip would be a success, she just knew it.

Chapter Eight

Maura was wide awake, dressed and packed for her trip by the time Bridget rang from the radio station the next morning and put her on air with the presenter.

She thoroughly enjoyed talking to him. It felt more like a chat with a very curious friend than a formal interview. He was very welcoming, apologised on behalf of the city of Dublin for the mugging incident and gave her lots of opportunities to promote Lorikeet Hill and the forthcoming cooking residency in Dominic Hanrahan's house.

The presenter himself brought up the snippet from the gossip column and said he'd heard she might like to take the opportunity to give the other side of the story. Maura took pleasure in quickly recounting what had happened at Lorikeet Hill. She was encouraged by his laughter as she painted the picture of Rob's antics and her final gesture with the vase of cold water.

"Well, as I always say, listeners, don't believe everything you hear or read in the papers. There are always two sides to every story. So, Maura, what delicious dishes have you got planned for our delicate Irish palates?"

Maura described a couple of the dishes she would be cooking and spoke about the Lorikeet Hill wines she would serve with them.

"It sounds very tempting, and after hearing about your way of dealing with critics, well, I'm sure you won't be getting any complaints!"

* * *

She was sitting on a delicate armchair in the hotel foyer with her bags beside her when Dominic and Carla came through the revolving doors. Dominic was polite, while Carla barely managed a smile, instead giving her a very pointed inspection, her mocking expression showing her contempt for Maura's clothes.

Maura felt her chin lift defiantly. She had dressed with great care this morning in a tailored fine-wool suit and knew she looked stylish and comfortable.

Carla broke away from her inspection to rummage in her large and obviously expensive handbag. With a malicious smile on her face she held out a folded newspaper.

"I've brought you yesterday's paper in case you didn't get the chance to see it. You got a very big mention, and you do know of course that it's Ireland's biggest-selling paper. Thousands of people all over the country would have read it," she added, smirking.

"And even more would have heard her on the radio this morning, wouldn't they, Maura?"

Maura spun around, smiling broadly at the sight of Cormac.

"What are you doing here?"

"I just had to say goodbye and congratulate you on your interview this morning. I don't think I've ever heard the presenter laugh so much."

"Yes, it was very entertaining," Dominic added in a quiet voice.

Maura looked at Dominic, surprised to see something approaching a smile on his face. She hadn't expected a millionaire businessman to do anything as ordinary as listen to the radio. She also hadn't expected him to have a sense of humour.

Not knowing what they were talking about, Carla looked back and forth at them, fury evident on her face.

Cormac put his arm around Maura. "Our little Aussie was interviewed on the radio this morning, and it was great listening, especially when you got to hear both sides of the story." He glanced at the newspaper in Carla's hand.

As Carla's eyes narrowed, Dominic smoothly broke in. "We haven't met. I'm Dominic Hanrahan."

Cormac put out his hand. "Yes, I've heard a lot about you. I'm Cormac Sheehan, of Graham's Wine Merchants. I understand you've stepped into the breach for Miss Carmody. I'm sure the Wine Society is very grateful." Cormac turned briskly from Dominic and to

Maura's surprise, swept her into his arms for a hug and a kiss. "Well, goodbye and good luck, Maura. Have a great time and I'll look forward to seeing you in Clare one night." He left with a flamboyant wave.

Dominic stood back silently. If he was surprised at the sudden friendship she had formed, he didn't show it. He checked his watch.

"We'd better be going, if we're to make Sligo for your first appointment. Do you have everything, Maura?"

Carla pouted and started to speak in a little girl's voice. "I wish I didn't have this appointment. I want to come with you."

Dominic touched her arm. "I'll call you tonight. Remember you can ring me if you need me."

Maura guessed it was a modelling appointment. Carla certainly had the looks and the body for it. It was Maura's turn to study Dominic and Carla closely, especially in light of all she now knew about their set-up. It was definitely an unusual arrangement. Carla was a pouting mixture of sex kitten and little girl, while Dominic seemed to be looking at her with almost clinical detachment. Watching his investment, Maura decided, imagining the sound of a cash register.

She suddenly wished again that the next four weeks were over and she was home, writing up the article, putting a golden gloss on everything. She could hardly leave now and write a four-page article on her two and a half days in Dublin. Unless it was a warning piece about muggers.

As Carla dragged out her farewell with Dominic, Maura settled herself into his luxurious car. When Dominic finally joined her, she became acutely aware of the strained silence between them. One half of her still wanted to apologise properly to him about the misunderstanding at Lorikeet Hill. God knows she and Nick needed this trip to be a success.

But the other half thought 'To hell with the apologies'. Now she knew his whole story she felt it wasn't up to her to make things any easier for him. All right, so he hadn't been responsible for Gemma's restaurant closing, but he certainly hadn't stopped Carla from feeding vicious gossip to her columnist friend. And if Cormac was right, he was using poor Bernadette's misfortune for his own ends.

If he was a moral vacuum, then any apology from her would just go to waste in any case. She held her chin up high. On Saturday night he had questioned her professionalism. She'd show him she was professional right down to the tips of her toes. She'd show him, and Carla and anyone else, that she had the ability to make a real go of this trip.

As they pulled into the Dublin traffic, she became aware that Dominic was saying something to her.

"I beg your pardon?" she queried, trying to sound calm and collected. "I didn't catch what you said."

"No, I gathered that," he answered, with a half smile. "You seemed to be fairly tied up with your own conversation."

Maura flushed with colour. She must have been talking aloud! She knew she had a rather bad habit of doing that, especially when she was trying to motivate herself. With any luck he wouldn't have understood a mumbled Australian accent.

Embarrassed, she tried to sound even more businesslike. "Well, you have my full attention now, if you could please repeat what you were saying."

"I asked, would you mind if I put on the radio?"

Oh, was that all? Maura thought. She nodded readily, grateful as the sound of classical music cut out any need for conversation. A week of this tension, she thought with a faint feeling of dread. She'd be worn out.

The music also gave her the opportunity to gaze out of the window at the scenery which was new to her yet still felt strangely familiar. The colours were definitely softer, the light not as bright as the Australian glare.

She recalled the brief conversation she had had with Nick that morning. She had finally had a chance to ring in the few minutes before Dominic arrived to collect her.

He had found the whole idea of the mystery food critic turning up in Dublin absolutely hilarious.

"That poor bloke," Nick had laughed. "The real critic was probably sitting at the next table watching all of this going on and wondering what sort of a nuthouse he'd walked in on!"

That hadn't even occurred to Maura. She'd been too

shocked at Dominic turning up to even think about the real critic. Well, it was too late to do anything about him now, she decided. And she couldn't do much from Dublin anyway. She changed the subject to Fran and was relieved to hear she was well.

"We had a bit of a scare the day after you left, when we thought the baby wanted to arrive early, but things have settled down again." Maura could hear the worry in Nick's voice, despite his attempts to reassure her that everything was fine.

He answered her unspoken question. "I'll ring you as soon as anything happens, you know that. And don't worry, really, Fran's fine, I'm fine, and Gemma's doing brilliantly in the kitchen too. We're dying to hear all your adventures, especially how you get on when you start looking around County Clare."

She had interrupted him there. "Nick, don't start on all that again."

"I won't, I won't, I promise. Just enjoy yourself and don't let that bloke give you a hard time!"

She had hung up determined even more to make a success of this trip, for Nick as much as for herself.

An hour into the journey, a lively burst of jazz from the radio heralded a food-discussion programme. Maura settled back and listened with interest, until Dominic reached over and switched stations, muttering something about the rubbish on the radio.

It certainly broke the silence between them. She turned in her seat to look right at him. "Just what is it with you and food?" she asked, genuinely puzzled. "First you talk about the hype and pretension of Australian food, then you tell me you've closed *OzTaste* down. Were you brought up in a monastery or something?"

He answered without looking at her but she saw a nerve twitch in his jaw.

"No, it was a normal house, as a matter of fact. A normal house where food was served because it's what your body needs to keep going, not because some new ingredient is suddenly trendy, or some desperate chef has travelled to some exotic country and stolen traditional ideas and called them his or her own."

She was astonished. "That's just inverted snobbery. Most chefs aren't like that at all."

"Did you ever actually read *OzTaste?*" he asked. "It was more of a food pornography magazine than a genuine discussion of cooking. Endless close up photographs of artistically arranged chillis and vanilla beans and other food most people never see, let alone eat. It was no wonder it hardly sold. I was amazed to hear it had lasted as long as it did."

"So you'll close down all the other magazines that don't match up with your ideal of what people should and shouldn't be eating, or wearing or enjoying, is that it? That's not publishing, that's making moral judgements." She was getting fired up now.

"Not at all," he said mildly. "I don't care in the least if some people choose to spend four hours every day concocting *jus* or wilting their spinach or whatever the latest fad is. But as a publisher my job is to publish magazines people will actually read."

She was indignant. "So it's goodbye to *Business Woman* as well, is it?" she said, naming another magazine in his stable. "Presumably you would also prefer women to stay at home and cook stews and bake their own bread, rather than be out working for a living?"

He acknowledged her sarcasm with a slight smile. "At the moment *Business Woman* isn't selling, so yes, I may look at closing it down."

"How can you make those sorts of judgements?" She was wide-eyed at his coolness.

"It's not a judgement, it's a business decision. If you put a particular dish on your menu at Lorikeet Hill every day for two years just because you liked it, yet no one ever ordered it, would you keep it on the menu?"

She took a deep breath. "Well, of course not."

"Then what's the difference? You'd be making a sound business decision, based on market research, and that's exactly what I'm doing with *OzTaste* and any other magazine that's not performing."

"But how can you just march into Australia and axe all these magazines? You don't even know the country, or the people."

"How can you march into Ireland with your Australian wine, and your Australian style of food, and presume everyone here will enjoy it too?"

"Because food and wine are universal. Everyone,

well, everyone except you by the sounds of things, enjoys good food and wine and relaxed company."

"I enjoy good food, good wine and good company, very much. And as much as it might surprise you, I like to cook too," he said quietly. "What I object to is when it is turned into some sort of high fashion."

She was about to argue the point again when their attention was taken by the sudden braking of the car ahead. She sat silently as the reason for the sudden stop emerged – a herd of cattle being driven across the road. She smiled to herself. She'd known if she waited long enough she'd see some of that touristy Ireland. If it had been Bernadette she was travelling with they would have enjoyed a laugh, maybe hopped out to take a photograph with the camera she had ready. Instead, neither she nor Dominic spoke a word.

The current affairs programme on the radio was the only sound in the car for some time.

Grateful she was saved from attempting a conversation for a little while, Maura watched the passing scenery with great interest, taking mental photographs and looking forward to checking her guidebooks and asking Bernadette what sights they would have driven past. The last thing she wanted to do was ask Dominic any questions. So far they hadn't seemed able to have a reasonable conversation. She closed her eyes for a moment. This couldn't go on between them. They had to work together. Lorikeet Hill needed this to work. She practised yet another apology in her head.

She opened her eyes, about to speak, when the sight of an enormous mountain rising ahead of them suddenly caught her attention. It had the most unusual shape, as though a whole layer had just been swiped off the top of it.

"That's Ben Bulben," Dominic spoke suddenly. "There's a little churchyard at the foot of it and the poet WB Yeats is buried there. He wrote his own epitaph in a poem called 'Under Ben Bulben'. It's on his gravestone – *Cast a cold eye, On life, on death, Horseman, pass by!*"

She looked at him in surprise.

He smiled across at her. "Did I surprise you? I've always thought everybody should know some poetry."

"I have to confess I know very little. I guess I didn't expect a hardnosed business man to have an interest in something so ethereal." She grinned suddenly, to take the edge off her words.

"Well, you know what they say, music and poetry are like food for the soul." He smiled again and she realised he too was offering her an olive branch.

They looked over at Ben Bulben again. "It's not quite Ayers Rock but it's pretty impressive, isn't it?" he said. A swirling layer of mist was drifting across the top, and the mountainside itself looked like it had been draped in great swathes of dark-green cloths.

She seized the opportunity to continue the conversation. "Did you see the Rock when you were in Australia last month?"

"Not this time. I saw it on my first trip there on

business, about five years ago. I try to have a few days' holiday on the end of each trip. Try out the latest restaurants, you know the sort of thing."

She knew he was teasing her, but wasn't sure enough of the new truce to snap a retort back. Instead she went on with her questioning.

"And had Carla been to Australia before?"

"Once." He didn't elaborate.

"On holiday?" she asked, quite curious where someone as exotic as Carla would go. The Gold Coast, probably. Or to one of the island resorts.

"No," Dominic answered shortly.

"Oh, was she working?" Maura asked. Perhaps Carla had worked as a model at one of the new gala Fashion Weeks. The sponsors had flown in quite a few international models to give the local industry a kick.

"No, she wasn't working." His voice was suddenly hard. She looked over at him in surprise. It was as though a shutter had come down on his face. She was about to say something when he pointedly leaned over and turned up the volume on the radio as the news came on.

Maura felt the chill settle in around them again. 'I bet it was business,' she thought. 'The business of keeping Carla happy so you can get her father's money.' Carla had probably taken a sudden fancy for a cruise on Sydney Harbour and Dominic hadn't dared to refuse her.

Chapter Nine

As the empty fields gave way to clusters of houses, Maura realised they were coming into Sligo. According to the notes the Wine Society had supplied, the first off-licence on her itinerary, The Auld Drop, was on the outskirts of the town and was run by a young man from the local area.

The shop was in a good position in the middle of a busy street. Maura felt a touch of excitement as she walked in through the front door. The wine-tasting in Dublin had felt like a party. This seemed like the real start to her promotional tour.

The manager had certainly gone to an enormous amount of trouble with the display, Maura thought, as she fought her way into the shop past all the props. But she wasn't quite sure if she could get the connection.

The floor was covered with thousands of foam balls, as if a dozen bean-bags had been opened and emptied everywhere. A pair of snow-skis were placed up against the counter. Maura guessed the foam balls were supposed to represent beach sand, and maybe snow-skis were the closest things to water-skis here in Ireland.

Standing beside the counter was a young woman wearing a brightly coloured knee-length dress and a ruffled white apron.

"Hello," Maura said tentatively. "This is Dominic Hanrahan from the Wine Society and I'm Maura Carmody, from Lorikeet Hill Wines. We're here for the wine-tasting."

The girl smiled broadly, put out her hand and gave a nervous cough. *"Guten Tag, Fraulein und Herr. Ich heisse Nancy."* She pulled her hand back suddenly and leaned down to operate something under the counter. The sound of accordion music suddenly filled the store.

Maura and Dominic both jumped at the noise. The young woman apologised profusely, before starting to speak directly to Maura in a very slow, very loud voice.

"You are very welcome. I just wanted to make you feel as much at home as possible. I love your wine here. And look, we've made a big sign especially in your honour."

She practically skipped toward the door, where she unfurled a big banner on which huge letters had been painted:

Meet an Austrian Winemaker Here Today.

Maura swallowed deeply, turning around just in time to see Dominic make a strange sound which turned into a cough. He busied himself with the bottles of wine on display.

"Nancy, I'm not sure how to say this," said Maura, "but I'm actually Australian, not Austrian."

Nancy looked completely shocked. "Australian? As in *Neighbours* Australia? *Home and Away* Australia? Down Under Australia?"

Maura nodded.

"What's an Australian doing in Austria making wine?" Nancy asked, in a puzzled voice.

"I'm not from Austria. I'm from Australia, where we make Australian wine," Maura said gently.

"You don't have any connections with Austria at all?" Nancy asked desperately.

"Uhm, I have seen *The Sound of Music* a few times," Maura offered.

A look of dismay came over Nancy's face. She began to speak very quickly. "I'm so sorry, I actually don't even work here. I normally work in the pharmacy across the way, but my brother's had the flu the last few days and I've been looking after the place for him. I was sure he said you were coming from Austria!"

Maura tried to make the best of it but the young woman was not to be consoled, as she tried in vain to remove the Austrian-style apron from around her waist.

Maura looked around at the foam balls and snow-skis and bit at her lip in an effort to stop herself from laughing, but to no avail.

Nancy looked up from her sobs and caught Maura's eye just as she started to laugh. A wan smile spread across the young girl's face, as she realised the funny side of it too.

"It's really not that bad," Maura said through her laughter. "Come on, we'll go ahead anyway."

Maura quickly set up a tasting table beside the wooden models of Austrian chalets, while Nancy hastily wrote some new signs. Nancy did manage to find one CD of Australian music, before Maura gently suggested Austrian accordion music might be a better lure than AC DC belting out heavy-metal anthems.

Within minutes quite a few people had wandered into the store, lured by the signs and the jaunty sound of Austrian music piping onto the footpath. The local shoppers didn't seem to mind in the least that Maura was Australian not Austrian, and the tasting and sales went along quite briskly.

Maura looked around the shop during a brief lull in the wine-tasting, suddenly realising that Dominic had disappeared. Well, thank you for your support, she thought, a little crossly. Several minutes later she saw him come back in, accompanied by a young woman carrying a bulky-looking camera around her neck.

Dominic seemed to be explaining something to her, at which the young woman stopped, looked around and burst into gales of laughter.

The pair of them came up to her at the wine-tasting table. "Maura, may I introduce Orla Keenan from the local newspaper. I thought that if Nancy doesn't mind, this might make a great photo story."

Orla had composed herself and was smiling at Maura.

"God help us, you must think you've arrived in the land of eejits altogether. Still, it's a great story, maybe even a front-page pic – much better coverage than you would have got normally." She winked.

Maura took back her mean thoughts, and gave Dominic a grateful smile. She would never have thought of contacting the local paper.

By the time they left an hour later, Nancy was greatly consoled by the attention the shop had received and by the steady stream of people who had come to have a look, many attracted by Orla setting up the photographic session outside the shop.

As they climbed back into the car and waved goodbye to Nancy, Maura looked over at Dominic. "Thanks for your help there," she smiled. "That was a great idea to contact the newspaper."

He inclined his head, and gave her a warm grin. "You're very welcome," he said softly.

Leaning her head back against the comfortable headrest, she thought again with a jolt how strikingly attractive he was. If only they hadn't got off to such a bad start. If only he wasn't with Carla. If only she hadn't found out he had sold a few years of his life for a few million dollars.

Chapter Ten

Rita rang on the car phone just as they were driving away from the final appointment of the day, a wine-tasting with the Sligo Wine Appreciation Club. It was past six and Maura's mind was swirling with the conversations she'd had. The entire day had flown by in a blur of off-licences, wine bottles and glasses. She hoped Nick's ears were burning with all the compliments his wine was receiving.

Dominic switched the phone into hands-free mode and Maura felt very selfconscious as she conducted her conversation, feeling like she was speaking into the glovebox. She quickly filled Rita in on their adventures so far, expressing her surprise at how short the travelling times had been.

"I thought we'd have to drive like demons to get from place to place when I looked at them all on the map," she said. "I was expecting Australian distances, I guess. This is a breeze."

Rita laughed at the story of the Austrian display, and thanked Maura for taking it in such good spirits. Then her voice became conspiratorial. "I've just had one of the poor off-licence owners from Kerry on the phone, complaining that Mrs Rogers had been in like a human tornado. He said he's spent days doing his display and she came in and completely rearranged it within seconds, while her poor husband cowered in the background."

Maura laughed out loud. "Which counties are they visiting?" she asked.

"Kerry, Cork and Waterford," Rita said. Her voice dropped to a whisper again, as if she was scared Mrs Rogers would overhear the conversation. "Actually, the Rogers were originally scheduled to travel around Wexford, Kilkenny and Carlow in the South East, until Mrs Rogers did her research and discovered that Kerry is one of the most popular counties in the country. So she made a fuss, threatened to pull out of the trip and cancel any funding to the Society unless we changed it around. So we had to."

Maura was taken aback at Rita's candour, but had to admit she loved hearing all the gossip from behind the scenes. Rita didn't seem to take any of it too seriously.

The line was getting crackly, but she could just make out Rita's words. "She tried to take Galway, as well, from you and Lorikeet Hill, until we explained about the twinning connection between the two Clares, and how it made sense for you to do the neighbouring counties too.

But I heard her asking how long it would take to drive from Cork to Galway, so you never know . . ."

The mobile phone suddenly went out of range and the connection was lost.

Dominic looked over. "Mrs Rogers is the terrifying woman from the cocktail party, I guess?"

Maura was about to elaborate, when a mental image of Mrs Rogers feeding gossip about her and Richard to Carla crossed her mind. She suddenly decided to keep quiet. Maybe she'd started to relax too much with Dominic. She had to remind herself of the Carla connection. And his deal with her father.

Instead, she smiled brightly. "That's her. Good heavens, you get some characters in this industry, don't you?"

Her airy reply surprised him, she could see that, and he was about to ask her another question when she made a point of looking at her itinerary again. She and Dominic weren't staying in Sligo that night, but moving on to a small town in Mayo, to give them an early start the next morning. She estimated less than an hour's travelling time. Good, she could have an early night. It was just what she needed. The jet-lag wasn't too bad but she was tired nevertheless.

Dominic was quiet as they drove through the town. She glanced over at him surreptitiously. They'd hardly exchanged a word all afternoon. Maura had been busy conducting the wine-tasting and every time she had looked over at Dominic, he'd been speaking on his mobile phone. Either Carla or work, she'd guessed. God knows how he'd managed to be able to take off a week like this, when he was in charge of an international company. But maybe that was one of the perks. You hired others to do the running around for you, while you managed from afar.

She looked at him again. He seemed worried about something.

She spoke impulsively, hoping she wasn't intruding on him. "Is everything all right, Dominic? I'm sorry to be so curious but I saw you on the phone. I realise this is keeping you away from your work and I really do appreciate you guiding me around, despite our shaky start. If you have to cut it short, really, I'll understand." She smiled across at him.

He looked at her for a long moment, as if he wasn't completely separated from his thoughts. Then a sudden grin changed his whole face. "No, I'm fine, work is absolutely fine. Everything's fine. But thanks for asking."

"You're welcome," she answered quietly, wondering if she was going soft in the head. Two days ago she was practically spitting at this man, now she was gently enquiring after his health. Hunger, that's what it was. She was getting lightheaded with hunger and that, mixed with the leftover jet-lag, was obviously a pretty potent combination.

Dominic spoke suddenly. "We've time for a pub meal if you're up to it, or would you rather drive straight on to the hotel we're staying in tonight?"

She was taken by surprise. "Actually, I'm ravenous. I'd love something to eat."

"Then eat you will," he said lightly, as he found a parking space not far from a pub advertising evening meals.

She glanced over again, trying to fathom his mood. Despite his easy manner, he was obviously preoccupied about something. She started to wonder if there was another problem with the trip. Perhaps there was a problem with Bernadette's house after all? She suddenly pulled herself up. What are you doing, Maura Carmody? she asked herself in exasperation. You're in beautiful Sligo, in beautiful Ireland, you're about to have your first authentic Irish pub meal instead of an Australian theme pub version. Now stop worrying and start enjoying yourself!

"Exactly," Dominic answered.

She looked up quickly. "I was doing it again?" He nodded. She caught his mood, and grinned up at him.

As they were waiting to cross the road, a gust of wind blew handfuls of her hair across his face. Apologising, she gathered the unruly tendrils back into a loose plait behind her head.

"You've got beautiful hair," he said, to her surprise. She looked up, about to babble on about it actually being a real bother to wash and how she'd always longed for thick straight hair. Then she stopped and cursed herself for behaving like a teenager out on a first date. Taking a deep breath, she looked up at him and gave what she hoped was a very grown-up smile. "Thank you," she said stiffly. Inside she groaned. Now she sounded like the Queen Mother thanking a loyal subject for shining her shoes, she thought. What was it about Dominic that kept unsettling her?

They walked into the pub, which was only half-full, but looked very comfortable. And it was warm, Maura thought with relief. The evening had turned very cold and she gratefully went over to a blazing log fire and warmed herself in front of it, looking at the blackboard menu hanging on the wall as she did.

"I'll order at the bar while I get you a drink, will I? What would you like – wine, Guinness?"

She shook her head. "Just a mineral water, please." She was feeling a bit lightheaded already, and an alcoholic drink would probably tip her over the edge.

"And food?" he asked.

Her choice was simple. "Seafood chowder for me," she said.

They were soon seated at a table close to the fire, steaming bowls of soup and freshly cut bread in front of them. Maura tasted it and sighed. "Oh, this is delicious. I love fish and seafood. I don't get to have it very often these days."

"But Australia's surrounded by sea – surely you can get hold of all sorts of exotic fish for Lorikeet Hill," he asked.

"Not really, Clare's too far from the coast and we can't always rely on getting fresh fish. I base most of our menus on what is produced locally, lamb and beef especially. It was great when I was in Sydney – we could experiment with lots of different fish dishes."

"That was the restaurant you owned with Richard Hillman, is that right?"

She looked up in surprise, before remembering the newspaper article. Of course he knew who Richard Hillman was. "No, it was Richard's restaurant, I was the apprentice really."

"But you were more than that . . . ?" Dominic left the question unfinished. It seemed it was his turn to probe.

"For a while," Maura answered, suddenly finding a spot on her wrist to scratch. It was a nervous habit she had when she found herself embarrassed or under scrutiny.

Dominic watched her movement with interest. "You don't like talking about it?"

Maura looked down. "No, it's not that, I must have been bitten by something," she improvised. "So tell me, how did you get started in magazine publishing?"

He gave a slight smile, acknowledging her swift change of subject. She'd half-expected him to evade her question, to stay mysterious, but to her surprise he seemed relaxed, almost pleased to talk about it.

"I'd wanted to be either a musician or a writer and thought it was as simple as that: you decided what you wanted to be, and then that's what you were. But it's not like that, of course, and my parents very cleverly talked me into studying for a degree in journalism here in Ireland."

"So you're a journalist?" Maura asked. "Did you work in newspapers here when you graduated?"

"No, I never completed the degree," he answered.

"Oh, why not?" Maura asked. Many of her friends had dropped out of courses midway and gone on to very interesting careers.

He looked up but not at her. "My parents were killed in a car accident when I was in my first year at college. I dropped out then, and didn't have the heart to continue. That's when I went to America. And I never really came back."

She watched him closely as he spoke. She had an odd feeling he hadn't told this story very often and was as surprised to be telling it as she was to be hearing it.

He explained that in his first year in New York he had just found work in Irish pubs and cheap restaurants. "Then I kept thinking about the writing and being a journalist after all, so I scratched all my savings together and started up a small street magazine for Irish people in New York.

"It wasn't exactly investigative reporting," he laughed softly as he remembered it. "I got most of the news from home out of old copies of the Irish newspapers in the library, or from phone calls with people back here. And it looked very rough and ready – but a lot of people started reading it. And because of that, advertisers got interested too, so it started to take off. Still a pretty basic print-job, mind you, and only once a fortnight, but it did very well. Then I did a foolish thing – overstretched myself and got into financial trouble. So I took a gamble and went to see one of the newspaper bosses to see if he'd help me through the bad times, with me paying him back when it came good. And he took a gamble on me." He grinned, the light suddenly coming back into his eyes.

"And that was Carla's father?" she guessed.

He gave her a surprised look. "Bernadette told you that?"

She just smiled mysteriously. Well, Bernadette probably would have told her if she'd known. She thought it best not to mention her source, just in case Dominic happened to know Cormac had a friend in the company.

"She's a better information service than Reuters," he said with a laugh, mistaking her silence for assent. "But yes, it was Carla's father. He realised it was an idea ready for its time," he explained. "There are always thousands of Irish people in New York looking for news from home, so we started producing a quality weekly paper, hired a couple of real writers to help me out and we actually reported on events in Ireland within days rather than months." Dominic took a sip of his drink, then continued his story.

"Henry Thomas, Carla's father, had an Irish great-grandmother, so he had an interest in the country. That one did so well, I was able to pay him back very quickly, so then he let me loose on my other ideas. I set up a music magazine, mostly focusing on new bands.

Then I started one to promote young American writers. We discovered a new hip writer from New York, which gave us a lot of kudos, and it just went from there. Henry was a great man, full of ideas himself. I miss him."

"And do you write yourself?" she asked.

"Ah, I used to, then I realised I had a better talent for recognising other people's genius."

"And now you travel the world?"

"Closing down magazines that don't suit my taste?" he finished, teasing her.

She blushed, glad the low light hid her rising colour.

He glanced at her, then continued. "Australia's a new market for the company, but yes, we've big plans there, and here too. That's the main part of my job now, researching possible markets and openings for new publications. Maybe you can convince me there's a market in Australia for a weekly magazine of restaurant reviews?"

She smiled wryly at him. She wasn't getting into all of that again. Finishing her drink, she looked at her watch and realised with a start it was nearly ten o'clock. The open fire, the food and the surprisingly easy conversation with Dominic had made the time sweep past.

He caught her glance and seemed surprised at the time himself.

"We'd better drive on," he said. "But we're not far away, you'll be asleep well before midnight, I promise."

Feeling pleasantly full and cosy in the warm car, Maura let her thoughts drift, enjoying the soft classical music playing from the radio. The car quickly left Sligo town behind, and she gazed out into the night, guessing that the large shadows on the horizon were mountains, and seeing tiny dots of lights sprinkled across the fields.

One day gone. It felt like a week already. Tomorrow they'd travel through Mayo and Galway and the day after that they would move on to County Clare. Maura felt herself tense at the idea but was determined not to think about it yet. There'll be plenty of time for that, she told herself. She leaned her head against the comfortable headrest and let her eyelids slowly close.

A sudden noise awoke her with a start. Her neck was sore and the side of her face felt cold from where she was leaning against the window. The car had stopped. Outside, it was very misty and a steady drizzle of rain was falling. There was no sign of any town lights – or of Dominic. Maura opened the door and then shrieked in fright as a figure stood up from a kneeling position beside her.

Dominic's voice was calm in the darkness. "It's okay, it's me. We've had a puncture, I've just changed the tyre. The spare is quite flat too – I'll have to get them both repaired in the morning. Luckily we haven't got much further to drive tonight."

"Oh, you should have woken me, I could have helped, or at least got out, made the car lighter." She knew she was babbling but they were standing uncomfortably close.

"I managed perfectly well. And you were in a very deep sleep, I didn't want to wake you."

She was embarrassed to think she had fallen asleep in front of him. She only hoped she hadn't started talking in her sleep, or even worse, snoring. If she knew one thing, it was that she wanted to keep her wits about her when she was with Dominic.

She got back into the car, rubbing her sore neck as she heard him move to the back of the car to put the flat tyre away. As she started to wake up properly, he climbed back into the driver's seat and looked over at her.

"You slept for quite a while. Are you still feeling jet-lagged?"

"Not too bad, I'm sure I'm nearly over it," she said, putting on a deceptively cheery voice.

"We're nearly there, I'm sure you'll be back asleep very soon."

Maura breathed deeply, looking forward to the idea of some time to herself in her own hotel room. She certainly felt more relaxed with Dominic than she had when they set off this morning, but the tension still ebbed and flowed between them.

She knew a lot of it was coming from her. She had felt herself growing to like him, especially in the occasional moments when he would relax or smile at her. Certainly, she couldn't deny the fact that he was a very attractive man. But every time she felt the attraction she made herself remember Dominic's deal with Carla's father. And Dominic's reasons for helping Bernadette. He might be charming and handsome, but that didn't mean she could trust him.

It was almost eleven thirty and the rain was still falling as they drove slowly through the narrow, cobbled streets of their destination for the evening. Dominic found the hotel with ease but it took more than five minutes to find a space in the crowded carpark. The hotel foyer was also bustling with activity and Maura could see groups of men and women gathered in the bar area. She was surprised at how busy it was.

The middle-aged receptionist smiled brightly at them as they walked toward the reception desk, carrying their suitcases, but it was a tense smile, Maura could tell. One of those professional 'I'll be nice to you as long as you don't give me a second's trouble' smiles. Maura had a version she used herself on particularly busy days at Lorikeet Hill.

"The rooms are booked under the name of the Wine Society, aren't they?" Dominic asked Maura as they reached the desk. She nodded. All the travelling and accommodation details had been sorted out weeks ago – she remembered sitting on the verandah at home in South Australia looking at the name of this hotel and trying to imagine what it would be like.

The receptionist ran her finger down a long list of names and slowly and carefully marked two small crosses beside their booking. She looked up and smiled the stiff smile again. "I hope you don't mind carrying your own bags up. As you can see, we've a terrible rush on tonight."

"No, that's fine," Maura answered, suddenly very weary and longing for her bed.

"That's grand, so," the older woman said with a distracted air, before dropping a key-ring onto the counter with a loud clatter. "So that's just the one double room, Mr and Mrs Carmody, straight up the stairs there to your left."

Chapter Eleven

Dominic and Maura spoke as one. "One double room?"

Dominic recovered first. "I'm sorry, there must be some mistake. Ms Carmody and myself are business associates. There should be two separate rooms."

"Well, I'm sorry, Mr Carmody . . ."

"It's Hanrahan, not Carmody," Dominic corrected her quietly.

"I'm sorry sir, yes, we did have the Wine Society booking as a two-room suite. But then we had this conference come in, and then we lost the use of two of the rooms because of storm damage to the drains last week, so we had to juggle the rooms around."

That storm again, Maura thought to herself. It was like the hounds of hell following her around, upsetting all her plans. Thank God she hadn't been in the country at the time. With her current run of luck she probably would have been swept up in a rogue tornado, never to be seen again.

The receptionist was continuing her explanation. "I'm sorry you weren't told about the change before you arrived. I'm sure someone meant to ring you but we've been so busy. Our room allocations manager must have assumed you were together because you both were booked under the same surname."

Maura realised immediately what had happened. The bookings were still under the Carmody surnames. She and Bernadette had thought it a sign of fate that they shared the same name, as a good start to their friendship. She hadn't imagined it getting her into this mess.

"Well, I'm sure it won't be a problem changing the booking into two separate rooms," Dominic said in a steady voice, but one that showed he expected to get his own way.

"Oh, I'm afraid that's impossible, sir. As you can see, we're completely full tonight. Indeed, I know for a fact there isn't a room free in the town tonight, or in the next town if it comes to that. You know what they say, if it doesn't rain it pours. We've got the Car Dealers Annual General Meeting, a group of local councillors up from Cork on a fact-finding trip, the ladies from the Catholic Women's League, a volleyball team from the North of England . . ."

Dominic interrupted her politely but firmly. "There must be another room in the hotel. Surely you can understand the situation?"

The woman's professional smile suddenly slipped.

She looked from left to right, then leaned forward over the counter until she was just inches from them.

"Sir, I have been up since four am this morning. It is now nearly midnight. I have had more complaints today than I have had in ten years. Taps not working. Beds not long enough. Views not interesting enough. Pillows not soft enough. I am tired. I want to go home to my bed. You look tired too. You both look like fine, normal people, I don't think either of you is hiding an axe in your bags.

"Let me give you some advice," she continued, as her voice got more and more gruff. "Turn the lights off while you're both getting undressed. Put a pillow between you to stop any overwhelming thoughts of lust. Say a rosary together before you sleep if you think it will help. I would even quickly build you another room if I could, but I am telling you . . ." the professional smile suddenly switched back on, " I really am sorry but there is no other room available tonight. Good evening to you both."

With that the woman placed a sign reading *Reception Closed until 7 am* with a bang on the desk in front of her, and walked purposefully out from behind the desk, heading straight for the bar.

Maura bit her lip. She wasn't sure whether she wanted to panic, to laugh or to cry.

Dominic broke the silence. "We can't really drive on any further with that tyre. I'll have to sleep in the car," he said.

"Don't be ridiculous," Maura answered quickly, pleased to be able to come across as the voice of reason. "It's raining, you'll be cold, we'll just have to manage. There's probably a couch or something like that in the room – one of us can sleep on that. Me, I'm the smallest. Come on, we won't get to sleep standing here all night."

She took up both bags firmly and moved toward the stairs, glad to see the weight stopped her hands from shaking. God knows she found it unsettling enough sitting in the same car as him, let alone sleeping in the same bedroom. Still, if it was big enough, they could even make up a small bed on the floor.

One second in their room put paid to any idea of sleeping on the couch. It was the smallest room she had ever seen. There was barely room for the double bed, let alone a couch. Two tiny bedside tables, with barely enough room to hold a phone on one and a lamp on the other, were crammed tight against the bed. There wasn't even room for an ensuite bathroom. She gathered from a sign pinned to the wall that they were supposed to use the facilities just down the corridor from the room.

If she'd been here on her wedding anniversary she might have found it cosy and romantic. But this was close to a hostage situation, sharing something the size of a cell.

Dominic's face gave nothing away. She could see the little muscle on his cheek twitch, but wasn't sure if it was anger, amusement or a sudden attack of unbridled lust. She didn't know which of the three would be worse.

She decided to be as brisk and businesslike as she could to break through her nervousness. "Well, we'll just have to make do. As the lady said, it's late and there's nowhere else we can go. We're both adults, I'm sure we can get through one night and we'll make sure to phone ahead and change the bookings in the other hotels first thing in the morning."

"Yes, first thing," he said, the smile still playing around his lips.

"Perhaps you'd like to have a quick drink in the bar while I get changed and ready for bed," she suggested. To her own ears she sounded like she had suddenly turned into Mary Poppins: 'Come on now, spit spot, none of this messing around or you won't get any supper.'

To her relief, Dominic seemed to think it was a perfectly reasonable suggestion. "I'll say goodnight now, then, you may be asleep by the time I come back in."

Some chance of that, she thought, as the door closed behind him. She looked around the room in exasperation. This wasn't exactly the night she'd been expecting. She'd imagined a quiet drink in a cosy bar before they went up to their rooms, and the opportunity to hear some of the traditional musicians the West of Ireland was apparently famous for. That hadn't seemed to be the preferred entertainment in the bar downstairs. To her untrained ear it had sounded more like country and western karaoke, with either the car dealers or the county councillors singing up a storm.

Maura looked again at the double bed taking up nearly all of the available space in the room. She knew she would lie rigid with nerves all night in case they happened to touch. "Stop being so ridiculous," she told herself crossly. She and Richard had lived together for nearly two years. She was twenty eight years old, a woman of the world. Why was she carrying on as though she was on day-release from the local convent?

As she found the tiny bathroom down the hall and got ready for bed, she spoke to herself in a firm voice, talking down her nerves. All she had to do to keep him away from her was leave her bank book lying around. Her paltry savings wouldn't compare with the aphrodisiac qualities of Carla's millions. She'd just climb into bed, fall asleep and before long it would be morning and back to business.

Then why was it she felt more awake than she had in days? Where was her jet-lag when she needed it most? She didn't even feel tired after her sleep in the car. Still, she'd hurry up, brush her teeth, change into her pyjamas . . . oh no, the thought suddenly hit her. She didn't usually sleep in pyjamas, and had brought just the one pair with her.

Nick and Fran had given them to her as a farewell present, laughing that every girl needed a pair of special pyjamas, just in case her hotel suddenly caught fire and she had to stand outside for hours watching the firemen at work.

Back in the room, she rummaged around in her case, hoping her memory had deceived her and they weren't as bad as she remembered. They were. But there was no choice. It was either wear them or go naked. It was the best of a bad choice. Keeping an ear out for Dominic's return, she pulled out the pyjamas and clambered into them as quickly as she could.

A sound in the corridor outside sent her hurtling for her side of the bed. She pulled up the covers to her chin, grabbed a book from the bedside table and lay as close to the edge as she could, trying to appear nonchalant. A moment later there was a gentle knock and Dominic's voice inquiring if it was all right to come in. She wondered whether to fake a snore but thought that would be too unconvincing altogether.

Her brief series of etiquette lessons at school had hardly prepared her for this situation. She would have been perfectly relaxed if Dominic were to ask her which fork went where, or how soon a fiancé should return the gifts after a wedding is called off. This was an unexplored situation entirely.

"Come in," she called, feeling like a child bride on her wedding night.

She couldn't be completely cool – she was about to sleep beside the man, for God's sake. There was no point pretending they were sitting beside each other on the bus. She could hardly strike up a quick conversation about the Irish soccer team's chances in the World Cup or his theories on Princess Diana's death.

He broke the silence. "Are you scared of spiders?" he asked mildly.

"Yes, why?"

"There's one walking across the pillow beside you. Perhaps you could brush it away with that upside-down Bible you're reading."

She leapt out of the bed even before he'd finished speaking. He was telling the truth, there was a spider on the other pillow, but it was a midget compared to the spiders she'd done battle with at home in Clare.

"That's not a real spider!" she said indignantly. "The spiders in Australia are ten times as big as that! God, we've got huntsmen and funnel webs and . . ." Her voice trailed off as she realised he wasn't paying her words much attention.

She caught sight of herself in the mirror stuck on the back of the bedroom door. From the neck up she looked fine. She had worn her hair down today and the fine misty rain had sent it into a tumble of ringlets. It was the neck down that was the trouble.

Nick and Fran had given her a pair of bright-green pyjamas, covered with shamrocks and with the words *I've got Irish Roots* emblazoned in huge letters across the front.

She looked down at her pyjamas. So did he. "They're a joke," she said.

"Yes, they are," he agreed.

"No, I mean they were given to me as a joke, normally I don't wear any pyjamas at all, I sleep better without any clothes on . . ." she was babbling to cover her embarrassment, and digging herself into a deeper and deeper hole with each word.

"Oh, never mind," she said, quickly climbed back into bed and pretended to become engrossed in the Bible as he left the room to take his turn in the shared bathroom down the corridor. When he returned, she didn't dare inspect his nightwear, but caught a glimpse of a light blue coloured shirt. She lay on her side, took up the Bible again and kept her eyes firmly fixed on *Revelations*.

She felt him climb into the bed beside her and murmured a reply when he wished her goodnight. But it was at least an hour before she fell asleep.

She woke suddenly at about four o'clock, the moonlight streaming into the room making it as bright as though the lamp were lit. Even in her sleep she had managed to keep clinging to her side of the bed. She thought if she looked closely in the morning she would be able to see claw-marks where she had gripped it so tightly. She had nothing to fear. Dominic was fast asleep, lying on his back.

But she was absolutely wide awake. She counted forward the hours to work out what time it would be in Australia. Early afternoon – no wonder she was feeling so alert.

The curtain billowed slightly, catching on the bedhead and letting even more moonlight into the room. It illuminated Dominic's side of the bed. Sitting up carefully, Maura took the opportunity to have a close look at him.

His shirt had become unbuttoned in his sleep and she could see the smooth, tanned skin of his chest. His face looked gentler in sleep, his hair tousled and falling onto his forehead. She suddenly wished he had made a pass at her. It was ridiculous, she'd spent hours unable to sleep in case he tried something on and now that he hadn't she was disappointed.

After Richard she'd lost faith that gentlemen existed. If it had been Richard in this position he would already have seduced her, waited until she'd fallen asleep and then gone downstairs to see who else he might be able to attract. She shook the thought of him out of her head. The problem was there hadn't been anyone since. She hadn't let any man near her in the years since she had left Sydney.

That was what this was all about, she told herself. It wasn't attraction, it was just that her sexuality was finally thawing. It had nothing to do with Dominic as such.

She felt comforted by her thoughts. She lay down again and tried to drift back into sleep, dismissing all thoughts of sexuality, thawed or otherwise.

She was startled back into complete wakefulness moments later with the feel of Dominic's arm moving gently around her. He murmured something in his sleep and pulled her body in close to his. Oh my God, he must think I'm Carla, Maura realised in horror, feeling his lips brush against the back of her neck.

She stiffened, waiting for him to say something or do something more, but there wasn't another sound. She moved her hand onto his arm to gently lift it away without waking him. His arm was bare and she held her breath as she felt the smooth, warm skin. She could feel the strength in his arm. Holding it still, she carefully looked around until she could see his face. He was definitely still fast asleep.

She suddenly realised she liked the feel of his arm around her, very much. Gently edging back in the bed, she moved until she could feel the warmth from his body. She stopped again, waiting to see if he would wake.

The room was dark and cosy and she could hear the rain begin outside again. She felt safe and warm and, she couldn't deny it, beginning to feel in need of something much more intimate than a sleepy embrace. She could feel her body start to catch fire and was shocked at herself. Think straight, she told herself. This is a complete stranger you are in bed with. He's practically a married man. You don't like him.

But while her mind was talking sense, her body was making its own decisions. She edged back even closer, until her body lay close against Dominic. She moved his arm gently around her, until his hand was just brushing against her. She felt an urge to press closer to him, to hold his hand tighter against her. Every part of her started to glow with the warmth of being held close against a strong male body again.

Damn the green flannelette pyjamas, she thought in a daze. Even the heroine in the Princess and the Pea fairytale would have been hard-pressed to feel anything through them. If only Nick and Fran had presented her with some flimsy, black lace nightwear.

She checked again to see that Dominic was still asleep and slowly turned within the circle of his arm until she was lying face to face with him. The strength of her desire had caught her completely off guard. He moved suddenly and she pulled back in an instant, holding herself very still and willing him to stay asleep. He settled again within a moment, lying on his back now, the movement pushing the covers away from his body.

She could see the strong hard muscles of his stomach, covered in a pathway of dark hair leading under the waistband of his pants. Richard had been slightly overweight, with a white flabby stomach – a chef's prerogative, he had always insisted. Looking now at Dominic, Maura couldn't believe how sexy a man's taut, naked stomach could be.

Reason had gone by now. She slowly and very carefully moved his shirt, letting it fall open and bare his chest completely to her gaze.

The door-handle suddenly rattled. Maura leapt back. It rattled again and the door moved as though someone was trying to get in. She made out voices, very drunk by the sound of the volume.

"The key doeshhn't work," one said.

"Gissh a look – it's the wrong number – this is seven not seventeen, that's why, *shhtupid*. Come on."

The interruption had the effect of a bucket of cold water over her. She pulled away as if she had suddenly been burnt and wriggled quickly to the very edge of the bed. What on earth had she been thinking of?

She hardly dared to look over at Dominic again, almost pleading aloud that he hadn't been woken by the commotion outside. He seemed to be fast asleep still. Thank God for the two drunks and their key, she thought, reason finally beating the still flickering desire. It must have been the jet-lag after all. She had obviously taken leave of her senses.

It took her more than an hour to fall asleep again, as she lay rigid on the very edge of the mattress. The dawn light was just starting to appear in the sky outside as she fell into a troubled sleep.

Chapter Twelve

Maura awoke at eight o'clock to the sound of the telephone beside the bed ringing. It was Rita once again, ringing to let her know a photographer from the local Mayo newspaper would be attending one of the wine-tastings that day.

Maura was glad to start the day with business, in order to dispel her thoughts about the happenings in the middle of the night. There was no sign of Dominic, thank heavens. He must have woken early.

She explained briefly to Rita about the problems with the hotel booking, deliberately making it sound much less of a bother than it had been, and not correcting Rita's assumption that the room they'd ended up with had two single beds, rather than a double.

"Oh, you're very good to take it so well. And I'm sure Dominic was the perfect gentleman."

He was fine, Maura thought in embarrassment. It was me who had the wandering hands.

After promising to ring ahead to ensure the rest of their hotel bookings were correct, Rita announced that the venue in Ennis had been changed because of the huge response.

"You'll be talking to at least one hundred people, isn't that brilliant?"

Maura agreed it was great news, while fighting a sudden attack of nerves. One hundred people? Promising Rita she'd be in touch again soon, she hung up and quickly gathered her bathroom things. After showering and dressing in record time, she nervously went back to the bedroom, hoping that Dominic was still downstairs having breakfast or out getting the tyres fixed or wherever it was he had disappeared to.

She longed for a cup of strong, black coffee, anything to settle her nerves and give her the strength to act as though absolutely nothing had happened during the night. She could feel herself blushing at the memory. What on earth had come over her?

She took a deep breath. She'd calmly go downstairs and have her breakfast and if Dominic was there she would just greet him politely and quickly re-establish the professional business relationship between them. She just hoped to God he was a deep sleeper.

She had just finished packing her bags when there was a brisk knock at the door.

She looked up, steeling herself to see Dominic and praying that the make-up she had applied would hide any sudden blushes. She had barely called "Come in" when the door flung open to admit a furious Carla.

"You slut!" she shouted at Maura, before striding over and slapping her sharply across the face. The shock sent Maura back onto the bed. "I knew I should have told you to keep your hands off him but you couldn't even last one night. I knew there was something going on between you, I've been watching the way you look at him – well, your secret's blown now."

Dominic came into the room right behind her. He ignored Maura's outraged gasp, speaking to Carla in a low soft voice. His tone was more suited to taming a wild cat than a hysterical woman, Maura thought, tentatively putting her hand up to her stinging face.

"It's not what you think, Carla. I told you there was a mix-up with the rooms. Absolutely nothing happened between us."

Maura hoped she imagined the quick glance Dominic gave her.

"Carla, I want you to calm down. Come downstairs with me again now and we'll have a quiet cup of tea together."

Carla allowed herself to be steered downstairs, flashing a glance at Maura as she left.

Maura sat back on the bed, breathing deeply. Enough was enough, she thought. What was supposed to be a business trip was fast descending into some sort of bedroom farce. This had to be sorted out or she would start to think she was in some strange Irish version of *Alice in Wonderland*.

"And thank you very much, Mr Hanrahan, for so stoutly coming to my defence when your charming girlfriend calls me a slut. Her bloody gossip-columnist friend has already tried to wreck my reputation here. I don't need any of this," Maura said aloud, dragging her heavy suitcase off the bed onto the floor.

"Yes, you do." Dominic stopped her rant with a few quiet words. He had silently come into the room behind her. There was no sign of Carla.

Maura spun around. "What do you mean 'I do'?"

"I know you need this trip to be a success. I've researched Lorikeet Hill's financial status. You're doing okay, but not brilliantly. You need these export sales. And I also know you've been commissioned to write an article about the trip."

She looked at him, shocked he seemed to know so much. Who on earth had told him?

"Bernadette," he answered, reading her mind. "And the Internet. I've read most of the Australian wine magazines on-line. I know you've had a bad season in South Australia, which means the vintage this year will be smaller than normal."

Maura glared at him, hating him knowing so much of her private business. At least he didn't seem to know about Nick and Fran.

"And I know your brother's wife is about to have a baby, so you're even more anxious to get your export sales moving."

Maura took a sharp breath.

He ignored her surprise. "I want to apologise on behalf of Carla. She arrived here unexpectedly this morning and came up to the room, just as I was going down for breakfast. She took one look at you asleep in the bed and jumped to the wrong conclusion, though I guess it was an understandable one. But I've assured her I'd done nothing for her to worry about."

Maura's over-anxious ears picked up Dominic's careful use of the word 'I'.

"We need to call a truce. I'll ask Carla to stop overreacting and to be civil to you. She's had some difficult times lately. I won't go into details, but her father died last year and Carla's on something of an unsteady voyage. I wasn't much older than her when my parents died, so I know how bad it can feel. Are your mother and father still alive?"

Maura shook her head, but said nothing, just glaring at him.

"Then you probably know how hard it can be sometimes. I'm sorry again that Carla slapped you, but I give you my word you and I can work together to make these next few weeks a success for both of us."

Maura had no time to comment. A stormy-faced Carla stalked into the room again and walked straight to Dominic, who put a protective arm around her.

"And Carla will be as much help to you as she can, won't you, Carla?"

The American girl nodded, giving Dominic an innocent look.

Maura, however, received a different look entirely. One of undisguised loathing.

* * *

"You have to stop letting people down like this, Carla, I've told you that before. I'll call them myself and reschedule it for you, will that make it easier?"

Walking out to the carpark after her quick breakfast, Maura shamelessly eavesdropped as she packed her briefcase into the back of the car. By the sound of things Carla had missed one of her modelling appointments.

Carla was now sobbing into Dominic's shoulder. It seemed that she had suffered an attack of insomnia during the night, worked herself into an anxiety state and decided that only Dominic would be able to help her. Not only that, but she had hailed a taxi to take her on the four-hour journey.

'I bet the taxi driver will be dining out on that story for a while, in more ways than one,' Maura thought with a grin, imagining a run of Dublin taxi drivers scouring the streets of Ireland for distraught American heiresses.

Dominic walked towards Maura, with a now sullen Carla beside him clutching his arm.

"Carla's going to travel with us through Mayo today, then catch the Dublin train from Galway later this afternoon, if that's okay with you," he said.

"That's fine," she answered brightly, surprised to have been asked. Though what else could she possibly have answered, she realised. No, Dominic knew that Maura really didn't have much choice. But by the looks of things Carla was certainly making Dominic earn every cent of those million dollars, Maura thought. If it had been her, she would have taken the poverty choice any day.

Maura offered Carla the front seat for the drive but the young woman insisted on taking the back, complaining that she was exhausted and wanted to sleep. Maura was tempted for a moment to throw a tantrum herself, just to see how Dominic would cope with two brats on his hands. But by the set of Dominic's jaw she guessed he wasn't in the mood for any sort of conversation. Maura sighed to herself, and took out the travel map from the glovebox to get her bearings and distract herself from the tense mood inside the car.

Westport was about an hour's drive away, and Maura was glad of the silence and the comfort of the moving car to daydream and enjoy the beauty of the scenery.

As she settled into her seat, her mind insisted on returning to the scene in the room in the middle of the night. In the fuss of Carla's arrival she had managed to put it all out of her mind. She almost hoped that she had imagined it. But her face flamed as she cast her mind back. She remembered it all very clearly. What would have happened if the drunken man hadn't tried the wrong door?

Not really wanting to think about it any more,

Maura dragged her attention back to the day ahead of them and looked through the notes the Society had supplied for this leg of the trip. Rita had done a great job organising all sorts of promotional activities. If the other Australian winemakers were being kept as busy as she was, then sales of Australian wine in Ireland would definitely get a big boost.

At least, one part of her mind thought about wine. The other part was still thinking about a naked male chest.

Chapter Thirteen

The Mayo countryside was absolutely spectacular – big mountains, moss-green fields, stone cottages. It was real picture-postcard Ireland. Maura stopped herself exclaiming aloud once or twice. There was something about the mood in the car that wasn't exactly conducive to excited chat about tourist sights. Dominic was still staring stonily ahead, Carla sulking in the back seat.

Maura wished again that she and Bernadette were travelling together – it would certainly have been more relaxed than this. Something had clicked between them and she knew they would have had a good laugh. Still, she'd be seeing plenty of Bernadette once she got to Dominic's house to do the cooking series.

She sat up straight in her seat as they drove down narrow winding roads into Westport, the main town in County Mayo. She had a reasonably busy schedule here, with two visits to off-licences to encourage them to sell Lorikeet Hill wine, before the afternoon presentation to the members of the local Chamber of Commerce and Rotary Club.

Carla opted to sit in the car, idly flicking through a fashion magazine, while Dominic and Maura called in to the off-licences. She was struck again by the friendliness and the interest in Australian wine. Nothing quite matched the Austrian snow display for inventiveness but she was thrilled to see the trouble the store managers had taken in their bid to win the trip to Australia.

There must have been a run on corks from the local hardware shop, she thought, seeing her second swagman's hat for the day, the corks bobbing around a smiling face. Maura turned her attention back to the store manager, who was supplying her with great detail about his many relatives who had settled in every part of Australia.

"Well, if you win the trip, make sure you fit in a trip to our winery," Maura smiled. "It's not quite as spectacular as Sydney Harbour or the Great Barrier Reef, but I can guarantee the hospitality." She tried to ignore the look Dominic shot her.

To Maura's amazement Carla expressed interest in watching her lunchtime slide presentation. She also seemed to suddenly discover manners, and even smiled at one or two of the businesspeople as she settled herself in a chair at the back of the meeting room in the local Town Hall.

Maura looked around at the attentive faces, feeling

slightly nervous about timing the slides to coincide with her speech. Carefully operating the ancient slide projector the Chamber had supplied, Maura took her audience through the winemaking process, from vineyard to bottling, giving them a taste of Lorikeet Hill's history and a feel for life in the Clare Valley as she did so.

Halfway through the slides, she realised she was actually enjoying herself. She and Nick had taken great care in choosing the right slides and subject matter. Without being conscious of it, they had also included lots of pictures of blue skies, which brought more than a few envious mutters. The drizzle continued outside.

Maura was pleased to see that she seemed to have everyone's interest. A few even began to interrupt her talk with questions, which she was happy to answer. She did her best to ignore Carla who had obviously become bored with polite behaviour and was now making a great show of looking out of the window and filing her nails.

Dominic seemed oblivious to Carla's rudeness and was watching Maura with close attention. She caught his intense glance once or twice but thinking back to the one public speaking course she had attended she decided to concentrate on the beaming man in the front row. "We finish each vintage with the Clare Valley Gourmet Weekend," she said brightly, as a slide came up showing groups of laughing people seated at tables scattered around the shining steel wine vats. It was one of the highlights of their year. Each winery presented their own food or linked with a leading South Australian restaurant and offered tastings of their new vintage wines with delicious entrée sizes of food. Lorikeet Hill was always a highly popular venue, not least because of the lively bands they always booked.

"And now to the reason we're all here today," Maura said, turning off the slide projector with relief. "It's time to taste the wine."

* * *

"Well done, Maura, you painted a very attractive picture today. I just wish we'd had the opportunity to fully experience Lorikeet Hill's charms when we were there last month," Dominic said, a glint in his eye, as they walked out to the car after the presentation.

She was surprised at his words. Had he forgiven her for the case of mistaken identity at last? "Thank you very much," she said graciously, a smile fighting its way onto her lips. "As I said today, we do try to make each guest's experience as memorable as possible."

"Oh, believe me, I'll never forget our time with you."

She was still smiling as they reached the car and she turned around, hoping to see Carla joining in this new relaxed mood. But Carla had reverted to a stony silence, barely giving Maura time to stow her briefcase and slides carefully under the back seat before clambering in.

"And now Galway," Dominic said, buckling his seat belt. "I'm sure you'll enjoy this part of the trip, Maura. We're about to see some of the most beautiful scenery in Ireland."

He was absolutely right. Maura felt her breath catch at the beauty unfolding around them. It sparked something inside her, she realised, wondering if it was a faint echo of her ancestors.

But it would take a cold heart not to be moved by this scenery, she thought, as a ray of sun highlighted a distant whitewashed cottage at the foot of a mountain.

"We've got time to stop if you'd like to take some photos," Dominic said, noticing her interest.

She nodded enthusiastically. She clambered out of the car and walked back a distance to get the best view. Dominic followed, making his way slowly to where she had clambered up onto a bank of earth on the side of the road.

"You've heard of peat, as in the whiskey-making process?" he asked.

She nodded.

"This is it, in its rawest form," he said. "It's called a turf bog."

Maura looked around at what had first looked like muddy fields. On a closer look she realised it wasn't that the crops had already been harvested, it was the mud itself that was the crop.

She said as much to Dominic, who gave a low laugh.

"Not exactly mud. It's actually old forests that have

146

been buried deep down under the earth for thousands of years."

"So it's something like coal?"

"Well, if it had been left for another few thousand years maybe. The turf is great stuff, you'll see it being used as fuel for open fires in Galway, and in the house you'll be staying at in Clare as well. It has a really distinctive smell when it's burning – when I was in America one of the local Irish pubs tried to artificially replicate the smell, just to stop us all from being homesick. It preserves things beautifully too. Archaeologists have found everything from ancient bits of oak to butter that was sunk hundreds of years ago."

"Butter?" Maura asked in surprise.

"Incredible, isn't it? Farmhands hundreds of years ago would bury their lunch under the earth to keep it fresh, and I guess every now and then they forgot where they had put it. People find all kinds of things buried in bogs."

"I'm surprised turf hasn't taken off as a beauty product if it's that good a preservative," she grinned up at him.

"Well, now there's a market. Perhaps when you get tired of wine and food," he smiled back.

She climbed back into the car, feeling energised by the wind on her cheeks. Now she was really starting to feel like she was in Ireland.

Carla's petulant voice from the back of the car broke the spell.

"I hope to God I don't miss my train with the time you were wasting back there."

"So do I," Maura said without thinking.

"What do you mean by that?" Carla snapped back quickly.

"I mean I would hate to think you'd have to catch a later train and miss your appointment," Maura said, chiding herself for her adolescent behaviour.

"What do you know about my appointment?" Carla was glaring at her now.

"Nothing at all," Maura answered, puzzled at the younger girl's sudden doggedness. "I just assumed it was a modelling appointment. That's what you do, isn't it?"

Carla sank back into her seat and smiled a satisfied smile. "I do, if the right job comes up. But I certainly don't waste my time on catalogues or silly parades in shopping centres. I did a fabulous shoot in Fiji one year. That's near your country isn't it?"

"Well, in the same hemisphere, I guess," Maura answered. But Carla wasn't exactly waiting on her answer.

"It was just fantastic. I was waited on hand and foot, and Raymond the photographer said I had the most delicate bone structure he'd ever seen. He said that I really was suited to . . ."

Maura wished she could block her ears against the torrent coming from the back seat. Two hours of sullen silence and then this – she knew which one she preferred. She glanced at Dominic, wondering how on earth he put up with it. But to her surprise he was smiling indulgently at Carla through the rear-view mirror. Her estimation of him plummeted yet again.

After what felt like days of uneasy quiet in the car, she was relieved to see they were coming into Galway. The reminder of Dominic's affection and financial attachment to Carla had made her feel uncomfortable again. She suddenly longed to phone Nick and Fran, to hear all their news and feel their uncomplicated love down the phone.

It was her turn to sit in the car while Dominic took Carla into the railway station and got her settled onto a train. She gave Maura the briefest of farewells, nothing more than a mumble, while Maura took pleasure in giving her a particularly cheery goodbye.

She glanced surreptitiously at Dominic on his return to see if his eyes were wet with tears but he seemed to have come through the ordeal of leaving Carla remarkably well. "Another day, another ten thousand dollars," she murmured.

"Pardon me?" Dominic looked over enquiringly.

"Oh, nothing, an old Australian saying just popped into my head," Maura smiled innocently back.

Dominic gave her a sharp look. "Our hotel is just down the road – would you like to go straight there or can I take you on a quick sightseeing tour, just to get your bearings?"

Maura was about to plead tiredness when a glimpse of the crowds streaming into the centre of town made her change her mind.

"A tour would be great," she said.

Chapter Fourteen

Dominic was just turning into the centre of Galway when the car-phone rang. He answered it briskly, flicking a switch to use the hands-free service again.

A cheery voice filled the car. "Hello there, this is Cormac Sheehan, looking for our beautiful Australian visitor. Maura, are you there too?"

She gave a surprised 'yes.'

"Hello, my lovely, how's it all going? I badgered Rita until she gave me your contact number. Are you a roaring success? No more Austrian surprises, I hope?"

Maura was too conscious of Dominic listening beside her to be able to respond openly to Cormac's unashamed flirting. Cormac seemed to realise the reason for her reticence and to her embarrassment played up to it.

"I realise you can't talk easily at the moment. I just wanted to say it looks like I will be able to get down to Clare in the next couple of weekends to take you out for a pint or two. I've been thinking about you, I can't wait to see you again."

He rang off before she had a chance to say that his visit might be inconvenient. She had no idea what awaited her yet. And she wanted to catch up with Bernadette.

Dominic looked over at her. "That was quick work."

"I was just being friendly," she said, slightly taken aback by what he was inferring.

He spoke calmly. "I didn't mean quick work on your part, I meant on Cormac's. And I'm not being critical. I'm not surprised in the least that you have an admirer. You're a very attractive woman."

As he gave her a long look, she suddenly had a flash of the goings-on the night before. She could feel the blush rising in her face.

Dominic spoke again. "I was just commenting on his persistence. I'm sorry if you took it as an insult."

She looked at him, about to protest when something in the sincerity of his look stopped her. She took a deep breath, prayed for a sudden dose of maturity and gave what she hoped was a gracious smile.

He drove on to show her around Galway before they checked into their hotel. As he pointed out several Galway landmarks she gazed across at him, trying to work him out. He seemed so controlled most of the time, yet every now and then she would get a glimpse of something else.

"Are you having trouble understanding my accent?

You seem to be giving me an odd look," he asked suddenly.

"Not at all," she said quickly. "I was just looking at the view through your window."

Dominic looked through the window. Outside was nothing but a row of very ordinary-looking warehouses.

"Yes, they certainly look very interesting," he said mildly.

Embarrassed at being caught looking at him, Maura was staring fixedly out of her side of the car when Dominic spoke again a few moments later. "There's a booklet in the glove compartment that you might like to see too. Rita gave me quite a collection before we left."

It was a beautifully produced guide to Galway, with a special section devoted to the history of the Claddagh rings.

"Oh, I've always loved those rings," she exclaimed, looking at a photograph of a delicately fashioned silver one and reading aloud the explanation of the simple design. *"With these hands I give you my heart and crown it with my love,"* she read softly to herself. "Oh, that's lovely." Nick had asked her to bring a special gift back for him to give to Fran. A Claddagh ring would be perfect.

She was about to ask Dominic if they would be difficult to find, when she nearly laughed aloud. As they drove down the main shopping street, every second shop seemed to be selling them or boasting a sign saying *Home of the Claddagh Ring*. The problem wouldn't be finding one but finding a unique one, she realised.

She liked the look of Galway very much. It was the most vibrant city she had ever seen. The winding streets and footpaths were crowded with people and cars and bicycles, all jostling for space. Every now and then the cars would come to a standstill as the footpaths overflowed, and people quite casually walked out onto the road as though that was their territory too.

There was the lively mix of people she had also noticed in Dublin. Businesspeople walking beside wide-eyed couples who were obviously tourists. Backpackers, hippies, New Agers, musicians, buskers, farmers. The streets of Galway were like a bubbling stream of all sorts of people. Dublin had felt busy but this was positively teeming with life.

The sun finally made an appearance for the day as they pulled up in front of their hotel, the Great Southern, right in the centre of the city.

"We've a busy day here tomorrow, haven't we?" Dominic asked, as he unloaded her suitcases from the car.

Maura nodded. "Five appointments altogether," she answered. "But no more slides until Ennis, thank God."

"That's a shame," he answered surprisingly. "I enjoyed your slide show very much, I learnt a lot myself."

She looked quickly across at him, pleased and embarrassed at his praise. They walked into the foyer and she was about to speak again when they both heard an all too familiar sound.

"Dominic?" the whining drawl called.

They both spun around. Carla was curled up in a corner of a sofa near the reception desk. Her mascara was smudged, her face blotchy and she looked as if she had been crying.

Maura looked at her in astonishment. Where on earth had she come from? Wasn't she supposed to be halfway to Dublin? She glanced across at Dominic and saw a nerve twitch in his cheek. She was amazed at his self-control.

"Carla, why aren't you on that train?" he asked in a suspiciously low voice.

Carla started to cry again, climbing up from the sofa and moving closer to Dominic, speaking in a child-like voice again. "I didn't like it, there were all these people crowded around me, shouting across at each other. I hated it. I made them stop and let me off, I couldn't . . ." She broke down in tears again.

Maura couldn't believe her eyes or ears. The girl was behaving like a five-year-old. Fighting her own curiosity, she diplomatically moved away. She heard Dominic's murmuring voice and watched out of the corner of her eye as Carla threw her arms around him. Dominic stood perfectly still, not responding.

'Trouble in banker's paradise,' Maura thought mischievously, as she walked up to the reception desk, praying there'd be no mix-up with the room tonight. Three of them together in one room would be just a bit too much.

With her own room key securely in one hand and

her luggage in the other, she waited politely for an opportunity to speak to Dominic. Unless there was another train back to Dublin tonight and he somehow managed to convince Carla to climb aboard, she had a suspicion he was going to be kept very busy this evening soothing his anxious girlfriend.

He suddenly caught her eye from where he sat on the sofa and after a quick word to Carla, stood up and came over to Maura.

"I'm sorry about this," he apologised, running his fingers through his hair anxiously. "She's not very well at the moment and is a bit upset."

A bit upset? Hysterical was probably closer to the mark, Maura thought.

Dominic was looking concerned. "I'd hoped to take you to one of the pubs or a restaurant, for a meal tonight, but I'm afraid I won't be able to do that after all." He nodded toward Carla. "Will you be able to manage with room service, or in the restaurant in the hotel?" he asked.

She was unexpectedly touched by his concern. He looked truly worried about Carla. "I'll be fine," she said, smiling. "Is there anything I can do to help here?" she asked, glancing over at Carla. She didn't like the girl but if she really was unwell . . .

"No," Dominic answered swiftly. "We'll cope. And she has promised me she'll return to Dublin in the morning, so please don't worry about this upsetting tomorrow's itinerary."

"I wasn't worried about that at all," she said, honestly. She was surprised he was.

A loud sniff from the sofa brought their attention back to Carla.

"You'd better go," Maura said, looking over at the other woman. "I'll see you in the morning."

"At ten?" he suggested. She nodded and said goodnight.

Upstairs in her beautiful room, she suddenly felt a wave of relief sweep over her. What a day. And what a start to her trip. She felt the sudden joy of unexpected solitude. She'd have a room-service meal for dinner, maybe watch an in-house movie or just give her tumbling thoughts a chance to settle. Then tomorrow she'd be ready for anything. Even Carla.

* * *

Over breakfast the next morning she glanced again at her Galway schedule. They had four off-licences to visit during the day, then a late afternoon wine-tasting with local traders, hoteliers, wine merchants and local media. *'And all very influential!'* Rita had handwritten on the notes.

Maura made her way downstairs to the foyer, to find Dominic waiting for her by the reception desk. There was no sign of Carla.

"Good morning," she said, about to enquire after her.

Dominic greeted her, then saved her the question.

"Carla's safely on her way back to Dublin this morning, I'm pleased to say," he said, with a slight grin. Maura was slightly taken aback to hear him say that about his girlfriend, but then again, after last night's performance, he probably was glad to see the back of her, temporarily at least. "My apologies again – I hope you were okay last night?" he asked.

She nodded, surprised once again at this softer side of his personality that kept making brief appearances. She had to keep reminding herself of all that Cormac had told her about him.

"I've looked through the itinerary this morning, and we're close enough to walk to all the appointments today, if you're happy to do that?"

She agreed readily. It was crisp, clear winter weather outside and after a day in the car she was ready for a good walk.

They soon reached the first off-licence, located in the front section of an old pub. Maura was pleased to see Lorikeet Hill wines prominently displayed in the front window, basking in the light from a round yellow lampshade spinning above them. She guessed that was supposed to be an Australian sun.

They were about to enter when Dominic's mobile phone rang. He answered it briefly, then asked his caller to hold for a moment.

He shook his head ruefully. "I'm sorry, again," he said to Maura. "I won't be a moment – do you want to go in ahead of me?"

Maura nodded and walked into the narrow little shop, her eyes squinting in the darkness. A middle-aged man smoking a pipe came out from a little room at the end of the shop.

"Can I help you, miss?" he asked, coughing slightly.

Maura introduced herself. "I just wanted to drop in and say hello, and thank you for your great window display. It looks brilliant."

The man beamed. "Well, hello there, Maura. I'm Dan O'Shea and aren't you a pet to say that about the display. Now, will you put in a good word for us with the judges? I fancy myself in a pair of shorts lying on the Gold Coast, can't you just see it yourself?"

Maura laughed. Dan looked like he'd be far more comfortable in a snug bar than a sunny beach and, by the twinkle in his eye, he thought the very same thing. "I'll do my best," she said with a wink. "That revolving sun might just do the trick. I hope it's all helping your sales of Australian wine, is it? We've a lot of competition with the French and the Spanish, though, haven't we?"

Dan leaned down and took a thoughtful suck of his pipe. "Well, now, it's all about what you like, isn't it? Some people like French wine. Some people like Spanish wine. There are those that like Italian wine too. And then there are the ones that like Australian wine. And they're the ones you want."

She blinked, trying to keep up. There was no denying his logic. "You're absolutely right," she said carefully.

Dan began an involved explanation of the differences between the wines from each country, and after some moments, Maura began looking nervously at her watch, hoping another customer might come in and give her an opportunity to politely leave. The bell at the door rang and they both looked up as Dominic came into the shop.

Maura took quick advantage of his arrival to interrupt Dan. "This is Dominic Hanrahan," she said, "my host from the Wine Society."

"And a great society it is too," Dan said. "It's good to meet you. Dominic, is it?"

Dominic nodded, about to say something, when Dan picked up from where he had left off. "Now, the French, their quality can vary widely from one region to the next – myself, I favour the Burgundy reds . . . "

Dan theorised for more than five minutes, in an almost breathless monologue, not giving them an opportunity to interrupt until he took a long pull on his pipe.

Dominic seized his chance and interrupted smoothly, as Maura watched with admiration. "I'm sorry to stop you there, Dan, but poor Maura has a very hectic schedule and it's my head that will roll if she doesn't make her other visits on time. Will you excuse us, and if we can find time to come back, we'll do our very best?"

"Of course, of course," Dan said, expansively, waving his pipe around until Maura was nervous a plug of tobacco would come sailing out. "It's a pleasure to meet you both, and Maura, don't forget to have a wee word with those judges now, will you?" he said, tapping the end of his nose in a secret code.

The other three winesellers weren't quite as voluble, but certainly as friendly. Maura had just arrived at one of the off-licences when a customer came in and bought two bottles of Lorikeet Hill wine.

"That lady behind you is from that very winery," the young shop assistant said, pointing at Maura.

The young man turned around. "Is he serious? This is your wine?"

Maura nodded. "Well, my brother actually made it. But I picked some of the grapes. A lot of sweat went into that wine, I can tell you!"

"Not too much, I hope. I was after a full-bodied red, not a watered-down one," he said with a grin. "Here, would you sign one of them for me?"

Maura blushed. She'd never been asked to do that before. "Well, if you're sure, I'd love to," she said, accepting a pen from the shop assistant. "It's not like a book, though, is it? One night and it'll be gone."

"Much more fun than a book, though," the customer grinned.

Maura thought for a second before writing in careful, small letters across the top of the label, grateful that Fran's designs always left plenty of white space. '*I hope you get a taste for it,*' she wrote, before signing her name with a flourish. She handed the bottle back. "I mean it, I hope you really enjoy it."

"We will," he said. He leaned forward conspiratorially. "I'm going to ask my girlfriend to marry me tonight – I'm hoping this will help her give the answer I want."

"Well, if it doesn't, you can drown your sorrows with the other bottle," the shop assistant said drily.

It was past seven o'clock by the time Maura and Dominic were walking back to the hotel. Night had fallen while they were at their final appointment for the day, and the city was now lit by streetlights and car headlights. The footpaths were packed again, as people going home from work for the evening blended with others just starting their nights out.

"That's it for Lorikeet Hill duties for the day, now, is it?" Dominic asked, as they dodged their way through the crowds back to the hotel.

"That's it," she said, sidestepping a trio of giggling teenagers. "I hope it's working. I'm hearing myself say the same things over and over again. I'll have to start embellishing them, to keep the interest levels up."

He grinned across at her, and she thought again with a jolt how handsome he was. He was in a suit still, but had removed his tie, and the white collar of his shirt was stark against his tanned skin. She suddenly had a mental image of him relaxed, laughing, in less formal clothes than the ones he was wearing today. A pair of faded black denim jeans, she decided. A thick woollen dark green jumper. With wind-ruffled hair.

A car beeping its horn at a gang of young men walking on the road beside her brought her back to reality. They were in front of their hotel and Dominic was saying something to her.

"Would you like to eat in the hotel tonight, or try one of the pubs or restaurants in town?" he was asking.

She suddenly had an urge to set some boundaries between the work trip and their spare time. "You really don't have to mind me all the time," she said earnestly. "I'm sure you've plenty of things you'd rather be doing, and I'm quite happy to get room service again or go out my own."

For a second she thought he looked slightly hurt. She told herself she'd imagined it. When he spoke again, his voice was quiet. "I've promised the Society I would take Bernadette's place this week, and I'm sure she wouldn't have left you to your own devices in Galway two nights in a row."

Of course, the Society. And his own research. Maybe he wanted to ask her for some tips on how to run a successful restaurant in the country, she thought suddenly.

He repeated his invitation again. "Would you like to come out with me?" His voice sounded surprisingly polite and sincere and she almost felt she was being asked out on a date. Oddly enough, the idea appealed to her, until a vision of Carla suddenly came into her mind.

Dominic was waiting for an answer. Maura suddenly thought back to the lively pubs and cafés they had passed. Oh, what the hell. What could he do? Bite her?

Sell her off to a visiting Arab? She could put up with a few more hours of the tension between them, and besides, she was dying to try a pint of Guinness and some more Irish food.

"I'd like that very much," she said.

He smiled.

Chapter Fifteen

They arranged to meet in an hour and Maura took the opportunity to shower and change.

She was in high spirits by the time she came downstairs to meet Dominic in the foyer. Her grin froze when she saw that he too had showered and changed.

He was wearing a pair of faded black jeans and a thick woollen dark-green jumper. It was as if he had read her mind. She suddenly felt like a child with a paper doll. If she had imagined him dressed in football gear would he suddenly have appeared in that? she wondered. He looked . . . she couldn't find the word for it. Strong. And very approachable. She gave him a big smile.

He seemed to be noticing her appearance too. She had dressed in a close-fitting dark-green top and a long, richly patterned skirt. She'd left her hair down and it fell in a mass of dark red curls around her shoulders and down her back.

He stopped looking first. "Would you like restaurant or pub food?" he asked.

"Oh, definitely a pub. Do you know I haven't had a pint of Guinness yet. Or heard any real Irish music. I'll have to complain to the Irish Tourist Board for false advertising," she said lightly, conscious that the relaxed mood between them had returned.

"Well, you're in the right town for pubs and music now," he said, smiling down at her. "We'll wander along until you find something that takes your fancy."

Maura was glad to find they were gathered up in the streams of people strolling down Shop Street. She felt a rush of excitement at the buzz of people around them. It seemed that even on a weeknight, the streets of Galway had an air of excitement, as people called out to friends, or wandered in and out of pubs and restaurants.

A pub with a brightly coloured mural out the front featuring musicians, writers and poets caught her eye. Dominic caught her interest and led her into its lively front bar.

There were very few seats left, though she noticed an entire corner empty except for a collection of instrument cases lined up along the bench seats.

"That's for the musicians later," Dominic explained, as he found a spare bench seat just beside the musician's corner.

She listened to the music playing in the background and recognised it immediately. The Waterboys, one of her favourite bands. She knew from reading about them that they weren't strictly Irish, but in her mind she had always associated their music with Ireland. She liked the coincidence, to be hearing them on her first visit to the country.

"They're one of my favourite bands too," Dominic said. She looked up. "The Waterboys. I saw you smiling. I saw them play live a couple of times – they were absolutely brilliant."

He must have put on a different personality too when he dressed up in his rugged windswept-poet costume, she thought. He didn't seem like the serious publishing mogul tonight. Or Carla's eagle-eyed minder. He just seemed like your every-day, run-of-the-mill, gorgeous, handsome, sexy, thirty-five-year-old Irishman, she thought, looking away quickly as he caught her staring at him again.

The dinner menu was short and simple, and she quickly chose a seafood platter, which promised smoked salmon, local oysters and poached salmon served with homemade tartare sauce.

"More seafood?" Dominic noticed.

"While I can get it," she smiled back.

Dominic offered to fetch two pints of Guinness from the bar and, while he waited by the long wooden counter, she took the opportunity to look around the pub. Every wall was painted with a bright mural, depicting well-known Irish actors, musicians and writers. There was also a collection of artifacts hanging from the ceiling: old buckets, washboards and what looked like old farming equipment, strung from wires and hanging precariously above the bar.

Irish theme pubs had become a boom business in Australia in the last two years, and Maura had been to her share of them on visits to Adelaide and Sydney. She'd always found the idea of them quite strange – you could interior-decorate until you were blue (or green) in the face, but you were never going to get the mood or atmosphere to mirror that of another country. Being in the real thing didn't make her change her mind. There was a history to this pub that you could nearly feel. The feeling with the Irish theme pubs that she had visited was an overwhelming air of fakery: as though, if the Irish decoration didn't work then next week it could just as easily be turned into an Arabian Nights theme pub or retro 1950s bar.

As they began to eat their meal, the musicians began to assemble in the corner. More and more people arrived into the pub. The seats around them filled up and she found herself pushed closer and closer up against Dominic. Reminded again too clearly of the night in the hotel room together, she felt a touch of shame, while at the same time enjoying the feeling of his thigh pressed close against hers. I'm like a schoolgirl at her first dance, she thought in embarrassment.

She turned the conversation around to the musicians, asking Dominic about the unfamiliar instruments as they began to tune up. He named the bodhrán, uileann pipes and the accordion, and told her about Sharon Shannon, a young accordion player from County Clare who had given the instrument a new lease of life in Irish traditional music.

"At least I can recognise a tin whistle," she said, remembering too late the CD she had played at top volume when Dominic and Carla had visited Lorikeet Hill in Australia. "You seem to know a lot about music – can you play any instruments yourself?" she asked quickly, hoping she hadn't reminded him of their unfortunate first meeting.

"Oh, I was marched off to classes for years when I was little. My father was a wonderful fiddle player and he wanted me to learn too. I played a lot when I was in Ireland, but not much after I went to America."

Maura was about to ask more when the musicians suddenly started up, launching straight into a lively tune that she recognised from tapes Terri used to play at home. The rhythms were absolutely infectious. Her feet started tapping, and she looked around the bar in pleasure at the reaction of the others in the crowd.

Maura felt the closed compartment in her mind open slightly and wondered about her emotional response to the Irish tunes. Maybe it was hereditary, maybe the music was stirring her more deeply the closer she came to County Clare . . .

As the musicians stopped for a break Dominic leaned toward her to ask if she would like another Guinness. She had just nodded when one of the musicians came up behind Dominic and clasped him on the shoulder.

"Dominic, is it you? Dominic Hanrahan?"

Dominic looked up and his face creased into smiles.

He stood up to greet the man. "Gerry Conway, I didn't recognise you with that beard! I don't believe it, how are you?"

"I'm great, just great. What are you doing back from New York? And who is this – your beautiful American wife?" The stranger looked at Maura admiringly.

"Ever the imagination, Gerry. Let me introduce you to Maura Carmody, from one of the New World wineries. I'm on a trade mission with her."

Maura stood up and shook hands with the man, who was looking astonished to see his old friend.

"This is Gerry Conway, an old school friend of mine," said Dominic. "We used to suffer fiddle classes in Cork together."

Maura listened as Gerry and Dominic had an animated conversation, catching up on twenty years in a very brief few minutes.

"This is brilliant," Gerry said, smiling broadly. "You have to join us for a tune, for old time's sake."

"I'll do nothing of the sort," Dominic said, attempting to take his seat again.

"Ah now, Maura, wouldn't you like to hear the magic this man can produce?"

"Sure," Maura agreed, enjoying the teasing Dominic's friend was giving him.

Dominic seemed about to take up the challenge, when a loud voice right behind them called his name, several times. Dominic, Gerry and Maura turned and stared.

"Dominic Hanrahan, isn't it? It is you, I know it is! What a coincidence!" It was Sylvie Rogers. "We've driven up from Cork for a night. We just had to look around Galway while we were in Ireland."

Maura's heart sank as Sylvie jostled her way past a group of people at a table next to them and walked up to Dominic.

She gave Maura a cursory glance, ignoring her fixed smile. "Laura, isn't it?" she dismissed her.

Maura swallowed a retort. "Maura, actually. Hello, Mrs Rogers, Mr Rogers." She nodded to the man behind Sylvie. He was carrying a number of large parcels that virtually obscured his face.

Sylvie turned her full offensive onto Dominic. "Mr Hanrahan, how lovely to see you again! I said to William as we were walking past, why, I'm sure that's Dominic Hanrahan the publisher," she gushed.

She hadn't forgotten *his* name, Maura noticed.

Sylvie moved closer to Dominic. "How wonderful to run into you like this. I had the most charming chat with your lovely ladyfriend Carla at the cocktail party on Saturday night. She was telling me all about your trip to Australia, and how you've turned the magazine world there upside-down. And planning to do the same thing here, a little bird tells me. So I thought to myself, now there's someone on the move, with energy and vision, like myself. So sit yourself down there, I've a few little business matters I'd like to discuss."

She grabbed his elbow and nearly pushed him onto the bench, plonking herself beside him. Gerry Conway quickly sized up the situation and, with a wink at Dominic, mouthed that he'd see him later.

Maura had no choice but to sit down in the small space left beside Sylvie, while William Rogers slunk in beside her. The four of them were jammed very close together. Luckily the musicians had started up again, giving herself and William something to look at. He didn't seem all that keen to make conversation, despite her best efforts. She wondered what his story was. His father Harry Rogers had been a legend in Australian winemaking circles, one of the few winemakers who had resisted the trend to pull up old vineyards and plant them with fruit-trees in the early days of the industry. As a result, The Glen property in New South Wales had some of the country's oldest Shiraz vineyards, which year after year produced award-winning, rich red wines. It was that vineyard that had made the family money, and kept it pouring in ever since.

William suddenly took a pack of cards out of his pocket. Was he going to suggest a game of Snap, Maura wondered. Then as she watched, he suddenly began flicking them through his hands, and over and around his fingers.

"That's very clever," she said. "Where did you learn to do that?"

"I don't spend a lot of time talking," he said, with a wry look in his wife's direction. Sylvie was still talking non-stop and loudly, and it was easy to hear that The Glen wines were, unsurprisingly, the current topic of conversation. William was continuing his explanation, all the while making the cards flip and skip around his hands. "And as you know, there's a lot of waiting around in the wine game. I needed a hobby, and this is it." He suddenly leaned close to her. "That's what I'd really like to do for a living," he said.

"Do card tricks? Can you make a living doing that?" she asked in amazement. She couldn't quite imagine it.

"I wanted to try, even as a part-time occupation, performing at kids' parties and fetes and things. But it wasn't quite in keeping with Sylvie's image of a winemaker, I'm afraid." To Maura's surprise, he suddenly started imitating his wife's voice. "'Now William, people won't take a man seriously as a winemaker if they've seen him take a Jack of Spades out of someone's ear, now will they?' She's right, of course, she always is." He sighed. "Anyway, I get plenty of time to myself to practise – the wine nearly makes itself these days."

That's not quite what I've heard, Maura thought, thinking back to the rumours she'd heard at the party about Sylvie hiring winemakers.

"But we travel a lot, and Sylvie keeps busy and happy, and if she's happy then I'm happy."

Maura looked closely at him and realised he actually meant it.

It seemed that was the end of their conversation. He

didn't ask her about Lorikeet Hill or South Australia or her trip so far, but simply went back to his card-shuffling.

She turned in Sylvie and Dominic's direction, just in time to see the older woman make a move to stand up, still talking nine to the dozen at Dominic.

"Good evening, then, and thank you for your time. I look forward to doing business with you," she was saying. As Maura watched, she took Dominic's hand firmly in hers and gave it half a dozen hefty shakes.

She barely looked at Maura as she sailed past, a gesture from her bringing William to his feet and trotting after her in a moment. He gave Maura a little wave goodbye.

"What was that?" Dominic asked. "Cyclone Sylvie?"

"I think you were in its path, not me," Maura laughed. "What on earth was she talking about?"

"Oh, just trying to drum up business," he said vaguely. "How did you get on with the husband?"

Maura shook her head in amazement, still not sure if she had imagined the conversation. She told him about the card tricks.

"Shame he can't make his wife disappear," he murmured.

Gerry Conway had obviously been keeping an eye on them and came over again. This time Dominic steadfastly refused to join the musicians, and instead Gerry fetched another round of drinks and joined them at their table.

"They can do without a fiddle player for a few songs,"

he said with a grin. "And anyway it's my band – what are they going to do, sack me?"

Maura watched with enjoyment as they caught up, wondering if she'd learn anything more about Dominic, and especially about Dominic and Carla. But she soon realised he was very skilled in evasive answers and she learnt more about Gerry and his relative success with his band than she did about Dominic. Carla didn't even rate a mention, Maura noticed curiously.

By the time Maura and Dominic walked through the still lively streets to their hotel their mood was lighthearted. The combination of the Guinness and the music had made her quite giddy and she invited him to join her for a final drink in the hotel bar before they went to their rooms.

He hesitated slightly, then agreed with a smile. They were heading into the bar when the receptionist called them over. "Mr Hanrahan?"

Dominic nodded.

"Two urgent messages for you, sir," she called.

Maura stood politely to one side, watching from the corner of her eye as he read the first message. He turned to her. His whole mood suddenly changed, his face hardened. Even his voice changed. The relaxed tone was replaced by a terse, clipped manner.

"I'm afraid I can't join you for a drink after all, something urgent has come up," he said.

"Oh, is Carla having trouble finding a taxi?" Even as she heard the words coming out of her mouth, she knew she had made a mistake. Her lighthearted remark fell very flat.

Dominic gave her a long look, shook his head in answer and then said a very formal good night.

Maura watched him walk up the stairs. "Damn," she said aloud.

Chapter Sixteen

As she sat eating breakfast in her hotel room on Friday morning, Maura's eyes kept straying to her itinerary for today. County Clare, at last. She felt a flicker of nervousness, though what she was afraid of she couldn't be sure. Finding out too much, or finding nothing at all?

"Or telling Nick either way," she spoke aloud, with a wry smile. If it hadn't been for his urging she would have let the opportunity go by. She hated to admit it, but he was right. Now she was this close, she would have to find out what she could. But in her own way, and in her own time, she vowed.

She had rung home when she got back to her room the night before, too worked up by the night out and the sudden end to the evening to go to bed straight away.

She'd been happy to hear from Nick that Fran was keeping well.

"She's getting tired of me asking how she is, but apart from that she's in great shape," he said. "But I've some

176

fantastic news, we've been chosen as a finalist in the Australian Restaurant Awards. And you'll never guess who one of the judges was!"

Maura named several well-known food writers, as Nick laughingly said no to each one.

"Tell me," she insisted finally.

"Do you remember the elderly couple who arrived just after poor Dominic and his girlfriend had dripped their way to their car?"

Maura wrinkled her brow, suddenly recalling a rather ill-tempered fellow and his wife who had seemed very unimpressed with the jollity in the kitchen.

"He was the critic from *OzTaste*, The Diner himself! He was moonlighting, judging for the Awards as well as writing his reviews."

"But we practically ignored the poor man!"

"I know, but he said in his Award nomination that we had, hang on, let me get it and read it to you – " He was back in a second. "Listen to this – *'Lorikeet Hill Winery Café has a remarkably unfussy and relaxed approach, coupled with an innovative and unusual mixture of dishes, which would be celebrated in a major city, let alone an isolated regional area.'* Isolated regional area?" he scoffed. "We're less than two hours from Adelaide!"

"Don't complain – if he thinks it's incredible that we can buy lemongrass and coriander out in the bush, it's not for us to shatter his illusions. Isn't it brilliant!" Maura was amazed.

"Thank God that Dominic copped all of that revenge

lunch or we wouldn't have had a hope in hell. We owe him a drink," Nick said with a laugh.

"I'll get through this trip first, then we'll see who owes who," she said.

"Well, hurry home, and start preparing your winning speech. I've a good feeling about this."

Gathering her luggage together, Maura's mind strayed again to the uncomfortable end to the previous evening with Dominic. She wondered again about the phone calls, and squirmed at her wisecrack about Carla and the taxi. It was getting to the stage she should just issue a blanket apology to this man to cover the rest of their time together.

She thought of the other Australian winemakers undertaking similar trips around Ireland this week, Sylvie and William in particular. She would bet her last dollar they weren't worrying about their hosts. As last night had proved, they were too busy networking and taking advantage of every opportunity to promote their winery. She decided then and there to do the same. Enough of this emotional carry-on. No more Miss Pleasant. It was time to get out there and behave like the New World businesswoman she was.

She came down the stairs carrying her suitcases, back erect and hoping she would look the part when Dominic set eyes on her. But the moment was lost when she scanned the foyer. There was no sign of him.

Instead, the receptionist called her name. "I'm sorry, madam, Mr Hanrahan had to leave suddenly this morning. He's left you this message."

Maura quickly opened the envelope and read his handwritten note.

Good morning, Maura,

My apologies for this short notice, but I've had to unexpectedly return to Dublin for the day. I've explained the situation to Rita, and she is driving to Galway this morning to meet you and manage today's itinerary. I'll meet you both in Ennis tonight.

Dominic Hanrahan

The phone calls the night before must have been important, Maura thought. She had just finished reading the note again, an odd feeling of disappointment trickling through her, when the receptionist called her name.

"You're in demand today, Miss Carmody," she smiled. "A phone call for you now."

It was Rita, calling en route from Dublin on her mobile phone. "Hello there, Maura, did you get Dominic's message? I'm afraid you're stuck with me for the day instead!"

Maura decided she didn't mind in the least. Today was going to be a very hectic day, and if she was honest with herself she found travelling in such close proximity to Dominic quite exhausting.

Rita was very enthusiastic about the day ahead. "I'll be with in you in less than an hour, and then we can head off to County Clare. There's been fantastic interest in your talk – we've had to move the venue yet again. And I've arranged another radio interview for you in Ennis this afternoon."

The idea of it made Maura very anxious. A few people in a council meeting-room she could handle. A hall full of expectant faces was a different matter. And she had a whole day ahead of her to feel nervous.

She decided to wile away the time before Rita arrived with another walk around Galway's streets, and a quick visit to one of the jeweller's to choose a Claddagh ring for Fran.

She found a nice, old-fashioned-looking shop and spent a pleasant half an hour looking over the different versions of the design, before finally settling on a slim, gold version with a tiny gemstone embedded in the heart.

Walking back to the hotel, she looked across the road and noticed one of the off-licences she and Dominic had visited the evening before. The winter morning sunlight was shining right on it, and she decided to take another quick photograph for Nick of the Lorikeet Hill display in the front window.

Walking up close and focusing her camera, she suddenly stopped and looked around, puzzled. She was sure this was the same off-licence – she certainly recognised the revolving sun-lamp – but there wasn't a single bottle of Lorikeet Hill wine in the window. The only Australian wine on display was Sylvie and William Rogers' Glen varieties. She rummaged in her bag and found her itinerary and rechecked the address, in case there happened to be two revolving-sun displays in Galway. No, it was definitely the same store.

Taking a deep breath, she climbed up the steps. From the back room she heard a small cough, and seconds later the old gentleman came out, the pipe still clenched in his teeth.

"Good morning, Mr O'Shea," she said hesitantly. "I hope you remember me, I'm Maura Carmody from South Australia, I was here yesterday . . ."

"Of course I remember you – you're going to make sure I win the trip, aren't you, Maura?" he asked, coughing again.

"Well, I'll do my best," she said nervously. "I'm sorry, I hope you don't mind me asking, but can you tell me what happened to the Lorikeet Hill display you had in the window?"

He looked surprised. "Oh, I thought you would have known about it. The gentleman you came in with yesterday called in, very bright and early this morning. I wasn't officially open, mind you, that would be against the law, just in here doing a bit of stocktaking, you know the way." He winked. "Anyway, your friend said he had to take all the Lorikeet Hill wine away. But he made sure we put another Australian wine in its place – look! Don't want to miss out on a chance for that trip, now, do I?" he grinned.

"No, I'm sure you don't," she smiled back, still very confused. Dominic had come in here this morning? An awful thought struck her but she tried to dismiss it. "Thanks again," she said hurriedly, heading for the door before the man struck up conversation again.

"And best of luck with the competition," she called, as she hurried down the steps.

Out on the pavement, she looked again at her itinerary. She found the address of the final off-licence she had visited yesterday, where a customer had come in and bought the Lorikeet Hill wine. This time trusting her sense of direction, she retraced her steps and came across the shop. The young man who had been behind the counter was on the pavement, cleaning the front window. The glass was covered in a soapy film and she couldn't see in to the display. She hurried up to him.

"Good morning, do you remember me?"

He looked a little surprised at her question, but smiled nevertheless. "Of course I do, my memory lasts at least twenty-four hours. How are you, Maura?"

"I'm well. I'm sorry to go right to the point, but can I have a look at your window display?"

"Of course you can," he said. "Hang on a second." He wiped away the soap bubbles with a quick movement.

As a clear porthole emerged, Maura looked closely. The front of the display was now devoted to all the other Australian wines, with a bottle of The Glen Cabernet Sauvignon perched in the front row. There was no sign of Lorikeet Hill wines. She suddenly realised her hunch was right.

The young man continued to wipe away the soap from the window. "Your guide – Dominic isn't it? – came around this morning and took all your wine away. He said there was some sort of a problem with it. To be honest, I wasn't quite awake myself. He said we should display these other Aussie ones instead." He looked concerned at her suddenly pale face. "Are they terrible wines? Dominic said they were all good."

Maura clenched her jaw. "Oh, he did, did he?" she said aloud. I bet he bloody did, she thought.

She had a clear mental image of Dominic talking to Sylvie in the pub the night before. What had Dominic said she was doing? That's right – 'just trying to drum up business'. And drumming up an absolute storm by the looks of these two store displays. And Maura would bet a thousand dollars the other Lorikeet Hill displays in Galway had miraculously disappeared too, in favour of The Glen wines. It was obvious. Sylvie had struck a deal to get Dominic to replace all the Lorikeet Hill wine in Galway with The Glen wine. That had probably been her on the phone the night before too.

Maura couldn't believe it. She had been completely taken in. That was why he had been so charming, to disarm her. Once a mercenary, always a mercenary. In the pub Sylvie had mentioned her conversation with Carla. That little brat was probably in on it as well.

She looked at her watch. She'd have to get moving, Rita would be waiting. She said goodbye to the puzzled young shop assistant and walked briskly back to her hotel, her thoughts racing. Would she tell Rita what she had discovered? No, she'd have it out with Dominic first. Rita was so grateful to Dominic for stepping into Bernadette's shoes she probably wouldn't dare upset him anyway. Maura would have to handle it herself tonight in Ennis when she saw Dominic again.

She pasted a smile on her face as she saw Rita waiting in the foyer of the hotel, and greeted her warmly. It was a relief to immerse herself in Rita's chatter and to hear all the news about the other winemakers' trips around the country. Maura mentioned that Sylvie and Dennis Rogers had turned up suddenly the night before, and watched Rita carefully to see if she had already heard as much from Dominic.

Her face gave nothing away. Rita just gave a merry laugh. "Didn't I warn you she would be trying to poach your territory? Really, that woman is incredible. I'm expecting her to pop up in Belfast or Longford any day now too!"

As long as Dominic has been there first, Maura thought grimly. He was probably on his way now, ready to sweet-talk some more innocent winesellers.

Chapter Seventeen

The rain started to fall as they left Galway and the swish of the windscreen wipers acted as a soothing rhythm to Maura's troubled thoughts. They had been driving for half an hour when she noticed with a start that they were passing from County Galway into County Clare, a fact marked by a simple roadside sign. As Rita slowed down so she could easily read the wording, Maura saw the last line on the sign: *Twinned with Clare, South Australia.*

"Do you want to stop and take a photo?" Rita asked, smiling at Maura's interest.

Maura shook her head, using the heavy rain as an excuse. "I'll wait for a fine day," she said.

"You'll be waiting," Rita said wryly.

The truth was Maura was too distracted. She had hoped to be clear-headed and rational today, not in this jumble of emotions.

She took a deep breath, and looked around, trying to calm herself.

She was in County Clare.

In a village somewhere near here her birth mother Catherine Shanley had grown up. Gone to school. Lived with her family. And then said farewell as she joined the emigration trail to America and Australia.

Maura's senses heightened. She gazed at the scenery around them, not sure if she was expecting it to look different or feel different to the other counties she had travelled through. It wasn't as if it was her home, she challenged herself. Her home was Australia. Was she expecting to suddenly feel a connection to this landscape that she hadn't felt in the other parts of Ireland?

Rita had gone silent, listening to a radio programme. Maura leant back against the headrest, throwing her mind back years.

She had always known that she had been adopted. Her mother Terri had been honest with her. When Maura was old enough to understand, Terri had gently explained that she had been unable to get pregnant again after Nick's birth, but had dearly wanted another child. "You were the answer to my prayers, Morey," she'd often said.

Maura didn't really remember Terri's husband – he'd deserted the family when Maura was only three – but her memories of Terri were vivid enough to fill the space he had left behind.

The idea of being adopted hadn't had much impact on her when she was young. But as a teenager she had become more and more curious.

On the morning of her sixteenth birthday Terri had come into her bedroom, given her an envelope, and then hugged her close.

"This is about my mother, isn't it?" Maura had asked Terri softly.

Terri had nodded gently, holding Maura's hand tightly. "She asked that you have this on your sixteenth birthday."

Terri had left her alone then, but it was some time before Maura had opened the envelope.

She read the short note from Catherine Shanley very slowly, taking in each word bit by bit. It was an apology, a wish that Maura might one day want to find her, and that she hoped Maura understood what a difficult decision giving her up had been. Catherine had written the telephone number of a priest in Adelaide who would always know how she could be contacted. There were other pieces of paper in the envelope. A copy of her birth certificate – father unknown. Maura had read the words slowly. A handwritten family history, explaining that Catherine Shanley and her parents John and Rosa were from a small village in the west of County Clare in Ireland. There was even a roughly drawn map, with the Shanley's house marked carefully on it. Maura couldn't pronounce the name of the village.

God knows what reaction Catherine Shanley had expected. But Maura could remember clearly the all-consuming rage she had felt as she read the letter. How dare this woman write to her? How dare she think she would want to find her? She had a mother. Terri was her mother. Who did this woman think she was?

Her fury had risen in seconds, powered with all the rage of a sixteen-year-old. She had stormed into the kitchen and, in front of Terri's amazed eyes, ripped the letter in four and thrown it onto the floor.

"I have a mother. I don't want some – some slut to try to claim me, with these pathetic words!" Maura had shouted.

In hindsight, Maura recognised that Terri must have been as pleased as she had been shocked at Maura's reaction. She must have always worried that Maura would rush to her birth mother, leaving her behind. In the fog of her anger, Maura had half-realised Terri's anguish. It had made her rail against the letter even more strongly.

"I don't want it – here, give it to me again, I'll burn it in front of you!" she had shouted.

Terri had quickly picked up the torn paper from the floor and pushed the pieces into her pocket, slowly shaking her head at the fierce look on Maura's face.

"No, that is a bit too dramatic, even for you, Morey," she had said, calling her by her pet name. "Let's forget about the letter, and you come here and give me a hug instead."

The sixteen-year-old had suddenly become the little girl again. Her tears this time were those of a child and not the she-devil of moments before. Maura still remembered the feeling of Terri's warm arms around her, soothing her with nonsense names.

They had never spoken of it again. Maura didn't want to, and Terri had never raised the subject. But after Terri had died, Maura and Nick had found Catherine's letter in her personal effects. The pieces had been stuck together with sticky tape. Terri hadn't added any note – she had just written Maura's name in strong letters across a new envelope, and placed the mended, folded letter inside. Maura knew Terri had wanted her to find it, and maybe in the calm of adulthood do something about it.

It was too late. By the time she had tracked down the path of clues laid down in the letter, it was only to hear from a very brusque matron in a rural hospital near Melbourne that the Irish nurse Catherine Shanley had died two years previously.

Maura's heart had been very heavy for months. She wasn't fanciful enough to think she had lost two mothers. Terri had been her mother. She hadn't known Catherine at all. She was mourning the idea of Catherine, she realised. Nothing more, nothing less.

But maybe that grief explained the strange few years that had followed. And explained why she had been powerless against Richard's ill-treatment of her. She hadn't known what her own place in the world was, let alone how to defend it.

Maura was glad the route she and Rita were taking through County Clare today did not pass Catherine Shanley's village. She was still fighting with herself about whether she wanted to seek out any of Catherine's family. They probably had no idea Maura existed. And she wasn't sure if she wanted them to know she did. "And what would I say to them anyway?"

"Say to who?" Rita's question interrupted her musing.

Maura gave her a puzzled look, not realising she had spoken aloud.

"I thought you'd asked me a question, something about saying something to somebody," Rita explained.

Maura blushed slightly. "Oh, I was rehearsing my talk for tonight, trying out some new commentary to the slides, don't mind me," she improvised.

She was glad of Rita's interruption, and pleased to see they were on the outskirts of Ennis, the main town in County Clare. Rita pointed out landmarks as they drove in, and Maura gently eased her mind back to the job at hand.

Within a minute of driving into the winding streets of Ennis, Maura realised what might have sparked all the interest in her talk that night. As they drove down the main shopping street, she noticed that almost every second shop had a poster with an Australian flag stuck to their window.

Free wine tonight, each poster blared. No wonder Rita had been forced to keep changing the venue, with promises like that being made. She only hoped the audience wouldn't be too disappointed with the few sips that she had to offer.

Rita drove on to the first off-licence on the itinerary,

a small shop in the middle of the town with a remarkably wide range of Australian wine. She had three shop visits today and then the interview on the local radio station. She was looking forward to that, having been told it would be as much about the Clare Valley as Lorikeet Hill Wines and tonight's tasting.

The visits and the radio interview went well. Maura was pleased her research into the origins of Clare hadn't gone to waste. She talked quite knowledgeably about Edward Gleeson, a wealthy landowner from near Lake Inchiquin in County Clare, who had settled in a valley in South Australia in the 1840s and named it after his home place.

The announcer finished the interview with another enthusiastic invitation to everyone to attend Maura's talk, cheerfully ignoring Maura's attempts to play down the wine-tasting part of the evening.

Maura had hoped to have a half an hour to herself to check through her notes and slides for that evening. But she fell into conversation with a producer at the radio station, who had been in South Australia the summer before and was keen to reminisce on her trips to the Flinders Ranges and Kangaroo Island. Rita whispered a reminder that it was nearly five o'clock and she had less than an hour to shower, change and get to the hall to set up.

Maura decided not to panic – she'd rehearsed her speech many times, and the slide show was a carbon copy of the one she had presented in Westport.

But even so, she felt the butterflies start up in her stomach when she and Rita arrived at the hall to find it absolutely jam-packed. She looked around to see if Dominic had arrived. If she had a moment, she wanted to get to the bottom of the wine-switching before she gave her talk. But there was no sign of him.

"Wow," Rita breathed, "there must be nearly two hundred people here."

One of the local County Councillors, Gerald Ramsey, greeted her effusively at the door, proudly walking her through the seated audience with his arm around her. She had met him the previous year, when he and a group of other Councillors had visited the Clare Valley as part of the twinning arrangements.

"It's a great pleasure and an honour to welcome you to Clare, Maura. As you can see, I've done all I can to promote the best wine in all of Australia," he said proudly.

She smiled nervously, thinking with alarm of the one dozen bottles of Lorikeet Hill wine on hand for the tasting that would follow her talk. At this rate, everyone would be lucky to smell a cork, let alone have a decent taste. And there'd be no chance of any sales, unless there were some empty bottle collectors in the audience tonight.

She tried to get Rita's attention to express her alarm, but she was busy talking to a young man with a camera and a notebook who was obviously from the local paper. She overhead him saying something about having the ideal headline for his story – *It's a long way from Clare to here*. She grinned to herself – she and Nick had used the same song title in their advertising a number of times.

Looking toward the door, she noticed with a start that Dominic had just arrived, carrying a cardboard box full of bottles. As she watched he handed the box to a young man dressed in a Wine Society T-shirt, then took out a mobile phone and made another call.

She was taken aback. Now what was he up to? She was about to approach him and have it out, but at that moment Rita came beside her and whispered good luck. Maura was led up the stairs onto the small stage and sat, a mixture of nerves and excitement, as Gerald Ramsey went to the microphone and heartily welcomed everyone.

Maura hardly took a word in as Gerald talked for almost twenty minutes about the twinning between the two regions and spoke in great detail about his most recent trip to Australia. She smiled politely at his story about his first confrontation with a kangaroo and how he had coped with the hot South Australian summers. By the looks on some of the faces in the front rows they had heard some of these stories a few times too.

Maura took the opportunity to try to count the number of people in the hall, trying to guess which of them would be likely wine-tasters and which had come along to learn about the Clare Valley. She noticed a few elderly women in one of the front rows, thinking with relief that they were unlikely wine drinkers. Then she noticed one of them nudge her partner, point to the table of bottles at the back of the hall and practically lick her lips.

She thought gratefully of the trial run in Westport. The patter she had rehearsed to lead into each slide had seemed to go down well. Mind you, the way Gerald was introducing her, tonight's audience was probably just expecting her to stand on stage and hurl bottles of wine out into the auditorium for them to catch.

In a sudden fog of nerves, she heard Gerald introduce her, and she stood up with shaking legs and walked toward the microphone.

Chapter Eighteen

Maura gazed out at all the faces looking expectantly up at her and took a deep breath.

"Hello, everyone, and thank you all very much for coming along tonight. From what Gerald's told me, you all have a pretty good idea already, but I thought I'd start my talk with a quick geography lesson, just to give you some idea of where Clare Valley is in the general scheme of things."

She clicked the slide remote-control button and turned around, expecting to see her first slide of a map of Australia, showing Lorikeet Hill's location in South Australia.

Instead it was an upside-down image of herself and Nick standing in front of Lorikeet Hill Winery Café. A few people in the audience started to snigger.

Maura's heart seemed to stop. She must have put the slides back in the wrong order after the talk in Westport, she thought in horror. In desperation, she ad-libbed.

"Well, the simplest way is just to remind you that Australia is indeed the land down under. From your point of view, this is how we look, upside down at the bottom of the world."

She was rewarded with a few more laughs.

"What I'd like to do tonight is briefly explain what Lorikeet Hill wine is all about." She clicked the button, expecting the next slide in her run-down of the winemaking process, an artistic photo showing rows of vineyards, bursting with fruit.

Instead it was a slide from the Gourmet Weekend, showing a gang of grinning people holding what was obviously not their first glass of red wine up to the camera.

With a cold rush down her back, and in a split second, Maura realised immediately what had happened. Carla must have meddled with her slides while she and Dominic were taking photos at the turf bog.

Maura had to stop herself swearing aloud. That little bitch, she thought. By God, she and Dominic made some double act. She thought quickly. She could hardly ask everyone to stop and wait while she did the laborious task of sorting the slides into the right way and the right order in the carousel.

She'd have to wing it. "Yes," she said, looking desperately at the slide. "That's exactly what Lorikeet Hill is all about. It's about good times, good friends and the taste of good wine."

She turned the slide projector off with a flourish,

attempting to mask her shaking hands and turned toward the audience again.

"You were probably all expecting a scientific lecture on the science of how wine is made. And I'm sorry to disappoint you. But it's not really that complicated. We take grapes, we crush them, the juice ferments, we blend it and keep our fingers crossed nothing goes wrong. Then we bottle it and you drink it. That's really simplified, of course, but the process is basically the same the world over, whether you're talking Old World, New World, Australian wine, Chilean wine, God knows, maybe one day even Hawaiian wine."

Thanks for my one feeble joke, Cormac, she thought in relief, as a few people in the crowd laughed.

"What I'm here to do tonight is to tell you why I think Australian wine, and especially Lorikeet Hill wine, is special."

She leaned back against a high stool beside the microphone, to give herself a relaxed look but in reality to stop her legs from shaking so violently.

"My brother makes it, and he is genuinely passionate about it. I think that helps. He's a great drinker, so that's a good first step. But he also loves the smells and the different tastes and the whole mystery and magic of it.

"One of the mysteries to me has always been why grapes grown in one part of South Australia produce wine that tastes completely different than wine made from grapes from another part of Australia or the rest of the world. Orange juice, or apple juice or tomato juice generally tastes the same, no matter where the fruit comes from.

"I think that maybe it helps that the Clare Valley is a very beautiful part of the world. I hadn't really realised how much I loved it until I went away from it for five years and lived in Sydney.

"I had my own idea of what Ireland would look like and you probably have your own idea of what Australia does, or should, look like. Most of South Australia is made up of long straight roads through flat, dry land. It's so different to the scenery I've seen the last couple of days as we drove through Galway, Sligo and Mayo and across the country from Dublin.

"I'm sure you're all used to it and hardly even notice how beautiful it is here. But as I look at it, I find myself thinking about all the thousands and thousands of people who have lived and worked and slept and picked over every plot of land in this country over many, many centuries."

Maura took a sip of water, before continuing. "Because that's what always strikes me about South Australia, and the whole of Australia. Its isolation and emptiness and mystery. There's a long Aboriginal history that we will probably never know everything about. And there are still places you can go there that maybe only you and one other person have ever stood on.

"I think that isolation and mystery helps make our wine taste different to French wine or German wine.

And of course we've only been producing wine in Australia for less than two hundred years, just a blink of an eye compared to Europe.

"And that is part of it, of course. When the first winemakers in the Clare Valley, stuck on the other side of the world using techniques from thousands of miles away, forgot something, they couldn't just turn to someone and say: sorry, what was that again? So they had to come up with their own ideas. And we've kept doing that.

"That explains a lot of the taste of Australian wine. But I also reckon the land itself has a lot to do with it. It's known a whole ancient civilisation, has had sun belting down on it for thousands of years, but very few people because of its sheer size. It's seen drought and bushfires and all sorts of strange animals running across it. But despite all that there is still something untouched about it. Something bold.

"And I reckon it's what's in the land that's coming through in our wine. A boldness, mixed with a lot of mystery, brought together by science."

There was a pause, and Maura realised with a shock that she actually had everyone's attention. She blinked a couple of times, suddenly feeling as though she'd been in a trance. She hadn't realised this was what she thought until she had heard herself say it.

She smiled suddenly. "Maybe you can help me solve another mystery tonight. Why isn't Australian wine outselling Guinness in Ireland?"

Everyone laughed. The mood was broken.

She took a deep breath and looked around. "Well, there's my theory on Australian winemaking. Now you should find out what it tastes like – if my assistants tonight are ready for you all?" She looked toward the back of the hall where two young men the Wine Society had roped in to assist with the tastings were waiting behind a long table covered with wineglasses. They nodded nervously.

"For those of you who had expected a more detailed explanation of winemaking, please come up and say hello to me afterwards and I'll do my best to answer your questions. And those of you who want to see the real thing, please take Gerald's word for it, and accept this as my invitation. Thank you for making me welcome in your Clare and I'll look forward to welcoming you all one day to my Clare."

She hardly heard Gerald's appreciative thank you, or his exhortation to everyone in the hall to line up in an orderly fashion.

She wanted to run outside and shout at the moon in sheer relief that the speech was over. Now that the adrenalin rush had gone, she felt her anger about Dominic's wine-switching and Carla's slide sabotage rise again. She could feel the damp curls at the back of her neck, where she had perspired from nervousness. And it wasn't over yet.

The queue for the tasting was snaking around the hall. Maura stepped carefully down the stairs where

Rita was waiting for her, with a warm smile and a hug of congratulations.

"That was terrific – well done! What a shame about the slides, did you drop them on the way here or something?" Rita asked.

"Nothing so simple, I'm sorry to say," Maura answered through gritted teeth, looking around for Dominic. She decided against filling Rita in on the whole situation just yet. She'd expected the imminent shortage of wine to be a more immediate worry for Rita, though the Irish girl seemed completely relaxed.

Maura looked around again. The room was quite festive by now. Everyone seemed to have had at least one free glass and she watched in amazement as great numbers of them went up to the table at the far end of the hall to buy a bottle or two to take home, at the special discounted price.

Through the queue of people heading toward the tasting table, she could see that Dominic was going into a back room and bringing out another box of bottles. Surely they had used up the stock by now, she wondered, unless he was performing a Wedding of Cana miracle and turning water into wine.

As she watched, he went back into the room and brought out another half dozen bottles.

"That room's like the magic pudding," she said aloud.

"What's that?" Rita asked with a distracted air, as she watched for the arrival of another local reporter.

"It's a famous Australian children's story – no matter how much you ate from this special pudding bowl, it was never empty. How on earth can there be any left to sell?" Maura asked. She was astonished there had been enough for so many tastings, let alone any sales at all.

"Dominic said he would look after it," Rita said in an undertone, before setting eyes on the reporter and going over to talk to her.

Maura watched puzzled as a young man walked in through the door carrying yet another box of wine. She wasn't sure, but from a distance it almost looked like The Glen trademark on the side of the box. The light was poor, but she was definitely sure it wasn't Lorikeet Hill's logo. She watched as Dominic took the box and handed the man what looked like a small bundle of notes.

No, she thought in shock. Surely he couldn't have done that as well. He had known a huge crowd was expected tonight and must have guessed they would run out of Lorikeet Hill wine. He'd probably discussed it with Sylvie Rogers last night and they'd seen it as the perfect opportunity to sell The Glen. By the looks of the crowd here tonight, no one really minded what brand of Australian wine they were drinking. From the queue it also looked like they were keen to buy as well.

Her temper rose like a geyser. Excusing herself from the group around her, she practically marched over to the wine-tasting table.

"I have to talk to you," she hissed at Dominic. He

looked up calmly from his unloading and followed her into the back room.

"Hello again, Maura," he said calmly.

She turned to him in a fury. Her embarrassment and near-disaster on stage overwhelmed her again and she could barely spit out the words.

"What the hell is going on here? First Carla does her best to sabotage my talk – and don't tell me you didn't know anything at all about her vicious little games. Then you trick all the Galway winesellers into displaying The Glen wines. And now you're running some sort of black market at Lorikeet Hill's expense. You know how important this trip is to our business. You're the one who suggested a truce – but it seems that making money at someone else's expense is just too hard a habit to break."

Dominic's eyes glittered at her but she was too worked up to notice the warning. His voice was very quiet and his body very still. "What are you talking about? What sabotage?"

"Carla did her best to wreck my talk tonight with her fun and games with my slides. And you've ruined everything for Lorikeet Hill in Galway with your 'business' with Sylvie Rogers. Now, I don't give a damn about whatever weird relationship you and Carla have or what sort of pact with the devil you've made to make yourself rich, but leave me, my brother and our business out of it, do you hear me?"

Dominic interrupted her. "No, *you* hear me. I don't

know anything about deals with Sylvie Rogers or your slides or what Carla did or didn't do. Or any trickery, or black market. And you don't know anything – anything – about my relationship with Carla, so keep your theories to yourself."

"Oh, I see," she said with heavy sarcasm. "They're all just theories, are they? So are you going to tell me you don't know anything about this sudden mysterious arrival of carton after carton of wine either? It's pretty obvious that you saw another handy opportunity to make a quick dollar. I saw you give that man some money."

Rita came in at that moment and heard the last of Maura's speech.

"Isn't he brilliant?" she said, smiling up at Dominic. "So he's filled you in on his whole brainwave, then. He wouldn't even let me tell you anything about it, in case you got worried or it made you nervous about tonight's talk. Thanks again, Dominic – you really got us out of a fix. And I'd say Lorikeet Hill has made some record sales tonight, Maura."

Maura felt a familiar sinking feeling. Rita mistook her shock for bewilderment.

"Ah, Dominic, have you kept it to yourself?" Rita laughed. She turned to Maura to explain. "When Dominic heard about the big number of people expected tonight he realised before I did that we'd have a shortage of Lorikeet Hill wine. He got on to every off-licence and pub and restaurant within an hour's drive of here and arranged for taxi drivers to collect and bring as much of your wine as they could. He even cleared all the Lorikeet Hill wine out of Galway himself, and brought it all along tonight. You saved the day, Dominic."

Maura closed her eyes slowly, hoping that when she opened them she would be a very, very long way away. Her wish didn't come true. Looking through the door into the busy hall, she noticed this time that while the boxes on the floor were all sorts of different brands and wineries, every bottle of wine being sold on the table had Fran's distinctive Lorikeet Hill bird logo.

"Our only problem now is how to deal with a temporary shortage of Lorikeet Hill wine in the west of Ireland, but I'm sure we'll cope, eh, Maura?" Rita asked with a grin.

"Oh, I'm sure we will," Maura answered in a very small voice.

She looked up at Dominic, shocked, and trying to send him a heartfelt apology with her eyes. She fervently wished Rita gone, so she could at least try to thank him and attempt to say sorry. But she knew from the look in his eyes that she had gone too far for a simple apology.

Rita was beaming with the success of the evening, and insisted that Maura and Dominic leave her to look after the clean-up herself. "Dominic, take that poor girl for a glass of champagne – she's got plenty to celebrate after all."

Champagne would be great, Maura thought. If I

could just get this foot out of my mouth so I could taste it.

Dominic waited outside the door while Maura fetched her coat and scarf. As the rain started again, Maura gathered the soft wool of the scarf around her, glad to have something to hide behind. Her temper had deflated like an empty balloon, and she felt full of shame about getting it all so wrong.

They walked along the now empty streets for nearly five minutes in silence, until Maura couldn't stand it any more.

"Dominic, please listen to me. I jumped to the wrong conclusion about you and the wine and I was upset about the slides and I took it out on you, I'm sorry. I have a terrible temper and I shouldn't have said what I did."

As she spoke, they ducked under a shop awning to escape a sudden blustery downpour. Dominic didn't answer.

"Dominic?" Maura implored softly, putting her hand on his arm to stop him from walking away.

She was taken aback when he pushed it away as though it burnt him. His eyes glittered at her, the irises looking black in the light from the shop window. He looked at her for what seemed like long minutes.

"I don't want to hear it, Maura," he almost whispered, his Irish accent now much stronger than any American tone. "You've said what you think of me and Carla. I don't think there's much more to add."

"But your relationship with Carla is none of my business, I don't know what made me say it."

"No, it isn't any of your business . . ." he said softly, his voice not as harsh as his words. She was sure he was going to add something and gazed up at him, almost begging him with her eyes to forgive her temper.

They looked at each other for a moment, and she held her breath as he slowly lifted his hand toward her face, as if he were going to stroke her cheek. A strange look crossed his face, then he seemed to mentally shake himself.

"You're getting wet, we'd better keep walking." His voice was low.

She followed him down the glistening, winding streets to their hotel. No receptionist to battle with, no arguments over the room tonight. Just a subdued good night to each other.

Maura let herself into her room, and fought back a longing to hurl herself onto the bed and burst into tears.

What did it matter? she tried to tell herself. Carla, and by association Dominic, had tried to ruin her talk tonight, for no other reason than malice. The wine trip was over. She'd have little to do with him while she was doing the cooking school. And tonight had been a great success, in publicity and sales – Rita kept telling her as much.

So why did she feel this strange, heavy sadness?

Chapter Nineteen

"Well, your photos don't do you justice, Maura, you're absolutely gorgeous in real life," Bernadette said as Maura and Dominic arrived at Ardmahon House. She gave Maura a big hug.

Maura embraced her with equal enthusiasm, feeling as though she was being reunited with a long-lost friend.

She pulled back from the hug and smiled at Bernadette. Her photos hadn't done her justice either, blurry and all as they were. They didn't capture the spark of mischief or the warmth in her eyes.

Bernadette was about fifty years old, curly-haired and – there was no other word for it – plump. But it suited her. She looked like a woman who had decided years ago there were better things in life to worry about than kilo-watching. Cooking and eating and entertaining people, for example.

"You look great too," Maura said. "And how are all your storm injuries? I wasn't sure if I'd be meeting you in a wheelchair or crutches or what."

Bernadette laughed. "I'm practically cured," she said, poking out her leg. A white bandage was just visible above a sturdy boot on her left foot. "It's a miracle, really – it was just a bad sprain, and I'm walking with no bother again now."

As Bernadette gave Maura another welcoming hug, she turned and gave Dominic a teasing smile.

"So how on earth have you managed to keep your hands off her for a whole week together? Lord, it would have tried the patience of a saint."

Maura gasped at Bernadette's cheekiness, but Dominic was obviously used to her saucy tongue. If she only knew they'd had trouble even talking to each other the past few hours, let alone anything else.

"Oh, I managed," Dominic said with a tight smile.

Bernadette raised an eyebrow in mock indignation, glancing back and forth at Maura and Dominic and noticing the tension between them.

"Well, I'm obviously not going to get any scandal out of you two today. So, Maura, you must be dying to have a look around this beautiful house. I've a head-start on you, I moved in yesterday, and I tell you, it's a dream come true." She turned to Dominic. "Thanks again for coming to the rescue, Dominic. You must have some great plans for it – the work you've had done is fantastic. It makes my place look like a stable."

Dominic smiled at Bernadette, but pointedly didn't elaborate on his future plans. "I'm glad you're settling in well. When's your first group of students arriving?"

"Not until Monday morning," Bernadette answered, "So we've the whole weekend to get ready for them. Have you time for a drink of something?"

Dominic looked up at the clock above the kitchen door. "I'm sorry, Bernadette, but I need to get back to Dublin as soon as possible, so I'll have to leave you to it." Maura noticed he was directing his comments to Bernadette. "I'm sure you'll find everything you need. If you don't, just ring me and I'll arrange for it to be delivered."

With a nod at them both, Dominic left the room. Maura looked after him, glad of the relief she felt now he was gone but oddly enough feeling a strange disappointment that she wouldn't be seeing him for a while. This morning's half-hour drive to Ardmahon House had been very tense, worse even than their first drive nearly a week ago. Maura had tried several times to apologise, to make conversation, but Dominic had seemed unmoved, even miles away. He hadn't been rude. Just distant. That was worse, she thought.

Bernadette watched her looking after Dominic and smiled knowingly.

"He's absolutely gorgeous, isn't he?" she said, breaking Maura's reverie.

To Maura's embarrassment, she felt a blush rising in her face.

Bernadette let out a great roar of laughter. "Don't be embarrassed. Heavens, if I was ten years younger I'd give you a run for your money myself."

As Maura started to protest that there was nothing between herself and Dominic, Bernadette just laughed her protests away. "I'm just teasing you, love. Sure, everyone here thinks Dominic is a handsome fellow. I'd be more surprised if you didn't notice it."

Everyone? Maura thought. Who is everyone? But Bernadette had tired of discussing Dominic's attractions and was pulling up a chair beside the long kitchen table.

"Come and look at the course schedules I've organised and tell me what you think and then we'll have a good nose around, now that Dominic has gone."

Maura immersed herself in the details of the next three weeks. Bernadette had done a great job organising all the bookings for her Australian Flavours series. There were three groups of eight people coming for the residential cooking classes, which would run Monday, Tuesday, Wednesday and Thursdays. Then each Friday and Saturday night the main dining-room would be transformed into a restaurant. Bernadette had even arranged for all her kitchen staff and waitresses to relocate to Dominic's house.

"Well, I'm glad you approve." Bernadette gave a dramatic sigh, knowing that Maura was delighted with everything. "Come on, now, you must be as curious as I am. Let's go exploring."

It took almost a half an hour to walk over the entire house and gardens. It was truly impressive. As they walked through the wide halls and immaculately decorated rooms, Maura couldn't begin to imagine the work that had gone into the renovations and rebuilding. She had heard from Cormac and Bernadette about the original state of the house.

"It's quite wonderful, isn't it?" Bernadette said as they walked through the final wing, which held half a dozen beautifully furnished bedrooms. "It's funny how your luck turns out, isn't it? The set-up here is actually better than at my own house. I never thought I'd say it, but that storm did us a good turn."

As they had walked around Bernadette had explained that the repairs to the storm damage at her house were coming along, but much more slowly than she would have liked. She admitted cheerfully to Maura that seeing Dominic's house had given her quite a few new ideas.

"I especially like the dining-room and living-rooms here," Bernadette elaborated, as they walked down the sweeping staircase together. "It would make a wonderful venue for exclusive house parties or top secret government conferences, don't you think?"

Maura looked around, noticing the beautifully landscaped gardens through the tall windows at the foot of the stairs. She nodded. It was very secluded and peaceful. It felt like they were hundreds of miles from anywhere, but it was really just a few hours from Dublin. Or London, if it came to that.

"When did Dominic buy it?" she asked curiously.

"About a year ago. It was completely run down – I

don't think anybody had lived in it for years and years. There used to be hundreds of these crumbling old castles and mansions all over Ireland, but they're like hen's teeth now. All sorts of retired pop-stars and bestselling authors snapped them up."

Maura tried to steer the conversation back from real estate matters to Dominic.

"Is his family from around here?" That would be just her luck, she thought. Dominic would turn out to be her second cousin or nephew.

"He's not from this area, I think he's from Cork or somewhere down south. Not that you can tell from his accent any more – he has that transatlantic mix, now, doesn't he?"

Maura said nothing, remembering with a spark of embarrassment her first meeting with him in Clare. She had been convinced it was an American accent.

Bernadette looked at her watch. "Enough sightseeing. Let's go down to the kitchen and have a good chat. And it's about time I tried some of your brother's wine, don't you think?"

Chapter Twenty

Bernadette was at the front door to welcome the first group of students as they arrived at Ardmahon House on Monday morning, in a mixture of hired cars, parents' vehicles and public buses.

Busy in the kitchen, Maura overheard the different conversations as Bernadette settled each of them into their bedrooms and showed them around the house, sounding as though she had lived there for years rather than moved in two days before.

Her experience showed, Maura thought. Bernadette had been running her residential cooking school for over ten years, holding long and short courses on everything from the Secrets of Cooking Potatoes to Christmas Dinners without the Fuss.

Bernadette had told her lots of stories over the weekend, as the two of them had visited local markets and stores, ordering goods and stocking up on the rest of the ingredients for the cooking school and restaurant in the week ahead. She had explained to Maura that her students came from all over Ireland, and sometimes all over the world.

"We have a lot of students who see this as something like a mini finishing school, but there's a great mix, actually," she'd explained. "In fact some of my students are middle-aged mums who just want a bit more confidence in their kitchen, or are bored with serving meat and three vegetables night after night. They want to spice up their lives a little bit, and where better place to start than the kitchen?" she had winked.

Maura had seen Bernadette's course list for the rest of the year and her series on the latest trends in Australian food and wine – with a very strong emphasis on Lorikeet Hill naturally – had fitted in very well alongside the forthcoming Cajun, Californian and Chinese cooking classes.

The first group of students – all women – were all pretty much under thirty years of age, Maura guessed, looking around at them as they found a place to sit in the roomy kitchen. The sudden relocation to Ardmahon House had meant the kitchen wasn't completely equipped as a demonstration kitchen – there was no overhead mirror, for example – but Bernadette had assured her that it wouldn't matter. "I keep the groups small to keep it informal and quite intimate, so they'll all be able to see what you're doing anyway. Just remember to speak slowly – that Aussie accent of yours can be the very devil to understand sometimes."

"No worries, mate," Maura had shot back.

Maura looked around nervously and eight pairs of nervous eyes looked back at her. She broke the silence by introducing herself and asking the students to say their names and give a little bit of background information about themselves as well.

Bernadette had suggested it as a good way to break the ice. "They're always shy with us and each other to start with," she'd said, with knowledge born of long experience, "but by the third night you wait and see. They'll be chattering away during your classes, then heading off down the road to the pub, larking up a storm and terrorising the poor local boys."

Ciara, Siobhan, Emer and Deirdre were Irish, from different parts of the country. Sally was from England. Angela was from Munich. The two shy girls hiding behind their long black hair were Regina and Selina, twin sisters from Spain.

As Maura started to talk, one of the twins started sobbing into a handkerchief held close to her eyes.

It was Selina. Maura looked over with concern. "Are you all right?"

There was no answer.

"Are you okay, Selina?" she asked again.

She looked over at Bernadette, who walked up and touched the girl on her shoulder. "Is everything ok? Are you feeling ill?" she asked with concern.

The girl burst into tears again, and suddenly let fly with a torrent of something that sounded like a mixture of Spanish, French and Italian to Maura's untrained ear.

Bernadette looked around the classroom. "I only stretch to German and Irish – can anyone give me a hand here? Regina, what did your sister say?"

Regina looked up nervously. "She doesn't want to be here," she translated helpfully. "She can't even think about cooking. Her heart is broken because our parents have forced her over here to do this course to keep her away from her boyfriend who she loves passionately."

"Oh, I see, of course," Bernadette said in a deadpan voice. She spoke softly to the upset girl. "Would you like a glass of water, Selina, or perhaps you'd rather go up to your room and lie down?"

Selina shook her head, replying in another bubbling stream of Spanish. The whole class looked over at Regina.

"She said she may as well be here as anywhere, because her heart belongs nowhere but with Carlos," Regina said, her flat voice somewhat spoiling the romantic effect of the words.

Maura bit back a smile and looked at Bernadette. The older woman winked at her and nodded.

"Well," Maura said, far more confidently than she felt. "Let's start with a rundown of what we're going to do together over the next three and a half days, and maybe that will take your mind off Carlos for a little while, Selina."

Maura outlined the programme in detail, pleased to see the girls' reactions. She and Bernadette had spent a lot of time working out which dishes to feature, and discovering which of the more exotic ingredients she would be allowed to bring into Ireland. The customs people had drawn the line at kangaroo steaks – she disliked them anyway – but she had been able to bring in a good supply of native bush food, which would be an important part of the class.

"I'm going to show you how to cook three different entrées, three main courses and three desserts," she explained. "And of course, given my winery connections, I'll also show you the best wines to serve with them, and give you a bit of background on the wine industry of Australia as well." Which I could now do asleep, standing on my head, she thought, especially after the Ennis talk. "And on Thursday morning, in our final class, we'll be a little less formal, and I'll show you a few surprises."

The girls took their seats on the stools dotted around the kitchen, while Maura stood in front of a whiteboard Bernadette had transported over from her own house, along with a huge quantity of kitchen equipment and all the bedding. It had taken three trips in a large van, she'd explained to Maura.

Maura wrote the words *Australian Cuisine* on the board and drew a big question mark beside it. "In a way, we should have called this Thai, Italian, Vietnamese, English, Irish, Hungarian and Chinese Flavours, rather than just Australian Flavours," she said, "because there really isn't a definitive Australian cuisine. It's a real blend of many other cultures, a bit like American food. Mind you, they have their fried chicken, and we have our Vegemite, but the reputation for great cuisines aren't built on ingredients like those.

"This week you'll get a little sample of cooking from all those countries, because I think that's what makes up the flavour of Australian food. We'll start this morning with entrées. I'll show you how I make them, talk you through each of the ingredients and then this afternoon it'll be your turn to make them, in time for your dinner tonight."

Maura wrote up the entrée menu on the whiteboard.

Crispy seafood rolls filled with scallops, fish, prawns, noodles, coriander and mint served with a chilli dipping sauce

A Thai-style spicy soup, made with chicken, lemongrass, mushrooms and pepper, cooked in a coconut-milk broth

Blue cheese, walnut and wild herb pastry fingers

She heard the murmurs of anticipation from the class as they read down the list. Bernadette gave her the thumbs up. They were on their way.

Tuesday was spent tutoring the students through three main courses, with Bernadette working with four of the girls and Maura demonstrating to the others. Despite some early caution with the spices, Maura was pleased to see they were getting a little more adventurous, happy to try everything from chilli to wild bush pepper.

She included a vegetarian dish in her choices of main courses – a delicious warm pumpkin, spinach and feta cheese salad. The Irish girls in particular were surprised to use pumpkin as the basis for the meal.

"We only have pumpkin in the house at Hallowe'en, and even then we only use the shell – the chickens get all the insides," Emer said with surprise when Maura first wrote the dishes up on the whiteboard.

"Well, your poor chickens are going to have to start looking elsewhere," she explained. "Pumpkin is a wonderful vegetable. In Australia we use it in soups and casseroles, and it makes a wonderful roasted vegetable too."

The other two main courses were chicken fillets baked with a seeded wild mustard crust, served on a bed of Asian greens and potato mash, and a delicious beef and mushroom casserole, flavoured with bush pepper and served with an unusual spiced peach side dish.

"I promise, they all are simple to prepare, look wonderful on the table and they're even good for you," Maura promised.

The students took to the cooking like ducks to water, even Selina, once she had managed to dry her tears. Maura demonstrated each dish step by step, before setting each student up with her own ingredients to try it for herself.

Maura and Bernadette had decided the final meal on the Thursday of each week would be a stereotypical Australian meal – a barbeque. Bernadette had managed to find a shop in Ennis that sold large portable barbeques and the metal contraption was now sitting out in the courtyard.

"It won't be the complete Aussie experience, I'm afraid," Bernadette said on the Wednesday night, looking up from the weather forecast in the newspaper. "Showers and gusty winds expected," she grinned. "Did you bring your sunbed with you?"

Maura looked over from the fridge, where she was putting away the big tray of marinating steaks. "I've taped some cricket commentaries – we can play those as background noise instead – then at least it will sound like an Australian summer," she suggested with a smile. She had just shut the fridge door when a loud bang followed by a high-pitched shriek made them both jump.

"What in God's name was that?" Bernadette looked over. "It wasn't a cat jumping on the roof, was it?"

"Not unless you've got cats the size of tigers here," Maura said. She looked up at the clock. Ten thirty pm.

"All the girls are back from the pub, aren't they?" she asked. Bernadette nodded. They had spent the morning cooking some rich, exotic desserts and the afternoon tasting the different varieties of Lorikeet Hill wines. The wine had given the girls enough of a buzz to send them off into Ennis to carry on in the pubs. Bernadette had let in the final pair, Ciara and Deirdre, just half an hour ago.

"There it is again," Maura whispered. The second bang was followed with heavy creaking sounds, one after the other.

"It sounds like someone walking on the roof of the conservatory," Maura said.

Bernadette listened too. "I think that's because it *is* someone walking on the roof of the conservatory. Whose room is directly above it?"

Maura thought for a moment. "Selina, isn't it?"

Bernadette nodded, before putting her finger to her mouth and beckoning Maura to follow her. They tiptoed out into the hall and carefully opened the front door, making sure to turn the hall light off. The moon was just bright enough to shed light onto the conservatory attached to the side of the house.

As they watched, they saw a leg emerge from Selina's bedroom window, followed by a whole body. Then another, this one holding a large bag. The two figures tiptoed as quietly as they could across the roof of the conservatory.

"It's Selina – and I'd bet a million pounds that's Carlos with the bag," Bernadette nearly laughed. "Oh, how romantic, this is just like Romeo and Juliet."

"It's not strong enough to hold them, is it?" Maura whispered in alarm.

"So far so good," Bernadette whispered back, "I think it's made with an iron frame, so it should be fairly strong. Anyway, if we call out they're liable to get a fright and lose their balance."

Maura and Bernadette held their breath, watching the two figures inch their way carefully across the frame of the conservatory, carefully avoiding the glass panes.

The couple had just reached the edge, safely away from the glass, when gravity stepped in. Selina suddenly lost her balance and as they watched, so did Carlos. In perfect unison, the two of them tripped and fell the six feet onto the gravel path below.

Maura and Bernadette ran toward the young couple, who were now slowly getting up to the sound of loud groans. "Romeo and Juliet?" Bernadette said under her breath to Maura as they came to their aid. "Abbott and Costello, more like it."

* * *

The next day the girls were full of the news of Selina and Carlos's attempted midnight flit.

"It's so romantic," Siobhan breathed, as she helped Maura prepare a potato dish which they would enjoy later with their farewell lunch of barbequed steaks and chicken breasts. "Imagine Carlos hitchhiking all the way from Madrid to rescue Selina."

Emer scoffed. "Rescue her? From what? This is a cooking school, not a home for delinquents."

Maura and Bernadette exchanged a glance. Last night they hadn't been so sure. Both Selina and Carlos had landed awkwardly, resulting in sprains and bruises. They were now, not so romantically, lying in bed in adjoining rooms waiting for their parents to come and fetch them. It wasn't quite the ending Carlos had planned.

"Well, back to the real world, girls," Bernadette broke up their gossiping session. "It's time to enjoy a true blue

Aussie barbie!" She was making a very bad attempt at an Australian accent. "And if you're all really good you can have some lamb tin for dessert."

Maura laughed aloud. "Lamb tin? Bernadette, that sounds disgusting. She means lamington, everyone, one of Australia's many gifts to the world of cuisine."

As she spoke, Maura brought out a tray of her surprise final dessert – squares of plain cake, dipped in rich chocolate icing and then covered in coconut. Maura had many memories of them from her childhood – lamingtons were a staple food at town fétes, country shows and in school lunches. "You won't find recipes for these in any classy Australian cookbook," she joked, as the girls looked down in surprise, "but there's nothing like them to finish a proper Aussie barbie."

Later that afternoon Maura and Bernadette sat in the now quiet kitchen, enjoying a glass of Lorikeet Hill wine. The barbeque lunch and the casual dessert had made a relaxing, informal end to the first week of classes. Maura had been buoyed by the warm comments she received from the students as they departed, each clutching a souvenir bottle of Lorikeet Hill wine and a folder filled with copies of all the recipes they had learnt during the week.

"Well done, Maura," Bernadette raised her glass.

Maura clinked hers against it. "Well done and thanks, Bernadette. I really enjoyed it – we make a great team, don't we?"

"We sure do," Bernadette smiled across. "We could

rival those two BBC cooks. We could call ourselves 'One Not So Much Fat as a Stone or Two Overweight Irish Lady and One Gorgeous Shapely Australian Lady'," she added with a laugh.

Maura laughed too. "Well, that's catchy. Do you know, I can't believe we spent all those months planning this, and it's a third of the way over already."

"We'll have to make sure you get to see some more of the country as well, before your month here is suddenly up," Bernadette said, as she leaned across to refill Maura's glass. "Is there anything you particularly want to do?"

Maura started to answer, to talk about the tourist sights in the West of Ireland she wanted to visit. Then to her own surprise she found herself telling Bernadette all about her adoption.

Bernadette sat quietly, taking in every word as Maura haltingly, then with more confidence explained the circumstances. With a beating heart, she said Catherine Shanley's name, half hoping that Bernadette would know her, and the search would end there and then.

Bernadette shook her head and Maura felt a mixture of relief and disappointment run through her.

"Forty years ago there were hundreds of young ones leaving from this area to go to America and Australia. It wouldn't have been an unusual occurrence. And many's the time you would just lose touch with the one that went away. Not like these days of e-mails and Internet and express post," Bernadette explained.

As she took a sip of wine, Maura gathered her

thoughts and tried to explain how she felt about going to Catherine Shanley's village.

"The thing is, I expected that once I arrived in Ireland I would get an overwhelming feeling about whether I wanted to find Catherine's family – my family I guess – or not. But I still don't know," she said hesitantly. "If anything, being away from Nick and Fran, and thinking about them about to have a baby has made me think more of them as being my family. And then when I do feel curious about Catherine and her family I start to feel disrespectful to Terri. As though now she's gone I'm trying to find my other family. I'd like to find out something about Catherine but only if I knew that what I would find out wasn't going to upset me." She laughed sheepishly. "That sounds cowardly, doesn't it?"

Bernadette didn't answer at first. Maura liked that about her. She always considered her answers, rather than just giving quick replies.

"No, it's not cowardly. I think it's very normal. It would be different if Catherine was still alive, and it would make some difference to your relationship with her if you were to see her homeplace and meet her family.

"But the fact that you are letting the thought of it go round and round your head means you haven't dismissed it entirely. You've two more weeks here yet, you don't have to decide today. Just keep mulling it over, and if you feel the need to go there, let me know and I'll help you all I can."

Maura was about to say something more when the

sound of the phone rang out through the open kitchen door. Bernadette groaned. The phone had been ringing a lot the last couple of days, as word of the restaurant nights got around. People had been keen to book a table and she had reluctantly had to tell each caller that apart from one or two seats the season was booked out.

Maura picked up the glasses and walked into the kitchen to hear Bernadette answer the call. Her heart jumped as she overheard the conversation.

"Dominic, hello! Yes, it's all going absolutely great, your kitchen is a paradise," Bernadette chatted away, breaking occasionally into a lively gust of laughter.

Maura watched surreptitiously. Bernadette was obviously getting the charming side of Dominic. It seemed he reserved the tense mood especially for her.

"We're absolutely booked out tomorrow night, but of course we can make room for you. Heavens, I can hardly turn our host away, can I? And Carla too, sure. Of course there's room for you to stay, we've left the whole east wing for you both. So we'll see you tomorrow, oh, later today, terrific. See you then."

Maura turned smiling eyes toward Bernadette. "And I thought the food critics would make me nervous. Now those two as well. That'll keep me on my toes."

"Well, as long as we keep you away from the vases of water, everything should be just fine."

Chapter Twenty-one

For reasons she didn't care to examine too closely, Maura was jumpy the rest of the afternoon. There were a few delivery vans making their way up Ardmahon House's long drive and she felt herself tense as soon as she heard the crunch of wheels turning on gravel.

By about five thirty she had a little knot of tension in her shoulders. Once again she heard the murmur of an engine and the sound of gravel. This one was definitely not a van.

She deliberately kept working, bent over the kitchen bench preparing vegetables for a base stock for the next night's dinner. The rhythm of the work calmed her nerves a little and she still didn't turn around, even as she heard the kitchen door open behind her.

Every muscle tensed as she heard heavy footsteps come across the tiled floor toward her. She suddenly felt a pair of cool hands cover her eyes.

A low musical voice whispered into her neck. "I couldn't stay away from you any longer." She jumped and spun around.

"Cormac!" she cried aloud. "You frightened the life out of me! What on earth are you doing here?"

"I told you, my lovely Aussie, I couldn't stay away from you a moment longer. I thought I'd drive over to Clare, try some of this wonderful cooking I've been hearing about, and then show you a few of the sights."

Maura shook her head in exasperation. "You really should have rung, I don't think we've any more places in the dining-room tomorrow night."

"There's plenty of room for old friends," Bernadette answered, coming into the kitchen in time to hear the last exchange. "Cormac, it's good to see you again – how is the wild world of Dublin wine-selling treating you these days?"

Maura had forgotten that Bernadette and Cormac knew each other through the Wine Society links. Bernadette obviously enjoyed Cormac's enthusiastic sense of humour and was soon extracting the latest Dublin gossip out of him.

Maura discovered soon enough that despite Cormac's flowery language, she hadn't been his only reason to travel west.

"I've just stitched up a very big deal with one of the ritzy Galway hotels and I couldn't miss the opportunity to call down to Clare and whisk you away for a night of celebrating, dining and romancing, could I now, Maura?"

he said in a theatrically flirtatious voice, sweeping her into a close hug.

Maura laughed despite herself, smiling over his shoulder at Bernadette, who was rolling her eyes at his antics.

Just at that moment the door opened again. Dominic walked in, carrying two suitcases.

Maura leapt out of Cormac's arms, as embarrassed as if she was a servant caught playing up in the master's kitchen.

Dominic took in the situation with a quick glance, his face expressionless. As he nodded in greeting to the three of them, through the open kitchen door Maura could hear Carla's voice shouting that she needed more help with her bags.

"You've obviously done your share for today, Dominic," Cormac said cheerfully. "I'll take on the next shift."

Watching through the window, Maura saw him approach Carla with mock servility. From this distance, it looked as if Carla was accepting his help as though it was only to be expected. Maura sighed. This was all she needed. It was bad enough that he and Carla would be dining here tomorrow night, let alone being around the day before.

As Bernadette struck up a conversation, filling Dominic in on the success of the first week of the cooking school, Maura returned to her cooking preparations, covering her nervousness with well-practised movements.

"We made a great team, didn't we, Maura?" Bernadette said in a pleased voice.

Maura nodded, busying herself with the heavy stock-pot.

"And it looks like you've a full house tonight and tomorrow night as well," Dominic said, with a glance through the window at Cormac, who was still being loaded down with luggage by an imperious Carla.

"He's not staying here," Maura said quickly, wanting to explain. "He's staying with friends a few miles away."

"He's very welcome to stay, Maura," he said in a soft voice, giving her a long look. "You're not a servant, you can invite all your boyfriends down if you want to."

How had he guessed that was how she had felt when he first walked in?

"I know perfectly well I'm nobody's servant and he's not my boyfriend," she said, a little sharply this time, only to be interrupted by Cormac returning to the kitchen, groaning theatrically under the weight of Carla's baggage. He had heard her last words.

"Ah, but it's not for want of trying, eh, Maura?" he said with a big hopeful grin.

Carla followed him in. She flicked a glance in Maura's direction, but didn't even attempt a greeting to either her or Bernadette.

"You remember Bernadette, Carla," Dominic prompted her like a father with a five-year-old child. "And Maura, of course."

Carla responded with a sullen hello, before turning her back on Dominic in a sulky movement.

Watching her closely, Maura thought that she wasn't looking her best. She looked very tired with dark shadows under her eyes, and seemed even thinner than usual. As Maura watched, Carla went to her pile of luggage on the floor and rummaged until she found a pack of cigarettes. She lit one up immediately, not bothering to ask for an ashtray, or to ask if anyone minded.

Maura minded very much. This was a working kitchen. Carla's smoking was unhygienic, let alone downright rude. She looked over at Dominic, waiting for him to ask Carla to put the cigarette out. It was his house after all. But he, Bernadette and Cormac had struck up a conversation about the house renovations and hadn't noticed what Carla was doing.

Maura took the matter into her own hands.

"I'd rather you didn't smoke in here, Carla," she said, her tone as icy as the look Carla gave her in return. "Maybe it's okay usually, but while I'm here this is a commercial kitchen, and I can't allow smoking."

"I don't give a damn," Carla said rudely, insolently taking a long draw. "As if a bit of smoke will have any effect on your food. God, if anything, it might improve it."

With that, the American girl blew a long stream of smoke in the direction of Maura's food preparations.

Maura felt her temper rise. The little brat. "I've asked you once, Carla. Put that cigarette out please," she said again, her voice level.

Carla simply turned away as if bored by the conversation.

Oh no you don't, Maura thought. She marched up behind her, snatched the cigarette from Carla's fingers and threw it out through the open kitchen door.

Carla gave a loud shriek.

Dominic and Cormac turned around in time to see Carla lift her hand as if she was going to strike Maura. "How dare you do that?" the girl shouted dramatically. "Who the hell do you think you are? This is Dominic's house and I'll smoke in here if I want to."

Dominic's quiet voice broke the stunned silence.

"Maura's right, Carla. You shouldn't smoke in here. Come on, we'll go upstairs and unpack. You can smoke in the living-room if you want to."

Carla flounced out, flashing Maura a narrow-eyed look as she went. She had obviously stayed at the house before and knew her way around, Maura realised through her outrage.

Cormac and Bernadette laughed at the look on Maura's face.

"Oh, you have a wild Irish temper as well as the Irish looks," Cormac smiled at her.

"That girl would have made Mother Teresa see red," she said, shaking her head in amazement. "She's done nothing but make my life difficult since I got here."

"Oh, don't mind her," Cormac said. "She's probably just jealous."

"Jealous?" Maura said. "Of what?"

"Oh, you never know," Cormac said teasingly. "She's probably noticed the way Dominic watches you sometimes. You know these rich people, they get very protective of their assets."

Maura looked at him in confusion. "What do you mean the way Dominic watches me sometimes?"

Cormac merely laughed at her again. "Forget it, and forget about her. She's obviously just used to getting her own way. You're probably the only person that's stood up to her in her life. Now come on, finish up whatever it is you have to do here, and let's head off for a drive. You're not opening the restaurant here tonight, are you?"

Maura shook her head.

"Then it's time you had a night off, isn't it, Bernadette?"

"It sure is," Bernadette agreed. "Get her out of this kitchen, Cormac, and I'll finish up here. Go up and get changed, Maura, and get out and see some sights before you think Ireland is nothing but the inside of off-licences and kitchens."

A half-hour later, calmer but still preoccupied by the skirmish with Carla, Maura climbed into Cormac's small blue car. She noticed with relief that Dominic's expensive car was gone.

As they made their way down the long drive, she forced a wide smile onto her face, and looked over at Cormac.

"I need a drink," she said.

Chapter Twenty-two

Maura settled back into the comfortable bench seat, and took a grateful sip of the hot whiskey Cormac had ordered from the bar. She looked around at the small pub, one of only a handful in the tiny village of Doolin.

On the journey Cormac had picked up on his concise tour of Ireland, pointing out stone circles and historic ruins in the fields alongside the winding roads. The blue skies were giving away to dark cloud, and by the time they pulled up in front of the pub a cold wind had struck up and heavy droplets of rain were falling.

She enjoyed Cormac's company. There was something uncomplicated about him, and his outrageous flirtation was obviously well-practised and not to be taken too seriously.

"Let's just pretend you're on holiday with me here, Maura," he had said, cheerfully slipping into tour-guide mode. "Doolin's famous for music and good pub food. This is picture-postcard Ireland for you now. And with any luck there will be some real Irish people for you to look at among all the Germans and Swiss and French and Australians and Americans in the pubs down here."

She'd seen what he meant within minutes of coming into the pub. The tables were packed with groups of tourists, recognisable by their backpacks and postcard-writing as much as their foreign voices.

Once again, one long bench had been kept empty, the positions claimed by a row of musical instruments, she was glad to see. She'd very much enjoyed the music session she and Dominic had walked into in Galway, despite the way the evening had ended. And at least she didn't have to give a series of talks tomorrow, like that time. She could relax a little, knowing that everything was ready for tomorrow night's dinner.

Cormac ordered her another hot whiskey before she had finished the first. She enjoyed the taste very much, the cloves and sugar and water diluting the strong spirit taste.

Cormac returned from the bar with the two steaming glasses and gestured over to the musicians' bench. A half a dozen men and women had now gathered and were taking violins and guitars from their cases, and doing a few lively snatches of tunes as warm-ups.

"You're in for a treat," Cormac leaned over to whisper. "It might be put on for the tourists tonight, but it's still a hell of a show."

Maura leaned back against the headrest and relaxed

as the music began to swell around them. All the postcard-writing was put away and the empty soup bowls pushed to one side, as all the customers gave their full attention to the music.

The sight of the empty dishes reminded Maura that she hadn't eaten properly since breakfast that morning. She'd had only a little bit of salad at lunchtime and it was now close to nine o'clock. Cormac affectionately placed his arm around her shoulders and she realised in the gentle haze of the whiskey that the weight of it was quite pleasant. It was a shame there was no spark between them, she thought mistily. He really was a lovely fellow.

But Cormac seemed to realise that she saw him just as a friend too, and was happily playing the genial host.

She stood up to go to the bathroom, and was surprised to find the room spinning slightly. She'd have to ask Cormac for a glass of water, she realised – the whiskey had obviously gone to her head a little bit.

But when she returned it was to find that Cormac had slipped up to the bar and bought her another. One more won't hurt, she decided. And she really was getting very accustomed to the distinctive smoky taste of the whiskey.

The music had changed from jigs and reels to some lively singing of traditional songs. She was surprised to realise she knew some of the tunes and was able to join in with many of the others.

"You've a lovely singing voice," Cormac leaned over to say. "You'll have to sing us a traditional Australian one yourself."

Maura shook her head and laughed. Her voice was okay, but nothing special. But others in the pub seemed to be volunteering to sing some of their national tunes, bravely starting without accompaniment, but giving the musicians grateful glances as they joined in once the tune became familiar to them.

The leader of the musicians applauded enthusiastically as one of the German visitors sat down, red-faced, having sung a lusty version of a traditional German folk song.

"Any other volunteers?"

To Maura's embarrassment, Cormac stood up and said, "We've an Australian here, I'm sure she'd love to sing us a good outback song, wouldn't you, Maura?"

Maura protested laughingly, as the other patrons urged her to give them a song. She was distracted for a second as she looked through the bar into the room beyond. The whiskey must have affected her eyesight. She could have sworn she saw Dominic and Carla in a group of people in the room through the bar. She shook her head, declining their offer.

But Cormac wasn't to be put off so easily and several others in the crowd continued to urge her on.

Feeling a little dazed, she stood shakily to her feet, looking around in vain for some other Australian in the pub who could help her. All of a sudden she was damned if she could remember the tune let alone the words of any Australian song. Exactly how many whiskeys had she had tonight?

A familiar tune suddenly popped into her head. Fuelled with Dutch courage, she decided she'd give it a go. What the hell, she was a long way from home. She smiled and nodded at Cormac.

"Good girl yourself," he smiled encouragingly. "Ladies and gentlemen, here's Maura Carmody all the way from Clare, South Australia, with a traditional Australian song."

Maura stood up, and half-closed her eyes, trying vainly to remember all the words of the tune in her head.

Smiling at Cormac and swaying ever so slightly, she began to sing. Midway through the second verse, she noticed some confused glances between several of the tourists and stopped, losing her confidence. "Is that an Australian song? I thought it was Scottish," she heard one beside her whisper. Through the whiskey haze, Maura mentally rewound the words she'd just been singing – something about Donald and Isle of Skye and lassies shouting about troosers. She suddenly realised that she'd launched into the Scottish ditty 'Donald, Where's Your Troosers?' How on earth had that come into her head? The last time she'd sung it was in a very bad student revue years before. Cormac seemed to find it completely hilarious, as Maura brought her hands up to her face to hide her embarrasment. The whiskey obviously had a lot to answer for.

"Oh, I'm sorry," she said, laughing through her fingers. "The wrong one came into my head."

The musicians didn't seem to mind, picking up the tune and gaily ending the song. Maura suddenly remembered the one Australian song she did know the words to. Feeling brave now and convinced she couldn't embarrass herself any further, she stood up again.

"I'll give it another go." With that, she began softly, singing the first verse of 'And the band played Waltzing Matilda', a lilting, haunting song about young Australian soldiers going off to the First World War.

To her surprise, the musicians all knew it very well, and one or two other people joined in the singing, until Maura no longer needed to lead them. She took her seat again in relief, shyly accepting Cormac's effusive compliments.

"That was gorgeous. Not a patch on the other for novelty value, but beautiful all the same," he whispered.

She leaned into him gratefully, her head spinning slightly. After a minute she opening her eyes and found herself looking straight at Dominic. She hadn't imagined it. He and Carla had come out from the back dining-room and must have seen not only her version of Eric Bogle's song, but by the sneering look Carla was giving her, they had obviously heard her surprise rendition of 'Donald, Where's Your Troosers?'

Maura resisted a temptation to poke her tongue out. She suddenly felt too weary – and to be honest with herself, too drunk – to be bothered about the pair of them. Feeling Dominic's eyes still on her, she leaned against Cormac and whispered, "Can you please take me home to bed?"

"Well, haven't I been just dying to hear you say that," Cormac laughed down at her. "Will you not just stay for one more? The musicians are just warming up."

"I really think I should lie down," she said, feeling a rush of nausea come over her.

Cormac looked at her closely, realising she wasn't used to the strong whiskey.

"Come on then, I'll take you back and between myself and Bernadette we'll have you safely tucked up in no time."

* * *

The sound of a gentle knock at the door awoke her the next morning. She lifted her head from the pillow, groaning softly as a dull headache made itself felt. She looked at her bedside clock. Five o'clock.

"Oh, no," she thought with a low moan, remembering the whiskies and her singing the night before. Cormac had reassured her the whole way back to Ardmahon House – no, she hadn't made a fool of herself and she didn't seem at all drunk to him. But Maura knew she had drunk far more than she should have and hoped she wouldn't pay for it too badly today. Not with forty certified foodies coming for dinner that night.

She barely remembered leaving the pub the night before. They had walked past Dominic and Carla on their way to the door. Maura had managed a feeble sort of smile, glad she had the support of Cormac's arm around her. In return, she had been ignored by Carla and received a distracted nod from Dominic. Maura thought they looked like they were in the middle of a furious row.

Maura lay back in the darkness, trying to work out just how bad she felt. She had just decided it was luckily more of an embarrassment hangover than a whiskey one, when there was another knock at the door. She heard Bernadette's voice calling her softly.

"I'm awake, come in," she answered.

"It's Nick, calling from Australia," Bernadette whispered. "He said he knows how early it is, but you have to get up."

Maura leapt out of her bed. The baby! She forgot about her headache as she practically sprinted down the stairs to the phone in the hallway.

"Nick, what is it, tell me!" she nearly shouted into the mouthpiece.

She could practically feel the smile in her brother's voice. "It's a little boy, can you hear him? I'm calling from Fran's hospital room."

Maura could just make out the sound of a baby crying in the background. "Is everything all right, is Fran all right, is the baby all right?" she asked in a rush.

Nick laughed down the line, sounding as relieved and happy as she was.

"Everything is just great. It all happened in a bit of a

rush, and Fran's pretty exhausted, but we've a little son and you've a little nephew. We're going to call him Quinn. It was our great-grandfather's name – what do you think?"

Maura thought it was beautiful. "I don't believe it, I saw a sign here for a village called Quin yesterday and I was thinking of you. Maybe it was an omen."

She then spoke briefly to Fran, who sounded as relaxed as ever, very tired but very happy.

She gently put the phone down and turned as Bernadette came down the stairs behind her. She was smiling broadly, having guessed what the call was about.

"Congratulations, Auntie Maura. Come and have a cup of tea and tell me everything." She looked closely at Maura. Maura grinned sheepishly back as Bernadette obviously recalled helping her to bed the evening before.

"No, perhaps we'll make it a strong black coffee."

* * *

There was no time to feel hungover or embarrassed once the preparations for the two nights of the restaurant got into full swing.

Maura felt the adrenalin rush, as she fell into the familiar pattern of organising a restaurant for two busy nights. There was the waiting staff to meet and brief, the menus to finalise, the usual last-minute hitches with supplies and getting used to the layout of the kitchen to serve fifty people a night. It was quite a different proposition to the relaxed cooking school.

She was aware that Dominic and Carla were around the house, but was glad the activity gave her enough reason to keep well away from the pair of them. Dominic was polite to her, but since her outburst in Ennis, he had built a wall around himself. She had given up trying to explain or apologise and had retreated to the same, unnatural politeness he was displaying. Their rare conversations were like stilted exchanges from an 18th century novel. "I am well, ma'am. And you?" "I too am well, sir."

If it wasn't making her feel so bad, she'd find it funny. And she knew Bernadette hadn't missed a trick. She seemed to be keeping a very close eye on both of them.

Carla seemed to have noticed the tension too and was enjoying it. She wandered into the kitchen late on Friday afternoon, deliberately leaning against one of the counters and whistling a Scottish tune under her breath to rile Maura. But Bernadette had saved Maura the effort by practically ordering her out of the kitchen.

"If you're not here to peel carrots, you're not welcome here, I'm afraid," she said, her wide smile masking any rudeness. To Maura's surprise and relief, Carla sauntered out.

The first night's dinner was a success. Maura knew it, even as her waiting staff carried out the last of the desserts. Cormac poked his head around the kitchen door toward the end of the night to shout his congratulations, giving her an enthusiastic thumbs-up sign.

"They all love it," he grinned at her. "They're calling for the chef. Come in and take a bow, before they're all too drunk to realise who you are."

She felt in her element. While she had enjoyed most of the wine-tasting evenings, and relished the compliments people had given about the wine, she had felt she had been accepting them on Nick's behalf. This time she knew it was her skill they were celebrating. Walking through the dining-room with Bernadette, meeting the tables of diners, who included quite a few food critics and writers from Dublin and London, she felt relaxed and confident.

She drew near Dominic and Carla's table on the other side of the room. They were sitting with two other couples and Maura overheard Carla telling the story of her experience at Lorikeet Hill for what must have been the hundredth time. Dominic seemed preoccupied and didn't react as Carla finished the story, but Maura cringed as she heard the others laughing politely. Still, she took solace in the fact that they had finished the meals she had cooked for them tonight.

She recalled her conversation with Dominic in the car on the first day together, when he had seemed scornful of the 'foodie industry'. She had tried to explain that it wasn't always an artificial world, that the combination of good food and wine sometimes almost weaved a magic spell. People relaxed when they were enjoying such spoiling, and she could see from the lively conversations going on around her that that was what was happening tonight.

She looked around the room again and found herself looking straight into Dominic's eyes. She had an odd feeling he knew exactly what she was thinking.

Chapter Twenty-three

The second week of the cooking school got off to a great start. One of the young Irish girls had even brought her equally young fiance along.

"We both spent a year backpacking around Australia and we loved the food," a bright-eyed Una explained in the introductory session on the first day. "We're getting married next month, and I thought I'm not going to be the one stuck in the kitchen while he sits in front of the telly banging his knife and fork together. So we've given ourselves this course as our wedding present."

Maura looked at Brian to see what he made of all that, but he was too busy gazing admiringly at Una to reply. He'd have followed her to a macrame course by the looks of things, she thought.

To Maura and Bernadette's amazement, the second group also contained a lovestruck young woman. Louisa spent the first day mooning about, apparently suffering from a broken heart and repeatedly writing her boyfriend's name in a trail of soy sauce on the counter. And a French girl at first seemed more interested in reading glossy magazines than learning the difference between coriander and basil in Asian-style broths.

But by day three the bewitching flavours had got to them all, and as Maura set up for her food equivalent of Blind Man's Bluff, she had everyone's attention.

"A lot of the dishes I've shown you this week have depended on one or two distinctive flavours to really give them that extra zing. So what I want to do now is give you a refresher course on some of those special ingredients, so you'll always know them in your supermarkets and greengrocers," she explained, as she brought out a series of covered bowls from under the counter.

As she spoke, she heard the door behind her open and turned around. Dominic was standing there with a stern-faced middle-aged woman beside him. He looked over at her, and half-smiled. "Excuse me," he said apologetically. "I'm just showing Eithne around, I won't be a moment."

Maura was thrown for a moment. Carla and Dominic had left for Dublin early on Saturday morning, and she hadn't known if she would see him again. She looked over at Bernadette who didn't look in the least bit surprised. She must have been expecting him.

She shot a look at Eithne, who was quietly inspecting the coolroom and kitchen equipment. Maura guessed she was a potential manager of the Ardmahon House country retreat.

She blinked and brought her attention back to the

students. "So we'll start with a few visual tests," she said.

She held up a tiny, bright red chilli. "Who can tell me what this is?"

The students relaxed. This was going to be easy. "Chilli," Una called. "And you have to be careful of the seeds, because they're the hottest bit, and you have to make sure to wash your hands very carefully after you've been handling them, and not to touch your eyes or you'll burn yourself," she finished breathlessly.

Maura nodded and smiled. "Exactly right. Especially about the heat. A tiny bit goes a long way with chilli, but it's a fantastic addition to any Asian-style dish, as you tasted yesterday."

Maura held up a number of other ingredients – bok choy or Chinese white cabbage, which she had ordered especially from a Galway greengrocer. She also showed the class a number of different noodles, including cellophane and hokkien noodles, which were a staple of Asian cooking but could be used so deliciously in many other sorts of dishes. She was pleased the students guessed most of them, and remembered the best ways to handle and cook them.

She'd been pleasantly surprised to find many of the Asian ingredients in the Ennis supermarket, and had said as much to Bernadette. "It's fascinating, isn't it, all the food from different countries gradually criss-crossing the world? Asian food in Ireland, Irish food in America, Indian food everywhere. I'd love to really trace how it all happened," she had said.

Out of the corner of her eye she saw Eithne whisper something to Dominic, who nodded. Eithne quietly opened the kitchen door, slipped out and carefully shut it behind her, but to Maura's discomfort Dominic stayed, even quietly moving a stool and sitting down to watch. If he was trying to unsettle her, it was working very well, she thought.

She moved on from the sight test and started telling her students about the growing use of native foods in Australian cooking.

She held up a few examples and explained how they could be used: wattle seeds, used to flavour everything from chocolate to flour and pasta; mountain pepper, which she used in sauces and as a marinade; and quandongs, a native Australian peach that could be used to make delicious jams and chutneys.

To amuse herself and Bernadette, she started to speak in what she thought was a very exaggerated Australian accent. "This bush tucker is really beaut. The blokes and the sheilas get stuck right into them with a few tinnies after an arvo at the footy or watching the Aussies beat the Poms at the cricket."

To her shock, the students – and Bernadette – continued looking at her with straight faces. She realised they hadn't noticed the difference. Her real accent was obviously as strong as the joke one, she realised, more than slightly embarrassed. To her slight relief, she saw a ghost of a grin cross Dominic's face. Thank heavens for small mercies, she thought to herself.

Returning to her normal voice, for all that it mattered, she brought the subject around to herbs, spices and other flavour ingredients.

"I'll need a few volunteers for this next test – I'm going to blindfold four of you and see if you can guess, just by the smell, what herb, spice or secret ingredient I am holding. So, any takers?"

They all seemed to be looking at their feet all of a sudden. "Please don't be shy, nobody gets punished if they get any wrong," she laughed.

Bernadette stepped forward. "I see we're going to need a bit of persuasion," she said. "Seeing as I'm allegedly in charge here, I can give a few orders. So, let me think – Una, Rachel, Fiona and let me think, yes, how about you, Dominic? We can test just how much you've learned in the last five minutes."

Dominic's head shot up, and he started to protest, but Bernadette was taking no excuses.

"No, I need four volunteers and you four will do very nicely."

The rest of the class, relieved that they hadn't been picked, settled down into their seats to watch with enjoyment, as the four guinea pigs made their way up to the front of the kitchen.

Maura lined up the four stools and stood ready with the silk scarves as they took their seats one by one. Dominic inclined his head as he took the seat on the end. Starting from the other end, Maura deftly began to tie the scarves around each person's eyes, checking that their eyes were covered, but their noses free. "You'll be relying totally on your sense of smell now, so concentrate," she said, talking quickly to mask a sudden attack of nerves as she came up to Dominic.

Standing behind him with the scarf in her hand she could smell the fresh, citrusy scent of his aftershave, and was suddenly overwhelmed with a memory of the night in the hotel room with him. As she carefully tied the scarf around his face, her wrist brushed against his skin and she knew for a fact that she had suddenly blushed red. She was struck with the thought that given very different circumstances, what she was doing could be a prelude to something very sensual indeed.

She stepped back from Dominic and snapped herself back into the present. "Now, if I can call upon my trusted assistant Bernadette to help me, we'll get started."

Maura directed Bernadette to walk along the four blindfolded people and hold a bowl containing one of the secret ingredients under their noses, while Maura spoke in general terms about how each one could be used. Once all four had smelt it, she asked for their guesses.

Coriander. Ginger. Lemongrass. Soy sauce. Basil. Coconut milk. Garlic. To her amazement, the only one who got most of them right was Dominic.

"Well, there we are," she said, still surprised. "Thank you to today's guineapigs. You can take your blindfolds off."

As they stood up and took them off, she turned to find Dominic right behind her.

"Congratulations," she said, looking up at him. "You surprised me."

She could see a glint of a smile in his eye, and was relieved to see something other than the coldness there had been between them since the night in Ennis.

"I might have grown up in a monastery," he said, a half-smile playing on his lips, as he referred to their heated discussion that first morning in the car, "but it was a very cultured one." She smiled at him, about to say something back, when one of her students came up to her asking a question about the nutritional value of coconut milk. By the time she had answered as best she could, Dominic had left the room.

Packing up that afternoon, she casually asked Bernadette where Dominic had gone.

Just as casually, Bernadette answered her. "Oh, back to Dublin for business, I think. And then next week he's off to Glasgow and London and probably Paris, I think. Magazine publishing's a heady world by the sound of things."

Rats, Maura thought childishly. She imagined she could still smell his aftershave from where her sleeve had brushed against his cheek when she was blindfolding him. The thought sent a little tremor down her back. What was happening to her? she wondered. She was carrying on like a teenager with a crush on a pop-star.

Bernadette interrupted her pleasant thoughts. "This might help you get over the disappointment," she teased. She held up a large envelope which had just arrived by international express mail.

"Nick's photos," she cried. "Oh, let's have a look." She fell upon the envelope, quickly ripping it open. Nick had sent enlargements of nearly a dozen photos of himself and Fran with tiny little Quinn. Maura felt tears come to her eyes as she looked at the three of them together. After all they had been through, it was a miracle to see Quinn. She looked in the envelope again and found a hastily written note.

Pictures paint a thousand words, don't they? We love him and so will you. The three of us can't wait to see you. Lots and lots of love, Nick, Fran and Quinn.

Maura felt a lump in her throat. "Oh, isn't he lovely, Bernadette, look," she said. "It's incredible, isn't it?"

Bernadette looked closely at each photo.

"He's gorgeous, absolutely gorgeous," she said. "They look so happy."

Maura was looking at one of the photos, a close-up of Fran gazing down at Quinn lying in her arms. Her look was soft and full of love.

She suddenly made a decision. "Are you free tomorrow afternoon, after the barbeque?"

Bernadette looked up and nodded. Maura had a feeling the older woman knew what she was about to ask.

She was right. Bernadette spoke first. "Of course I'll take you to your mother's village," she said softly.

Chapter Twenty-four

The sky was grey, but the light clear as they climbed into Bernadette's small car the next afternoon after saying goodbye to the second group of students. Maura's manner had been easy, but her mind was preoccupied.

"I've a few books on tracing your Irish ancestors, but I suppose they're not exactly applicable in your case?" Bernadette asked with a smile, looking across and noticing Maura's tension.

Maura shook her head. She'd read all those books. They tended to concentrate on great grandparents and ancient shipping records. She knew exactly where her Irish ancestors were from, right down to the address of their house. She had the practical side covered – it was the emotional side she was having difficulty with.

"So tell me again what you know about Catherine and her family," Bernadette asked, as they turned off the main road onto a much bumpier and narrower one.

Maura turned in her seat toward Bernadette. "Apart from what details she left in her letter, not much. I talked to one of the nurses she last worked with, and she told me a little bit more. I know she left Ireland for America when she was about twenty-three, then travelled on to Australia. I don't know why she left America, or Ireland, if it comes to that."

"And your father?" Bernadette asked gently.

"Nothing, not a word. The nurse at the hospital said that Catherine had talked about her daughter, but not about the father. She said she thought it might have been a married man, but she wasn't sure. And there's no way to find out now. She wrote *'father unknown'* on my birth certificate."

Bernadette looked closely at her. "Do you want to know?"

Maura laughed nervously. "I think trying to find out about a long-lost mother will do me for starters, don't you? At least she knew she had me. He may not even know I exist. Besides, I didn't grow up with a father in my life, so it's not something I know about anyway. I guess all I hope is that it was a great romance between them, even if it was short but sweet. I hope it was, I'd hate to think it was something awful." She was quiet for a moment. "Anyway, I've done all my crying and ranting and raving about who or what or why. I've decided that if I don't find out anything about her today, then I'm not going to look any further."

"Then let's hope you do find something,"

Bernadette said. "So let's work out where to start looking and asking questions about her. What age would she have been now if she was still alive? Did she write of any friends in Ireland? What did her parents do for a living?"

"I feel like I'm travelling with Miss Marple," Maura said, trying to lighten the situation. Bernadette just smiled at her.

Maura carefully unfolded the note her mother had left for her sixteenth birthday. She'd been clutching it tightly since they left the house. She knew every word off by heart, but scanned the lines again.

"Her parents were called John and Rosa, and he was a farmer. Catherine was thirty-four when I was born, so she would have been sixty-two now."

"So we're looking for people around sixty who may have grown up with her here. Well, in a village as small as this one is, there's sure to be someone who remembers her."

"What do you suggest? Will we round up all the sixty-plus aged women into a room and interrogate the lot of them?"

"That's one way," Bernadette said, looking over at Maura. She knew Maura well enough now to know that her light words were masking a dose of nerves. "But why don't we take it a bit more slowly?"

Maura took a deep breath. Now that she was this close she wanted to stand in the middle of the village and shout at the top of her lungs. "Does anyone want to meet Catherine Shanley's surprise daughter? Here I am."

"Would you like to go to your grandparents' house first – Catherine's letter gave you directions, didn't you say?"

Maura was silent for a moment. She'd often imagined turning up at her grandparents' house. Sometimes in her mind they welcomed her, other times they had been cold and unforgiving. She bought herself some more time. "Her parents would be very elderly, if they're still living there. I'd probably give them the fright of their lives if I just turned up at the door."

Bernadette agreed silently. "Then what about a look around the village first, maybe find out what we can first from someone local?"

Maura nodded.

"Right, so, where would we find people aged about sixty in a town like this, to get us started?" Bernadette thought aloud.

"In the hospital?" Maura suggested. "Doctors or nurses or cleaning ladies and cooks."

"No hospitals in these little villages," Bernadette answered. "Everyone travels into Ennis these days."

"Shop-owners. Publicans or their wives," Maura suggested again.

"The very thing," Bernadette answered. She had a feeling there'd be little else in this village other than a shop and a pub or two. "We'll try all of them, just to get a feel for the place."

Maura looked at her watch. "It's a bit early for pubs, isn't it?"

"God, you really do think we're all heathens, don't you? I was thinking of a cup of tea, you minx. That'll get the chat going. Now, what story will we go in with? Presumably you don't want to just charge on in there and ask if anyone knew your mother?"

Maura shook her head.

"Rule number one in these situations, keep your story simple and stick to the truth as much as possible. Let's say you used to do some volunteer work as a cook in a little rural hospital in South Australia, say, just a couple of nights a week while you were studying to be a chef. And who did you work with only this lovely nursing sister called Catherine Shanley from Ireland who used to make her home town sound so gorgeous you always wanted to visit it if you were ever over here."

Maura laughed despite herself. "I'll need to write notes on my hand to remember all of that."

"Don't worry, I'll get you back on track if you get stuck," Bernadette promised.

They pulled into the town. Maura's immediate thought was it would have been hard for Catherine to make this place sound gorgeous and alluring to a potential tourist. There wasn't much to remark about at all. It wasn't one of County Clare's beautiful seaside villages and didn't seem to boast any historic houses or ancient ruins. It was just a jumble of little houses and a small row of shops and pubs, all looking a little gloomy in the grey afternoon light.

"What would Catherine have done if she had stayed here?" Maura whispered.

"She must have asked herself the same question," Bernadette said, looking around. "Perhaps that's why she left."

They walked into the first shop on the street and bought some peppermints from a surly young man behind the counter. He barely grunted at them as he took their money.

Bernadette shook her head ruefully as they came out into the street. "There's that famous Irish hospitality for you," she laughed. "And I bet he wonders why business is quiet."

"Now, watch your tongue, that could be my second cousin you're talking about there," Maura said sternly.

"Well, now, I did notice a resemblance," Bernadette teased.

They walked on, past a combination hardware and undertaker shop. Maura shook her head at Bernadette's enquiring look. "Maybe as a last resort," she said.

There were two pubs to choose from. As they walked into the first, their eyes taking a moment to adjust to the low light inside, they saw they were the only customers. The elderly man behind the bar served them in near silence, more interested in reading his newspaper than having a chat.

They drank their lukewarm tea, looking around as

the front door opened again and two elderly men came in and joined the uncommunicative barman. They too took out newspapers and the three sat companionably reading and sipping their pints. The arrival of two younger fellows, with a sulky-looking teenage girl, added a bit of noise. The two boys set up the pool table for the latest in what sounded like a long-running tournament. The girl sat in a chair on the edge of the room, watching both boys, as she twirled a piece of her long hair round and round her finger.

Maura tried to imagine Catherine in this pub as a young girl, and couldn't. She couldn't imagine herself here either. It had been fairly quiet growing up in the Clare Valley, but nothing like this.

Bernadette leaned over. "Do you want to ask any of them any questions?"

Maura shook her head quickly.

"Then we'll try the other one and hope for better luck there."

They walked the short distance up the road to the other pub, which looked very similar to the one they had just left, apart from the addition of a cheerful-looking window box of red geraniums on one of the windowsills.

The welcome couldn't have been more different. The woman behind the bar started chatting to them as soon as they set foot over the threshold.

"I thought you'd come in here eventually – I saw you go into Down the Road," she said, with a disparaging nod of her head, meaning the pub they had just left. "Lord, I don't know why that man bothers opening for the general public – sure, he only talks to the people he knows. It might as well be a private men's club the way he carries on. Now, what can I get the two of you?"

Bernadette and Maura exchanged glances. They'd get on much better here.

Bernadette answered. "My Australian friend and I would love a cup of tea each, please."

"Oh, you're from Australia," the lady looked over at Maura with friendly curiosity. "You're very welcome, are you travelling around the whole country?"

Maura decided to stick with the truth for the time being.

"I'm here in Clare for a few weeks, running some cooking classes with my friend here at Ardmahon House," she answered.

"Oh yes, I heard something about that on the radio, an Australian cooking school. What are you having – barbeques every night?" The woman gave a loud laugh.

"Well, maybe just a few," Maura smiled back, hoping she wouldn't hear any kangaroo-steak jokes.

The lady arranged their pots of tea and cups on the bar in front of her, introducing herself as Dymphna Hogan. Maura and Bernadette took up the unspoken invitation, pulling bar stools up close to the worn wooden edge.

Bernadette got the conversation flowing without any bother. "Yes, Maura has been whipping up a storm all around Clare with her great Australian wine and food."

Dymphna looked around her barshelves with an exaggerated grimace. "I'm afraid we're not getting much call for wine from any country in here just yet. No call for it from the locals, and we're not exactly on the real tourist trail yet, if we ever will be. What we need is a reclusive pop-star or a moving statue miracle to get the tourists flocking in. All we've got to impress the visitors with is our great Irish charm and that old fellow down the road doesn't help a scrap there, I'll tell you that."

Bernadette interrupted her. "Not much for the young ones here then, I guess. Are you a local yourself?"

Dymphna answered cheerfully. "Lord no, your great-grandparents have to have been born and bred here before you can call yourself a local," she said. "My husband and I bought this pub about fifteen years ago. I'm from Wicklow myself. Of course, our kids didn't stick around. One's in Dublin, one's in London, the other in Nicaragua of all places."

Maura ventured a question, taking a deep breath and hoping the fibs would flow freely.

"I worked in a hospital in Australia for a while with a lady who was from around here – maybe you knew of her? Her name was Catherine Shanley. I think she would have been about your age."

The woman stopped serving and cocked her head to one side. "What did you say her name was again?"

"Catherine Shanley," Maura repeated.

"And you met her in Australia?"

Maura nodded.

Dymphna thought for a while. "Shanley's a common enough surname around here, and I think quite a few young ones from this area went to Australia. But she would have been before my time, I'd say. I can't say I remember hearing her name or not – sorry, love."

"Oh, well, that's a shame," Maura said quickly, but conscious of a rush of relief. The search would end here, but she could at least tell Nick – and herself – that she had tried.

But Dymphna was still thinking. "Hang on a moment, let me ask someone else if they knew your friend. She's lived here all her life." She called out to a woman carrying a mop and bucket through to the other side of the bar.

"Eileen, do you remember a Catherine Shanley, born here about sixty years ago? This young lady here worked with her in some hospital in Australia."

The older woman came over. "Australia, did you say?"

Maura nodded.

"I went through school with a Catherine Shanley. Though she called herself Kate sometimes, or even Katie, depending on her mood. Ah, she fancied herself that one, you'd never know from one day to the next what name she'd answer to. We all had to call her Cecilia one week, when she decided she preferred her confirmation name to her real name. She wouldn't answer to anything else, not even when the teacher called her."

Eileen put down her mop and looked right at Maura. "Where did you say you met her – nursing?"

Maura nodded, not daring to add anything else, and hoping to God she wasn't the spitting image of her mother.

To her surprise Eileen gave an unpleasant laugh. "Well, that's a bit of a comedown for that one, that's for sure. She had great plans for herself. You'll see me in Hollywood, Eileen, she'd say to me one week. Or another week it would be the Olympics – she was going to be the world's greatest female sprinter. Or the best painter. Aye, she really fancied herself."

"So whose daughter was she?" Dymphna asked Eileen, evidently getting into the spirit of the conversation. Bernadette gave Maura a reassuring smile. It was off and running without much help from them after all.

"John and Rosa – they used to live in that stone cottage just outside the town." Eileen said. "You remember Rosa, Dymphna – the old one who cleaned the church for years."

Maura gave Bernadette a quick look before she spoke again. "Yes, that would be the Catherine I met, she said her parents' names were John and Rosa." She paused for a brief moment. "Are they still living here?"

Eileen shook her head. "No, John died about ten years ago and she didn't last that long after him. God rest their souls."

Maura was conscious of only the barest shimmer of feeling at the news.

Eileen was curious now, the mop forgotten. "You met Catherine nursing, did you say? I don't remember Rosa saying she was a nurse over there. Mind you, I don't think she heard from her very much. I can't imagine her as a nurse, not that one. She wouldn't have struck me as the nursing kind, more likely to fill her patients up with sleeping tablets and head out for a night, she was."

Maura felt her indignation rise. She had no idea if Catherine had always been a nurse, be it a good or a bad one, but she didn't like this woman's tone.

"Oh, Catherine was a wonderful nurse, in fact she was the Assistant Matron in the hospital," she heard herself say. "She even won awards. There was a whole file of letters from people writing to thank Catherine for the wonderful job she had done looking after their relatives."

Maura felt Bernadette turn and look at her.

Eileen's eyes narrowed. "Well, perhaps she'd had a change for the better during her travels. All she used to say to me was 'You wait and see, Eileen, I'll make my mark in the world, I'll rise above this place'. I was sick of hearing her say it. She fancied herself, that one," Eileen repeated, with a loud sniff.

The door behind them opened and an overweight fellow, looking in his mid-sixties, shambled in, straight to the other end of the bar. Dymphna had started pulling his pint of Guinness before he had sat down. He grunted a hello at them all. "Ask him about Catherine Shanley, he knew all about her," Eileen said surprisingly. With another loud sniff she picked up her mop again and went through to the other bar.

Dymphna leaned over toward them. "That's Jim McBride, Eileen's husband," she said in an undertone to Maura and Bernadette. "Not that you'd guess, eh? She thinks he drinks too much. He thinks she cleans too much. I like the pair of them – she keeps my floors clean while he keeps my till full."

She suddenly spoke louder. "Jim, this is – what were your names, loves?"

Maura and Bernadette introduced themselves.

"Maura here worked with Catherine Shanley in Australia, and was in here asking about her. Do you remember Catherine at all?"

The old fellow turned around, a beaming smile on his face.

"Ah, Catherine," he said wistfully, "there was a great young one."

They all heard Eileen's grunt from the other room. She wasn't missing a word.

"You were a good friend of Catherine's in Australia, did you say?" Jim asked Maura.

"I only knew her for a few months, really," Maura said quickly. "She was a nurse at a hospital I worked in. She mentioned she was from here so while I was in the area I thought I'd have a look around."

Jim shook his head. "Ah, she was a great girl altogether. She had great spirit, like mercury, or quicksilver – you'd try to get your hands on her and you wouldn't be able to hold her." He gave a cheerful, musical laugh, the sound quite unexpected from someone his age.

Bernadette reached under the table and squeezed Maura's hand.

"I bet she stirred up trouble in that hospital. I can't imagine Catherine taking orders from anyone." He laughed his young man's laugh again.

Maura added more embroidery to her imaginary tapestry of Catherine's life.

"Well, she was the one in charge when I met her, so I don't know about that. She was a wonderful teacher though, all of the student nurses said she was an inspiration. She was so patient, always ready to go that extra mile for them," she added for good measure.

"Really?" Jim mused. "Well, yes, she had a way with people."

Eileen suddenly appeared behind Jim. "I already told her that Catherine fancied herself." With another sweep of her mop, she flounced into the men's toilets, making a loud noise of disgust as she did so. The door was propped open with a bar stool.

Jim leaned back against the bar and rolled his eyes. "Thirty-five years we've been married and she's still jealous of Catherine." The laugh rolled out of him again.

"Jealous?" Bernadette asked.

Jim laughed again. "Me and Catherine were childhood sweethearts. Sure, it only lasted about two years, and we were just kids. But then she left me high and dry and I had to settle for second best, didn't I, Eileen?"

The toilet door slammed in answer.

"You went out with Catherine?" Maura asked, her eyes widening.

"Ah, in the rosy days of youthful sunshine," the old man said, closing his eyes dramatically. "But I just wasn't good enough for her in the end. She left me for Dublin, then I heard she emigrated. So she ended up in Australia, eh?"

Maura nodded, tensing in expectation of his next question.

"Where is she now, do you know? Married with a clatter of kids outback somewhere?"

"She died a few years ago," Maura said quietly. "I don't know much more – we lost contact really, after I finished working at the hospital." She was amazed how quickly the lies were flowing. She noticed that Jim seemed quite upset by the news that Catherine had passed away.

"Has she any family left here at all?" Bernadette broke in, sensing Maura's discomfort.

"Oh, Lord no, I don't think so," the old man answered. "Her parents are long passed away and she was the only child. And now she's gone too." He shook his head regretfully.

"There wouldn't be that many left in this village any more that would remember any of them," Dymphna said.

"Sad isn't it, the price of emigration, whole families just disappear, nothing left behind of them."

Maura felt strange suddenly, her lips locked tight.

Dymphna spoke again. "It's like I was saying before, we're not on the tourist track. In a few years even more of our young ones will have moved on. If you don't want to farm or run a shop or a pub, there's not much here to keep you."

Maura found her voice. "No, I guess not." Turning to Jim, she asked, "Would you have a photo of her? I'd be curious to see what she looked like when she was younger." She knew it was an odd question, but she had left caution behind. Her heart was beating quickly, as if she was on the verge of a discovery.

"Would you now?" the old fellow said. "Ah, isn't her image engraved in my mind. Golden hair soft as silk, flowing straight down to her waist, a face like an angel, a voice like molten gold . . ."

Eileen stomped back in. "What a load of rubbish! She had short red hair and she looked as much like an angel as you look like Pierce Brosnan."

Jim winked at Maura. "Oh, just an old man getting things muddled." He pinched Eileen's cheek affectionately. "No, love, sure didn't I marry the best-looking girl in town, and you know it."

Maura and Bernadette looked closely at Eileen. It was hard to tell what she might have looked like as a young woman. Years of scowling had permanently set her face in a spiderweb of wrinkles.

Jim went on. "No, Catherine was a grand-looking girl. Cheeky eyes. As Eileen said, short red hair. She cut it off when she was just a girl – her mother wanted her to wear it long and in a fit she cut it off to spite her one night. Ah, she was a bold one, that one. You'd tell her to do one thing and she'd do another, just out of badness." He sighed in affectionate memory. Meanwhile, Eileen had virtually scrubbed the tiled floor to the bare earth below.

Bernadette nudged the conversation along again. "So you don't have a photo then?"

"Ah, sure, it's what, over forty years ago now? I'd hardly seen a camera back then."

Eileen grunted. "She'd be in one of those photos in the exhibition," she muttered in Maura's direction.

Maura spun around, trying not to appear over-enthusiastic. She'd arouse their suspicions if she became any more curious about someone she had briefly worked with years before.

"Which exhibition is that?"

Dymphna remembered it too. "That's right, in the local parish hall. It's a display of old newspaper cuttings and photos and school reports from the last fifty years in the area. It's the closest we get to a heritage centre. I told you, we had to do something to get the tourists in."

Bernadette finished her tea and looked at her watch. "Well, we've got a few minutes before we have to get going – we may as well take a look, do our best for local tourism, eh?" She smiled at Dymphna.

Thanking them all for their help, Maura followed Bernadette out into the milky sunshine, blinking rapidly to try to release the tension behind her eyes.

Bernadette looked at her carefully. "Do you want to have a look or do you want to just get out of here?"

Maura took a breath. "Let's have a look."

They looked down the street. An elaborately painted sign reading *Heritage Centre* was attached to the front door of an old stone building. Bernadette walked in first, dropping several pound coins into the basket by the door and smiling at the obviously bored teenager sitting reading a glossy magazine. She seemed relieved when they declined her offer of a guided tour.

The budget had obviously been used up on the entrance sign. The exhibition consisted of four display boards, decorated with about a dozen large photocopies of newspaper clippings. In one corner stood a store dummy dressed in a strange selection of fancy dress and period costume and in another corner was an old tractor wheel and three hay bales.

Maura quickly found the most likely photograph – a slightly faded, enlarged school group photograph, titled *In Twenty Years Time*? The caption explained that the children, boys and girls aged between ten and twelve, had been invited to come to school dressed as their dream occupation. Some were dressed as nurses. One or two were in cowboy gear. One was in a full nun's habit, looking solemnly out from the headgear.

Holding her breath, Maura quickly scanned along

the rows of names. She found the one she was looking for. Catherine Shanley was at the end of the front row, staring defiantly into the camera. According to the caption, she had come dressed as a movie star. She was in a badly-fitting sparkling dress, in shoes at least twice her size, with a tiara balanced precariously in her mop of red curls. She even had a ratty-looking fur stole around her neck.

Maura looked at it closely, memorising every detail, trying to get a sense of the woman her mother might have been from the bright-eyed child in the photograph. Her stomach felt tense and she knew her hands were clenched at her sides, as she silently cursed the poor quality of the photocopied photograph.

Bernadette came up beside her and looked closely at the photograph. Matching the name in the caption she squeezed Maura's arm, before laughing aloud.

"Well, there's an expression I'd recognise. Look at the mischief in that one."

Maura had noticed the resemblance herself. She felt a sudden tightening in her throat. Jim in the pub had been right. This girl had obviously had great plans for herself. She'd wanted to be something. But instead she'd ended up alone and pregnant and dead before her time, out in the middle of nowhere in rural Australia.

Her mother.

"Do you want another cup of tea, or a look at your grandparents' old house?" Bernadette whispered beside her.

Maura shook her head, unable to speak.

"Do you want to go back to Ardmahon House?" Bernadette asked gently.

Maura nodded, gratefully feeling Bernadette's arm around her shoulders as they walked to the car.

They had driven a few miles out of the village when a look over at Maura made Bernadette pull over.

"Are you okay?' she asked.

Maura nodded, attempting a smile. It faltered on her lips. Turning toward Bernadette, she burst into huge racking sobs.

Chapter Twenty-five

Bernadette smiled her thanks as Maura passed another section of one of the Sunday newspapers across to her. The remains of their breakfast of bacon and eggs were on trays at their feet, their armchairs pulled in close to the sitting-room fire.

Maura finished the colour magazine she had been reading and stretched luxuriously, wriggling her toes in the warmth of the fire.

"I'm exhausted," she said, yawning, closing her eyes. "That was a big night last night."

"Oh, I didn't think it was too bad," Bernadette looked across. "What was it, two spilt bowls of soup, one complaining sourpuss and one returned meal because the mountain pepper sauce was too hot? Nothing a complimentary glass of your brother's excellent Cabernet Sauvignon didn't put right."

Maura kept her eyes shut. "No, you're right of

course. We've just had a dream-run up till now, so I guess I was surprised to have any problems."

She didn't explain the real reason she was so tired. She'd had great difficulty sleeping since their afternoon in Catherine Shanley's village. Her mind was busy during the days, distracted by the intensive preparations in the kitchen for the two full houses in the restaurant on Friday and Saturday night.

But come midnight or one o'clock, as she climbed into bed, all the conversations in the pub and the image of the little girl in the film-star costume kept coming back into her mind. She would eventually fall asleep, only to have fitful troubled dreams of herself lying sick in a small hospital in Ireland, being nursed by Catherine, or turning up at the village pub to find Catherine serving behind the bar. And last night she had dreamt vividly again of Terri's death. She had woken up crying, as though it had just happened.

Bernadette poured them each another coffee, still reviewing the previous evening. "The table of eight were great gas, did you get much of a chance to talk to them? They were mad about your food – the older man said he'd been out to Australia three times before but this was the best Australian food he'd ever tasted."

Maura roused herself with effort. "It's those Irish ingredients," she answered, "nothing to do with the cooking."

"And Dominic certainly enjoyed his meal," Bernadette said, shooting Maura a glance under her lashes to see how she would react. "All the restaurants in Dublin must have suddenly closed down – that's the second weekend he's been here, had you noticed?"

Maura just smiled and said nothing. Had she noticed? Had she what! She seemed to have grown a pair of invisible antennae that started humming furiously whenever Dominic was within five kilometres of Ardmahon House. His sudden arrivals weren't helping her already taut nerves either. She wished he would give a little more warning before he turned up, even if it was his house.

She'd had only a few brief conversations with him, but each one had unsettled her. She had a feeling that he had forgiven her for her outburst in Ennis. Certainly, he didn't seem angry with her, and the coldness had thawed between them too. Now there was just a strange awkwardness. Maura didn't like it. It had been bad enough being a teenager the first time around, all jumping hormones and embarrassed silences. She wasn't ready for a second run at it.

She had surreptitiously kept an eye on him in the restaurant the night before. Carla had hardly picked at her food, making a great act of choosing the smallest entrée on the menu and drawing attention to the slenderness of her waist. She had worn clothes to emphasise her slight figure too, Maura had noticed, remembering that her outfit had been made not so much of material as some sort of gauze. She was surprised you couldn't physically see the tiny leaves of lettuce make their way down into Carla's stomach.

But Dominic had ordered adventurously, trying the most unusual of the dishes on the menu. Not only that, but he had sent back compliments with the young Ennis girl waiting on their table.

"The dark-haired man at the window table said to tell you that the chicken was the finest he has ever tasted," she had said breathlessly, still flushed in her cheeks from the attention Dominic had obviously given her. "He said to make sure to tell you it had exactly the right amount of spice to suit him."

Maura grinned despite herself.

"Please tell him the chef accepts his comments with immense gratitude," Maura said in as serious a voice as she could manage. "And please ask him if he is ready for a refreshing glass of water."

The waitress was about to obediently return to Dominic's table with the message when Maura stopped her. If she wanted to tease him, she'd do it herself. "No, no message after all. Just thank him for his kind words," she said to the confused girl.

Maura had started to think perhaps she and Dominic could manage a proper conversation again and had looked forward to seeing him at breakfast. But by the time she had come down this morning Dominic's car was no longer in the driveway.

Now Maura stretched again, before leaning down and folding the newspapers into a neat pile. "Do you feel like a walk?" she asked Bernadette. "We've got the whole afternoon free, haven't we?"

"We sure do. That's a great idea – I'm supposed to give this foot of mine some regular exercise," Bernadette answered, flexing her left foot, which was now free of bandages. "We just need to have a quick look over this week's classes, and then we're free as birds."

Maura fetched the students' folders from the kitchen and sat down in front of the fire again to run through them. She wanted to check that all the introductory notes and recipes were inside, the name-tags were done and that each of the new students had been allocated a bedroom.

She counted the folders under her breath, frowned, then counted them again. "Nine? Have we had an extra booking this week?"

Bernadette looked up, slightly embarrassed. "Ah yes, I was asked last night if we had room for one more, and, really, it was an offer I couldn't refuse."

"Someone asked you last night?" Maura asked, puzzled. "At the dinner? That's late notice, isn't it? I mean, it's great, of course we've room for one more, I'm just surprised they left it so late. Who is it anyway?" she asked, rifling through the folders again, this time looking at the students' names.

She found the newly written folder just as Bernadette coughed slightly.

"Carla?" Maura said in amazement.

"Carla," Bernadette confirmed, a little sheepishly.

Maura looked over in shock. "Carla is doing my

cooking course? Bernadette, Carla doesn't like food. It's like a teetotaller joining Alcoholics Anonymous. What do we teach her – how to boil water and roll her own cigarettes?"

Bernadette explained. "I don't think it's the course so much as the company we're providing."

Maura was even more surprised at that. "Company? She loathes me and she ignores you."

She suddenly remembered Bernadette and Dominic having a lengthy conversation toward the end of the evening. Carla had gone upstairs to her room straight after the meal and many of the other diners had left. Maura had been in conversation with one of the wine importers from Dublin, but had been unable to stop herself from glancing up, and now and then disconcertingly finding Dominic looking over at her too.

"Are you doing this as a favour to Dominic?" Maura asked.

"In a manner of speaking," Bernadette said, in a strange tone of voice.

Maura was suddenly embarrassed she had reacted badly to Bernadette taking on an extra student. "I'm sorry, I've no right to tell you how many students you can take on. I'm just surprised it's Carla, that's all."

"I was too," Bernadette admitted. "But Dominic's going to be in the UK all this week for business. Carla was going to go with him, but apparently that doesn't suit now, so he's asked if we would mind her staying on here. I said no, of course not. And actually it was my suggestion that she do the cooking course. You know the saying, the devil makes work for idle hands."

Does that apply when the girl in question is already a she-devil? Maura wondered. "I would have thought she'd prefer to stay in Dublin," Maura asked innocently. "Bright lights, night clubs, all of her model friends . . ."

Bernadette raised her eyebrows. "From what Dominic hinted, it's those model friends that he wants to keep her away from."

Maura smiled. In case any of them happened to know and accidentally blurted out the details of his deal with her father probably. Well, the week ahead would be more of a challenge than she expected. She only hoped Carla didn't disrupt the classes for the other students.

"So she's still here, I guess," she said, with a glance upstairs.

Bernadette looked at her watch. It was nearly midday. "She is, but I doubt we'll see her for some time yet. Why don't we have that walk and if she's up when we get back she can give us a hand setting up the rooms for the other students."

"Oh, I can just see that," Maura laughed, as they walked out into the hallway to fetch their coats and scarves.

They walked for nearly an hour, taking it slowly, the cold breeze whipping at their cheeks. Hardly a car passed them as they walked along the narrow tree-lined lane that ran past Ardmahon House, almost to the edge of the Burren, the strange lunar-landscaped area of County Clare. Maura had not heard of it before she arrived in Ireland. Areas like the Ring of Kerry and Blarney Castle were the popular tourist haunts, but she had fallen in love with the Burren. The grey rocky landscape had a strange kind of beauty and the limestone seemed to affect the surrounding light as well, making it sharper and clearer.

"I've come out again without my camera," she groaned, as they stopped to catch their breath and look out over the landscape. "I'm going to have to buy some postcards and try to pass them off as my own work for that article at this rate."

"You've over a week left," Bernadette soothed her. "Plenty of time to take lots of photos. Now come on, we'd better be going back, it looks like there's rain coming."

Carla was ambling out of the sitting-room as they let themselves in through the big front door.

"Good afternoon," Bernadette called brightly. To their surprise, Carla didn't ignore them.

"You had a phone call while you were out, Maura," the young woman said, pointing at the hall table. "I took a message."

Maura picked up the note and read it with some difficulty. Carla's writing was very scrawled and she hadn't taken a number. "Is it Tim McBild?" she tried to pronounce it.

Carla sauntered over. She always walked as if a thousand eyes were on her, Maura noticed. "I couldn't really understand his accent," she drawled. "It was Tim or Jim somebody. McDaid or Mcsomething. He sounded like an old guy."

"Did he leave a number?" Maura asked.

"No, he said he'd call back later," Carla said in a bored voice, before sauntering into the sitting-room again. Seconds later they heard loud music as the television was switched on, then the door to the hall was slammed shut.

"Who's Tim McDaid or McBild?" Maura asked Bernadette. "He's not a parent, is he? I don't remember any students with that surname."

"If it's McBride, isn't he the old fellow we met on Thursday – the one that knew your mother?"

"Of course, that's who it is – Jim McBride," Maura said, relieved to remember. "But why would he be ringing here?"

The phone began to ring as she spoke. "I guess you're about to find out," Bernadette smiled. "I'll leave you to it," she mouthed, as Maura picked up the phone receiver. "Good afternoon, Ardmahon House, Maura Carmody speaking," she said brightly.

"Hello, Maura, this is Jim McBride speaking." His voice was low and she could hear what sounded like pub noises in the background. She was about to speak when he spoke hurriedly. "I met you in the pub on Thursday."

"Oh hello, Mr McBride," Maura replied. "I remember you of course."

There was a pause, then he spoke again. "Yes, you were in asking about your mother."

Maura took a deep breath. "Oh, no, you must have misheard me. I was asking about a lady I used to work with in Australia."

Jim's voice was very kind. "Maura, I guessed the moment I saw you. You're the image of Catherine. And there's not many in the world with that shade of dark-red hair. I'm only surprised Eileen didn't pick up on it as well. But as you know she gets very upset when she thinks about Catherine – she's probably tried to block out the memory of her face." He laughed fondly.

Maura suddenly had a shocking thought. She dropped all the pretence. "Mr McBride, are you my father? Is that why you're ringing?"

The old man gave his youthful laugh again. "No, Maura, I'm not. You wouldn't be as good-looking as you are if I'd been your father. No, I'm not him. And call me Jim, not Mr McBride, won't you?"

He spoke hurriedly again, his voice serious. "But listen, I didn't tell the whole truth when I said I didn't have any photos of Catherine. I've a few bits and pieces. Would you have an hour to meet me? Can I show them to you?"

She immediately said yes. Jim named a village just five miles away, in the opposite direction to his home village. "There's a small pub called Moloney's there.

People may see us and people may talk, but then isn't that the nature of country life?" he said. "It'll give Eileen a little something extra to worry about."

In less than ten minutes she was strapped into Bernadette's little car and negotiating her way down the narrow lane, following Jim's directions. Bernadette had handed over her car keys without hesitation. "Do you want me to come with you?" she had asked. Maura had thought for a moment and then shook her head.

"No, but thank you very much for offering," she said quietly. "I think I need to do this one on my own."

Chapter Twenty-six

Jim McBride was sitting up on a high stool at the end of the bar when Maura came in. She noticed a brown paper package on the stool beside him and fought an impulse to snatch it up and run out the door with it.

Jim smiled shyly at her. "Hello, Maura, can I get you something to drink?" He was staring intently at her and then smiled again. "You really are the image of her. Sit yourself down and we'll get you settled with a drink and now we've a bit of privacy, I'll tell you what I know about your mother."

Maura barely took in her surroundings as she waited for the pot of tea Jim had ordered. Jim seemed equally nervous, reluctant to start any conversation until the barman had served them and retreated to the other end of the pub.

They were finally on their own. Maura looked at him. "Thank you for ringing," she said softly. "It was a shock to find out the little I did about Catherine." She couldn't bring herself to say the words 'my mother'. "The idea of her running off to Australia so young has been going round and round in my head since you told me. Did something terrible happen to her here as a child?" she asked, in a rush.

Jim laughed his soft, rippling laugh again. "No, nothing terrible happened to her here. Have you been reading *Angela's Ashes*? Lord, not every Irish child of that generation had a terrible childhood, and Catherine and I certainly didn't. No, she just wanted adventure, more than she was ever going to find here. She only lasted in America for less than a year, then she took a notion to go to Australia and, as you well know, that's where she ended up."

"Did you hear from her after she left, then?" Maura whispered.

Jim lowered his voice even more. "A letter every few months or so, for the first five years she went away. Then myself and Eileen got together, and well, Eileen is a very jealous woman, and she wasn't at all happy with the idea of me exchanging mail with an old girlfriend, so she put a stop to it."

"How did she do that?" Maura asked, surprised.

Jim looked sheepish. "She said she wouldn't, uhm, let me treat her as my wife, if you know what I mean, unless I behaved like a proper husband and left past girlfriends in the past. So I wrote to Catherine one last time and asked her to stop writing. And after one last letter she did." He gave a short laugh. "One of the few times she obeyed my wishes – the sun must have made her soft in the head, eh?" he laughed.

Maura's eyes were drawn to the brown-paper parcel again. "You've got five years' worth of Catherine's letters there?"

Jim nodded, almost proudly.

"Didn't Eileen make you throw them away?"

"Well, she thought I had, but my friend here," he nodded in the direction of the barman, "he said he'd mind them for me, as a favour like. I always knew I couldn't throw them away and now you're here, I'm glad I didn't. I must have known you would turn up one day, eh?" He laughed softly again, and took a long, slow swallow of his pint.

"And can you –" Maura tried again, "would you tell me a little about what she got up to, what was in her letters?"

"Of course I will, love, that's why I telephoned you and wanted to meet up with you. They are great reading altogether. She was a lively scrap of a thing, full of fun, and it seems Australia was the right place for her. You worked in a hospital with her, did you say? I still can't imagine her as a nurse." He shook his head, smiling.

Maura looked embarrassed. "Jim, I made all that up, about working in a hospital with Catherine. It wasn't true. I was just trying to find out what I could about her. She was a nurse but I never got to meet her."

Jim turned fully around on his stool and looked

Maura full in the face. His eyes were full of feeling. "Ah, love, I didn't realise that at all. I knew you were fishing for information, but I thought you had actually met her. Oh, I'm so sorry – so you've no idea of her at all? All that stuff you said about her being the award-winning nursing sister, then, is that not true?"

Maura shook her head, even more embarrassed. "I don't know. I spoke briefly to the matron and one of the nurses in the last hospital she worked in, but when they told me Catherine had died a few months before, I was too shocked really to ask much. And after I left I didn't ever really want to go back."

Jim nodded, taking another swallow. "Aye, I guess you wouldn't," he said softly. He brightened suddenly. "I suspected it wasn't the whole truth, though, especially when you were telling the stories about her being a great teacher. Catherine would never have had the patience, she was a quick learner herself and could never understand it if other people couldn't keep up with her. But you certainly convinced Eileen. You should have heard her that night! 'Imagine that Catherine coming to anything, God, I'd never have believed it'," he said, imitating his wife's voice, then smiled again. "We needn't worry about enlightening her, need we?"

Maura shook her head. She suddenly felt as though she was imagining this entire conversation. The whole scene. She was standing in a smoky pub on a wet Sunday afternoon in County Clare, hearing about her

Irish mother. She'd actually begun to think of her as that. Not biological mother, or birth mother, or any other term. Her mother.

Jim spoke again. "You're a cook, is that what you told Dymphna on Thursday?"

Maura nodded.

"Catherine worked as a cook for a while herself. Maybe it's in your genes?"

"Catherine was a cook?" Maura said, surprised. "I thought she was always a nurse?"

"Not when I was writing to her. That must have come later, after – " he looked at Maura and she knew they were both thinking about Catherine getting pregnant. "Well, after some other things had happened in her life. No, she worked as a cook for six months in some sort of roadside café in a place called Darwin, do you know it?"

Maura nodded. It was the capital city of the Northern Territory, the tropical top end of Australia. She'd never been there, but knew its reputation as a frontier town. She couldn't imagine what it would have been like for a young Irish girl in 1960s Australia.

"How on earth did she get there?" Maura asked.

"Oh, she met some other travellers, and they all hitched a lift up with a truck driver. It's all in the letters, photos and all."

"You've got photos of her when she was my age?" Maura asked. She was still feeling her way through the twists and turns of Jim's revelations.

"Oh yes," Jim answered. "I've four or five of them. That's how I knew you were her daughter as soon as I laid eyes on you. What age are you, Maura?"

"Twenty-eight," Maura answered.

"Just a few years' difference from Catherine's age in the photos. She had a strong face, like you do. You'll probably get even better looking as you get older. I always thought Catherine would. Mind you, we stopped contact when she turned twenty-six, when Eileen stepped in," he reminded her again. "I was sorry not to get any more letters – it was just when things were getting interesting for her too, by the sound of things."

"Did she mention my, uhm –"

"Father?" Jim finished her question for her. "I really don't know, love. She talked about this fellow or that fellow, but maybe she was just trying to make me jealous, eh?" he laughed for a second, before noticing the tense expression on Maura's face. "No, she didn't, Maura, I'm sure of it. All of that happened a few years later, going by your age. Anyway, as I said, she was too busy travelling and having adventures by the sound of things." He patted the letters again.

"Could I see the photos?" Maura finally asked, unable to bear it any more.

Jim looked surprised. "See them? Lord God, you can have them. And all the letters too. It's years since I read them, but do you know, I can still nearly remember them word for word. But you have them – you'll enjoy reading them, I'm sure. Ah, she was great gas altogether, you'll see for yourself."

Maura gently picked up the package. She didn't want to open it here, in this little pub, with curious eyes glancing over at them. Jim seemed to understand. He patted her arm.

"Away you go, love. Take them with you. They're yours now."

"Thank you, Jim," she said simply. She suddenly leaned forward and gave him a hug.

He pretended to protest but she could hear the smile in his voice. "Get on with you now. And safe travelling back to Australia. Sure, maybe I'll see you out there myself one day." He laughed happily at his own joke.

Outside in the cool air, Maura held the package close to her chest. Not really thinking clearly, she climbed into Bernadette's car and drove back in the direction of Ardmahon House. Halfway there she saw a road veering to the right, into the heart of the Burren. Hardly looking behind her, she turned the wheel and drove off up the rough road, barely feeling the bumps and lurches.

A gateway across the road suddenly halted her movement. She climbed out of the car, shivering as a wild gust of wind threw the door open wide and tossed her hair out of its loose band. Her curls flying around her face, Maura slammed the door against the wind, and pulling her coat and the package close against her body, set off walking across the rocks.

She didn't know where she was, or where she was

going. She just knew she had to walk, had to be as alone as she could be when she read the letters and looked at the photos. The glittering, silver light seemed to suit her mood. She stumbled several times, nearly catching her foot in the tight clusters of rocks. Rounding a corner, the wind nearly forcing her up against a metre-high boulder, she caught her breath as she came across a tiny lake, just a dozen metres across. Beside it was a large group of rocks. She walked toward it, finding shelter against the wind.

She pulled the package out from under her coat, and with shaking hands, carefully undid the tape around it.

The photos were in a separate envelope, and she took them out, one by one, looking carefully at each of them. They were old-fashioned, the colours still bright, each print with a white border. Catherine standing on a beach, dressed in a full swimsuit, grinning at the camera. Catherine smiling at an unnamed girlfriend, standing at Sydney Harbour, the Harbour Bridge in the background. Catherine feeding a kangaroo in a wildlife park. And one photo obviously taken at the café in Darwin of Catherine proudly standing in front of a giant-sized frypan, holding a pair of kitchen tongs. In the background were two beaming young men, truck drivers perhaps, holding their knives and forks in the air, waiting for their breakfast.

Maura laughed aloud, her eyes filling with sudden tears, as she noticed a feature of the two posed photos. Catherine had a wide-eyed look in each, as if she was willing herself not to blink. It was a look Maura recognised straight away.

She fumbled with the envelopes containing the letters and then read each one, slowly and carefully. Catherine's writing was fluid, with great loops and plenty of misspellings, as if she was in too much of a hurry to have time to spell correctly. She and Jim must have been great friends. The letters weren't from a fleeing girl to the boyfriend she left behind, but from a young woman spilling over with stories to a close friend. Eileen had had nothing to worry about, Maura thought.

Catherine was glad to be away from America – she had found it too hard and too fast and too crowded. Sydney was fun, and lively, and the most beautiful place she had ever seen. But she still wanted to see more. Darwin was hot, flat and hard work but made her feel like she was really in Australia, cooking huge steaks to serve to tanned, cheeky blokes. She joked at the accents, expressed amazement at the heat, wrote of her occasional homesickness for Ireland.

Her reply to Jim's letter asking her to stop writing to him because of Eileen was also in the package. Maura noticed with a fleeting grin that it had been addressed to the pub, not Jim's home address. Catherine didn't seem at all put out, instead teasing Jim that this was a sign of his life ahead, under Eileen's thumb and jumping to her bidding. 'Don't say I didn't warn you!' she had written in her sloping handwriting.

She wrote that she was planning to leave Darwin and try Melbourne or Adelaide as her next stop. She'd heard Irish barmaids were always in demand. And Irish nurses. That was the first hint of the new career, Maura realised. Catherine had signed off cheerily, writing that she hoped one day to return to Ireland for a visit and she would be sure to arrive at Jim's house 'wearing my prettiest dress and brightest lipstick, especially for Eileen!'

By the end of the final letter, Maura could feel the tears streaming down her face. Roughly wiping them away, she started again, reading every letter once more, taking them in word by word.

When she finished the second time, she leaned back against the grey rock behind her. They were the sort of letters she might have written to one of her friends when she first went to Sydney. They weren't of a sad, homesick girl, fleeing a terrible past, or a terrified girl in a new country. They were from a lively, adventurous young woman, amazed to find herself on the other side of the world and determined to try everything she could.

And maybe that's where I came in, Maura thought to herself. Maybe Catherine met someone lovely on her travels, got swept along with the excitement and then realised she was pregnant and alone. It was too far away to come back to Ireland, and anyway, Maura could imagine very easily that an unmarried pregnant Catherine would not have been very welcome in her home village.

And so she had given Maura up for adoption. And Terri had received her with loving arms. Maura wished now that she had found the courage, and the need, to go looking for Catherine earlier. When it wasn't too late.

She felt a sudden rush of anger. Why hadn't her mother come looking for *her*? Was she too busy having more adventures? She looked down at Catherine's letters and photographs, suddenly wanting to tear them up. Rip them into tiny squares. With shaking hands, she grasped the corners of the first letter, ready to tear it apart. She imagined the gusts of wind teasing the pieces out of her hand and sending them flying across the grey rock and the rippling surface of the water.

But she couldn't do it.

Instead, she slid down against the stone, the letters clutched against her and buried her face in her arms.

It was some time before she lifted her head. She breathed deeply, taking in the cool, clean air, slowly focusing on the rocks and the lake nearby. After a moment, she gently unfolded the letters, and slowly read them once again.

They were a glimpse into Catherine's life. Now Maura could imagine what meeting her, having a conversation with her might have been like. Perhaps she wasn't the ghostly figure, the sad, downtrodden old Irish lady Maura had imagined her to be. The homesick, sad nurse stuck in the regional hospital.

Maybe she had been full of spark until the end. Or maybe she had become bitter. But at least now Maura had a fragment of memory to think about, a tiny sample of what Catherine had once been like.

She knew then what she would do with the letters. They weren't hers to throw away, or to keep. They belonged to Jim.

Before she walked back to the car, she looked at each photo again for a long moment. Her mother at Sydney Harbour, at the wildlife park, on the beach. And the one taken in the kitchen, her mother wide-eyed, laughing into the camera, waving the cooking tongs at the photographer.

Maura smiled slowly.

She'd ask Jim if she could keep that one.

Chapter Twenty-seven

Maura welcomed her final group of students to the course, doing her best to ignore Carla's sullen presence in the corner of the kitchen.

With now practised ease Maura gave her introductory spiel on the makeup of modern Australian cuisine and how she would aim to give them all first-hand experience of it over the next few days.

"We'll be trying seafood, and new ways with beef and chicken, as well as some delicious desserts," she promised, as she handed out course notes listing the recipes they would be trialling.

"I can't eat meat, I'm a vegetarian," Carla's distinctive voice came from the corner.

Maura's brow furrowed. "Are you, Carla? I'm sure I saw you trying some Thai chicken kebabs last week in the restaurant here?"

Carla actually blushed slightly. "I started this morning," she said, boldly. "Meat is murder."

Maura counted to ten. "That's fine, Carla, you can

just watch during that section of the class. We'll be doing some dishes without meat later in the day. I'm sure you'll enjoy learning how to cook those," she said, in a tone of voice she'd only expect to use on a particularly disobedient child.

But later in the day it seemed Carla had suddenly become allergic to eggs. And then wheat products. "She's a medical marvel," Maura whispered to Bernadette. "At this rate she'll be allergic to oxygen by the end of the day."

"Chance would be a fine thing," Bernadette whispered back. She was less concerned with Carla's sudden food intolerances than the effect her disruptiveness was having on the others in the class. The younger ones seemed in awe of the American girl's glamour and good looks, and had started to enjoy her snide remarks to Maura. Carla's sudden commitment to vegetarianism, involving graphic descriptions of abattoir conditions and battery-hen farming, appeared to be turning the heads of one or two in particular.

At the lunchtime break Bernadette came up with a solution. "What about I start up a different class in the corner?" she suggested. "An all-vegetarian, all-wholefood, no salt, no spices, no flavour class. I'm sure Carla will be in it, and if any of the others want to join in then they can, what do you think?"

Maura nodded. It was worth a try. At the rate they were going, Carla would have them all marching on nearby farms with placards, demanding the immediate release of their sheep and chickens.

She wasn't surprised when three of the girls joined the renegade class. Maura worked on determinedly on the other side of the kitchen, instructing her group in the creation of the delicious entrées of crispy seafood rolls and Thai-style soup.

The spicy aromas acted like an invisible lure. One by one the girls drifted across, keen to taste and try the techniques themselves. Soon there was only Carla and Bernadette on the other side of the kitchen, concocting a plain lentil salad.

That night Maura and Bernadette were amazed to hear Carla offer to lead the group off on a tour of the local pubs.

Bernadette shut her eyes in exhaustion as they left Ardmahon House in a pair of taxis. "She's probably kidnapping the lot of them, brainwashing them against the evils of cooking schools," she said with a sigh.

"They're not kids," Maura replied, "We can hardly banish them all to their rooms, can we?"

Bernadette shook her head. "Nope. Anyway, with any luck they'll all come back roaring drunk tonight, be hungover tomorrow and then be putty in our hands."

"Are we supposed to keep an eye on Carla twenty-four hours a day?" Maura asked.

"Dominic wasn't specific," Bernadette answered. "He just said it would be better for her to be here than in Dublin. She's started to hang around with a pretty fast crowd there by all accounts."

Maura raised an eyebrow. "Should we give her a

blood-test each morning, do you think? We could give Dominic a written report at the end of the week."

Bernadette grinned. "Now, Maura, claws back in please."

Maura laughed, realising she'd been caught out. "Nothing of the sort," she fudged. It just disturbed her that Dominic could be so concerned with Carla, when it was obvious that Carla was mightily self-obsessed.

Maura woke suddenly in the early hours of Tuesday morning, immediately alert. She checked the time on the bedside clock. 3 am. She had heard an odd noise outside and lay very still, waiting for it again. Not another Romeo and Juliet re-enactment, she hoped. Apart from Carla, this group of students seemed happily single – at least there hadn't been any lovelorn tears so far. She waited again for the noise that had woken her. It was a motorcycle idling in the courtyard downstairs, she realised. She silently climbed out of her bed, tiptoeing across the room to her large bay window which overlooked the sweeping courtyard at the front of the house.

There was enough moonlight to be able to see Carla as she clambered down from the back of the small motorbike, removing her helmet as she did so. As Maura watched, the rider took off his helmet as well. From the distance, she could just make out a young man, his cropped blonde hair shining white in the light. She watched as Carla leaned against him, her hand on the young man's face. Then she moved closer and

Maura held her breath as they suddenly started kissing passionately, the man's hand confidently tracing the outlines of Carla's body through the tight-fitting black dress she was wearing.

Maura was shocked. This was what Carla got up to when Dominic was away? She saw the man's hand move even further up Carla's skirt, and the kiss turn more passionate.

Embarrassed, Maura let the curtain drop, not wanting to see any more. She tiptoed back to her bed, climbing in under the covers again, only half-awake and dazed by what she'd seen. The saying about mice playing when the cat's away ran through her head. She lay still, unable to stop herself from listening out for the sound of the motorbike starting up again. The sound didn't come. Instead, a few minutes later she heard the faint sound of the front door opening downstairs and heard muffled giggles as Carla and her companion made their way slowly up the stairs.

Maura was wide awake now, not sure if she was imagining it all. The man's deep voice confirmed her suspicion. Carla was taking him into her room.

The house was silent again. But Maura couldn't sleep. She dozed fitfully, waking again just before dawn when the sound of a motorbike starting in the courtyard below woke her. She climbed out of bed and went to the window again, just in time to see the bike disappear down the tree-lined drive. She didn't care about Carla. But she suddenly felt sorry for Dominic. Deal or no deal with Carla's father, she knew what it felt like to be two-timed.

That morning the students seemed a bit bleary-eyed, but nonetheless still keen to learn. There was no sign of Carla.

Niamh, one of the Irish girls, passed on a message that Carla had a sudden migraine and probably wouldn't be down that day. Maura felt a rush of relief.

But Carla emerged again late that afternoon, coming into the kitchen just as Maura was introducing the desserts section of the course.

Maura looked over at the American girl as she came in, noting the shadows under her eyes. She smiled a welcome, determined that Carla wouldn't unsettle her.

Bernadette took the lead. "Hello, Carla, you're just in time for our desserts class," she said brightly. "Maura, what will we be enjoying today?" She motioned Maura to continue.

Maura wrote the list of desserts up on the whiteboard:

Wholemeal pancakes served with mandarin and passionfruit sauce

Grilled figs and grapes in a spiced yoghurt sauce

Peach sorbet with a side dish of fresh peaches stirfried with Tasmanian leatherwood honey and toasted almonds

She could almost hear the students licking their lips as they read through the list.

The kitchen was soon an aromatic mix of smells, as each student worked through the steps. Carla actually seemed interested in learning to cook the sweet dishes, and Maura watched in amazement as she ate an entire serving of the pancakes and half of the grilled figs dessert.

After a break, Maura joined the rest of the class in the sitting-room, where they would be enjoying an informal wine-tasting session. Carla was missing again.

"She went upstairs," one of the students offered helpfully, when Bernadette noticed her absence. "She said she wasn't feeling well again."

Bernadette looked over at Maura. "I'll just make sure she's okay," Maura said, biting her lip to stop any further comment. "Bernadette, perhaps you'd start by explaining about the different sorts of glasses."

Bernadette nodded. She'd been expecting a showdown between Maura and Carla and this seemed as good a time as any.

Leaving the room as Bernadette started explaining the difference between the designs of white wine and red wineglasses, Maura walked up the staircase. Carla was still staying in the east wing she shared with Dominic when he was there, a beautifully designed two-bedroom suite, with a sitting-room that looked over the fields surrounding the house.

The door was ajar and Maura knocked softly. There was no answer and she was about to go downstairs again when she heard a retching sound coming from the bathroom, followed by the unmistakeable sound of vomiting.

"Carla?" Maura called, suddenly concerned. "Are you all right?" There was no answer. She walked toward the bathroom. The noise came again, quickly followed by the sound of a tap running. Maura was about to knock on the bathroom door, when Carla emerged. She jumped to see Maura.

"What are you doing here?" she snapped.

Maura was put out. "I was just checking that you were okay. I'm sorry to intrude, I heard you – " she chose her words carefully "I heard you being ill, is everything okay?"

To her surprise, Carla ignored her reference to the sounds from the bathroom. "I'm fine," she said defiantly, though Maura noticed her eyes seemed teary, her mascara a little smudged. She seemed to be hiding a bottle of tablets behind her back. "It's that time of the month, I get a bit queasy," she said, staring Maura right in the face, daring her to ask any more questions.

Maura acknowledged her answer with a slight nod. "Well, we're just starting the wine-tasting session, if you feel up to it. You're welcome to just come and watch if you don't feel able to do any tastings."

Carla gazed coldly at her. "Your brother's wine?" she drawled, her tone showing her contempt.

Maura felt her patience start to disappear. "Not just his – we're tasting French and Italian wines as well today. Would you like to come back down?"

Carla shrugged. "I've nothing better to do, I guess." She stepped toward the door. "After you," she said.

* * *

Maura had just finished clearing the kitchen that night when she received a surprise phone call from Joel, her food writer friend. It was early morning in Sydney and Maura could just picture him, probably stretched out on a deckchair on his balcony overlooking Bondi Beach.

"Can you believe it?" he shouted down the phone. "I'll be in London on Thursday night! Twelve thousand miles of flying just to do one story. I'm only there for three days, so you've no excuse, you have to come and meet me."

Maura made him slow down and explain the situation again.

"It's a story for the *Sydney Morning Herald*, about the popularity of Australian chefs overseas. It's come completely out of the blue. They want me to try out their restaurants, talk to a few of them, interview the owners, you know the sort of thing," he explained excitedly.

He coaxed her again. "I'm only there for three days, darling. You have to come over and meet me, there's no excuse."

"I'll do my best," Maura said laughing, promising to call back as soon as she'd had a chance to look at her diary and talk to Bernadette.

"Of course you can manage it," Bernadette said

immediately. "And you should see London while you're this close. You can go over on Thursday night after the class finishes, see Joel and then come back on the Friday in time for dinner. I can manage all the preparations here for you – this new Australian cuisine isn't that difficult once you get the hang of it!

"And I know just the hotel for you, right in the best part of London. Dominic stays there and says it's great. Actually, he's there this week, you might even run into him," she added casually, as she reached for her address book.

Maura wrote down the details of the London hotel, only half registering Bernadette's comments about Dominic. She quickly rang Joel back and made the arrangements to meet.

"So I'll see you Thursday night at the restaurant. It'll be brilliant, I can't wait," she said enthusiastically.

As she turned from the phone, the smile still on her face, she was surprised to see Carla walking out of the dining-room alone.

"So you're going to London," Carla said in her distinctive drawl, making no apologies for eavesdropping. "Catching up with an old friend, by the sound of it."

What was it about Carla that made her want to slap her face, Maura wondered. "Yes," she countered, "a very old and very dear friend. I can't wait to see him again."

"A lover, is it?" Carla asked, looking Maura up and down dismissively, as if amazed she could possibly attract a man.

"Oh, even better than that," Maura answered quickly, her temper rising. "A man who loves me for who I am, not who my family is, or how much money I've got."

Carla's eyes narrowed. "I doubt they exist."

"I'm sure you do," Maura answered as coldly.

Bernadette's call from the kitchen stopped the argument. Shaking her head, Maura thought with relief of the surprise trip to London. With all that had happened in the past three weeks, she was more exhausted than she'd been in a long time. A night out with an old friend was exactly what she needed.

Chapter Twenty-eight

Bernadette insisted on driving Maura to Shannon Airport, just a short distance from Ardmahon House, urging her to enjoy the quick break. "You know you can trust me to get everything ready – anyway, there's plenty of canned soup in the cupboard as a back-up, isn't there?"

The flight took less than an hour and after arriving into Heathrow airport and facing the throngs heading toward the underground, Maura decided to splash out and catch a taxi direct from the airport to the restaurant in the centre of London where she was meeting Joel.

Walking down the grand staircase into the main dining-room, she was glad she had worn her red dress again and taken advantage of the long cab ride to reapply her make-up and arrange her hair in an elegant style.

It was the most luxurious restaurant she had ever seen.

Each wall featured an elaborate combination of mirrors and handpainted murals. The chairs were works of art. Every waitress was exquisitely beautiful, wearing clothes that wouldn't have looked out of place on a catwalk.

She had just been directed by a supermodel look-alike to her table when she heard a familiar purring voice behind her. It was Joel, dressed to the nines, looking like the cat that had got the cream. "It's a home away from home, darling, isn't it?" he laughed, as Maura greeted him warmly.

He took his seat and swiftly ordered two glasses of champagne for them. "This is an absolute swizz, sweetheart," he said, grinning from ear to ear. "All this way to talk to six Aussie blokes. I could have telephoned from Sydney and got the whole thing over and done with in less than an hour. They might be the world's best chefs but believe me they'd make terrible chatshow guests. Articulate they are not." He rolled his eyes.

As they fell into their usual easy conversation, swapping Sydney gossip with rural Irish tales, she laughed as Joel ostentatiously placed his mobile phone on the table between them.

"Just fitting in with the natives, my little colleen," he said. Maura glanced around. Sure enough, there seemed to be a mobile phone beside nearly every plate in the restaurant. The wall-length mirrors made it seem even more bizarre, as tables reflected tables.

She pulled her attention back to Joel, who was

outlining his research for the story. "I've been trying to set up an interview with the owner of this restaurant since I knew I was coming over," he confided, "but he seems to be the busiest man in London. Hopefully I'll get twenty minutes with him here tomorrow – his PR said she'd ring tonight to confirm."

The phone thankfully stayed silent while they ate their meal. The food matched the décor in every way, rich and sumptuous, with incredible attention to detail.

As they ate, Maura brought Joel up to date with the story about the critic's visit to Lorikeet Hill and the problem with the mistaken identity. He was especially amazed at the news of Dominic turning up in Dublin.

"Darling, I hope I didn't get you into trouble," Joel was aghast. "I should have found out exactly what that critic looked like. And me and my big mouth. I shouldn't have breathed a word about the takeover."

Maura swept his concerns away. "It doesn't matter, really, none of it. It was all absolutely fine," she pretended. "And it sounds like you're still getting plenty of work. Let's forget about all that – tell me about life in Sydney."

Joel was great company, Maura thought, wiping away tears of laughter after a particularly scandalous story about one of the newspaper food writers. He fitted in perfectly here, his flamboyant style well-suited to their surroundings.

Even the bathrooms were magnificent, Maura thought later. Like the inside of a Hollywood starlet's powder puff. There was even another beautiful woman stationed permanently inside, waiting to turn on the bathroom taps, give out soap and offer a spray from a selection of very exclusive perfumes. Maura laughed to herself at the thought of borrowing that particular idea at Lorikeet Hill. She could imagine the shock some of her regular customers would get if they entered the tiny cubicle and found a waitress waiting there for them, hand-towel at the ready.

Joel had just regaled her with a tale he had heard second or third-hand about Richard's work in London when his mobile phone finally rang. He mischievously let it ring until he had caught their fellow diners' attention, then picked it up.

It was the restaurant owner's personal assistant, ringing to tell him that the only opportunity for the interview would be within the next hour, as her employer had to unexpectedly fly to Paris in the morning.

Maura brushed off Joel's apologies for the sudden end to the evening. "Of course I understand. You can't possibly say no – that's why you're here, isn't it?"

After an effusive farewell from Joel, Maura caught a taxi to her hotel, only a few miles away. Bernadette was right – it looked charming. She had just checked in and was about to go straight to her room when the sound of gentle music from the small hotel bar caught her attention.

Looking at her watch, she decided it was far too early to go to bed yet. She was in London after all. How often did that happen? She'd have a glass of champagne, catch up on some letter-writing and have a good look at some Londoners.

As she took her seat at a quiet window table, she looked around the bar, enjoying the elegance and sophistication of the other patrons. There were several couples in evening wear. A well-dressed family group. A trio of businessmen in suits. And Dominic Hanrahan.

Dominic? Surely not. She looked over again, suddenly embarrassed. It was him. Bernadette had told her Dominic was staying here, but she'd put it to the back of her mind, not really expecting to see him. He appeared to be in the middle of a business meeting and didn't seem to have noticed her.

Not sure why she was doing it, Maura quickly shifted around in her seat, looking intently out of the window onto the street. With her back to the room, she hoped Dominic might not recognise her.

She had nearly finished her drink and was writing a postcard to Gemma when a hand on her shoulder made her jump.

"Well, well, so you've given up restaurants and taken up high-class prostitution instead, have you? You've probably got more talent for it than you'll ever have for cooking."

She looked up in shock, even after three years immediately recognising her ex-boyfriend's voice. "Richard! What are you doing here?"

"You can thank your dear friend Joel," he said

surprisingly. He ignored her unwelcoming stare, and pulled up a chair beside her, dragging it uncomfortably close. "I've been out tonight with the restaurant owner Joel's interviewing and I was still with him when Joel turned up. And you know Joel and his big, big mouth – he just happened to let slip you were in London and staying at this hotel. So I came right here. I knew you'd come looking for me eventually – I'm just surprised it took you so long."

She realised in a second by the slur to his words that Richard was very drunk. And by the odd glitter in his eyes he'd taken something a bit stronger than alcohol as well. As Richard moved his chair in even closer to her, she could see immediately that the years hadn't been kind to him. His hair was receding, and he'd become even flabbier. The arrogant tilt to his jaw hadn't disappeared though.

"Still on your own, I see," he taunted her, leaning close enough for her to get a strong whiff of alcohol. "I told you, and that idiot friend of yours, that it was a mistake to leave me. What was her name? Gemma, wasn't it?"

She didn't even bother to nod. Richard knew Gemma's name perfectly well.

"How is dear Gemma? Has she managed to find any work yet? Such a shame about that magazine review, wasn't it? And I hear you're serving chops and mashed potatoes in some football canteen in the country. Found your true calling, did you?"

"Leave me alone, Richard," she said, her nerves jangling.

Richard's mood changed in an instant. "'Leave me alone, Richard'," he mocked. "How dare you say that to me. And how dare you walk off on me like you did? Don't you know I was the best you'll ever get, you little fool." He swayed dangerously toward her, putting his hand on her leg to steady himself.

Maura sat rigid. She'd seen this mood up close before. His hand came up to her forehead. From a distance it would look like a caress, but she breathed in sharply as he took hold of a curl and tugged it hard enough to hurt her.

"Nothing to say, Maura? Still need your friends to hide behind, do you?" he slurred.

She felt the anger rise, a cool, clear fury, unlike the hesitant confusion she'd often felt in similar situations with him.

"Take your hands off me now or I'll call for security," she said, finding a calm, strong voice.

"Oh, big brave girl, aren't you?" he taunted her. "Come on, darling, remember the old times. I know you've missed me."

"I mean it, Richard. You mean nothing to me. Get away from me now or I call for the police," she repeated.

Richard twisted her hair again. "Listen to me, you little fool . . ."

A quiet voice behind them stopped his words.

"Is this man bothering you, Maura?"

Dominic's voice.

Richard turned around before she did. "Who the hell are you?" he growled at the newcomer.

Maura looked quickly up at Dominic. He was on his own – no sign of the other businessmen. His meeting must have finished.

His arrival had distracted Richard enough for him to loosen his hold on Maura's hair. She put her hand up to his wrist and gave it a sharp twist, digging in her nails as she did so. In his state he barely noticed the pain.

"No, he's not bothering me at all," she answered Dominic. "And we needn't worry about introductions. He's just some old drunk and I was leaving anyway."

She stood up, gathering her belongings in one quick movement. Smiling fixedly, and taking great pleasure in turning her back on Richard, she surprised Dominic as much as herself by kissing him on the cheek and taking his hand.

"It's wonderful to see you, darling," she said deliberately loudly for Richard to hear. "I hope all your meetings went well."

She was conscious of Richard looking blearily back and forth between the two of them, rubbing his wrist where her nails had dug in. He seemed about to speak when Maura interrupted.

"Goodnight, Richard. And goodbye, Richard," she said politely, virtually marching Dominic out into the foyer.

Her nerve started to fail her once they were back in the bright light.

"That's how you deal with 'just some old drunk'?" Dominic said, looking down at her with a half smile. "I must remember to stay sober around you."

She didn't reply, too shook up to respond to teasing. Dominic looked closely at her over-bright eyes, and seemed to realise it had been serious.

"That was Richard the chef, I gather?" he prompted softly.

She looked up at him. He had a good memory. "It was," she said quietly.

He looked down at her bags. "You're staying here, I believe?"

She nodded. Bernadette must have telephoned and told him. "I'm just in London for the night, I met up with an old friend from Sydney. But this wasn't quite the night I was expecting . . ." She knew she was babbling, but she couldn't quite believe all that had just happened.

His voice was concerned as he looked down at her again. "Maura, are you all right? Would you like me to see you to your room?"

She nodded, still distracted. She kept mentally replaying the encounter with Richard. Through her shock, she felt relief at how she had handled it. She had never really had a final showdown with him. After their last fight, she had not seen him again, not feeling strong enough to do so. The ending of their relationship had always felt slightly undefined in her mind. Not any more.

Wordlessly, she followed Dominic as he escorted her to her room. He had just said goodnight when he noticed her hands had started to shake. She could hardly get the key in the lock.

"You seem to have had more of a shock than you realise," he said gently. "Would you like a drink of something?"

She thought for a moment, then nodded, attempting a smile. "I'd rather not go back to that bar though." She thought of Richard waiting there.

Dominic seemed to understand. "I've a bar in my room, just up on the next floor. Would you like a glass of wine or something stronger?" he asked.

Maura nodded. As she followed him up the stairs, she started to explain the situation. Dominic hushed her.

"Let's get you settled with a drink, then you can tell me the whole story if you want to."

His room was lit with two warm red lamps, the double bed turned down by the maids, the couch covered with his luggage.

Dominic gently steered her toward the side of the bed. "Sit here for a moment, while I clear a space for you to sit and get you a drink."

Sitting in the quiet of his room, she suddenly had a delayed reaction to Richard's insults. She remembered him pulling at her hair, and the aggression in his eyes as he had leaned toward her. Before she knew it her eyes had filled with tears.

"Ah, Maura," Dominic said, turning back to her immediately. He sat close beside her and, without a word, she turned into the circle of his arms.

"Shh," he soothed her. "Don't mind him, he can't get you now, I'm here, I'll look after you, you're fine . . ."

She recognised the tone of voice as one he used sometimes with Carla. It was a rhythmic, gentle tumble of words that relaxed her as easily as she had seen it do to Carla. For once the thought of Carla didn't raise her hackles. Carla seemed a very long way away.

She tried to sit up straight in his arms. "I'm sorry," she said, embarrassed now. "It was just the shock of seeing him, it was the last thing I expected. You'd think in a place as big as London – " she stopped. "I thought I was over him, I mean, I am over him, I just didn't expect him to be so . . ."

"Horrible?" Dominic prompted, with a smile.

"Horrible," Maura echoed in a small voice, nearly smiling. "Yes, horrible." She sat up straight again, the movement causing a lock of hair to fall into her eyes.

Almost absentmindedly Dominic reached up and gently stroked it away from her face. The gesture didn't stop there. His finger began to slowly trace the side of her face, across her cheekbone and down across her lips.

Maura held her breath, looking straight into his eyes.

"He's a very stupid man," Dominic whispered.

She went very still.

"And I've been a very stupid man," he said, seconds before he leaned forward and brushed his lips against hers.

Maura closed her eyes as she felt every sense spring alive. She could smell a musky scent off him, a mixture of fresh shampoo on his hair and the faint aftershave she already associated with him. Her breath caught in her throat as his lips moved from her lips to her neck.

"Now it's my turn to look at you in the dark," he whispered. Her eyes shot open. He smiled down at her. "But I miss the green pyjamas."

Her face burned as she remembered the night in the Mayo hotel room. "You were awake?" she whispered, aghast.

"Wide awake. In every way," he added softly. His eyes looked deep into hers as he gently moved to kiss her lips again.

Before she knew it, the gentle caress had turned into a passionate deep kiss. She was shocked at the response in her body. The night in the hotel room she had convinced herself she was responding to Dominic as an attractive stranger. Now she was responding to him as Dominic.

The kiss seemed to last forever. There was gentleness and strength all at the same time. Silently they fell back onto his bed. Their clothes seemed to fall away. In the dusky light in the room she gazed at the sight of Dominic's naked body lying against hers. Her fingertips seemed red hot as they travelled the length of his body, her lips curving into a smile as she heard him gasp in pleasure. They didn't speak. There didn't seem to be any words that needed saying. The only noise in the room was the whisper of their bodies moving against the sheets and their slow moans of pleasure as they explored each other.

Ireland seemed worlds away. The trip together felt like a decade ago. All she wanted now was the feel of his hard body against hers and in her. When it happened it was as if it was all she had ever wanted. She brought her body up to meet his, again and again, almost dizzy with the pleasure of it. She felt as though she was nothing but a jangle of senses, of touch and taste and feeling. It was beautiful.

At the moment of ecstasy she looked right into his eyes, her eyes widening as he looked right back at her.

"Maura," she heard him whisper, before they closed their eyes as the pleasure travelled in long, flowing waves through them.

In the middle of the night they woke again.

"What about Carla?" she whispered.

"What about Cormac?" he whispered back. He laughed at her immediate indignation. "I'm teasing you, I know there's nothing between you and Cormac."

"But you and Carla?" she whispered back, trying to tease, but suddenly too conscious of their real situation.

He was suddenly serious. Their kisses stopped as he rose above her and gave her a long, searching look.

"Oh, Maura, Carla doesn't even come into it," he said in a quiet voice, leaning down to kiss her mouth gently. "Believe me when I tell you I'm not doing this lightly." His voice suddenly became urgent. "I've wanted this since I met you. Carla . . ." he stopped suddenly. "I need to tell you everything about Carla, but tonight isn't the time. I made a promise to her father and it's a very long, very complicated story. I promise I'll tell you as soon as I can. Will you trust me?"

She looked up at him, searching deep into his eyes. So the deal with Carla's father was real. But maybe there was more to it than she thought. Too many times she had misread him, misunderstood situations with him. She nodded, smiling, her mind already distracted by the wonderful things his hands were doing.

"I'll tell you everything, soon, I promise. But trust me tonight?" he whispered again.

She did. Somewhere in her heart, she did trust him. And right now there were other things she wanted to do than think about Carla.

Chapter Twenty-nine

She woke up to the luxurious feeling of a gentle fingertip lazily tracing the contours of her face, then moving down her neck and further down, under the edge of the cool, cotton sheet. She slowly opened her eyes, a smile curving across her face.

Dominic was lying on his side, leaning on one arm, lazily running his finger along her body.

She smiled tentatively. "Good morning, Dominic."

"Good morning, Miss Carmody," he grinned. "I see we're back on polite terms again. And there was me thinking we'd broken some ice last night between us."

Broken some ice? Maura thought. They'd smashed a whole fridgeful of it.

Her body still tingled in memory. She slowly woke up, trying to let everything sink in. She was in a hotel bedroom with Dominic. She had had sex with Dominic. Several times. They'd been responsible about safe sex, so there was nothing to worry about there. But she could still hardly believe it. Oh my God, she thought.

She must have spoken the last thought aloud. Dominic suddenly looked concerned.

"Maura," he said softly, "Please don't regret it, it was beautiful, I was sure you wanted it as much as I did. I felt sure you did."

She looked back at him. There was no point pretending otherwise. "Probably more than you did," she said. It was cards on the table time. "I think I've fancied you since that first day at Lorikeet Hill." She grinned suddenly.

"Oh, of course. I suspected as much when you served such terrible food. And I suppose the vase of water was to make sure I didn't mistake your true feelings," he said solemnly.

"It was that obvious, was it?" Maura replied. "I really must learn to be more subtle."

He reached for her again, Maura feeling a strange sense of unreality as once again a slow kiss began to build into something more. Feeling herself start to go lightheaded, she tried to grasp at some logical thought. This was just too strange. She was lying in bed with Dominic – and it felt wonderful. Then an image of Carla flashed into her head again.

Maura pulled back from the kiss, her body practically shouting in disappointment. She began to speak quickly, rushing to explain her feelings. "Dominic, I just have to say something. I need you to know that I don't usually get at all involved with people who are already in relationships. I've had it done to me and I hated it. I can't pretend I like her and I don't particularly want to stop what we're doing, but it's really not what I usually would do to another woman, sleep with her boyfriend like this."

She suddenly remembered Carla's midnight flit with the motorbike rider, but decided to keep that one to herself. It was getting complicated enough as it was with the three of them, let alone bringing in a friend of Carla's.

Dominic looked at her, his initial confusion giving way to a smile that started in his eyes and slowly reached his lips. "Maura, are you talking about Carla?'

She nodded.

"Maura, this might come as a surprise, but Carla and I aren't lovers. I know it can look like that and sometimes it's been quite convenient for people to think that, but we're not. We never have been."

Her face betrayed her amazement. He smiled at her again, punctuating his words with swift kisses to her face.

"Maura, I want to tell you everything about me and Carla, but it's not just my story to tell. I have to talk to her first. I have a loyalty to her as well as to the arrangement I made with her father."

That deal again. She'd hoped she'd imagined him talking about it the night before and that Cormac had everything wrong. But now Dominic had mentioned it again. It was like a dark cloud had slipped into the lightness in the room. Maura didn't want to think about

Carla, or Carla's father or any deals, especially deals as mysterious and complicated as this one was becoming.

Dominic seemed to feel the same way.

"I've got an idea," he said, kissing her lightly again. "Until I get the chance to talk to her, let's declare all talk of Carla, or her father, even Ardmahon House out-of-bounds."

Maura smiled her agreement, moving closer to him in the bed and enjoying the luxurious feel of his hand stroking her back.

"Maura," he murmured her name slowly. "I've wanted to ask you, how did an Australian girl get to have such an Irish name?"

Maura shut her eyes, her face warm against his naked chest. In a soft voice, she explained about Catherine Shanley, and how Terri had chosen an Irish name for her adopted daughter, to make sure there were some links between them.

He looked closely at her and she could feel his interest and curiosity. He had a clear, calm way of looking at her, listening to her.

"Your mother was Irish?" he asked softly. "Where was she from?"

Maura waited for a moment, before realising that she wanted to tell Dominic the whole story. She didn't look up at him, just lay in his arms, slowly telling him all that had happened since she arrived in Ireland. His gentle hands on her back soothed her as she spoke, his soft voice gently asking her questions.

The story told, they didn't speak for some minutes. But his hands were speaking a language of their own. Maura felt warm, protected. He kissed her gently on her face, then more passionately. Once again, words were forgotten as they gave themselves up to touch.

Some time later Dominic murmured into her hair. "What time does your flight back to Shannon leave today?"

Good God, she'd forgotten all about that and the restaurant for a moment. Poor Bernadette could end up with all the preparations. She leapt from the bed, knowing and enjoying that Dominic was taking in every inch of her.

She found her ticket in her bag. "Three o'clock," she read aloud.

Dominic reached out to the bedside cabinet and picked up his watch. "Then we've a few hours yet. What will we do to amuse ourselves?"

"What do you mean?" she asked, puzzled.

"Well, much as I'd like to stay in bed with you all day, we'll have plenty of time for that other days."

She liked the sound of that.

"Won't we?" he said again, quietly.

She smiled down at him. And nodded.

He drew her back onto the bed beside him. "So what had you planned to do today?" he asked, lazily tracing her shoulderline again and making it very hard to concentrate. Her insides were melting.

Her voice was husky. "Something a proper tourist

would do. A London bus tour maybe, something that doesn't take long."

"Would you mind if I came with you?" he asked suddenly.

"Mind? I'd love it," she admitted. "But don't you have meetings or business to do?"

"I rescheduled them this morning, while you were still sleeping. One of the bonuses of being the boss," he explained with a grin.

"So I'm in your hands for the day," Maura said, well aware of the double meaning.

Dominic made the phrase reality, touching her softly, and pulling her body in close against his. "Well, if you put it like that," he whispered, "who am I to say no?"

By eleven they were climbing onto a tourist bus, rugged up against the cold wind.

Maura couldn't shake off the feeling of unreality, but was happy to go along with every second of it. As the bus pulled out from the kerb, the tour guide began her spiel, pointing out landmarks and painting a picture of London's history.

Or Maura assumed she did. The commentary was just a soundtrack to her own soft conversation with Dominic. The subjects of Carla and Ardmahon House may have been out-of-bounds, but there seemed to be a hundred other things to talk about. She looked up at him, amazed to see him so relaxed, feeling the sensual charge of his finger tracing the top of her hand. They laughed and talked so much that the guide began shooting cross glances across at them.

"Have you got the general idea?" Dominic said quietly.

Maura nodded. Holding hands, they both jumped from the bus as it slowed to go round a corner near Hyde Park. She felt like a naughty teenager.

"I'd rather walk with you anyway," he said, one arm gently across her back. As they walked into Hyde Park they passed a small souvenir stall.

"Wait a moment?" He put his hand on her arm. She stood, pulling her coat in tightly around her, watching as he had an animated conversation with the stall-holder and laughed at something the young man said. She already knew a line appeared in Dominic's right cheek when he grinned. And that his eyes creased into laughter first. And that his dark hair was starting to go very slightly grey. She had noticed all these things intimately over the last twelve hours and she hugged them to her like a secret.

He walked toward her, offering a small paper bag. "A little present for you. You can't come to London and leave without a souvenir. Especially a rare one like this."

She smiled, accepting the package. It was a bright red London bus brooch, complete with smiling passengers waving through the windows. She laughed to see it. "It is beautiful, really exquisite," she said, solemnly. "Thank you so much, Dominic, I'll treasure it."

"I was sure you would." He smiled down at her.

* * *

He insisted on coming to Heathrow airport in the taxi with her, despite her protests.

"Would a gentleman leave his lady to battle the traffic of London alone? Of course he wouldn't." He kissed her gently on the mouth. "I'll be back in Ireland tomorrow night – we've a lot to talk about, to tell each other, Maura," he said softly.

She was suddenly overwhelmed with a rush of feeling. She didn't really trust herself to speak. She kissed him goodbye.

He was still waiting as she went through the check-in and through to the departure lounge. She caught sight of her reflection in a wall mirror. There was no other word for it, she thought. She was glowing.

Chapter Thirty

Bernadette collected her from Shannon Airport.

"Well, there's a girl that's enjoyed a break," she said with a laugh, noticing Maura's sparkling eyes. "The bright lights suit you, by the looks of things."

"Something like that," Maura said with a smile. It was too soon to share her secret with anyone. She satisfied Bernadette's curiosity with tales about Joel, and rapturous descriptions of the restaurant. The rest she kept to herself.

Bernadette had been true to her word. All the preparations were ready for the weekend's restaurant nights. Maura laughed as Bernadette showed her the extra tables in the dining-room, all hastily borrowed from one of the big hotels in Ennis.

"I just couldn't say no to the bookings. How do you possibly turn down the food editors from the big magazines and three famous pop-stars. Haven't we plenty of food to go around?" she said with a grin.

There didn't seem to be any sign of Carla in the house.

"She told me she's having a night out in Galway," Bernadette explained as they continued the preparations in the kitchen. "I tried diplomatically to let her know that Dominic didn't really want her going too far from the house, but she was having none of that." Bernadette laughed. "She left not long after you did yesterday, some fellow in a motorbike picked her up, an old friend from her modelling agency I think she said."

Maura said nothing, busying herself at the sink washing fresh herbs from the garden. Bernadette continued chatting away.

"But she'll be back tomorrow, she's booked in a whole gang of her Dublin pals."

"That's great," Maura said brightly. She didn't mind in the least. In the mood she was in she would happily serve every person Carla had ever met.

Bernadette gave her an odd look, as if puzzled at her sudden enthusiasm for Carla. "And Dominic rang a little while ago, to say he'd be back on the last flight tomorrow night, in time for the final course," she said.

Maura hid her face again, surprised at the rush of feeling hearing his name gave her. "Oh, really," she said noncommittally. She hugged her secret close, half-wanting to tell Bernadette everything, but also needing to keep it all to herself for a little while longer.

* * *

Saturday evening was chilly, and as the guests arrived at Ardmahon House in small groups they moved gratefully into the drawing-room to enjoy a pre-dinner drink and the warmth of the open fire.

Maura moved easily among them, her nerves sharply alive, an air of excitement making her eyes sparkle and skin glow. She knew it was partly the excitement of tonight being the final night in the cooking residency, but mostly her anticipation of Dominic's imminent return.

She had dressed with great care, deliberately choosing an elegant green dress that highlighted the rich red of her hair. It wasn't the most practical of dresses but she wanted to be sure she looked good out in the dining-room, even if she had to cover herself in a voluminous apron in the kitchen.

"You look terrific," Bernadette said warmly, noticing her mood. "Who'd have thought we'd get to the final night so quickly – it all seems a bit unreal, doesn't it?"

Maura spontaneously hugged the older woman. "It's been wonderful," she said, "and it's been fantastic working with you, Bernadette. Don't start me, or I'll get all sentimental and ruin the meals tonight."

She spoke briefly to a food writer from one of the Dublin newspapers, who in turn introduced her to a magazine editor over from Glasgow. Cormac had arrived again unexpectedly, with a young woman who was obviously much more responsive and interested in his flirtations than Maura had ever been. He was slightly less attentive to Maura this time, but still managed to overload her with outrageous compliments.

Following the format of the previous evenings,

Maura gave a short speech explaining a little about Australian food and outlining the night's menu, before inviting everyone to move into the dining-room.

She and Bernadette had decided on a different approach for the last two nights – rather than three distinct courses, they were serving five smaller courses, allowing the diners to try even more flavours. This style of dining was hard work for the waitresses, who had barely taken one course out than they were collecting the plates, but it was a great way of demonstrating the wide range of Australian cooking styles.

As she spoke, she noticed Carla whispering away to one of her friends, pointing to Maura as she spoke. The friend giggled at Carla's words. Maura felt uncomfortable for a moment, feeling self-conscious about the way she looked compared to all their style and glamour, until the thought of Dominic's intentions that night calmed her. All day she had let thoughts leap into her head about him, about their night together and the possibilities of what would happen between them now. Carla was the least of her concerns.

The guests moved through into the dining-room, the lively buzz of their conversations drifting through to Maura in the kitchen, where the preparations were in full swing.

There were five helpers, each working away setting up the array of dishes.

The first course was a choice between an Asian-style sweet-potato soup or a rich, intensely flavoured fish soup, served with wattle-seed rolls, baked fresh that evening and still warm from the oven. This was followed by an artistically arranged selection of seafood, each prepared by a different method – salmon with an Australian native spice and black pepper crust, grilled prawns, satayed scallops, freshly made seafood spring rolls and a morsel of smoked salmon. Each plate also held a selection of dipping sauces made using the Australian bush herbs Maura had brought with her.

The next course was entrée-sized chicken pieces, which Maura had marinated in soy and ginger, then quickly grilled. It was served on wilted spinach and bok choy, nestling on a bed of sesame-oil-flavoured Hokkien noodles.

The Lorikeet Hill wines were perfectly matched to each dish too. Through the course of the evening, her guests would enjoy the whole range of Nick's winemaking skills, from the light fresh Riesling he was becoming known for, right through to the rich, fruit-filled Shiraz that was almost a meal in itself.

The final savoury course was what she had dubbed the Lorikeet Hill Platter. Each round white plate had six different tastes beautifully arranged upon it – marinated local lamb, fillet of beef cooked with Australian native pepperberries, poached salmon in coconut milk, a tiny smoked chicken pie, just a taste of lemon myrtle pasta in olive oil and a wild mushroom tart baked with light, crispy pastry. A mixed salad of greens flavoured with a delicate dressing added colour.

Just before the platters were served, the mushroom tarts would be coated with a rich sauce from a pan bubbling on the stove, a heady mix of garlic, olive oil and herbs. She would pour the rich mixture over the mushrooms, sprinkle with local vintage cheese and give the lot a blast under the grill to half-melt the cheese and allow the garlic and olive oil to run through the mushrooms.

The platters were almost ready – only the mushroom tarts were needed now. As Maura stirred the garlic and olive oil concoction, she realised parsley was missing. Damn. She looked around but there was only a sprig or two left on the wide counter. She remembered there was a large tub of it growing in the greenhouse at the end of the garden. She had a few minutes and dashed out to pick some, asking Shona, her kitchen assistant, to keep stirring while she did so.

It was a beautifully clear night, cold but crisp and as Maura walked quickly down to the greenhouse she breathed in the fragrant air, feeling the tremble of excitement in her again. Dominic would be here soon.

As she entered the kitchen again, a large bunch of fresh parsley in her hand, she was surprised to see Carla leave through the door back into the dining-room.

"What was she doing in here?" she asked Shona, who was still stirring the saucepan, quite red-faced from the steam and heat rising from the stove. Since the time Bernadette had chased her out with a threat of enforced carrot peeling, apart from attending the course Carla had avoided the kitchen. "She said she needed a few bottles of mineral water for her table and asked me to get them for her from the coolroom, was that all right?" the young girl asked anxiously.

"Of course," Maura answered quickly. "It's just you have to make sure you keep stirring this sauce, it sticks so easily," she said, taking over quickly and checking that the garlic hadn't stuck to the bottom of the pan.

"Oh, it's okay," Shona said, smiling nervously. "She stirred it for me while I got her the water."

"Oh, good," Maura reassured her helper, looking into the pan. Carla cooking, now there was a novel thought. Maybe the course had taught her something. As she looked into the pan, she noticed a strange greenish film forming on top of it. That was odd. She took a spoon and had a quick taste, nearly gagging at the flavour.

"Shona, did you see Carla add anything to this?" she asked quickly.

Shona shook her head vigorously. "No, of course not. Well, I was only in the coolroom for a moment, but I don't think she did."

Maura felt a rush of sudden anxiety. A moment would have been all Carla needed. She looked around quickly. Under the sink counter beside the stove was an opened bottle of industrial strength disinfectant, which they used each night to scour the floor. Maura had a sudden feeling of foreboding. She carefully tasted the sauce again, nearly choking.

"She wouldn't have," Maura said softly to herself. Then she thought again. Yes, Carla would have.

Maura quickly called Bernadette over, from where she was supervising the assembly of the last of the platters. The trays of mushroom tarts were ready for the grill.

"Smell this," Maura asked her urgently.

Bernadette pulled a face as she sniffed the sauce. "That's disgusting, what is it?"

"Carla's specialty," Maura almost hissed. "I think she's poured disinfectant into the sauce."

Bernadette looked at her aghast. "When, just now?"

Maura nodded. "I'll explain later. We'll have to forget about the mushrooms tonight. This could have killed someone, or made them very, very sick."

Maura spoke urgently to the kitchen staff. Without giving a reason, she explained that the platters would have to be hastily rearranged, to hide the gap where the mushroom tarts should have been. Luckily she always over-catered. There would still be plenty on each platter. She would just have to hope that four courses down the line no-one would remember her speech at the beginning of the evening previewing what tonight's platters would contain.

The staff moved quickly, as Maura poured the sauce down the sink to avoid the possibility of anyone accidentally having a taste. She kept a tiny bit in a jar. "Forensic purposes," she said grimly to Bernadette. "God help me, I'll kill her myself, if she doesn't get me first."

The murmur of voices from the dining-room soothed her worry that everyone might be getting anxious, waiting for the next course. The Lorikeet Hill wine was obviously flowing freely. She still had a few more minutes.

Looking out into the dining-room, she noticed through her anxiety that Dominic had arrived. She was too agitated at the moment to react as she watched him take his seat at Carla's table. Carla had seemed almost glittering tonight, a strange nervous excitement surrounding her. Maura knew why now.

The newly arranged platters were ready. With a deep sigh of relief, Maura watched as the waiting staff moved efficiently to deliver the plates to all the tables. She heard the murmur of voices rise and fall again, as the diners started to enjoy the elaborate range of flavours.

Bernadette touched her arm. "Are you all right?"

Maura nodded, giving her a half smile. "Good thing she used green disinfectant," she said with a small laugh. "If it had been one of the other clear bleaches I might not have noticed."

Bernadette shook her head grimly. There was no time to discuss it now, with the dessert plates still to be prepared. Maura was again giving each diner a selection of tastes, including a sharp citrus tart, home-made honey icecream, using blue-gum honey she had brought with her from the Clare Valley and a tiny chocolate truffle flavoured with macadamia nut. She also hadn't been able to resist serving pavlova, a rich meringue dessert that had been invented in Australia, served with fruit salad and plenty of rich local cream.

They were halfway through the preparations when

one of the waiters came running through the kitchen door.

"Someone's sick, quick, we have to call an ambulance!"

Maura and Bernadette moved quickly out into the dining-room, half-knowing what they'd see.

Carla was groaning and writhing in her seat. "I've been poisoned," she was shouting. "It must have been a toadstool!" The other diners were twisting in their seats to watch the commotion.

Maura felt a fierce coldness run through her. So that had been her game.

She walked quickly towards Carla's table, her anger increasing at the sight of Dominic, his concerned face close to Carla, his arm around her. His platter lay untouched in front of him.

"What's happening here?" she asked, icy calm.

Carla looked up, a dramatic grimace on her face. As Maura came close, she gave another groan, doubling over and clutching her stomach.

"It's her fault," she groaned, pointing at Maura. "She's served us poisonous toadstools instead of mushrooms!" She gave another long groan.

The other tables had gone quiet. Maura noticed through Carla's fuss that the other diners were looking at their plates, wondering if they too were about to be struck down.

"There weren't any mushrooms on the platter tonight, Carla," she said quietly.

Carla groaned. "Yes, there were, and you've given

me a poisonous one. I thought it looked like a toadstool. Ohhh," she clutched her stomach again.

"No, Carla, there weren't any mushrooms tonight, I changed the ingredients at the last minute," Maura said calmly. Her voice carried through the quiet dining-room and she half-noticed people around her looking at their platters. She heard one man say confidently to his partner that he certainly hadn't seen any mushrooms on his platter.

"Yes, there were, in those little tarts I saw in the kitchen," Carla seemed to be recovering with amazing speed.

Maura gestured toward Dominic's untouched platter. "Perhaps you could show them to me," she said, her voice now dangerously low.

Carla looked at Dominic's platter. Her expression changed to one of mutinous anger as she realised the truth of Maura's statement.

Maura looked quickly at Dominic, too preoccupied to take in the loaded look he gave her.

Carla's recovery was as sudden as it was miraculous. She swept her platter to the floor. "Your food is rubbish, anyway, mushrooms or no mushrooms."

There were shocked gasps from the other diners. This was becoming quite a floor show. They'd expected great food and wine, but this after-dinner entertainment was quite a bonus.

Dominic suddenly stirred from his shocked amazement. "Come outside now, Carla," he said, his voice dangerously firm. "That's enough."

Carla was almost dragged by Dominic from the dining-room, followed by two of her friends who seemed as puzzled at her behaviour as everyone else.

Maura took a deep breath and faced the dining-room, forcing a smile onto her face.

"I do apologise, everyone," she said, as confidently as she could manage. "I can assure you all there were absolutely no mushrooms, poisonous or otherwise, in your meal. Please enjoy the rest of this course, and in a little while I hope you'll enjoy our selection of desserts."

The thought of the forthcoming desserts seemed to have an immediate calming effect. Maura was relieved to see the low murmur of voices and the clink of cutlery and glasses start up again almost immediately.

Thank God the wine's relaxed them, she thought to herself, as she helped the waiter quickly pick up Carla's discarded platter from the floor. She saw with relief that Bernadette was moving around the dining-room, making light of Carla's display and helping to soothe the patrons.

The rest of the dinner passed in a blur. Maura busied herself in the kitchen, listening with relief to the enthusiastic compliments the waiting staff were bringing in to her.

There was no opportunity to seek out Dominic, or Carla, though she noticed neither returned to their table. As liqueurs were served, she returned to the dining-room, stopping to talk briefly to the people at each table, and be introduced to the food writers and other influential guests, only half-hearing their remarks.

It was past one before the kitchen was cleared. She sent the staff out to enjoy a drink in the now empty dining-room, and leaned back against the counter, closing her eyes.

"What the hell was all that about?" she dimly heard Bernadette ask.

"You tell me," she said wearily. This was no time to explain all that had happened between her and Dominic. She had an inkling Carla had suspected something, and tonight's action was her last-ditch effort to ruin Maura's trip once and for all. "All I know is that if anyone had eaten that sauce there would have been a lot of very sick people here tonight. Maybe even worse." She had inspected the bottle of disinfectant again. It was a lethal mixture.

Bernadette looked at her closely. "You're nearly asleep on your feet. I'll finish up here. Go to your bed, girl, before you collapse in front of me. We'll talk about it tomorrow."

Maura nodded, too strung out to argue.

This wasn't the night she'd been hoping for. She hadn't expected Carla to react delightedly to whatever Dominic was going to say to her tonight, but she hadn't expected anything as bad as this.

Up in her room, she showered and changed into a long black slip, the closest thing she had to something sexy. God knows she wasn't going to put on the green pyjamas. She knew Dominic was just down the hall. Her hands were shaking as she waited for him to come to her room.

By two, puzzled that he hadn't appeared, she could wait no longer. She went out into the corridor and looked down the hall. Carla and Dominic used the main double suite of rooms whenever they stayed here.

She tiptoed down toward their suite. The light was on, the door slightly ajar. Knocking quietly, she walked in silently. There was no-one in the sitting-room that adjoined the main bedroom. She moved almost in slow motion toward the main bedroom. The door was half-open. She could hear the rise and fall of voices. She was dazed with tiredness and an overwhelming feeling to get things out in the open there and then. She and Dominic could talk about it all in front of Carla if they had to.

The plush carpet muffled the sound of her footsteps. She was in front of the open door, taking in the scene for a long moment before the sight fully registered in her tired brain.

Carla was completely naked, lying on top of the bedcover. Dominic was naked from the waist up. Maura's eyes took in the look of his naked back, glowing in the lamplight.

He was leaning over Carla, gently brushing back the hair from her forehead. Maura's skin tingled, as she remembered the feel of his fingers doing the same thing to her.

She could hear his words clearly. "I promised your

father," he was saying to Carla in a soothing, low voice. "I won't let him down, I'll always be there for you."

Maura took a deep breath in shock. She couldn't believe what she was hearing. Her gasp made Dominic look up and his eyes widened in surprise.

"Maura," he breathed.

Maura suddenly came out of her stupor. Her eyes hardened as she took in the loving scene before her.

"Now I'm the stupid one," she said, coldly and clearly.

Only a last shred of dignity stopped her from running out of the room. Ignoring Dominic's harsh whisper for her to wait, she barely registered her journey as she passed through the sitting-room again, out into the corridor. She quickly found her room, pushed the door shut, and locked it with a quick movement.

Only when she was inside did the real reaction set in. She leaned her forehead against the wooden panel of the door, feeling her breath come in short gasps.

The word 'fool' kept going through her mind. Gone was the pleasure of the memory of her night with Dominic, which had been rippling through her all day, like a special secret. Instead she felt embarrassment and shame and anger. She'd been absolutely, completely taken in. He would never leave Carla. Whatever was between them was too strong.

It seemed like hours, but could only have been minutes later, that she heard Dominic's voice through the door.

"Maura, let me in, let me explain," he said urgently.

She shook her head, not daring to answer. "Go away," she whispered, so softly he couldn't have heard. "Leave me alone."

She knew there was only the door between them. She could feel his hand against the door knob, hear his voice imploring her to listen to him. Her face still pressed against the wood, she just whispered again. "Leave me alone," over and over.

He finally went away.

It was a long time before she straightened, her head spinning. She didn't undress, didn't wash. She just took a few unsteady steps and fell forward onto her bed. Something sharp pricked against her arm. She rose up and saw the London bus brooch lying on the bedcover, the clasp open. She picked it up and hurled it across the room.

When sleep came, it was troubled and full of turmoil. She imagined noises in the corridor, footsteps running up and down outside her room, loud voices and sudden snatches of conversations.

She slept finally, just as the dawn was breaking.

Chapter Thirty-one

Bernadette was alone in the kitchen when Maura finally came down the next morning. It was past noon. Bernadette took one look at her drawn face and pulled her into a hug.

"Do you want to talk about it?" she said softly. "Do you want to tell me what's going on?"

Maura started to speak, looking anxiously at the door. Bernadette guessed her thoughts.

"They're not here. Carla was taken away in an ambulance last night. Dominic is with her."

Maura laughed a strange, bitter laugh. "More food poisoning?" she asked. "God, she doesn't give up, does she?"

Bernadette shook her head. She was completely confused herself. "She took an overdose of something, we don't know what it was. It happened after everyone had gone to bed, we think."

Maura looked up at her. "She looked all right when

I saw her, perfectly happy," she managed to say, before the image of Dominic leaning over Carla hit her again. Her voice broke.

As Bernadette enveloped her in her arms again, Maura told her everything. "I thought there was really something between us," she whispered. "I feel so stupid, how could I have been so stupid?"

Bernadette hushed her. "Ssh, love, you haven't been stupid at all. There's more to this than either of us know yet. I've seen Dominic look at you, seen the way he watches you all the time. I don't think this is the end of it."

"I heard him talking to her, I heard what he said," Maura said, the anger giving her spirit again. She looked up at Bernadette, the tears dried now. "He'll never leave her, I know that now. I was just a silly one-night stand."

"Not so silly, by the sound of things," Bernadette said quietly.

A flash of their night together took Maura unawares. Trust me, she remembered him saying. Like a fool she had.

"Yes, silly," she said, biting her lip to stop the tears again. She took a deep breath and looked up at Bernadette. "I was stupid. Never again. I've learnt my lesson now."

Bernadette just shook her head. "There are always two sides to a story," she said.

"Oh, yes," Maura laughed a mocking laugh. "And here's what they are. Dominic is at dear Carla's hospital bedside, her little stunt having worked a treat. I am here, embarrassed and shamed. In three days' time I go back to Australia. We all live happily ever after. *The End*. That's both sides of the story." She heard the bitterness in her own voice but didn't care.

Maura didn't want to talk about it again that morning. She felt bad about rejecting Bernadette's repeated attempts to give Dominic the benefit of the doubt, finally asking her to stop mentioning his name. The house seemed very quiet. A weak winter sun was shining, and she took her coffee out into the garden. She looked around, trying to memorise it but knowing she didn't really need to. Every image of the last month was imprinted deep in her mind. Her discoveries about Catherine. The visits to the wine-sellers. The talk in Ennis. The cooking schools. And Dominic. Her mind kept returning to him.

Rita phoned a little later, to congratulate Maura on the success of the trip and to report on the increase in Lorikeet Hill sales around the country. The whole exchange had been very worthwhile for all the Australian winemakers, it seemed.

"We'll have to do it again soon," Rita said enthusiastically, before saying goodbye. Maura was grateful for all she had done. Perhaps one day she would come back to Ireland. But it would never again be the place she had imagined.

Bernadette guessed her mood and ignoring her protests bundled her into the car for a day of touring.

"You'll just mope all day if you're stuck inside. Come on, girl, you've three days left in the wonderful west of Ireland, let's at least have a look at some of it."

Maura reluctantly agreed. Bernadette was right, she felt like moping. In fact, she felt like hurling herself on the bed and howling. She felt embarrassed for being taken in by Dominic, furious at Carla for her part in it. And she felt sad – that was the worse feeling of all. As though a wonderful dream had ended suddenly.

Bernadette drove at a furious pace, determined to show Maura as much as possible. They travelled across the Burren to the Cliffs of Moher, then stopped at a whitewashed pub in the seaside village of Ballyvaughan. As they settled by an open fire, with glasses of Guinness and big bowls of steaming chowder in front of them, Maura felt some tension slide from her body. Bernadette noticed it and gave her a big smile.

"That's my girl, you have to keep your spirits up at times like this. I'm sorry to sound like a broken record, but a story's not a story till you've reached the end. And I don't think we've heard the last of this one."

Maura laughed despite herself. "Bernadette, you sound like some mysterious sorcerer. What next, a spell on all of us? Look, I'm overreacting. It was a holiday romance that ended badly, that's all. If I can tell myself that, you can too. It's all over, I was stupid, I'll never see Dominic or Carla again, and that's that."

Maura knew immediately her brave words weren't fooling Bernadette.

"Don't do what I did, and live to regret it," the older woman said.

"What did you do? One night of passion and your life changed in an instant?" Even as she spoke Maura knew she'd hit on a nerve.

Bernadette smiled ruefully. "Bull's-eye. Twenty years ago and I still remember it."

Maura felt contrite for her lightheartedness. "Oh, Bernadette, I'm sorry, tell me, what happened?"

"It was quite a different story to yours, but I know how you're feeling now. We were like you and Dominic are together – always conscious of each other. There was a real attraction but neither of us would admit it."

Maura blinked. Had she and Dominic been like that? As obvious as that?

Bernadette continued. "I was thirty, very stubborn. I had my chance but I was too proud to do anything about it. He finally gave up trying to convince me. It was on his wedding day that I realised how wrong I had been."

"And you kept your heart for him for the rest of your life?" Maura breathed.

Bernadette threw back her head and laughed. "Oh, God no! There's been a few since then. But I think I let the best one get away from me." She put on a mock deep voice. "Don't make the same mistake I did, my girl."

Maura felt a little better and smiled up at her. "Too late for this one, but if it happens again, I won't, I promise."

"Good girl yourself," Bernadette encouraged her. "I tell you, things will turn out for the best. They usually do."

As they drove back, Maura felt an echo of her old spirit come back. She tried to think of the bright side. The export trip had been a success. In just a few days she'd be home in Clare, meeting little Quinn and enjoying sitting down with Nick and Fran, telling them all the good news about the response in Ireland to Lorikeet Hill wine.

Bernadette and Maura drove up the long avenue to Ardmahon House. They were going to pack up their belongings from there this afternoon, and spend the last two nights at Bernadette's house, where the repairs were all but finished.

"Just in time, we're about to be overrun by builders again here," Bernadette explained. "Dominic said . . ."

Maura shot her a look. They had agreed not to talk about Dominic or Carla any more.

"I can tell you this," Bernadette protested. "They're having more renovations done, though God knows what there is left to do."

They let themselves in through the front door. The answering machine by the telephone was flicking at them, the number display showing they had missed five calls. Bernadette pressed it absentmindedly as she passed by.

"More desperate diners, insisting we open up for one more night probably," she said, walking past.

The first two messages were hang-ups and then her brother Nick's voice suddenly filled the hallway. Maura hardly recognised it.

"Maura, it's me, can you ring me on this number? It's urgent." He had left two other messages, less than half an hour apart, his voice becoming increasingly more anxious as he repeated the international number for Maura to call.

Maura looked at Bernadette, worry freezing her blood. She didn't recognise the number in South Australia, only realising from the area code that it was in the Adelaide area.

After a frustrating ten-minute delay, while a soft-toned operator explained that the lines were temporarily congested, she finally got through. A brisk voice answered. Maura didn't catch what she said.

"Is Nick Carmody there? It's his sister, calling from Ireland," she asked urgently. Bernadette stood by, concerned and watchful.

"Just one moment, I'll put you through," the voice said.

Nick must have snatched up the phone as soon as it rang.

"Maura, thank God you got the message," she heard him whisper. "We're at the children's hospital in Adelaide. It's Quinn."

Chapter Thirty-two

Maura's heart nearly stopped. "Nick, what is it?" she whispered.

Nick's voice was shaking. "He nearly died, Maura. Fran got to him just in time. She went to check on him in the middle of the night and he wasn't breathing."

Maura could feel Nick's anguish down the phone, as he tried to tell her what had happened.

"She gave him mouth to mouth and revived him and he was rushed to hospital. We don't know if he'll live."

12,000 miles away, Maura felt a rush of clarity.

"I'm leaving now, Nick," she said, suddenly calm. "I'll be home as soon as I can." She barely said goodbye to him.

Bernadette had heard the conversation and took her cue from Maura. While Maura ran upstairs to pack, Bernadette rang nearby Shannon Airport. There was a flight leaving in an hour that would get her to London.

From there she'd try for the next available flight to Adelaide.

They drove to Shannon in near silence. At the departure gate Maura hugged Bernadette close, hoping the touch would convey all that she wished she could say.

"Will you call me when you get the chance?" Bernadette asked, nearly in tears herself.

Maura nodded.

"God love you all," Bernadette said, giving her a final hug.

The flight to London passed quickly. At the international desk Maura urgently explained what had happened, willing the man to help her. She smiled gratefully as he managed to find her a seat on a flight to Australia leaving in the next couple of hours.

The journey was like a long, drawn-out nightmare. All she wanted was to be home, not sitting close to two strangers who kept giving her curious glances. She had put on her headphones within seconds of settling into her seat and sat with her eyes shut, pointedly ignoring any attempts at conversation. She had nothing to say. She wanted to see Nick and Fran and Quinn. Nobody and nothing else.

Her thoughts were troubled, the snatched sleep unsatisfying. Only a month before she had travelled the same route in reverse, filled with excitement and anticipation. Now Ireland, Catherine, and Dominic hardly featured in her thoughts. The worry of Quinn's illness took everything else away.

She had insisted neither Nick or Fran meet her at the airport. As she gathered her bags, for a second she longed for the homecoming they had originally planned. Nick and Fran and little Quinn were to have been waiting there at the arrivals gate. Right now she should have been holding Quinn for the first time.

Catching sight of herself in one of the mirrors on the airport pillars, she realised and didn't care that she looked a mess in the now crumpled dress she'd been wearing on her day-trip with Bernadette.

Squinting her eyes against the bright Adelaide morning sunshine, Maura made her way alone to the taxi rank and directed the driver to the children's hospital.

She saw Nick and Fran before they saw her. They were pressed close to a tiny cot at the end of a ward. She stood back for a moment, as she took in the scene. Quinn was motionless, with tubes coming from his nose and his tiny arms. Fran was gently stroking his little face.

Maura must have made a noise, for they both turned around slowly. Their faces were drawn, and they were barely able to raise a smile as she came toward them. "How is he, how are you all?" she whispered, as she looked down at her little nephew.

His tiny chest was barely rising up and down, and his pale skin was marked with bruises from where the doctors had taken blood samples. An oxygen-measuring device clipped to one of his fingers looked enormous beside his little hand.

He had a thatch of pitch-black hair, and she could

see a likeness to Nick in his little nose and the shape of his chin.

Fran didn't answer, not looking up from her little son. Maura realised she was still in terrible shock. Nick gave Maura a wan smile.

"He's alive," he whispered back. "That'll do us for now."

With a tired nod of agreement from Fran, Maura and Nick went out into the foyer, where a couple of couches were set up next to a coin-operated coffee machine.

"Coffee?" she asked Nick, who replied with a weary nod.

Maura got two cups of lukewarm coffee that smelled more of antiseptic than caffeine, and sat close to her brother on one of the sofas.

She glanced at a young couple sitting across from them. Both man and woman were racked with grief, the tears pouring down their cheeks. Maura couldn't begin to imagine what terrible news they had just had. She turned her attention back to Nick.

At her glance he tried to pull himself together. "Thanks for getting here so quickly, how was your flight? How was everything?"

Maura shrugged the questions away. "Forget all that for now. Tell me everything," she said gently.

Nick started to shudder, and she watched helplessly as tears started pouring down his face. "We thought he was gone," he managed to say. "He was turning blue, Maura. We thought we'd lost him."

"What happened?" she asked softly.

"He'd been a bit snuffly during the day, but we just thought he had a slight cold. We all went to bed early, and then Fran suddenly woke in the middle of the night, she doesn't know why, and went to his cot. That's when she realised he wasn't breathing. Thank God she knew what to do. What if it had been me who had woken up, I wouldn't have known what to do, he would have died . . ." The words were lost in Nick's sobs.

As he calmed, he continued the story. Fran had run into their bedroom with Quinn in her arms and started giving him mouth to mouth resuscitation.

"I called for an ambulance straight away. It seemed like hours before they arrived, but thank God it was only minutes. It's a terrible thing to say, but we were lucky, there'd been a car accident on the main road and the helicopter had been called to bring the injured man to hospital. They were able to take Quinn as well."

Nick answered her unspoken question.

"There was only room for Fran. I followed them in the car. It was the worst drive I've ever had. I just prayed and prayed that they would get there in time. The hospital was alerted that he was on his way and they put him on a ventilator as soon as he arrived.

"The doctors are still doing tests to find out what happened. All I keep thinking is that it was an absolute miracle that Fran went in when she did, and that she knew what to do. If it had been me . . ." he shuddered again.

Maura held him close.

"We couldn't bear to lose him, Maura," Nick looked up at her, his eyes glazed. "We love him so much. We've only had him a month, surely he couldn't be taken from us so soon?"

Maura held her brother close. "He'll be okay, won't he?"

Nick shook, trying to nod. "We don't know. We don't know. He's had three scares even since we've been in hospital. He's just suddenly stopped breathing. They've got him lying on a monitor, and they've checked for infections and run blood tests. But they still won't say for sure what's wrong."

Maura held him close. "He'll be okay, Nick. You're in the right place, he'll be okay."

She shut her eyes, fighting back her own panic and anguish.

Chapter Thirty-three

"It could be a few more days before I get up there – are you sure you're right to hang on?"

On the phone in the hospital foyer, Maura listened with relief as Gemma insisted that she was perfectly capable of looking after both the café and the winery.

"I owe you one, Gemma, thanks so much," Maura said wearily. Saying goodbye, she hung up the handset of the public phone and leant her forehead against the cool plastic. She read the obscene graffiti scratched into the wall, but it didn't register. In the three days she'd been back, the turmoil of her life hadn't calmed.

She worked out the time difference and quickly rang Bernadette. By the noise in the background, she had the builders in again.

Bernadette was very relieved to hear that Quinn was gradually improving.

"And how are you feeling, love? You mustn't know what side of the world you're on at all?"

"That's about it," Maura admitted. "I'm just tired, I guess, and I feel like I haven't really had a chance yet to think about everything that's happened."

There was a pause, then Bernadette spoke again, quickly.

"Dominic called by, very anxious for news of you . . ."

Maura interrupted her there. "Bernadette, I'm sorry, please don't talk to me about him, or to him about me, not just yet. I'll be ready to laugh it all off in a few months – just now I can't really handle it." Maura knew she was lying to herself. She was anxious for details of Dominic but the last thing she wanted was for Bernadette to know the extent of her heartache.

Bernadette wasn't that easily put off, though, and tried to mention Dominic again.

"Sorry, Bern, someone urgently needs to use the phone," Maura fibbed again. "I'll ring you again soon." She said goodbye and hung up quickly.

Over the next two days, Maura, Nick and Fran took turns sitting by Quinn's little cot, not wanting him to wake up and not have someone who loved him sitting close by. They each snatched some sleep back at the hotel room they were staying in, quickly showering then coming back to the hospital to let someone else take their turn having a rest.

The doctors were cautiously optimistic, but reluctant to announce a firm prognosis until they had finished running a series of tests.

Maura confronted the ward sister late on her third

afternoon back in Adelaide. They had had a frustrating morning, waiting for Quinn's specialist to turn up. Two hours past the appointment time, the ward sister had informed them that the specialist had been called away and wouldn't be in to see them and Quinn until the next morning. Nick and Fran had received the news calmly, so used to shocks and let-downs that another one hardly registered on them.

Maura wasn't so easily put off and followed the sister back to the ward office. "What do you mean he's been called away?" she asked the young woman, once Nick and Fran were out of earshot. "Isn't Quinn important enough? What is it, a golf game, I guess?" Her voice was tight with anger. The thought of Nick and Fran waiting with taut nerves on the results of the tests fuelled her temper.

The sister gently steered her back to the ward, hushing her as she did so. "We need to be as quiet as we can, for everyone's sake," she whispered, her hand on Maura's arm.

A wave of tiredness swept over her. "I'm sorry, I just feel useless for Nick and Fran. There must be something we can do?" she pleaded as she thought of her little nephew.

"Just keep willing him to get better – we always think they pick up those feelings," the nurse said with a sudden smile. "He's a little battler, you can tell just by looking at him."

A day passed before the specialist finally appeared

and brought good news with him. The tests showed that Quinn had suffered from a series of sleep apnoea episodes. "It's more common in adults than babies," the doctor explained. "The easiest way to explain what happens is that the sleeping person simply forgets to breathe. An adult will eventually wake up enough to take a deep breath but in a baby it can be much more serious."

Maura looked across at Nick and Fran, knowing they were both remembering the first frightening night, when Fran had found Quinn in his cot.

The doctor continued. "The tests have also detected a weakness in one of his lungs, and we want to keep a close eye on that, and keep him here until all the risk has passed." He went on to advise that when Nick and Fran took Quinn home they should install a monitoring device in his cot, which would send off an alarm if he stopped breathing again during his sleep. "But he's a strong little fellow," he said, touching Quinn lightly on the head. "He's going to be fine."

As the doctor moved on to his next patient, they were quiet, letting his words sink in. Fran held Quinn close against her chest, gently kissing his little dark head. She smiled at Maura and Nick, for what seemed like the first time in days. They grinned back at her. The relief trickled through them.

As the day passed, Maura watched Fran gradually emerge from the barricade of worry she had built around herself. Her eyes cleared, the tension eased from her body and she seemed to become aware of everything around her again.

Maura smiled at her. "Welcome back, Fran."

Fran smiled back. "Welcome back too, Maura."

The mood changed from that moment on. As they sat around Quinn's cot, Maura started telling stories about her trip to Ireland, deliberately keeping it light.

It wasn't until Fran was at the hotel later that afternoon that Maura told Nick the whole story about her trip to Catherine's village. She was surprised how easy it was to talk about it. She wasn't running away from it any more. She'd actually done it, discovered something about her mother. Nick didn't say much at first – that wasn't his way, she knew that. But he listened intently as she spoke, and she knew that he was carefully watching her face as she related the story.

As Fran came back into the ward, Maura changed the subject. Fran knew the sketchy details, and Maura didn't mind if Nick told her everything later. But for the time being she wanted it just between her and Nick.

"Just in time, Fran," Maura looked up with a smile, noticing that Fran looked years younger now the tension had eased. "I was just about to give Nick the rundown on how Lorikeet Hill was greeted by cheering crowds in every Irish village."

Nick was hungry for all the details about the response to his wine, and Maura noticed with pleasure that he avidly read the notebook in which she had written every comment she had heard about it.

"I'm proud of you," he said unexpectedly, as they sat in the foyer later in the day, again attempting to drink the terrible coffee.

She looked up suddenly from the newspaper she was reading. "Pardon?" she said, not sure if she'd heard him correctly.

"I'm proud of you."

"Don't be silly," she said hurriedly, unused to comments like this from her brother. "It was your wine, I just had to talk about it."

"I'm not talking about the wine. I'm talking about you looking for Catherine and the fact that you did it. Terri would have been really glad you did."

Maura felt her eyes fill with tears. She blinked them away. She tried to think of some wisecrack to lessen the mood, lighten the moment, then realised she didn't need to do that with Nick any more.

"Thanks," she said softly. "I'm glad too."

Chapter Thirty-four

"Has anyone else noticed this is the third day in a row I've worn this T-shirt?" Fran asked the next afternoon in the hospital. Clothes and food and sleep had hardly mattered in the first worrying days, but now the storm had passed, all sorts of ordinary things were becoming important again.

"Do you want me to go shopping and get you some fresh things?" Maura asked, looking up from her impromptu desk at the bedside cabinet. She was trying to make a start on her magazine article.

"I've a cupboard of these at home," Fran answered. "It's a waste to buy new ones. If it won't bother you both looking at me, it won't kill me to wear it for a few more days," she added with a grin.

Maura volunteered immediately. "Look, why don't I drive up to Clare, pack a few suitcases of fresh clothes for us all, and check on the winery and café while I'm there?"

She could tell Nick was relieved at the idea. While Gemma and one of Nick's fellow winemakers in the Valley had been keeping an eye on the most urgent matters, she was sure he must be getting slightly anxious about being away.

"Can you check if the new tanks have arrived yet?" Nick asked, confirming her thoughts.

"And could you give our garden at home a good watering?" Fran asked. "It's been so dry, I just hope everything's survived these past few days."

"And could you check the water pump in the back vineyard is still working?" Nick added.

Maura laughed as the list got longer. She stood up, deciding to make a start for Clare there and then. "Why don't I get going with this for starters and you can ring me if you think of anything else." She said goodbye to little Quinn, smiling as she noticed again the healthy pink glow coming into his skin. His eyes were getting brighter and more alert every day too. He was well on the way back.

As she headed north, driving with the late afternoon traffic, it took some time to get used to the stiff gear-change in Nick and Fran's battered old four-wheel drive. She hit the end of the peak hour, a stream of traffic around her, as she drove through Adelaide's flat northern suburbs – a series of car yards, suburban shopping centres and housing developments.

Once she was clear of the town of Gawler, forty minutes north of Adelaide, she knew she would virtually have the road to herself. She had done this trip many times in her life, and could name the small towns along the way with ease, knowing each bend and turn of the highway.

She looked at the scenery with fresh eyes, comparing it to the Irish countryside. She remembered the way she had described it to people in Ireland. She'd talked about the space and the isolation. As the sun set, throwing huge splashes of dark pink into the sky to her left, she noticed that space even more, especially after the confinement of the past seven days, on the plane and in the hospital.

The spectacle of the sunset had a soothing effect on her as the car filled with the strange pink light she always associated with late summer in South Australia. For the first time since she'd arrived home, she let herself dwell completely on Dominic and the last night she had seen him, caressing a naked Carla.

She didn't feel angry this time. Instead, as she recalled that evening, she felt the tears start to well up. Cross with herself, she roughly wiped them away with the back of her hand. She pretended it was a release of tension, a mixture of the worry about Quinn and the shock and jet-lag of her sudden departure. But she knew, if she was honest with herself, that most of it was sorrow about losing Dominic.

She had felt so close to him that night in London, emotionally as well as physically. She kept getting flashes of memories from their trip together, the strange tension and awareness that had been between them since the moment they met, her dawning realisation of her strong attraction to him. She had hugged the secret of him close, after London really believing that there was the possibility of something, somehow, between them.

She cried aloud, feeling some relief as she drove faster than the speed limit. It made her feel a little better. No happier, but better. She hadn't felt like this when she and Richard had finished. Did that mean that he hadn't been her true love and Dominic was? Or was this just a fantasy too, and her reaction worse because of that?

As she drove further, she felt a weary calmness. In the fading light, she noticed the yellow paddocks lining both sides of the road. It looked like there hadn't been any rain at all in the month she'd been in Ireland. All along the roadside was high yellow grass, and she could see plenty of rough undergrowth under the trees in the paddocks either side of the road. She frowned as she noticed it. The Mid-North of South Australia had suffered terrible bushfires several years before, and many of the trees had only this year grown back enough new, light-green leaves to hide the black stumps. It looked like all the natural bushfire fuel had grown back too.

She felt the familiar skip in her heart as she drove around the sweeping corner into the village of Auburn and read the sign welcoming her to the Clare Valley.

The green of the vines was as calming and beautiful as ever. She was impatient to be home now, and had to keep a careful eye on the speedo to stop herself from driving too fast in her haste. The villages of Leasingham, Watervale, Penwortham and Sevenhill flashed by.

Just on the outskirts of Clare, she saw the sign for Lorikeet Hill on the main road and laughed aloud. Nick must have had it freshly painted while she was away. He'd added a line to the bottom: *Now enjoyed in Ireland*.

She pulled into Lorikeet Hill's driveway, the heavy wheels crunching on the gravel. She didn't get out of the car immediately, taking a moment to lean back against the seat, and savour the view around her. As she did, the front door opened and she saw Gemma come out onto the verandah, followed by a well-built man wearing an Akubra hat. As she watched, Gemma pulled him into her arms and gave him a very long, very passionate kiss.

Maura grinned. So that was why Gemma was so keen to stay on.

The noise of the door of the four-wheel drive creaking open caught their attention and they both spun around. To her surprise, Maura recognised the man as Keith Drewer, a successful local farmer who had been several years ahead of her at school.

"Hello, Gemma, hello, Keith," she called, an amused tone in her voice.

Gemma pulled back from Keith and ran toward Maura with a beaming smile.

"Welcome home, it's great to see you!" she smiled, throwing her arms around her friend.

Maura hugged her back, whispering as she did so. "Sorry to interrupt, will I come back later?"

"Don't be ridiculous," Gemma laughed out loud, and threw a remark over her shoulder. "It's fine, Keith's just leaving, aren't you, darling?" Gemma exaggerated the endearment and Maura was amused to see Keith blush.

Imagine, Gemma, with him of all people. He was a country boy through and through and Gemma was Sydney glamour from her head to her toes. But from the looks they were giving each other – and their tousled clothes – something had obviously clicked between them.

Keith politely asked her about her trip, before Gemma practically pushed him into the car. "See you tomorrow, Keith. I've got a night of talking to my dear friend ahead of me."

After Keith drove off, Gemma hugged Maura close again, then stood back and held her at arm's length.

"How are you, darl? How's Quinn, how's Nick, how's Fran, how was Ireland, how is everything?"

Maura smiled back. "Quinn is getting better in leaps and bounds and so are Nick and Fran. Get us a bottle and a glass each, a seat on the verandah, and I'll tell you everything."

As Gemma fetched some chilled drinks, Maura stretched out on the comfortable garden seat on the café verandah, and felt her muscles relax. She could hear

Gemma bustling around in the kitchen and she smiled to herself. They had a good night of chat ahead of them. She could just see her own cottage through the trees in the adjoining paddock. She was looking forward to sleeping in her own bedroom for the first time in weeks. It was nice to be home.

Gemma broke into her reverie, coming out onto the verandah carrying a tray laden with a bottle of sparkling wine in an ice bucket, glasses, little bowls of locally grown olives and the portable phone.

Maura raised an eyebrow at the phone. "That desperate for bookings, are we, or are you expecting a call yourself?"

Gemma started to deny it, before bursting out laughing. "Well, he said he might ring. But let's forget Keith for a moment," she said, passing her a fizzing glass. "It's great to have you back, Morey. Tell me everything, every single detail."

Nick had obviously already told Gemma about Bernadette's accident and the sudden appearance of Dominic, but Gemma was hungry for all the facts direct from Maura.

They took turn and turn about, Maura keenly hearing all the details of Gemma's meeting with Keith, when she had called him to source some local lamb for the café.

"It was like a slow motion film, Morey – our eyes locked, our hearts leapt and I had to stop myself from running into his arms then and there."

Maura laughed uproariously. "And you haven't stopped yourself since by the looks of things."

"It's the country air, it gives a girl a great appetite, as you've often told me yourself."

Maura shook her head at Gemma's boldness. "Well, good luck to you, it looks like it's doing you the world of good."

Gemma stretched luxuriously. "I'm a new woman, believe me. Now, what about you, did you manage a quick windswept romance with any rugged Irish poets or red-faced bottle-shop owners?"

To Maura's surprise, she didn't tell Gemma anything about her feelings for Dominic. Nor about the night in the Mayo hotel room, or the night in London, let alone what had happened the night she had found Dominic with Carla. She couldn't explain why, even to herself. It was too raw at the moment, she guessed. Instead she lightheartedly changed the subject, asking Gemma to fill her in on the latest Clare Valley winery gossip.

The mood was easy, until once again Gemma shifted the focus back onto Ireland, tentatively raising the subject of Catherine. She knew of Maura's confused feelings about her birth mother and was curious and sympathetic as Maura haltingly told the story.

Gemma carefully pressed for detail and Maura was glad of her interest, feeling herself coming to terms with it all even more as she spoke her thoughts aloud.

Around ten in the evening, the phone rang. It was

Fran, calling with good news from the hospital. The specialist had been in again earlier in the evening, just after Maura had left.

Fran reported that Quinn's lungs were definitely getting stronger.

"The doctor reckons the last monitor will be removed in the next couple of days," Fran said in a happy voice, "and Quinn'll be breathing completely on his own again."

Maura passed on the good news to Gemma. "Around these parts, good news means more good wine," Gemma announced, filling both their glasses. They had barely taken a sip when the phone rang again.

"Keith?" Maura suggested.

Gemma gave a saucy smile, before answering the phone in an exaggerated husky voice. "Lorikeet Hill Winery Café, hello," she breathed. "Maura Carmody, yes, this is her number. Who is this, please?"

Maura looked up in amazement, her brow creasing. Who knew that she was back in Clare already?

Gemma repeated the caller's name for Maura's benefit. "Dominic Hanrahan," she said, arching an eyebrow in query at Maura.

Maura felt her blood chill suddenly and shook her head violently. "I'm not here yet," she mouthed, her eyes wide.

Gemma didn't miss a beat. "Maura is actually still in Adelaide at the hospital with her family," she said smoothly. "Yes, he's much better, yes, it's a great relief.

Shall I give Maura a message? No, well, I'll tell her you called. Goodnight."

Gemma hung up, turned to Maura and made a whooping sound.

"That's Dominic? What a gorgeous voice! What's he doing ringing here and how does he know so much about Quinn?" she shot the questions.

Maura didn't answer, her thoughts a whirl. Bernadette must have filled him in on the situation with Quinn, and given him her number.

Gemma looked at her closely again. "Why are you being so weird and silent, girlie? What haven't you told me about this Irish trip? You haven't left out the juicy bits by any chance? Why would he be ringing here?"

Maura rubbed at her wrist. Gemma knew that sign too. "This is Gemma," she said. "Your oldest and dearest friend. I tell you everything, you tell me everything, remember the rule? Spill the beans, kiddo."

Maura shifted in her seat. "Well, maybe something happened between me and Dominic."

"Maybe? Maybe what?"

"Well, maybe I fell for him and maybe we slept together and maybe I made a fool of myself," Maura said in a rush, looking up defiantly.

Gemma pulled her chair closer to Maura's, and settled in comfortably, grinning at her friend. "Now, this is more like it. Let's work backwards. What do you mean you made a fool of yourself?"

Feeling herself tense as she spoke, Maura briefly

explained the situation and how she had walked in on Carla and Dominic in bed.

"Maybe he was telling her what had happened between you and him," said Gemma, always anxious to see both sides of the story.

"That's right, without their clothes on, the way you normally have those sorts of conversations," Maura said bitterly.

"You said she was naked but he had his trousers on?" Gemma was pressing for the nitty-gritty details.

"So I guess I interrupted them. Thank God I didn't walk in a few minutes later . . ." Maura's voice tailed off.

Gemma's brow creased. "Well, let's go back to admissions one and two. You said maybe you slept with him. Don't you know for sure?"

Maura brought up her hands to cover her face. "Yes, I know for sure, Gemma, don't make this any bloody harder than it is."

Gemma smiled at her friend. "I'm not trying to make it hard, I'm just mad to hear the details and you're being very cagey. So what happened?"

"I told you about running into Richard in London."

"Yes."

"Well, I ran into Dominic the same night. At the same time."

Gemma clapped her hands together. "Fantastic! A tug of love between two men!"

Maura cast her mind back. "No, it wasn't like that at

all. I was a bit shaken after Richard suddenly turned up, and Dominic was staying in the same hotel and, well, he looked after me."

"He certainly did," Gemma grinned, then was serious again. "How did you end up staying in the same hotel?"

"Bernadette highly recommended it to me – "

Gemma raised an eyebrow. "Doing a bit of matchmaking, by any chance?"

Maura started to deny it, then remembered that Bernadette had been quite firm that she stay in that particular hotel. And she had mentioned that Dominic was staying there too. And Dominic hadn't been at all surprised to see her in London . . .

"No, it must have been just a coincidence," she said, though starting to doubt it herself.

From her expression, Gemma wasn't convinced, but she went on with her questioning. "So you met in the hotel. And then what happened?"

"Well, I was a bit nervous about going up to my hotel room on my own."

"Well, of course you were," Gemma said with a laugh.

"Don't tease me, I was. Richard was furious, I had this image of him following me up to my room . . ."

Gemma's face went serious, as she remembered a couple of incidents with Richard in Sydney. "No, you were probably dead right. So you stayed with Dominic in his room instead. And?"

Maura started to speak, then stopped, a smile slowly spreading across her face. "And you're not getting all the details, so don't ask. But it was . . ." she searched for the word. "It was wonderful."

"Then what happened?"

"We talked about Carla and he asked me to trust him and wait for him to talk to her, and like a fool I did. And look where that got me."

Gemma looked puzzled. "Then what's he doing ringing you here?"

"I don't know. Maybe he's feeling guilty about me, now that he and Carla are desperately in love again. I guess he wants to salve his conscience or something."

"Why don't you talk to him next time he rings and find out?"

"There probably won't be a next time," Maura said defiantly. "Look, Gem, it was a holiday romance that went wrong. In fact, it was never even right."

"But still, why would – " Gemma was interrupted by the sound of the phone ringing again. Maura nearly leapt from her seat, while Gemma snatched up the receiver.

She grinned broadly and then started murmuring in a throaty voice that nearly made Maura choke on her wine. "Keith, darling, I've just been thinking about you."

Maura rolled her eyes, and picked up her glass and moved further down the verandah to give Gemma some privacy.

A Taste For It

She leaned against the rail, moving the glass from one hand to another. Her heart was still racing. Dominic had rung. Should she have taken the call? She was glad she hadn't. What if her voice gave away her feelings to him? At least this way he hadn't realised that she had almost fallen in love with him. That gave her some shred of pride to hang on to. It was better to just forget about him, she reasoned. As if she could, another voice reasoned back.

Gemma joined her again. "As if you could what?"

Maura shook her head, smiling at her friend. "Just talking to myself as usual. How's Keith?"

Gemma looked slightly sheepish. "Actually, he's coming over again, he says he can't wait until tomorrow to see me. Do you mind?"

Maura shook her head. "Not in the least. You've been very patient with all my yabbering tonight already. I'm exhausted anyway and I'm longing for my own bed again. Go for your life."

"Oh Lord, don't put ideas in my head!" Gemma said with a suggestive laugh. She noticed Maura's newly quiet mood, and leaned over and stroked her friend's arm.

"It's good to have you back home. And don't worry about Dominic and silly old Carla. It'll all work out for the best."

"You sound like Bernadette," Maura muttered, as she stifled a yawn.

"Then you're a lucky girl, you've got two wise

379

friends. Now, will I walk you home? I can lock up when I come back."

Maura shook her head. "No, you wait here for Keith, it's only two minutes away. See you in the morning." She hugged her friend close, then walked down to get her small suitcase from the car. She'd leave the rest of the luggage till the morning.

The walk through the vineyard to her own cottage was soothing, the wine she had drunk making her pleasantly foggy-minded. Inside, she walked around her little house, noticing with a smile the big bunches of flowers Gemma had placed around the rooms. She had taken great care of the cottage in the month she had been there, Maura could tell. The spare room, now full of Gemma's belongings, looked like a different room.

Lying in bed, Maura heard Keith's car pull up at the café. She heard their murmured laughs and voices as Gemma locked all the doors, and their whispered conversation as they walked down the vineyard path and let themselves into the cottage.

Soon after there was a long silence from the spare bedroom, which didn't need much interpreting. Maura curled up in a ball, glad to be home and in her own bed.

But by two o'clock she was still wide awake, tossing and turning for what felt like the hundredth time. The question wouldn't go away. Why had Dominic rung?

Chapter Thirty-five

No matter how much she watched it, the phone didn't ring for her the next day.

"Ring him, will you?" Gemma eventually insisted. "You're like a scalded cat every time it rings and you're making me jumpy now too."

"I don't have his number," she answered feebly.

Gemma snorted. "Don't be ridiculous. The Wine Society in Dublin would have it, or you could ring directories. Or surely Bernadette would have it?"

Maura answered in a small voice. "Yes, she would have it, but I'm not going to ask her for it."

Gemma looked at her friend in astonishment. "Who is this weak-kneed creature in front of me? Has she lost her marbles during the flight home? Has she become a meek and timid Stepford Wife . . .?" Gemma was in full flight.

Maura stood up, laughing, waving her arms in the air. "Enough, enough. I'll do something about it, I promise."

"That's the girl! Ring Bernadette now and get his number."

"I can't," Maura answered.

Gemma looked as if she was about to wind herself up again. "Can't? Can't? Why not?"

"Because it's three in the morning in Ireland," Maura said silkily.

Gemma looked at her watch. "Then ring her later."

"I'll be on the road to Adelaide by then," Maura answered, delighted with herself. "It'll just have to wait another day."

Gemma shook her head in mock disappointment. "Who'd have thought you would just give in as easily as that? Where is the courage of your convictions?"

"Gemma," Maura said warningly. "You're starting to sound like a football coach. I'm not like you, I can't just go charging in there. I feel like a fool already, I don't want to make it any worse. Please just leave me to sort out how I feel, will you?"

Gemma was about to speak again but a glance at Maura's face changed her mind. Maura really was hurting about this. Gemma had thought it was a harmless fling, but she knew her friend well enough to see that Dominic had shaken her. And he was the first man she had even mentioned since Richard. Gemma wisely decided to keep her mouth shut. Not permanently, she assured herself. But for the moment at least.

Nick and Fran were delighted to see Maura back in

Adelaide, and even more delighted to see the bags of clothes and supplies she was carrying.

Quinn was like a different baby. Maura could see an enormous change in just two days. She delighted in watching a little personality emerge from what had been a gravely ill baby. She was even able to hold him and felt a rush of love for the little boy lying in her arms. She couldn't begin to imagine how Nick and Fran must have felt, coming so close to losing him.

The doctors wanted Quinn to stay in for another week, to be completely sure his lungs were strong again, but the worry was all but gone.

A week to the day of her return from Ireland, she and Nick sat again in the foyer area of the ward.

"This coffee has got worse, if that's possible," she grimaced.

Nick laughed, pulling a face as he too took a sip from his cup. He suddenly looked serious.

"Are you okay? Apart from Quinn, and Catherine, and the sudden return, I mean. As if that isn't enough. You don't seem yourself."

"I'm fine," she consoled him. "Just jet-lag, I guess."

"One week later?" Nick wasn't easily put off. "Did something else happen you're not telling me about?"

"It's a long story, but nothing to worry about. I'll tell you the whole lot one day," she said with a wry smile.

Nick looked at her closely. "You're not worried about the winery or the café, are you? Please don't be – I really reckon we're on the way up."

"So do I. No, I'm not worried about it at all. Just wait till I get my article written and sent off to the magazine, we'll be turning the punters away."

Nick's face cleared. "Oh God, that commission, you haven't had a chance to finish it, I guess, have you?"

Maura gratefully accepted the article as an excuse for her distracted air. "Well, I've done a few notes but I've a couple of weeks yet."

"Look, things are fine here with Quinn now, why don't you go back to Clare and your computer and get cracking on them? Gemma said she's happy to stay on and help run the café for as long as we need her to. Fran and I are fine here, and besides, we'll be back with Quinn in a week ourselves. How about it? It's time you had a bit of time to yourself."

Once he'd assured her he meant it sincerely, Maura was happy to take up his suggestion.

Within twenty-four hours, she was back in Clare again. As she started writing up the magazine article, she was pleased at how easily the anecdotes came, and how she was able to put a gloss on the whole trip. To her surprise, she was also contacted by the food and wine writer from one of the national newspapers and interviewed for a feature story on the Irish trade trip.

Reading the newspaper article several days later, she saw the journalist had referred to Lorikeet Hill as one of the regional finalists in the forthcoming Australian Restaurant Awards.

"Oh God, I'd forgotten all about those Awards, with

everything else that's happened," she said to Gemma as they read their newspapers over breakfast. "What happens next? I've never been nominated before."

"They do a second round of judging, I think," Gemma said.

"So we have to go through it all with that critic again, do we? I'll get nervous every time an elderly man comes into the place."

Gemma frowned as she tried to remember the judging process. "No, I think they send different judges this time around, so there's no favouritism. The South Australian writers judge the Victorian restaurants, the West Australian ones do the Queensland ones, etcetera etcetera."

Maura thought of their bookings register, and looked worried. "This looks like being our busiest time as it is."

"Don't worry about a thing," Gemma soothed. "I'm sure they'll give us a bit of warning."

Whether it was the write-up in the national newspaper, or just the long spell of fine March weather, but a rush of phone calls over the next few days saw Lorikeet Hill completely booked out for the next couple of weeks.

Maura spoke to Nick on the phone. "I think it's just as well I'm here with Gemma, she's going to be flat out. We've decided to try opening up for Friday and Saturday nights until the Gourmet Weekend in May, just to meet the demand. What do you think?"

Nick was enthusiastic. "Go for it, I reckon. Are you sure you don't want me to come back? Quinn's getting better every hour. I'm sure Fran would understand if I came home for a few days."

Maura was insistent he stayed where he was. "Everything's fine, honestly. Gemma and I can handle it."

By Saturday she was wishing Nick *was* on hand. The café was booked out, and the phone was still ringing with enquiries for tables.

She had been perfectly relaxed at ten o'clock that morning, when she had given Bernadette a quick ring, using the fax phone to keep the main line clear for bookings. She was featuring a light potato and leek soup on the menu that evening, and wanted Bernadette's recipe for Irish brown bread to serve with it.

Bernadette had been delighted to hear from her. In the rush of the last week, they had only managed a couple of hurried e-mails to each other, and they had both avoided any real news, sticking to "I'm fine, how are you, how is Quinn?" messages. Bernadette was thrilled to hear that Quinn was making such progress.

"That must be a relief for you all, what a time you must have all had."

Maura readily agreed. "And now I can talk a bit more calmly, how are things with you?"

Bernadette explained that the house restorations were nearly completed. "You won't believe it, but we've actually had five days clear of rain, so we've been working like demons to make the most of it," she said with a laugh.

There was a faint pause, and Maura knew in her heart that Bernadette was about to mention Dominic again. The pause lengthened, and Maura realised Bernadette was waiting for Maura to ask for news. Almost despite herself, she asked a quick question.

"So, any word from Dublin?"

"Oh, Cormac's doing just fine, he's still seeing the young one he brought to your final dinner – that's almost a record for him."

Maura couldn't help but laugh. "No, I don't mean Cormac, you brat."

"I thought I wasn't allowed to mention anyone else to you," Bernadette said innocently.

"You know who I'm talking about, Bernadette Carmody. He happened to ring here the other night and I wondered how he might have known I was back in South Australia. I wondered if by any chance he had been talking to a certain well-known chef from the West of Ireland who might have been saying more than she should have on behalf of her dear Australian friend?"

"Jesus, Mary and Joseph," Bernadette said, the mock-outrage obvious in her voice even 12,000 miles away. "Sure, why would I want to involve myself in private business between two young people who obviously already know their own minds?"

"What do you mean he knows his own mind

already? What did he say?" Maura couldn't stop herself from asking.

"Well, we only had a quick conversation last week, just before he left for America . . ." Bernadette said slowly.

Maura's heart fell. He'd obviously taken Carla back to New York to recover from her little turn. She was about to swallow her pride, and ask for the whole story, when Gemma stuck her head around the door.

"Sorry, Bernadette, can you hold for a moment?" Maura looked over at Gemma, who was unusually fussed.

"I need to talk to you, it's urgent," Gemma hissed.

Maura nodded at her friend, actually quite glad of the interruption. Dominic's phone call the other night had strangely lifted her spirits. Hearing this latest update from Bernadette, she felt them plummet again. "Bernadette, I'm sorry, I have to go. I'll talk to you again soon – and thanks for the recipe." She said a quick goodbye, before giving Gemma her full attention.

"Sorry, darl," Gemma said, almost breathless. "I've just had a call from the tourism department. Can you believe it, they want to bring the bloody judges for the Awards here tonight!"

"But we're booked out!"

"I told them that and they didn't even apologise. They said they're turning up like this at all the restaurants, to see how well everyone copes under pressure, and to make sure they're not getting preferential treatment."

Maura groaned. "How many of them?"

Gemma swallowed. "Four."

"Four judges? What is this, the Culinary Olympics?"

"Well, the woman said there'll be a couple of judges, one of the sponsors and a tourism representative. I hope that's it. She said they would make themselves known when they arrived, so it's not completely anonymous."

Maura felt her stress levels rise. "Can we make room for them?"

Gemma had the bookings register with her. "Let's see – we've got a twenty-first birthday party, two work dinners, a few smaller parties and lots of couples . . ."

"Where do we put them, out in the winery with the vats?"

"Calm down, darl –" Gemma said under her breath, as she looked closely at the bookings. "I've got it – we can move all the cosy couples inside so they'll be very cosy indeed and like magic your VIPs get the best table in the house, out on the verandah under the moonlight."

Maura glanced over the list. Gemma was right, that would work well. Luckily, it was a balmy March evening. The table on the end of the verandah would be one of the nicest spots in the café. She looked at her friend. "Now I know why you're called Gemma. Because you're an absolute gem, do you know that?"

Gemma gave a flamboyant bow. "Here at your service, ma'am."

Chapter Thirty-six

By eight o'clock the mood in the kitchen was one of controlled mayhem. The twenty-first party had arrived half an hour earlier than expected, already full of champagne and hungry as hounds.

Maura switched completely into professional mode, overseeing the preparations her assistants were making and methodically working her way through the orders.

She and Gemma had decided on a limited menu for the evenings. It was easier to keep a quality control on all the ingredients, and also allowed for smooth running of the preparations. As a large order of ten came in from one table, she was glad of their decision.

From the kitchen, she could hear Gemma greeting each group warmly and professionally. Gemma was a terrific cook, but her real skill was as front of house, Maura had always thought. She had a real knack for relaxing all the diners, helping everyone slip into a mood receptive to good food and wine.

Maura was relieved to just stay in the kitchen and concentrate on cooking the food as close to perfection as she could. This was the ideal situation. She sometimes found it a strain managing both roles of chef and front of house.

Gemma had assembled a good team while Maura had been away. Annie had gone back to her studies, and Rob had set off on a round Australia trip, but Maura was very impressed with the two new waiters working the tables tonight. Gemma could run this place in a second, she thought.

Gemma walked into the kitchen at that moment, with the order from a table of six celebrating a silver wedding anniversary.

"It's past eight o'clock, our guests of honour will be here any moment," she said in a doom-filled voice.

Maura pursed her lips. "Don't fall for that hype, Gemma," she said mock-primly. "They are all our guests of honour – you know what they taught us at cooking school."

Gemma winked back at her, the reception bell stopping her cheeky reply. Maura could hear her effusively greeting another party of diners.

Five minutes later she was back in the kitchen.

"They're here, they're here! I'm a bag of nerves," she said dramatically.

Maura looked up from where she was gently ladling sauce onto an array of large white plates. She smiled at her friend. "Well? What are they like?"

"Three men, one lady. The woman is tiny and nervous-looking. One of the men looks like he's closer to the grave than his dinner. The second man looks like he wants to forget the food and go straight for the wine, and the third one's a real dish. If it wasn't for Keith I'd be in full flirt mode tonight." Gemma laughed at Maura's expression.

Maura knew she was joking. Keith had been around almost every night since she had been back, smitten with Gemma and enjoying every outrageous piece of behaviour she came up with. Maura was pleased to see Gemma so happy, and Keith was great for supplies, she admitted to herself. His farm produced some of the highest quality lamb in the district, and the best of it had suddenly become readily available to Lorikeet Hill for a very reasonable price indeed.

"I'll have a look at them later, once the rush has passed," Maura said, handing the plates to her assistant to finish the preparation. "Go give them that Gemma charm, my friend."

The orders came in a flurry for the next hour. The new wine waiter was rushed off her feet, but very impressed with the range the guests were ordering. She reported breathlessly to Maura each time any of the tables ordered one of the more expensive wines. The Award judges' table seemed to be topping the lot.

"That's their second bottle of Nick's special Shiraz," she said in amazement. "They know their stuff."

"More compliments to the chef," Gemma said,

coming into the kitchen with six more empty plates. "This group's from Adelaide – they read all about you and your Irish trip in that newspaper article and said they just had to drive up and try it for themselves. Well done!"

Maura smiled. The Irish trip was well and truly paying off, and that was before the glossy magazine article came out, or the export orders for the wine were confirmed. Nick would be very happy.

Gemma was in high spirits, happily exchanging cheeky remarks with all the guests and keeping the orders bubbling along. Maura thanked her stars she was on hand for this sudden rush of bookings, and wondered if Gemma would be interested in staying on permanently. If this quantity of bookings kept up, and it looked like it would, there would certainly be enough work for her. She had mentioned several times that she was tired of Sydney, and now there was the Keith factor as well . . .

Gemma came into the kitchen again, carrying empty plates from the judging table. "Extravagant compliments to the chef, my dear," she said. "And one sends special compliments on the wonderful bread. He wants to know if it's a house specialty."

Maura laughed. It was made from the recipe she had got from Bernadette earlier that day. "What did you say?" she asked Gemma.

"I said I thought it was an old Irish recipe, that it went back years in your family."

"Well, eight hours, at least."

An hour later, all the main courses were served and being enjoyed. Only the desserts were still to go out and her two kitchen assistants had those well in hand.

Maura followed her usual ritual, and poured herself a glass of wine, the one drink she allowed herself on the nights she was cooking. She relaxed back against the counter. Her assistants were still in a flurry, but she knew her work was really over for another night.

Gemma popped in again with another update on the happenings in the café. Maura loved hearing her impressions of all the diners. It was like sending a spy out into a battlefield and getting an hourly report.

"The twenty-first birthday party family is having a ball, though I'd say a fight is brewing. The father's just made an emotional speech, which has made the mother and the birthday girl cry, but the older daughter is furious and hissing to everyone that he never said those nice things about her at her birthday party.

"The romantic couple in the corner celebrating their engagement are now having a full-on row. I heard him say, 'It wasn't love, it was just for the sex, it's you I want to marry,' but I reckon he's about to get his ring shoved down his throat, so that's probably the last time we'll see them here, I'd say."

"And the judges?" Maura asked.

Gemma grinned widely. "They're having the time of their life. Lots of wine and chat, and now they're getting excited about their desserts. They even saw a possum run across the lawn, which the woman judge went mad for – what did she say? Oh yes – 'Look, we're dining in a rustic wonderland.'"

Maura groaned. "She said that about a possum? I should have arranged for a flock of sheep to run past."

"I asked them if all this high praise meant you had the Award in the bag."

"Gem, you didn't!"

"Of course I did. There's no point skirting around the issue, or treating them like heads of state."

"I suppose I should go out and meet them now the rush is over."

Gemma agreed. "They really want to meet you. And like I said, one of them's especially worth a look. He could be just what you need to get rid of all those Irish memories."

Maura glanced around the kitchen. Everything was under control. "I'll just freshen up and then I'll be out in two ticks."

She slipped into the staff bathroom, brushed out her hair and quickly applied a little bit of make-up. Was she the only one who could see the sad look in her eyes? Gemma said she was looking well again, that she had lost the haunted look she'd had when she first returned, but Maura felt not all of her had come back yet.

She walked out of the kitchen into the main dining-room. As she moved from table to table, exchanging a quick word with the diners, she could tell it had been a good night. Except for the couple in the corner, who were very obviously still in the middle of an extremely angry conversation. She diplomatically avoided them.

She accepted a glass of champagne from the twenty-first party, and walked out the front door onto the verandah. If anything, it was hotter outside than in the kitchen. The usual evening coolness hadn't arrived, and a strange dry heat was still in the air.

The table at the very end of the verandah was easily the best in the café, and she was glad they had been able to adjust the bookings to let the judges sit there. From the hum of conversation coming from them, they too were having a good night. Gemma had obviously done a great job keeping their wineglasses filled. She'd made sure they were going back to their hotel in the sole local taxi, so there were no restraints on them at all, by the looks of things.

Maura thought she recognised the two people facing her as she moved toward their table. The older man was from the tourism association and had dined at Lorikeet Hill a number of times before. The man beside him was vaguely familiar too, and she realised she had seen his face in photographs illustrating food articles. So he was one of the judges. That was good, she liked his writing.

She was about to walk up to their table and introduce herself, when the man with his back to her suddenly laughed. It was a very familiar sound. Even as she stopped dead still, and looked closely at the back of his head, she knew the answer.

It was Dominic.

Chapter Thirty-seven

"You can't stay in here, Maura, for God's sake."

"Well, I'm not going out there again." Maura's voice was muffled from her hiding-place in the wine laboratory. One sight of Dominic and she had hightailed it back through the café and out into the dark winery.

"Are you sure it's him? I thought you said he was in America," Gemma asked in a confused voice.

"That's what Bernadette said. Of course I'm sure it's him. And I'm not going out there, I can't talk to him like this."

"No, not if you're hiding under a laboratory table, " Gemma said mildly. "But they are expecting to meet you and you can't stay in here all night."

Maura was shaking. "Gem, I just can't. What the hell is he doing here anyway? Is Carla with him?"

"The American model? No, he seems to be on his own, and he certainly didn't mention that he'd left someone back in his hotel room. Call it a mad hunch, but I'd say he's here because he wants to talk to you, wouldn't you?"

Maura was obstinate. "I'm not going out there. I'm too tired. I look a mess. I'm not ready for this."

Gemma suddenly became serious. "Quite apart from the fact that the love of your life is sitting twenty metres away ..." she ignored Maura's protests about her turn of phrase, "quite apart from that minor matter, they are the Award judges. It's important you talk to them."

"You've already charmed them and it's my food they're judging, not my personality. Tell them I've got a migraine all of a sudden. Tell them I've been abducted by aliens."

Gemma laughed at her. "Maura, you're behaving like a fourteen-year-old."

"I don't care if I'm behaving like an eight-year-old. I swear, Gem, I can't go back out there tonight. Please, will you handle it?"

Gemma turned the laboratory light on. Maura looked genuinely in shock.

"You know that you should talk to them? And especially to him?" she said, but Maura could tell she was softening.

"I know what I should do, but please, I just can't."

"He's gorgeous," Gemma said, as if that made it all okay.

"I know that," Maura said in exasperation. "But I'm still not coming in." She had a brainwave. "Tell him I've had to go back to Adelaide suddenly."

"In the middle of the night? No way."

Maura thought for a moment. "Then tell them one of the staff has collapsed and I've had to take them home. I'll come back later if I can."

"And will you?"

Maura looked at her friend. "I might."

Gemma shook her head at her and then laughed. "Who ever said country life was quiet, hey? I'll see you at home."

Maura waited until Gemma had gone back into the restaurant, before using the cover of the trees to skirt around the edge of the garden, taking the long way via the main road back down to her cottage.

Letting herself in, she decided against turning on any lights – her cottage was too clearly visible from the café verandah.

Her mind was a whirl. Dominic was here. Less than 500 metres away. She kept imagining she could hear his voice. He was so close, yet she just couldn't make herself go back to the café.

If only she'd had some warning.

She imagined herself, calmly taking the news he was part of the judging party. She would have dressed smartly and sophisticatedly, slicked her hair back into an elegant style, found a long cigarette holder and a cigarette from somewhere, and strolled sensually up the lawn toward him. "Oh, hello, Dominic, what a charming surprise," she would have purred.

As if. She didn't need a mirror to know the reality

was a long way from that. Her hair was a tumbled mess. She could smell cooking scents on her skin. And she was probably still white with shock.

It was far, far better she stayed at the cottage, out of harm's way, and waited for Gemma to come home with the whole story.

She sat at the kitchen table.

Hummed a tune.

Drummed her fingers.

Poured a glass of wine.

Drank half of it.

It was no good. She had to have another look at him.

Tiptoeing through the dark house, she found a pair of binoculars in the cupboard under the kitchen sink. She'd never tested them, but remembered the saleswoman's pitch that they could work at night.

Maura slowly crept out onto the verandah, nervous that Dominic and the other guests would choose that moment to look across the vineyard to her cottage. She moved into the garden, keeping close to the trees, feeling her heart beating.

Reaching the spot where she expected to have a clear view of the café verandah, with the advantage of a large bush to hide behind, she nearly cursed aloud. The bush had grown so much that she couldn't see over it any more. She'd have to go up higher.

She looked around, still clutching the binoculars, when the rainwater tank beside the house caught her eye. Perfect. It was about two metres high, but perhaps if she swung herself over from the fence beside it, she could land on top of it. Holding the binoculars' strap in her teeth, she prayed she was still agile enough. She climbed the fence and propelled herself into the air.

The sound she made as she landed on the top of the tank sounded to her ears like a thousand car crashes. She lay very still, willing the others not to have heard. The night seemed deathly silent for a moment, and then she heard the sound of conversation and light laughter drift over again.

Releasing a breath, she settled herself across the top of the tank, thankful the drought meant the tank was practically empty and she wasn't lying in a puddle. She held up the binoculars, straining to get a sharp image. It seemed like minutes passed before her eyes adjusted enough. A sharp image of the man from the tourism association suddenly came into view. He looked like he was finishing his coffee. They were obviously about to leave.

Holding her breath in anticipation, she carefully moved the eyepiece until she was focused on Dominic. It was him. Absolutely, positively. Her gaze lingered on his face.

As she watched, Gemma came into the picture. Maura could hear light sounds of laughter as they obviously reacted to something Gemma had said. Then to her horror, she saw Gemma turn and point in what seemed exactly in her direction. They all turned, and for a moment it felt as though Dominic was looking directly at her.

She dropped flat onto her front, horrified, and felt the binoculars slip from her fingers as she did so. She heard a little tinkle, as they bumped into something on the way down. Then a smash as they hit the ground.

The noise brought her to her senses. She suddenly realised how ridiculous she was being. Twenty-eight years old, and she was hiding on top of a tank, spying on a man. "Maura Carmody, you ought to be ashamed of yourself," she groaned.

She prayed that Gemma wouldn't suddenly come home and catch her up here. She quickly slid her way down and scampered across the garden back into the house.

It was nearly midnight before Gemma arrived back. Turning on the kitchen light, she jumped at the sight of Maura sitting at the kitchen table, a half empty bottle of wine beside her.

"You frightened the life out of me! Have you been lurking in the dark all this time?" Gemma said.

Maura could see she was trying not to laugh. "Don't tease me, Gem," she warned, her expression serious. She quickly poured her friend a glass of wine. "Well?"

Gemma cheerfully accepted the glass. "Really, if my performance tonight doesn't win you the Award and me a whopping great pay-rise, I don't know what will."

"Gemma, to hell with the Award, what happened with Dominic after I left?" Maura asked. She had prudently decided not to mention her own tank-climbing episode.

Gemma gave her a wide-eyed look. "I thought you didn't want to know why he's here. That's certainly the impression I got as you ran off into the night."

"Gemma!" Maura pleaded. "Please!"

Gemma relented. "Well, they stayed until just after eleven. It was a little difficult to talk to your Dominic in front of the others, but you'll be glad – or terrified – to hear that he's staying on in Clare for a couple of days. His publishing house is sponsoring the Awards, by the way, if you're wondering how he managed to wangle an invitation tonight. The others are going back in the morning, there's more judging to do in Adelaide apparently."

"He's staying on? In Clare? Why?" Maura leapt up.

"I guess the answers are all in here," Gemma said, pulling an envelope from her pocket and handing it to Maura.

With shaking hands, Maura pulled out the sheet of paper. Dominic had written just a short note, in firm black handwriting:

Maura, Will you talk to me? Please ring me and I'll come to you. Dominic. He had added a mobile phone number.

"Well?" Gemma looked over.

She looked up. "He wants me to ring him." She read the note again, then looked over at Gemma again, her face quite pale. "But it's too late now. I'll do it in the morning."

Gemma looked at her watch. "It's only just past midnight. The phones do work this time of night."

Maura shook her head. She was too nervous to speak to him now. "The morning will be fine," she said, trying for a firm voice. She changed the subject. "More wine?"

Gemma grinned knowingly, then obediently held out her glass.

* * *

By nine o'clock the next morning, Maura had read the note many times over, trying to read between the lines. But it was straightforward, the message clear. He wanted to tell her something. The problem was, what? She thought briefly about bolting again, but squared her shoulders. He was an honourable man, she knew that in her heart. Even if he had come all this way to explain that what had happened between them in London was a mistake, and that he and Carla were happy together, then at least she would know.

Before she could have second thoughts, she rang his mobile number. There was a brief pause, then she heard his voice.

"Dominic, it's Maura." She knew her voice was shaking. "I got your note."

"Will you see me?" he asked quietly.

Her heart was pounding. "Yes, can you come here at twelve today? To Lorikeet Hill?" She wanted to be on safe ground, on her territory.

"Yes, of course." He paused. "Thank you, Maura."

They hung up then, at the same time. She was

annoyed to feel her heart beating quickly, and took a deep breath to calm herself. There was certainly nothing to go on from that brief exchange. It was probably the shortest phone conversation she'd had in her life.

She made a cup of coffee and came out onto the front steps where Gemma was sitting, legs bare in the already hot sunshine. Looking around, Maura realised it was dangerous weather, well suited to the drama of the past twenty-four hours. The whole sky to the east of the house was a strange dusky colour and a gusty hot wind was whipping around the trees.

"Well?" Gemma looked up.

"He's coming to Lorikeet Hill at twelve today."

"Good girl," Gemma said proudly. "I liked him. There's something decent about him."

"Yes," said Maura. "Very decent of him to come all this way to tell me it's all over before it even started."

Gemma shot her a look. "So you've become psychic all of a sudden and know exactly what he's come to tell you? You may as well cancel the meeting then."

Maura poked out her tongue and was about to answer back, when Keith's car pulled up in front of the house. He was taking Gemma to the Barossa Valley, an hour's drive away, for a day's wine-tasting.

Gemma hugged her goodbye. "Good luck," she said. "I hope you sort it all out. And listen to what he has to say, won't you?"

Chapter Thirty-eight

Maura waved as they drove off down the gravel road. She looked at her watch. Not even nine thirty. She had more than two hours to fill before he arrived, and she was too nervous to spend it in front of a mirror putting on make-up or trying to decide what to wear.

She looked around the house. There was nothing to do here. Gemma was meticulously tidy and had the whole place in perfect order. There were no preparations to be done at the café either.

Maura suddenly thought of Nick and Fran's house. They would be back with Quinn in just a few days and the last thing they would want to do was a big clean-up. She'd go out there and scrub their place for a couple of hours. That would keep her busy, and keep her mind off Dominic, for a little while anyway.

She took the back roads through the yellow scrubby paddocks to Nick and Fran's house, noticing again the strange light in the sky. The wind had become even fiercer too, whipping up clouds of red dust in front of the car, once so quickly that she had to suddenly brake because she couldn't see anything in front of her.

She turned on the radio, and wasn't surprised to hear a news report that a spot bushfire had broken out in scrubland about forty kilometres north of Clare. The volunteer fire-fighters had it well under control, she was relieved to hear, but it gave her an uneasy feeling. The hills around Clare had even more undergrowth than the flat plains to the north.

She let herself into Nick and Fran's house, and took pleasure in vacuuming the carpets, mopping the floors and cleaning the windows. She had given it a basic tidy-up the last time she had come out here to collect some clothes for them, but this was the sort of good physical work she needed to keep her mind from the imminent meeting with Dominic.

By the time she finished, it was nearly eleven thirty. Just time to get home, wash and change, and be ready to meet him at Lorikeet Hill. She carefully locked the front door, noticing again the strange haze in the sky, which only slightly blocked out the searing heat of the sun. The forecast was for 35 degrees and it felt like it was nearly that already. As she climbed into her car, she thought she caught a faint smell of smoke. She wasn't surprised. The winds were so fierce there was every chance the smoke from the fires would be swept down as far as Clare.

She had just driven up onto the rise of the hill when

she braked suddenly, the tyres spinning on the gravel road. "Oh my God," she said aloud.

The row of hills on the horizon were blanketed in smoke, the sky above them coloured a glowing pink, shimmering and changing hues even as she watched.

"Fire," she breathed. Climbing out of the car, she could just hear the sound of the fire sirens in Clare, sending out a signal to all the volunteer fire-fighters to hurry to the station. There were no such things as full-time fire-fighters here.

The smoke made it difficult to get her bearings for a moment, and she had taken a back road to Nick and Fran's that she didn't often use. But she realised in one horrible moment that the fire front was heading west. If they couldn't stop it, Lorikeet Hill would be right in its path.

"No, no way!" she screamed aloud. Not after all they had done, all the effort they had put into it. And especially after all Nick and Fran had been through with Quinn. There was no way she was going to let them come back to find Lorikeet Hill burnt to the ground.

She drove like a demon through the paddock roads, heading toward the main road. She looked at her watch, eleven forty-five. She couldn't let herself think of Dominic, just hoped that he too had heard about the fire. If she had a chance, she would ring him.

Minutes later, she knew there'd be no chance for a phone call, let alone a meeting. The fire was obviously devouring the kindling dry undergrowth on the hills to the west of Clare. The smoke was billowing down in great choking gusts onto the main road. It was nearly impossible to drive through the clouds of smoke and whirling dust that were sweeping down from the hill.

She was only a couple of hundred metres from Lorikeet Hill and saw to her relief that two of the fire trucks had already reached there. She pulled the car to a stop and ran toward one of the fire-fighters, recognising him immediately as an old school friend.

"Kym, thank God you're here, what can I do?"

"Maura, you shouldn't be here, you know that, it's dangerous. How did you get past the roadblock? The cops are stopping all the cars from both directions."

"I took the back road," she said quickly, not explaining that she would have broken the road block in any case. "What can I do?" she repeated.

Kym looked around quickly. The other fire-fighters were already dragging hoses toward the shed that housed Nick's wine laboratory and barrels. "We've got the wine covered. Can you do the café?" he shouted, the roar of the wind making it difficult to hear. She nodded.

"Wet everything down, block off the downpipes and fill up the gutters with water. We'll fight off the best of it. And wrap some material around your nose and mouth, to help you breathe through the smoke."

As Maura ran to do what she was told, she felt the adrenalin rush through her, blocking out the panic she had felt previously. Thank God she and Nick had listened to all the fire warnings about protecting their property.

They had ensured that the grass and undergrowth was kept well down around Lorikeet Hill and her cottage. That barrier would give them some protection, she knew that. She had seen photographs taken the morning after bushfires. Whole paddocks of blackened earth, broken up by a tiny island of green in which a house stood, saved only because the owner had taken the right precautions.

The smoke was thick all around them now. She could barely see in front of her as she dragged a ladder and hose from the garden shed. The fire-fighters were shouting frantically around her. They wanted the road to act as a fire-break to the main front. The only problem was the unpredictable wind. The gusts could drive the flames across the highway. Lorikeet Hill would be right in its path.

Maura could hear the roar of the wind and an undercurrent of a loud crackling noise. Branches snapped and gum trees exploded, the oil inside them igniting in the heat of the flames. The fire front was getting closer.

Kym snatched three towels from the clothesline and threw them to her as he ran past. "Use these to block the downpipes, Maura," he shouted.

She dragged the ladder against the front verandah of the café and clambered up it. She crammed the towels into the downpipes and turned on the hose. A powerful stream of water flowed into the gutters. That would help stop any sparks falling on to the roof and setting it alight.

"We've got about five minutes," she heard one of the

fire-fighters shout into a two-way radio. "The front's changing direction – it's headed this way."

Another surge of adrenalin ran through her. She looked at her watch. It was twelve noon. The thought of Dominic flashed through her mind. He'd be safe. He would have been stopped by the police roadblock.

"Well done, Maura," Kym shouted as he ran past, his voice only just audible over the roar of the wind. Maura gave him a thumbs-up sign. She started coughing, glad of the cloth around her face which was keeping some of the smoke and ash from her lungs.

The ladder gave her a high vantage point and her blood pumped as she saw, in glimpses between the billowing smoke clouds, the red glow of the fire burning its way down the hillside towards them. The main road was their last defence.

Maura knew that it wasn't just the first rush of fire that caused the damage. It was the second wave, the slow creeping carpet of flames that stayed and caused the most harm. That was started by burning leaves being flicked through the air or gusts of wind carrying whole fiery branches.

Climbing quickly down the ladder, Maura ran up to the fire truck and shouted to the fire-fighter in charge, an older man called Len. She knew him from his full-time job in the local post office but she hadn't realised he was a volunteer fire-fighter too.

"What else can I do?" she shouted over the sound of the two-way radio and the roar of the wind.

Len leaned down to her. "We're as ready as we can be. The front'll be here any minute."

They all braced themselves, hoses directed at the undergrowth on the edge of the road. The fire would have to catch there if it was going to make the jump over the road. If it didn't, or couldn't, it would burn sideways and then back on itself. It would have already devoured a lot of the bush fuel, and Maura knew the hope was that it would burn itself out.

The noise was incredible. She thought she heard the sound of glass exploding and remembered the abandoned old shed across the road. It must have been right in the path of the fire.

She looked up, her eyes smarting from the smoke and the tiny specks of ash that were hurling through the air. She gasped as she saw a whole burning branch whip past, throwing out sparks as it did so. It landed on the roof of the café and to her horror, caught under one of the eaves.

"Kym, Len!" she screamed. But they were too busy to hear her, their attention focused on the flames roaring by the main road only a hundred metres away.

As she watched, the branch on the roof flamed up again. She grabbed the ladder and dragged it around under the eaves. She clambered up and snatched hold of the hose. It was caught in the gutter. The branch was burning fiercely. If any sparks managed to fall down through the iron roof, there was plenty of fuel to inflame it. She tugged at the hose again, feeling the ladder shake as she did so.

"Come on!" she roared, trying to pull the hose free. She gave a furious tug and it suddenly came free. She directed the force of water at the branch, shouting as she did so. *"Go out!"* Her eyes were filling with smoke and tears. Finally it looked like the branch had stopped burning. The air was now so thick with smoke she could hardly see. She put her hand on the gutter to ease herself down the ladder. As she did so, she felt a great gust of wind.

The ladder suddenly gave way under her. She felt a sharp blow as she knocked her head against the edge of the roof and fell to the ground.

Chapter Thirty-nine

Her first sensation was one of agonising pain. She felt as if a layer of skin was being slowly scraped off her right arm and a blowtorch directed at her raw flesh. Something was wrenching at her skull. She screamed aloud and felt the blessed relief of unconsciousness slide over her again.

Later she heard voices and shouts around her and she felt her body being carried and carefully placed into a vehicle. She was dimly aware that it must be an ambulance, but she was unable to form any words or ask any questions.

Her head was spinning. Pounding. The blowtorch against her arm wouldn't stop. She could smell a bitter mix of smoke and ash and an underlying acrid odour. In a dazed horror she recognised it as the smell of her own burnt hair and flesh.

She willed herself to faint again, to leave this behind until she was ready for it. She tried to ask what had happened with the fire, whether they had been able to drive it back but the chorus of soothing voices started up again, tumbling over each other to implore her to lie still.

In the midst of it, she thought of Dominic. She had to find him, she had to talk to him, hear what he had to say.

The chorus wouldn't let her. The voices solidified into gentle hands that slowly stroked her forehead, briefly easing the pounding pain, soothing her for a moment. She managed to say his name. There was no answer from the voices. She said it again and imagined she heard his voice in reply.

The heavy sleep suddenly claimed her again.

Chapter Forty

Maura sensed the light on her. She could feel warmth on her face and frowned for a moment, not opening her eyes. Her cottage bedroom didn't face the morning sunshine, so what was the light that was waking her up so early? And it must be early. She didn't feel like she'd had nearly enough sleep.

Eyes still tightly shut, she moved her left hand up to her face. As she did, she felt her hair. All three inches of it. Her eyes snapped open. What had happened to her hair? She looked around in a panic. This wasn't her bedroom. It looked like a hospital room. She tried to sit up and gasped as a sharp pain shot down her arm.

The noise caused a male figure at the window to suddenly turn toward her.

"Dominic?" Maura said haltingly. She had barely spoken his name before he had covered the short distance from the window to her bedside. He didn't speak, just looked at her searchingly.

"Dominic," she said again, a little stronger this time. "What's happened? Where am I?"

Still he didn't reply. Instead he moved as if to touch her right arm, then suddenly pulled his hand away. She looked down and saw her arm was completely covered in bandages. She tentatively tried to move it and was rewarded with another agonising dart of pain.

She suddenly remembered it all. "I was in the fire, wasn't I?"

He nodded. When he finally spoke, his voice was very quiet. "You're in the Clare Hospital. We think a gust of wind blew you off the roof. You were knocked out, and a burning branch landed on you."

So the nightmare of the blowtorch had been reality. "And Lorikeet Hill? My cottage?" she whispered, steeling herself for the awful news.

Dominic smiled gently at her. "All saved. You lost a couple of trees from the far end of the garden, but they managed to fight the fire back at the main road. A shed was lost in the field across the highway, but apart from you, there was no serious damage."

She remembered it now. She was supposed to have met Dominic there at noon. "What time is it now?"

"It's Wednesday afternoon," he answered softly.

She sat up again. "Wednesday? But the fire was on Sunday."

He lifted his hand and gently touched her forehead. "You've been in and out of consciousness since then. The doctors have had you on some very powerful painkillers."

It was all becoming too much. She struggled to understand why Dominic was still in Clare. "That means you've been here for days. You shouldn't be here. You're supposed to be in New York. Bernadette told me," she said, confused.

"I came to talk to you and I wasn't going anywhere until I'd done that. You'd disappeared on me once before and I was determined you wouldn't this time. Though the fire was a pretty good diversion, I'll give you that." He gave a ghost of a grin.

She tried to smile back, hardly recognising the feeling as her lips moved. She was about to speak again when a noise at the door made them both look around. It was her brother.

"You're awake," Nick said. "Oh, Maura, you've had us worried."

She saw wide smiles pass between Nick and Dominic and noticed an easy familiarity between them. "Have you two met each other?" she said, struggling to be polite.

Nick laughed. "Met each other? We've been practically living together in the hospital, haven't we, Dom?"

Dom? Maura looked up in surprise.

"Dom wouldn't leave your bedside," Nick went on, fully aware of the impact of what he was saying. "We had to prise him away to make sure he got some sleep himself. It was only when the doctors said you were on the mend and that you'd gone from concussion to a deep sleep that he would even go outside."

Maura wanted to close her eyes and open them again to see if this strange scene would go away. She tried it but nothing changed. Instead, there was another noise at the door, and they all turned to see a nurse come in, carrying some medication. She smiled over at Maura. "Welcome back, Maura."

Maura tried to smile back, completely bewildered now. She felt herself spinning a little. As she did, she heard Gemma's voice from the corridor. It was all too much, too quickly.

She fell back into the quiet comfort of sleep.

A nurse's cool hand on her wrist woke her the next time. The room was blessedly dark, and she saw by a tiny clock on her bedside that it was eight o'clock.

"Is it morning or night-time?" she whispered to the young woman standing beside her bed.

"It's Wednesday night-time," the nurse whispered back. "You've had another good long sleep. I think perhaps you overdid it with the visitors this afternoon. Maybe take in single ones rather than coach-loads for the first few days, hey?" she smiled down at her.

Maura felt much better, the peace and darkness of the room calming her. She read the nurse's name badge. Jenny. "Jenny, what's happened to me, am I all right?"

"Only the doctors are supposed to tell you that but I'll let you in on a secret – you're going to be absolutely fine."

"But my arm, my head? Will I be scarred?" she asked anxiously.

"Hardly at all. You picked the best place in the world to have an accident like that – you were surrounded by fire-fighters who knew their first aid and knew exactly what to do. They put cold water on the burn on your arm straight away, stopped your head wound from bleeding, and called an ambulance. Your hair was the worst casualty. The doctors had no choice, it was singed so badly and they needed to check the cut on your head. I've heard your friend Gemma stood over them like a fashion consultant while they cut it – you would have been proud of her." The nurse grinned down at her.

Maura asked the nurse if she could see the damage for herself and was handed a mirror. Apart from some bruises on her cheek, she didn't look too different. That's if she ignored the spiky crop of hair where her long curls used to be.

The nurse watched her closely. "I don't know what your hair was like before, but that elfin look really suits you."

Right now Maura didn't really care about her hair. There were other more urgent matters to think about. She glanced at the door.

The nurse seemed to read her mind. "Your Irish guardian angel is just outside," she gestured to the corridor, "if that's who you're looking for. He's never been far away."

"Would it be all right if I spoke to him? And would it be all right if he was my only visitor for a little while?" she asked softly.

The nurse finished her temperature and pulse checks and nodded. "Of course it would be. I'll put up a *Do Not Disturb* sign. Just don't get too excited, okay?" she added as she left the room.

Maura gave a weak smile. Concussion or not, it was time to sort things out between them.

There was a faint knock at the door, then Dominic was in the room again with her. There was a long moment when neither of them spoke. She looked closely at him.

Dominic spoke first. "You're back with us, aren't you? I can see some of that fight back in your eyes. How are you feeling?"

"I'm much better, thank you," she said, strangely polite. Then she couldn't wait any longer. "Dominic, why are you still here?"

"I wanted to make sure you were better. If it hadn't been for our appointment you mightn't have been at Lorikeet Hill at the time of the fire. I wanted to make sure you recovered."

She looked away. 'Our appointment.' So that was it. He must have an over-developed conscience. He'd come to tell her about his love for Carla. And he'd stayed because he felt guilty about her injuries.

"Wrong on all counts."

She looked back at him in surprise.

"You really are going to have to stop speaking your thoughts aloud," he said with a wide grin. "You'll never make a high-powered businesswoman at this rate – you'll give away your secrets at every meeting."

She was confused again and this time she definitely knew the concussion wasn't to blame.

"So why are you here then?" she spoke now, looking closely in his eyes for clues.

"I had to tell you something and see if you had anything to say back to me. I hope you have. I think you do."

Now he was talking in strange rhymes and riddles. This time her face showed her thoughts.

"Ah, Maura, I'm sorry, I'm going too fast. I need to start at the beginning. I want to tell you all about Carla, tell you the whole story," Dominic answered, suddenly deadly serious. "Are you up for talking now, are you not too tired?" His voice was concerned.

She shook her head. "I'm fine, please, tell me."

He moved closer, and sat in the chair close to her bed. "I wanted to tell you about Carla that night in London. Even before that. But I owed her some loyalty and I didn't quite believe what I was feeling for you. I couldn't decide if you felt something for me or if you loathed me. It was like a storm in my head. Sometimes it made me want to tell you everything, so you'd think better of me. But at other times I was happy for you to think the worst, because you seemed to think so badly of me anyway."

"What is there between you and Carla?" Maura whispered, trying to take in everything Dominic was saying and distracted by the gentle touch of his hand on her face.

"There's nothing between us," he said firmly. "There

never has been, no matter what you've heard." He sat up suddenly, putting a small space between them. When he spoke again, his voice was quiet.

"Maura, Carla has a serious eating disorder. She's a very sick woman."

Maura looked up at him in shock.

"She started starving herself when she was just a teenager, trying to get into modelling. But she thought she wasn't getting thin quickly enough, so she started using diet pills and diuretics and laxative tablets – you name it, she tried it."

Dominic was looking down at her hand, his fingers lightly stroking it, as he continued his story.

"It could be worse, I guess. Her best friend in New York moved on to speed, and then on to heroin. I know Carla tried it once or twice, she said everyone did it. That was when Carla's father asked me to help her. He'd been doing all he could, then he found out he was dying. He was more worried about her than himself. I couldn't say no. I didn't want to say no. He was more than a boss to me. I promised him I'd help her get better and to keep her – and her friends – away from her inheritance, until she got a grip on her life again."

Maura started to ask a question but then sank back into her pillow again. She wanted to hear everything from Dominic first.

He noticed her movement. "I can guess what you probably heard. That I had conned her father? That I'd been bribed to be with her?"

Maura nodded.

He smiled grimly. "They were all lies. There was never any money in it for me. There were worse stories too. When I cut off her money-flow to keep her junkie friends away, they spread rumours that I was the main dealer in town. That I was trying to get Carla addicted as a way of moving in on her money."

A nerve in his jaw twitched. Maura remained silent.

"We started travelling a lot, half for my business, half to keep her away from her friends and keep her on treatment. She came to Australia with me twice. There's a clinic in Sydney that's had good success with eating disorders. But she wouldn't stay there. She wouldn't stick to any treatment.

"So I brought her back to Ireland this year, to a clinic just outside Dublin. It's one of the best in the world. But she kept skipping appointments or storming out mid-session. Sometimes she'd go missing for a few hours or even a day or two."

Maura thought back to Carla's sudden arrival by taxi to Mayo. And the urgent phone messages Dominic kept getting during their trip together. It was all falling into place. She looked closely at Dominic, trying to imagine what he had been through.

He looked steadily back at her. "So I made a deal with her. I would set up Ardmahon House in Clare as a temporary clinic. Eithne, the woman I was showing around that day during your class, was going to run the treatment programme in the house."

"So she's there now?" Maura asked in a quiet voice.

Dominic shook his head. "Her overdose that night made us realise it was much more serious than we thought. It's gone beyond an eating disorder. She's done serious damage to her kidneys and her heart. She's back in New York, in a private clinic. The doctors have told me she's become too dependent on me, that all the dramas are part of the illness. She knows it's up to her now. She's the only one who can drag herself out of it and it's going to be a long, slow process, years probably. I've had to tell her all that."

Maura took a quick breath, thinking with shame of the remarks she'd made to Bernadette about Carla and food. She remembered hearing Carla being sick in the bathroom at Ardmahon House, after she had eaten the desserts. She guessed now that Carla had taken something to make herself throw up.

She couldn't be silent any longer. She needed to know everything. "But what about that night in Ardmahon House?" Her voice shook as she recalled the evening. "I saw you in bed with her. You were both naked," she whispered.

His hand gently touched her cheek again. "Your face that night has haunted me. I tried to explain but you wouldn't let me."

Maura remembered how she had felt, leaning against the door while Dominic pleaded to talk to her. And then he had been gone the next morning.

Dominic looked searchingly into her eyes. "Carla

was naked, Maura, I wasn't. And it absolutely wasn't what you thought it was."

He took a deep breath. His expression told her the memory of that night caused him pain as well. "After that scene in the restaurant, her friends stormed off, back to Galway or Dublin or wherever they'd arrived from. I wouldn't let her go. The mood she was in, I didn't trust either them or her. She calmed down enough to decide she'd take a bath, then go to bed. A separate room. It always was," he added, looking solemnly at Maura. She believed him.

"She'd been in the bathroom for nearly an hour and then she wouldn't answer me when I called her. It took nearly five minutes to get the door open. She was lying in the bath, nearly unconscious. I thought at first she was dead."

Dominic answered her unspoken question.

"She'd swallowed some pills, Valium or Prozac or a bit of everything, I never found out exactly what. I pulled her out of the bath, and she suddenly came to and was violently sick over the both of us. I'd just called the ambulance, lain her on the bed and taken my wet shirt off, when you walked in."

He closed his eyes for a moment. "I stayed with her until the ambulance officers arrived, then ran to talk to you. When I came back, she'd tricked the ambulance woman into letting her use the bathroom and had tried to take another handful of pills. That's when it got really serious. She was rushed to Ennis hospital, then to

Dublin by helicopter. I went with her, and that's why I was gone the next morning.

"I rang you but I kept getting the answering machine. Carla was conscious again by that stage, so I drove back to Ardmahon House to see you, hoping it wasn't too late. It was late Sunday afternoon by the time I arrived."

Maura thought back. By that time she had heard the news about Quinn and was on her way back to Australia.

"I met Bernadette just as she was coming back from dropping you at Shannon Airport. She explained everything that had happened. I felt terrible for you and your family and I couldn't call you then, I had to wait. So Bernadette and I stayed up all night talking. That's when I decided to come to Australia to find you again, to talk to you. I flew to New York, to finalise the clinic arrangements for Carla, then flew on to Adelaide. The Awards judging gave me the perfect excuse to arrive unannounced. I just wanted to get here, to see you."

Maura struggled to sit up, grimacing as the burnt skin on her arm stretched. "Did you tell Carla . . ." Maura searched for the words.

"Tell her about us?" he helped her.

She nodded.

"I rang her straight after I'd said goodbye to you at the airport in London, after our night together." His hand was gently stroking her left arm. She felt a slow ripple of feeling flicker through her body. Dominic continued his explanation. "She had already guessed something was happening between you and me. She reacted badly. Not from jealousy – I think she realised that if I wasn't always around then she'd have no choice but to stand on her own two feet. It was time for her to make the decision and she was furious. That's why she tried that food-poisoning trick, to make a fuss and keep you away from me. It was a terrible night. All I wanted was to be with you."

He took a ragged breath. "I wrote you a letter a million times in my head, but I couldn't get the words right. There was too much to be said. And it was all still new between us. I wanted to touch you again, to hold you, not explain how I felt on a scrap of paper. And I worried that you wouldn't read it anyway, not after what you thought you had seen."

She agreed silently. She probably wouldn't have read it, would have torn it up there and then.

Dominic moved closer to her. "I've had four days of sitting here, rehearsing what I want to say to you and imagining your answer. I've gone through every single possibility. Sometimes you say exactly what I want you to say, sometimes you speak your mind. I love you for both those things, so I can hardly complain, can I?" He laughed softly, as he gently stroked her hand again.

She felt a stirring of excitement as she tried to keep up with his words. "What did you say, Dominic?"

"I said I've gone through every possibility . . ."

She interrupted. "Not that bit, the end bit."

He frowned, obviously trying to recall his words. "I

said I can hardly complain if you speak your own mind . . ."

Maura was almost climbing from the bed in her impatience. "No, the other bit."

Realisation dawned on his face. "Oh yes, the bit where I said I love you. That's the bit I came here to say." His voice softened. "I meant to be much more romantic, not just blurt it out in mid-conversation like that. But I haven't had much practice at these things," he said. "Let me try again. I'm in love with you, Maura. That night in London I asked you to trust me, but I knew I had to earn it. I'll spend all the years in the world earning that trust if I need to."

As he noticed a smile start to appear on her lips, he visibly started to relax. Then to her surprise, his whole tone of voice suddenly changed and became businesslike.

"I've had an idea, a great idea for a new food magazine and I know for certain that an international magazine publisher is right behind it." He smiled. "A monthly series, tracing the food from different countries and their impact on the rest of the world. You know, Irish food in America, Indian food in Britain, Asian food in Australia. Not a food glamour magazine, more like cultural history, with recipes thrown in, to widen the appeal."

Dominic appeared oblivious to her look of surprise. It was identical to the idea she had discussed with Bernadette. He was continuing his spiel, fighting a smile that kept crossing his lips. "All I need now is a bright, clever chef who can also write and talk about food . . . and would travel all around the world with me if I asked her to. A bright, clever chef who could travel safe in the knowledge that her friend Gemma was extremely keen to settle in Clare and run the very successful Lorikeet Hill Winery Café."

"How do you know that? How do you know all these things?" Maura was taken aback.

"There's been a lot of very interesting conversations in the hospital waiting-room these past few days," he smiled. "I've learnt a lot of things, especially about a brave, beautiful, spirited woman called Maura."

His hand found hers on the bed. "Can I ask you four questions?"

She nodded.

"Will you travel the world with me?"

She nodded.

"Will you work on the magazine with me?"

She nodded.

"Could you love me?"

She nodded.

"Will you think about marrying me?"

She grinned and nodded her head, once, very firmly. His arms came around her, unfortunately dragging her bandaged arm against the bedcover. She winced as a shot of pain went up her arm.

Dominic tried again, attempting to hold her close but only getting tangled in the drip tubes suspended from the stand next to her bed. He extricated himself. "That will just have to wait," he said, trying not to laugh. He reached into his pocket and brought out a small velvet box. "This is for you," he said.

He helped her open it. She smiled as she looked inside. Nestling on top of the black velvet was the little red London bus brooch she had thrown across her bedroom at Ardmahon House.

"Bernadette found it, embedded in the curtains in your room. She had a feeling I might know something about it, and gave it to me. Would you like it back?"

She gave a big smile. "I'd love it back," she said softly, holding her breath as he gently pinned it on to her hospital gown.

"There's something else in the box for you," he said. She lifted up the velvet square and took a deep breath. An exquisite silver ring etched with tiny Celtic designs lay there.

"I had it made especially for you," he said, gently taking it out. He went to put it on her finger.

They both looked down. Her right hand and arm was completely bandaged.

He grinned. "It'll have to go on your left hand, won't it?" he asked.

Maura grinned back. "I guess so," she said.

Dominic eased it onto her ring finger, then leaned his lips against her forehead. As he did so, the bell in the corridor chimed, signalling the end of the visiting hours. Outside, they could hear a siren blare as an ambulance came up the drive, stopping abruptly with a squeal of brakes.

She could feel his laughter.

"It's not quite an isolated beach, with a setting sun and soaring violins, but will it do?" he asked.

Maura nodded.

He looked down at her. "You still haven't really answered my four questions," he said.

She smiled up at him. As his eyes searched her face, the look in Maura's eyes answered for her.

She spelt it out. "Yes, yes, yes and yes." She reached up and gently stroked the side of his face. She couldn't believe all he had said or all she was feeling.

"How on earth did you know?" she asked. "How did you know I felt all this about you?" Then she suddenly guessed.

"Bernadette told you?" she asked.

Dominic smiled down at her.

"Bernadette told me," he answered.

Then he kissed her on the lips. Very, very gently.

Epilogue

The sound of a spoon being tapped repeatedly against a glass competed for attention with the conversations taking place in the marquee.

Eventually losing patience, Councillor Gerald Ramsey stepped up on to the small stage and took hold of the microphone, sending an ear-splitting squeal into the crowd.

"Hello, hello, can you all hear me?" he said, clearly enunciating his words.

"Unfortunately," a wit called out.

"Yes, yes, very funny," Gerald said, looking around and trying to spot the culprit.

Standing on the small stage beside him, Maura and Bernadette tried unsuccessfully to fight back grins as Gerald appealed again for order.

"Well, good afternoon, ladies and gentlemen, boys and girls, and welcome to this very special occasion," Gerald said, leaning in close to the microphone to better project his voice.

There were at least eighty people seated in the marquee set up on the front lawn of Ardmahon House, and several dozen more stood outside in the sunshine. Thankfully, the forecast rain had not come, and they were all enjoying a blast of August Irish sunshine.

As Gerald embarked on what promised to be a long introductory speech, Maura absentmindedly stroked her wrist, feeling the raised crescent-shaped scar that was the only reminder of her burn injuries.

It was over two years since that time, since Dominic's sudden arrival in South Australia had turned her life upside-down. She thought of their wedding day, in the tiny chapel in the hills north of Lorikeet Hill. The three months of travelling that followed, as they worked to set up the international food magazine. And the steady, unfolding relationship between them.

Smiling to herself, Maura remembered a few of their more fiery moments. She couldn't say it had been all smooth sailing – they'd taken the turbulent, more scenic route, she thought. Looking out into the crowd, Maura caught Dominic's eyes on her. She winked at him surreptitiously and grinned as he winked back.

Maura concentrated on Gerald's speech again, as he drew attention to the newly painted sign that had been installed at the front gate just that morning:

Ardmahon House Restaurant and Cooking School

It was Bernadette who had suggested going into business together. The classes at her Cloneely Lodge cooking school had become so popular she needed to move to bigger premises. Ardmahon House had plenty of room. And Maura and Bernadette already knew they worked well together.

Neither Maura nor Dominic had needed much persuading. While Maura had enjoyed working with Dominic to set up the magazine, her first love had always been cooking. It had been no hardship to hand the magazine responsibilities over to a bright young editor, a Donegal woman newly returned from London.

Six months of hectic activity had followed, as they called in the builders once again. The old stables that backed on to Ardmahon House were completely renovated. They installed a large-scale teaching kitchen and a modern function room, with plenty of room and all the facilities they would need.

A sudden noise at the back of the marquee stopped the Councillor mid-speech. The audience turned around, just in time to see Maura's nephew Quinn duck under the heavily-laden table, chasing a bright red ball. Fran leapt forward, catching the huge bouquet of flowers Joel had sent, as Nick reached under the table and picked up a wriggling Quinn.

"Sorry," Fran whispered, looking embarrassed. Maura smiled. It didn't matter at all. She was so pleased that Nick, Fran and Quinn had made the trip to Ireland, she didn't care if Quinn brought down the entire marquee. At two years of age, he was mischievous enough to try just that.

Maura would have loved to see Gemma here today

too, but her friend had needed to stay in South Australia to manage the renovations taking place at Lorikeet Hill. Under Gemma's lively management, the café had gone from strength to strength – helped along by the fact it had been highly commended in the Australian Restaurant Awards for two years running. Gemma had promised Maura she would see her again soon though – she and Keith had put Ireland at the top of their list of potential honeymoon destinations.

Maura could see Cormac and Rita among a lively group over from Dublin for the day. There was no sign of Carla, even though she'd grudgingly accepted the invitation they had sent to her in New York. She still hadn't come around to the idea of Maura and Dominic's marriage. Maura thought it was just as well Carla's treatment programme was taking place in America. She had seen Carla only three or four times in the past two years and had a feeling that they would never be more than acquaintances.

The sound of light applause interrupted her thoughts. Maura looked on with pleasure as Gerald invited Bernadette to say a few words about their new partnership.

Bernadette enthusiastically outlined their plans to make Ardmahon House one of Ireland's finest restaurants and cooking schools. They were expanding their range of classes, she explained, and even had plans for a range of theme weekends, with guest speakers on a wide range of topics.

Gerald proposed a toast, and as he did so Bernadette put her arm around Maura.

"To us, partner," she said proudly, while glasses clinked around them.

As Maura moved through the crowd afterwards, Jim McBride came up beside her. Maura had been pleased he and Eileen had accepted her invitation.

"It's great to have you home for keeps like this," he whispered, then added in an undertone. "Your mother would be proud of you."

"Thank you, Jim," she said, touched by his words. He tipped his hat at her politely and moved away to talk to a neighbour.

With a moment to herself, Maura looked around the crowded marquee, taking in the sight of the guests talking, laughing and enjoying the fine food and wine.

Feeling a hand gently caress her back, she knew without looking it was Dominic. She turned around and smiled up at him.

Jim was right, Maura thought.

She really was home.

THE END